betrayal

of fools

Lyn J Pickering

From the author of Opus Dei

Forest of Lebanon Publications
ISBN 978-0-620-71877-6

To the persecuted such as Saudi Arabian, Raif Badawi, for whom my main character is named.
And to the persecuted church:

> *Blessed are they which are persecuted for righteousness' sake: for theirs is the kingdom of heaven. Blessed are ye, when men shall revile you, and persecute you, and shall say all manner of evil against you falsely, for my sake. Rejoice and be exceeding glad; for great is your reward in heaven; for so persecuted they the prophets which were before you.*
> *Matthew 5:10-12*

'While the peoples of the world are still stunned by the accomplished fact of revolution, still in such a condition of terror and uncertainty, they should recognise once for all that we are so strong, so inexpugnable, so superabundantly filled with power, that in no case shall we take any account of them and so far from paying any attention to their opinions or wishes, we are ready and able to crush with irresistible power, all expression or manifestation thereof...'
Protocols of Zion.

"Soon, we will be in direct confrontation. So watch for us, for we are with you, watching."
Abu Bakr al-Baghdadi, Caliph of ISIS
Warning to the United States of America.

On *4th July, 2016, the spacecraft, Juno, went into orbit around "the biggest, baddest planet" Jupiter. Launched five years before, NASA's timing, as the craft manoeuvred into the planet's powerful magnetosphere, was perfect. But why was this day and this particular year chosen to remember the American year of Independence in such a manner? What set 2016 apart from any other year?*

But I talk in riddles here, and only when the end of this tale is reached will you begin to understand. Let the play begin.

Chapter 1   Betrayal

On the beach not far from where Eugenia stood, a small black-clad figure wearing a broad-brimmed straw hat bent to the task at hand. Beside her chair and under it, fishing nets were laid out in streaks of green, brown, blue, and purple. She worked nimbly at her repairs, her wrinkled fingers obviously still adroit with years of patient labour. Eugenia allowed her vision to stray beyond the colourful scene to where the sea, ever-advancing and retreating, became pallid in its enduring effort to integrate itself with the pebbled beach. A whitewashed village spilled over the hills to Eugenia's left and, as always, she was struck by the simple integrity of the old buildings in comparison with the self-conscious planning of the new complexes mushrooming along the Spanish coast.

Catching her skirt, she bunched it with one hand and, with her sandals in her other, strolled down towards the waves. There was the lightest of breezes that teased the free hem of her dress and flipped the ends of her hair around her face. The unexpected chill of the sea between her toes caused Eugenia to catch her breath. She stood still, allowing the small waves to roll in, suck at her ankles and the sand beneath her toes before retreating. Gulls wheeled and circled between sea and sky announcing their presence with triumphant cries as they rode the wind.

When she toiled back up the beach half an hour later the old woman was still there. She paused, looked up, and, holding onto her hat in the stiff breeze, smiled briefly in acknowledgment of Eugenia's raised hand before returning to her work. Eugenia retrieved her shoulder bag from the car, brushed the knots from her hair and tied it back into a pony tail. The hem of her skirt clung damp against her calves and she shook it out as she slipped on her sandals. This was a perfect day, the end of her 'varsity year; exams behind her and home and family ahead. In another year she would complete her degree and finally make her own way in the world.

There was time for a coffee before heading back onto the highway. She started the engine of her Fiat and made her slow way through the narrow streets of the village until she reached the square. The sudden burst of sound and the unexpected sight of the men startled her. Eugenia glanced over her shoulder but there was no possibility of turning back. As unobtrusively as possible, she locked the driver's door. Her hands gripped the steering wheel as the crowd surged towards her. Their black uniforms identified them immediately as jihadists. The lower half of their faces were banded with black scarves but as they crowded around the vehicle, she could see the zealous intensity of their eyes.

"Out!"

Still, she sat, white-faced and terrified, unable to respond.

"Out!"

Slowly, Eugenia leaned over and unlocked the door. She moved clumsily, her legs seemed incapable of obeying. Foremost in her thoughts were images she had seen of beheadings in the Middle East. She stood before the mob staring at them, not knowing whether she was looking into the face of death. And suddenly she was disinterested as though her emotions had detached and like the sea gulls on the beach, had become observers of the world below without being part of it.

One Muslim addressed her in perfect Spanish. "Whore," he said, casting his eyes contemptuously over her. "Look at you! You are dirt! Go home and be thankful that we don't do today what should be done with a woman like you. Soon, you and your kind will learn what it is to be a woman. You will learn your place when we cover every Spanish woman with the *niqab*[1]!" He turned away from her and, for a moment, Eugenia thought it was over. Without warning, he swung round and lashed out hitting her across the mouth with the

---

[1] Islamic covering

back of his hand. She collapsed instantly under the blow and lay whimpering with shock and pain, one hand clutched to her face.

"Get up, whore!" She was shunted contemptuously with the butt of his rifle. "Get up and get out before I kill you."

Eugenia scrambled frantically to her feet. Blood trickled down her chin and the taste of it filled her mouth making her want to gag.

As she turned towards her car, one of the men smashed her windscreen with a paving stone and then booted the door. Her assailant pushed her towards the vehicle, forced the dented door open, and thrust her into the driver's seat.

"If we see you here again, we will kill you," he said. "Al-Andalus is ours and you Spanish will learn to live under our rule or die like dogs at our hands."

Eugenia started the car and drove slowly forward; the men parted like a swathe before her as she crossed the square but their eyes bored into her. Her body shook uncontrollably and, as she drove out of the village, she began to sob.

* * *

Alexander Wesley-Smith leaned across the charge office desk.

"Come on, Sergio," he said, "You know me. You've known me for years and you've known Eugenia since she was a child!" he demonstrated vaguely with one hand against his knee. "How can you say you can't help me? My daughter was assaulted—she could have been killed! These men are thugs and the Guardia must stop them."

Captain Sergio Fernandez, head of the Provincial Headquarters was a man in his late fifties, near retirement. His face was weathered and his expression tired. He smoothed back the thin wisps of hair above his ears and shook his head.

"We're faced with an impossible situation here," he said and his voice was toneless. "Basically Lex, it is hands-off with these *Salafists*[2]," he shrugged, "we're ordered not to go after them for these minor incidents."

---

[2] Adherents to the laws of the first three generations after the Prophet Muhammad

Alexander straightened up and looked at his friend in disbelief. "Come on, Sergio, you can't be serious. This is not minor! A crime has been committed here. You've seen Eugenia's face…"

The police chief glanced apologetically at the young woman. Her right eye was closed and her mouth was swollen. He fanned his hands as if to demonstrate his ineffectuality but could not meet Lex's gaze.

"I'll submit a report," he said at length, "but don't expect action. Perhaps it's fear. The number of Muslims in Spain is increasing. They're powerful already. People are afraid to report these activities in the villages. Perhaps the government is also afraid…" He shrugged uncomfortably.

"I can't just walk away from this as if nothing has happened!"

Eugenia took her father's arm as Lex's voice rose in annoyance. "It's okay, Papa," she said. "Really, it's okay."

He glanced at her, his face still taut with anger. "It's not okay, sweetheart. If the Guardia refuses to act, what's going to happen? We could find ourselves in the middle of something beyond Spain's ability to control!"

Sergio massaged the bridge of his nose between finger and thumb, the gesture was weary. "That case in Brussels earlier this year, you remember, Lex? French Muslim. The guy murdered four people in a Jewish museum."

Alexander nodded.

"He's just been released from prison. The authorities knew him, they knew what he stood for and they knew he was dangerous, but there was no surveillance."

"They picked him up though?"

"In Marseilles on a drug swoop. They were lucky. He was about to take a boat to Algeria complete with his weapons and ISIS flag."

"So arrests are being made," Lex said pointedly.

"Some," Sergio admitted. "But these guys go into prison, which are Islamic hotbeds, and come out more radical than before. The situation is pretty much out of control. There was an earlier case in France. The guy's name was Moussa Merah. Before he killed four Jews and three soldiers, he had served several sentences in French prisons. He joined some jihadist organisation and fought in Afghanistan. When he came back to France it was known—but again, no surveillance. In that case, there was a gun fight and Merah was killed. Now," he shrugged, "he's a martyr of the faith. The youths revere the guy." The Captain wiped his mouth with the back of his hand and his knuckles clenched into a fist. He held it against his mouth for a moment as though to stem a possible flow of words. "Let me see the car."

He came round the counter, donned his cap, and together they walked out into the sunlight. The little Fiat was parked across the road from the police station and Sergio walked around it, his face expressionless.

"I'll give you a report that will satisfy the insurance," he said at length. "But let me tell you, Alexander, the less you speak about Islam in general, the better. Don't ask me why, I don't understand it any better than the next man. It's just better, that's all!"

Alexander shook his head angrily. "If that's the truth, things are worse than I thought," he said. He turned to his daughter.

"Are you all right to drive?"

Eugenia nodded. "I'm fine, Papa."

"I'll see you back at the house."

Alexander Wesley-Smith had arrived in Frigiliana with his young Spanish wife, twenty-five years before. They had met in England, but one visit to the little hillside village had captivated Lex and they stayed. In those early years, there were few other resident foreigners in the area and Lex's arrival caused something of a stir. He and Adriana bought a peasant cottage in the hills above the village, revamped it, and added on to it as the children arrived. Lex had an inheritance that gave them a fair monthly income and allowed him to indulge in his passion as a novelist. His books sold few copies and he spent hours on social networking, studying marketing strategies on the web with little obvious success, but he laboured on optimistically, certain that the breakthrough would come in time. Adriana, on the other hand, painted and exhibited regularly in Malaga and various galleries in the surrounding area, bringing her an independent income. Her pictures were abstract, flamboyant and an excellent reflection of her character.

Juan was born two years after their marriage and Eugenia a year after that. Both were now at the University of Granada, Juan in mathematics and science and Eugenia in fine arts. Life had treated the family well. They grew olives, grapes and avocados. Lex made a passable wine and they had a regular supply of olive oil. Adriana grew vegetables and herbs for the table and they raised chickens. The attack on Eugenia was one of the few major upsets they had ever had to face.

"They are barbarians!" Adriana declared when she and Lex were alone that evening. "Young brutes with no outlet for their emotions!"

"If Sergio's right, it's more than that. The problem could be national."

Adriana gave a brief flourish of her fingers in dismissal. "Non, non! Exaggeration, Lex. I don't believe that."

Lex's eyes searched his wife's face briefly and decided not to pursue it. "Genie is going to need our help to come through this. She was badly frightened."

Adriana nodded more soberly. "I can see that. She was hurt physically, poor baby; but the threats and verbal abuse have possibly hurt her more." She sat down on the edge of the bed, kicked off her shoes, plumped up the pillows, and leaned back against the headboard. "I'm happy that she is going to be home for a while, I could not have borne the thought of her returning to university with this on her mind."

Lex pulled his shirt over his head and felt under the pillow for his pyjamas. Adriana glanced at him and smiled to herself. His hair, which curled down below the nape of his neck, was greying and had thinned to nothing over the crown. He was one of those with an expressive, often pensive, face. Anger, when it came, was deliberated and seldom explosive. Mostly, people warmed to his ready smile even as she had so many years ago. The overall picture was still attractive, she decided. No oversized belly or thickened features; perhaps she would still take time to paint him someday. It was a thought she had toyed with now and then, but there were always more pressing images that sought to find expression, and those were the ones that sold.

"So, you will need to spend some time with your daughter," Adriana said. "I will be busy for the next two weeks preparing for the exhibition in Nerja."

He raised his eyebrows at her. "So, you're abdicating?"

"I didn't say that. Of course not! But you know there's a lot to be done before the opening." Her expression sobered. "Are you going to pursue this case, Lex?"

"Of course! Our friend, Captain Sergio, seems to think we should drop it," he said with heavy irony. "I have no intention of letting it go!"

"Just don't endanger the family," she said suddenly. "You won't take things into your own hands?"

He slipped into bed.

"Not unless I have to, but I don't intend to let those bastards get away with it that easily!"

Chapter 2   Betrayal

Dust and smoke rose through the air and where the sun was able to penetrate, formed a bright veil. From a distance, the billows, like a low cloud formation, were almost pleasing to the eye. The taxi driver was reluctant to go any further but Moussa urged him on as the fighter jets wheeled away in the direction of the Damascus' military airport at al-Mezzeh. The action, for now, appeared to be over.

"I'll pay you double if you go in."

The driver grumbled and muttered something under his breath, but reticence gave way to greed. He drove slowly through Hamoryah where the streets were deceptively quiet and then into Zamalka.

"Turn right here," Moussa Ahmadi instructed. "Left."

From the back seat, Raif could sense his father's tension by the set of his shoulders. To the sixteen-year-old, the streets had become an unfamiliar maze. Sandbags blocked doorways and piles of rubble forced the driver to mount the pavement or take detours through back-streets. Everywhere there were scenes of panic. Men shouted and gesticulated, women ululated and wept. Some scrabbled frantically with bare hands at the ruin that was once a home. The heat was cloying. Sweat mingled with the dust and trickled down Raif's arms. He could see it forming dark rivulets on the necks of the two men in the front seat of the taxi. As they turned into the street where his grand-parents lived, Raif drew an involuntary breath. Neighbours had already gathered in the tiny front garden. The building had been brutally crushed. The blast had demolished even the low wall and gate fronting the street and spewed broken brick and plaster into the road.

As the taxi drew to a halt, Moussa flung the passenger door open and ran towards the knot of spectators. Raif saw his father's gestures, his disbelief, and his fury. He saw his shoulders slump and the involuntary burying of his head in his hands. And, at that instant, hatred flamed in Raif's breast and the thought of revenge was first formed.

Raif's father was a civil engineer who had gained his degree in Italy. When the fighting started in 2011, he saw the writing on the wall and reluctantly began making plans to leave the country. The death of his parents simply confirmed his decision, so when a job offer came up in Malaga the following year, he accepted it. Already, many of the suburbs of Damascus were in rebel hands and Assad's troops were bombing the strongholds. Civilians were leaving in droves, many of them abandoning their possessions as they fled ahead of the clashes. Moussa Ahmadi was one of the fortunate ones who had money outside the country and a pre-arranged work permit.

After his wife's death from cancer in 2005, Moussa's sister, Sabeen, assumed the maternal role. There was laughter before the war; the home in Syria had always been abuzz with cousins, grandparents, and neighbourhood friends. The women gathered in the kitchen gossiping as they chopped onions and parsley and crushed garlic for the next meal—it was the women who comforted the young ones and shooed the older children to the garden. Over weekends, the men gathered in the front room, drinking endless cups of sweet Turkish coffee, smoking American cigarettes, and discussing Syrian politics. But that was all before the outbreak of civil war. Then the shortages were felt most keenly in the cities. Power cuts took place almost daily and often lasted for several days at a stretch. Water supply was sporadic as pipes were damaged and only temporarily repaired when the fighting died down. Sewage spilled through broken drains into the streets. The hunt for food and the avoidance of danger became a daily challenge.

For Raif and his siblings, the move to Spain was a mixture of relief and heartache. Much of the wider family stayed behind. Shortly after the transition, they received news that Aunt Sabeen's family, as well as two of Moussa's brothers with their wives and children, had fled with the refugees into Jordan.

Much to Aunt Sabeen's disapproval, her brother had never imposed, or even encouraged, attendance at a mosque on Raif and his siblings in their formative years in Syria. Moussa's time in Italy had freed him from most religious constraints. Outwardly, he kept up some show of adherence to Islam in order to keep parents and clients happy but within the home, he dropped all pretences. He ate during Ramadan, kept the best whisky in his drinks cabinet and treated the pronouncements of the imams with quiet contempt. Raif in turn gave religion little thought beyond that which was taught him at school.

Now that Aunt Sabeen was no longer with them, Raif's nineteen-year-old sister, Amal, took over the role of home-maker. Raif and his younger sister, Layla, were enrolled in Muslim schools and began the challenge of mastering Spanish alongside their other subjects.

"They teach us in Arabic, English, and Spanish," Raif complained when his father questioned him after his first day. "It's difficult, *Baba*. My grades will suffer."

Moussa shrugged. "Be thankful. You at least have an education here. In Syria, you were more out of school than in."

"But Spanish, *Baba*!"

"Is a new language such a burden to you? We all have to learn!" His father's tone conveyed irritation. "I had to learn Italian—do you think they tutored us in Arabic at university?"

"No, *Baba*, but..."

"There are no buts. You have a brain, go and learn!"

After four months in Malaga, Raif had begun to grasp the rudiments of the Spanish tongue and now understood how difficult it must have been for his father; venturing out as a young man to gain a degree in a foreign country could not have been easy for him. Yet Moussa had qualified with his peers and gone on to become a successful engineer in Syria.

There were aspects of the new school that he chose not to discuss with his father. Islamic studies were by far the most important part of the curriculum and lectures dominated after-school activities. They were not only well-attended there was also an infectious fervour in the young men that gathered to hear the imam speak.

"Malaga was conquered by the Moors under a force sent by Tariq Ibn Zyan in the year 711. It was lost once more to the *kafur*[3] in the 15th Century. Why did the city fall?" He answered his own question, "It was not through the will of Allah but through the weakness of the emir. These leaders abandoned the teachings of the

---

[3] Unbeliever

Qur'an. They became like women, weak in the flesh, filling their big bellies with the delicacies of the Western World. For a while, Granada absorbed Malaga in an effort to prevent its fall but the forces of the enemy prevailed and Al-Andalus was lost to our people. This was the righteous judgment of Allah." The imam paused and stroked his beard; his cheeks were sunken with age but his dark eyes were vibrant with the message he was imparting to his followers. "But, may his name be praised, we are back in our land and in time the infidel will be forced out—forever!"

Raif would take a bus back to their apartment and allow his mind to mull over the imam's teachings. "You must eat and drink the words of the Holy Qur'an and do its works. Each young man is to keep guard over his own life and the lives of his friends. You are to become warriors for the sacred cause of jihad. Let no one stand in your path—it is your duty to fight for the land and to bring it back under the power of Islam. Pray, *shebab*[4], pray that the victory may be ours!"

Raif bought an Arabic copy of the Qur'an and read avidly when the family retired for the night. He began to attend the local mosque and, whenever possible, in the seclusion of his bedroom, he bowed in prayer with his face towards Mecca at the times appointed to the great Prophet by the angel Gibril. As his interest grew, it alarmed him to realise that his father's rebellion, once perceived as strength was in fact weakness. Moussa had succumbed to Western temptations and had betrayed the cause of Islam. But it was not done for a son to challenge such things.

Raif was already certain he was among those chosen to raise the banner of Islam in the West, but first, there was another sacred mission that must be completed. He had decided that in 2014, he would return to Syria to help free his home country from the power of Bashir al-Assad's regime.

---

[4] Men

Chapter 3   Betrayal

Malaga is flanked on one side by the Mediterranean Sea and, on the other, by the dominant slopes of the Mountain of the Lighthouse, known by the Arabs as Djabal Faro. The city is a treasure trove of old and new. Ancient Moorish buildings link hands with gracious Spanish homes, broad city squares, a bull ring, fish markets, and churches. Narrow cobbled streets open onto fountains, museums, and parks. Red geraniums flow over window boxes against dazzling whitewashed walls. Slick modern shops in the town centre give way to ochre buildings with arches accentuated in dusky pink over the balconies. On the coast lies the yacht harbour where white hulls reflect deep into the quiet backwater against the quays.

Ever since she could remember, shopping trips to the city had been one of Eugenia's greatest pleasures. Roving the outdoor fish and vegetable markets as a child held a particular magic. Trestle tables groaned under heaps of pink and silver fish; water redolent with the scent of the ocean flowed over the cobbles and gurgled into the drains. Men with heavy legs clad in waterproofs would clap their hands together for warmth while they shouted their wares to passers-by, their breath a white cloud against the morning chill. Women sat on wooden crates, clasping their chapped hands around steaming cups of coffee. Beneath their black skirts, thickened ankles were hidden under the wrinkles of heavy woolen stockings.

Once she was old enough to see above the counters without being lifted, Eugenia delighted in the colourful displays in the vegetable market; neatly piled red and yellow peppers, plump red tomatoes and purple brinjals; strings of garlic and clusters of red onions which hung from the stall canopies. There were barrels of green and black olives, boxes heaped with red and green chillies, gleaming stacks of apples, baskets of almonds and apricots. The fresh produce markets had been driven indoors with the advent of the EU but, in recent years, Eugenia's interests had also progressed beyond the markets to the boutiques, art galleries, and coffee shops.

Since the incident with the Salafists, she had become painfully aware of the presence of Islam. Here in Malaga, it was outwardly peaceful and her fears seemed irrational, but she was unable to shake off the feeling whenever she was faced with a dark stare from a Muslim in the street, that he might have been one of those in the village square. Her tormentors had been masked, except for the eyes: they might recognise her, but she could not know them. For the first time in her adult life, Eugenia was afraid of being alone—even in broad daylight in the city streets.

There was a small café near the Picasso Museum and Eugenia was relieved to find her friend was already waiting at a table on the sidewalk.

She shrugged off her jacket and hung it over the back of a chair before sitting down.

"So glad you could get here, Rosa!"

"I've never been known to refuse a lunch date!"

Eugenia chuckled. "So, have you ordered?"

"Not yet." She raised a hand but the waiter was already on his way. They ordered salads and coffee and Rosa stretched her legs out in the sun. She was wearing a blue halter-neck top and denim shorts, and her long blond hair was caught in a straight plait down her back. She regarded Eugenia from behind her sunglasses.

"You've had a bit of excitement."

"You could say so!"

"Has your car been repaired?"

Eugenia nodded. "I got it back last week."

"So, what happened?"

Eugenia filled in the details of the attack over lunch. Rosa stirred her coffee absently, removed her glasses and laid them down on the table.

"How are you feeling now?"

Eugenia looked down at her hands. "Quite honestly, I'm scared," she admitted. "Does it sound dramatic to say that my life's been turned on its head? My parents have always supported immigration and encouraged us kids to treat everyone as equals. That is part of my life and I don't want it to change, but this militancy is something else. It's happening in Iraq and places like that, I know. But somehow…" she tailed off.

"Not in Spain?"

Eugenia looked up sharply. "Did you see it coming?"

"Not until recently," Rosa admitted. "But France and Germany are having problems—assaults, things like that. I don't suppose we should expect Spain to be any different."

"Papa says that this upsurge in aggression is tied to Israel's attacks on Gaza. He thinks it will simmer down eventually."

"Israel!" Rosa dismissed the country with a flick of her fingers. "They are swine, Eugenia. The level of aggression against Gaza has been horrific! We've all seen the photos—civilians, women and children. Are we supposed to show some sort of sympathy for Israel when they act without compassion against a weaker nation? I don't blame the Muslims; they are quite within their right to protest."

Eugenia heard the familiar words many times and for the first time wondered if she knew what they meant. She had seen the pictures of swastikas spray-painted on the synagogues, of Muslim women wearing *niqab* with placards bearing the slogans, 'Hitler was right,' 'Slaughter to the West,' and 'Your holocaust is coming'. Hitler, in his attempted genocide of the Jewish people, had slaughtered six million. Islam was not only saying this was right and the job must be completed, but that the Western world was next on the agenda.

Just ten short days ago, she had faced a group of militants and with one stroke they had tarnished her world and turned her belief system on its head. Their words still rang in her ears, "If we see you here again, we will kill you! Al-Andalus is ours and you Spanish will learn to live under our rule or die like dogs at our hands." That threat expunged the political correctness she had been raised to accept; everything she read and heard from this point onward would inevitably be seen in the light of the Islam she had experienced firsthand. Eugenia steered the conversation to safer ground.

"So, what will you be doing over vac?" she asked.

Rosa drew the plait over her shoulder and fingered it idly. "I plan to rest as much as possible," she smiled languidly. "I've downloaded a few books. Oh, and did you hear that Angelique's throwing a party next week?"

Their lunch arrived at the table and Eugenia ate absently. She had the distinct feeling that she had moved on; things that were important a couple of weeks back held no attraction anymore. She supposed the phase would pass and, at some point, life would regain its charm. Rosa chattered on seemingly unaware of how quiet her

friend had become. Eugenia called for the bill and handed the
waiter her card.

"Great to see you, Rosa," she said. "See you around."

Eugenia was not the only one deeply troubled by the jihadist
threat. Lex Wesley-Smith was not just disturbed and angered by the
danger his daughter had been exposed to, he was concerned for
Andalucía and for Spain. Adriana dismissed it, somewhat uneasily,
as an isolated incident and refused to discuss it any further. Lex
knew his wife well enough to know this was her response to fear and
to leave her to deal with it in her own way.

Was it possible for a small band of men to destabilise a nation?
He doubted it. Then why were these occurrences being ignored by
those in power; surely it made sense to nip something of this sort in
the bud?

Guardia Captain, Sergio Fernandez, had written his report and
assured Lex that it had been forwarded to the relevant authorities.
The car insurance had paid out without a murmur, but that was it.
To all intents and purposes, the case was buried. As Lex saw it, he
had a choice—he could pursue the matter, write to the media, or
challenge the local government but he was afraid that it might have
the effect of endangering Eugenia further. So, what was the
answer?

It came to him in the shower, which is where most of Lex's
revelation was received. He would simply do what he was best
equipped to do; he would write a novel exposing Muslim intention to
restore Spain to Islam. He agreed with himself that this was the
coward's way out, but tackling a group of armed foreigners was the
job of an army, not an individual.

Despite his support of Gaza over many years, Alexander Wesley-
Smith realised he knew nothing of Islam. He would need to research
the project thoroughly before picking up the quill, so to speak. But
he had Eugenia's description of the jihadists in the village square—it
was a starting point, perhaps even a first chapter, and he would see
where it led from there.

Chapter 4   Betrayal

Moussa Ahmadi had very little problem settling into his new job. English was the one language in common in the office but, with his knowledge of Italian, he soon picked up enough Spanish to carry him through most situations. The company had landed a large contract in Lebanon and Moussa was employed for his ability to handle both the communication with the Lebanese and, with a team, the oversight of the project on the ground. Travel between Spain and Lebanon was part of the deal and meant that he would often be away from home. During those times, the household was placed in the hands of Raif and his sister, Amal.

The approach by his son early in 2014, a day after he arrived back from one of his business trips, took Moussa by surprise.

"*Baba*, I would like your permission and blessing to return home."

Moussa glanced at his son's earnest expression, picked up the remote, and turned the television off.

"What for?"

Raif took an involuntary breath. "*Baba*, I intend to fight for Syria."

For a long moment, Moussa Ahmadi toyed with the remote tossing it from hand to hand. At length, he looked up. "Raif, you are twenty years old; I had hoped you would begin to prepare for university."

"Perhaps later, *Baba*," he said. "For now, Syria is more important to me. Assad must be ousted."

"How do you intend to get there?"

"There is an organization that will send me."

For the first time, Raif saw the anger rise in his father's face. "What organization?" His voice was dangerously quiet.

"The imam at the mosque in Malaga is in contact with AQI. It's an Iraqi-based group of *mujahideen*[5]."

---

[5] One who engages in jihad

"Al Qaeda in Iraq. I know exactly who they are!" Moussa ground out. "Sit down! I want to know if you fully understand what you are doing."

Raif sat. He looked at his father's familiar features; dark eyes under heavy brows, long nose, and full lips. Moussa was a big man, tall and broad-shouldered with a bit of a belly that had developed with middle-age.

"How long have you had this in mind?"

"For two years, perhaps more." Raif looked down at his hands. He had prepared himself to face his father's wrath, but not for the hurt which now replaced the anger in his eyes.

"And how long have you been attending mosque?"

"For a little more than that, *Baba*."

"I should have seen it coming. I thought when we moved to Spain that you would be free of that sort of radicalism but, if possible, these groups are more radical in Europe than they were at home."

"I wasn't influenced by the imams," Raif protested. "This was my own decision."

Moussa looked at him pityingly. "So, they never preached jihad in the mosques?" he asked sarcastically. "What did they say then? Was it all about the five pillars of Islam, profession of the faith, prayer five times a day, giving *zakat*[6], making *Hajj*[7]?"

Raif coloured. "I didn't say jihad was not preached," he replied, "only that the decision to fight was mine. In a way, it began when your parents were killed."

"Getting rid of Assad is not going to change anything in Syria now," Moussa said. "Al Nusra and al Qaeda are fighting one another for dominance. In fact, there are a dozen factions squabbling among themselves. These men are rubbish, they are destroyers! There's nothing noble to fight for, Raif. Going to fight a war that is pointless won't atone for your grandparents' death, but it may cost you your life."

"I know that and I am prepared to die."

"Which would deprive me of a son as well as my parents," the irony in Moussa's voice did not hide his sorrow. "I can see you have

---

[6] Religious duty - tithe to the poor
[7] Another pillar of Islam – pilgrimage to Mecca

made up your mind. So go! I won't stop you but I hope you will see the stupidity of your decision before it is too late."

Three weeks later, Raif flew into Turkey with two other young men from Malaga. The parting had not been easy. Amal, and Layla, Raif's younger sister, were tearful. Amal had been bitter at first, accusing him of selfishness.

"We rely on you, Raif, when *Baba*'s away. You are the man of the family. How am I supposed to cope without you?"

He shook his head. "Believe me, I'm sorry, Amal. It doesn't even make much sense to me at the moment, but I have to do this." She banged the pots and pans around the kitchen just like Aunt Sabeen used to when she was angry, and Raif was forced to hide a smile. "You will manage, Amal, I know you will. And if I fail *Baba*, you will make him proud."

"And what? Am I supposed to look after Layla until she's old enough to marry, while you go off adventuring? Do I not have a life?"

Raif caught her in his arms and kissed her cheek. She smiled up at him but her eyes were tearful.

"Whatever happens, Raif, I know you are not doing this lightly and I'll always be proud of you."

March 2014

Amal's words rang in his ears as they crossed the Turkish border into northern Iraq and drove to the camp on the outskirts of Mosul. As they leaped down off the back of the truck, the men were welcomed, issued with a khaki uniform, boots, and black headscarf, assigned their tents and directed to the ablution block. "When you have showered, come to the mess," they were told. "Tomorrow you will begin training."

They were hot, tired, dusty, and stiff after the drive so the promise of a shower and a hot meal was more than welcome. The men lined up impatiently at the showers. The water was cold and there was pandemonium whenever anyone took more than a couple of minutes to complete their ablutions, nevertheless, Raif made his way to the mess feeling refreshed and ready for a meal. The hall was packed and the queue long. Places at the bare trestle tables were almost filled to capacity but, as he waited to be served, he realised that no one lingered over their meal. A kitchen worker wearing a discoloured *thobe*[8] slapped a helping of rice and sauce onto Raif's tin plate without looking in his direction. He helped himself to a couple of rounds of Arabic bread and glanced around for a seat. As someone got up to leave, Raif took his place on the bench and introduced himself to the man next to him.

"*Marhabba.* You are billeted with me I think?"

"A couple of beds down," he acknowledged. "I'm Farid Al-Balawi."

"Raif. Did you come in with our convoy?"

Farid nodded, tore a strip off his bread and used it to scoop a mouthful of rice and chicken to his mouth. He grimaced. "Food's lousy; I'm beginning to miss my mother. Yes, I was on one of the trucks; it was a rough ride!"

"But you are Syrian."

"From the south, Quneitra. By your accent, I would say you are from the same region."

"My family's from Damascus, but we left Syria four years ago," Raif said.

Despite Farid's assertion about the food, he was making short work of it. Raif took the first mouthful and allowed his thoughts to stray nostalgically to Amal's home cooking. The two men finished their meal, washed their plates, filled their mugs with coffee, and walked out of the mess together. The temperature had dropped and the sky was salted with myriad stars against the black expanse of desert.

"So you came back to fight?" Farid asked. "There's jihad enough to fight in the West. Why didn't you stay there?"

"My business is with Assad," Raif replied shortly and he received a grin in reply. "How did you come to be in the convoy from Turkey?"

"My uncle was an officer serving under Assad," he said slowly. "My family fled north a few months ago when he was executed."

Raif glanced at him sharply. "Why? What did he do?"

Farid shrugged. "He was accused of passing information to Hezbollah. We weren't given details."

---

[8] Basic ankle length robe

"So you got out?"

"My father was also serving with Assad at that point. When his brother was killed he defected to Al Nusra. The rest of us left." He seemed unwilling to say anything further and together they breathed in the vastness of desert and sky. Behind them, the mess emptied of men, and the clamour of voices dulled to a distant murmur.

Raif yawned. "I'm ready to turn in," he said. "How about you?"

Farid nodded.

The tents stretched out with military precision in rows of six on the desert sands. Behind them, a cliff face offered some protection from wind and sun, but even at night, it was a bleak picture.

At 4.00 am the camp snapped awake to a short blast of a bugle. Everyone tumbled off their cots, picked up their towels and trudged up to the ablution block to perform ritual cleansing before gathering together in the prayer room attached to the long concrete shed that served as a mess.

Raif Ahmadi sat cross-legged in his row on the tiled floor of the training centre building that had once served as a recreation hall. It was incongruously painted in lilac but the black flags of the Islamic State had been taped onto the walls in an attempt to add a level of militancy. A bearded imam chanted the *adhan*[9] to the assembled rows of men. He read a passage from the Qur'an, concluding with prayers as the men bowed four times towards Mecca, their foreheads pressed to the ground. This was followed by a routine exhortation from the *raqib*[10]. Emphasis was laid on obedience and discipline. Men who failed to follow orders would be shot. Their destination was Syria, but first, they were to face arduous training.

"Syria is a place for men, not boys!" the *raqib* shouted. "You are still boys! Where are the beards?" There was laughter as some of the younger men fingered their chins. "Only men will go on to Syria," he declared. Men who have learned to know the enemy, to face the enemy, and to kill the enemy! The highest calling of the Qur'an is to kill and be killed for the sake of Allah, blessed be his name. Today, you will take your first steps."

---

[9] Statement of faith. Recitation of Takbir (God is Great) followed by the Shahada (No god but God, Muhammad is the messenger of God)

[10] Sergeant

Black flags waved languidly in the slight desert breeze but as the day wore on and the sun rose higher in the sky they hung limp and listless. The relentless heat during training was becoming Raif's greatest enemy and he soon understood that the headscarf was an absolute necessity in the desert conditions. Sweating into that and the cloth of the uniform retained the vital body fluids that would otherwise have evaporated instantly. He was continually plagued by thirst and his body screamed for relief.

"Is there no end to this torture?" Farid Al-Balawi demanded as he flopped down beside Raif and passed him the carafe of water. "When I thought it was impossible to do another press-up, the *raqib* ordered fifty more and when my feet said they could not take another step, we were commanded to run another two kilometres!"

Raif lifted his head from between his knees and sat up wearily. "I didn't think it was possible for any human-being to do what we've done today," he replied. "Right now I ache from head to toe."

"I'm beginning to see prayer as a respite from agony!" Farid said.

"Those breaks are vital," he agreed, "coming as they do, just a heartbeat before death!" He grinned, "Associating prayer times with relief from pain is to the advantage of the imams. If we're not corpses by the end of this training, we are sure to be holy."

An incident in the third week would remain with Raif forever. One of the twelve men in his tent, Rami Mansour, was quiet and reserved. Whereas most of the recruits spent the rare moments of free time sleeping or swapping stories, Rami buried himself in the Qur'an. As the days went by, it was easy to see that he was not coping with the physical regimen.

It was searingly hot when they were told to fill their rucksacks with rocks and run to the crest of the cliff behind the mess buildings. On the south side, there was a path that wound up the hill just wide enough for the recruits to run in single file. Limbs burned with agony and trembled under the weight of the back-packs. Each man focused within himself, or prayed to Allah for the strength to make it to the top. None dared give in. Raif was aware that Rami ran ahead of him on the path and he knew that he was slowing. They were close to the top when he stopped.

"Come on, Rami. There are others behind us."

He gave a click of the tongue. *"La."*

"You can do it!"

Rami's legs sagged beneath him and he dropped onto the verge. He frantically pulled the scarf away from his face. His skin held an unhealthy pallor and he was blue around the lips.

The *raqib* pushed through the blockage behind them, "What's going on?" His eyes behind his black face-mask blazed with anger. "Who has stopped?"

"It's Rami Mansour," Raif said. "He's sick."

"The boy is not sick. He's lazy!" He grabbed him by the shoulder of his uniform. "Get up!"

Rami stared at him with unseeing eyes and did not move.

The *raqib* cursed, "I said, get up! I order you to get up!"

"He can't," Raif said quietly, "He's ill."

The man swung his Kalashnikov toward Raif's stomach. "Are you arguing with me?"

"*La.*"

"Then shut up!" Without further warning, the *raqib* aimed his weapon at Rami's chest and fired. Mansour's back arched and he flipped over, his body lurched sideways restrained by the heavy rucksack. His chest rattled and a trickle of blood spilled from the corner of his mouth. One hand clenched twice and then relaxed.

Raif recoiled in shock.

"What are you waiting for?" The dark eyes behind the headscarf menaced Raif. "Get up there. Run!"

His legs were like rubber as he forced himself to continue up the narrow track. Somehow he made it to the summit and looked back at the men who were still toiling behind him like a line of ants. They appeared to move very slowly, heads down, making a circuit around the still body that lay just inside the path.

Much later, Raif admitted what he would have done to no man while he was at the camp: after Rami Mansour's death he would gladly have fled, except that pride alone prevented him from going home to admit defeat to his father and to Amal.

Fear sobered all the men for the remaining weeks of their training and tempered every action. But as they began to revel in the heightened levels of fitness and learned to handle weapons, to fire Kalashnikovs and rocket launchers, a new sense of excitement drove them on. Ahead lay the goal—the promise of action.

Chapter 5   Betrayal

They marry ideology, a sophistication of strategic and tactical military prowess. They are tremendously well-funded. This is beyond anything we have ever seen. So we must prepare for anything.
Chuck Hagel – Defense Secretary.

The withdrawal of U.S. troops had been followed by an Iraqi crackdown by government forces on tribal militias across Iraq. Unrest escalated in Anbar and Raif and Farid were involved in some minor skirmishes in the Ramadi area. It whet their appetite for battle, as Farid said, without satisfying their need for a real meal.

When the Caliphate took control of the Iraqi city of Mosul in June 2014, it bulldozed the border between Iraq and Syria to ensure the free flow of weapons and rebel fighters. The two men were part of a contingent of sixty fighters who travelled from northern Iraq into Syria. Raif experienced a sense of anticipation and anxiety as he readied himself to face action in his home country but no amount of training could have prepared him for the things that lay ahead.

The trucks rolled into Raqqa late the following night after a gruelling journey and the men were billeted in the town. Farid and Raif stuck together, never questioning from that first meeting, the friendship that had developed between them. They were assigned a room in one of the many homes that had been abandoned by those who had fled the fighting. Two days later they were among *mujahideen* sent to Aleppo where they fought alongside other rebel forces to regain control of the city. The shelling of government-held parts of Aleppo was intense, but June 17th saw the capture of the western neighbourhood of Rashideen and ISIS moved in to mop up.

They had been trained in Iraq with automatic assault rifles and machine guns to work as a team, some shooting, others reloading, all the time maintaining a continuous volume of fire against the enemy positions. This was how Raif Ahmadi had visualised an attack against Assad's forces and now that he was engaged in battle, it was exhilarating. There was the same rush of adrenalin he had once felt in virtual battle in computer games; wound up, on another plane, tense with fear and excitement and almost unable to breathe. With his back against a wall, he reloaded his automatic rifle. Repetitious calls of *"Allahu Akbar,"* sounded over and over, their cries replacing the song of birds long-flown from the city since the bombardments began.

"Allahu Akbar! Allahu Akbar!" preceded and followed every round of gunfire, every rocket launched, and every concussive blast from the heavy artillery. The phrase had become a mantra against the enemy; against the very real possibility of sudden death.

The ratatat of automatic gunfire beat a sharp tattoo against the massive explosions which rocked the already shattered buildings around him. Everything was wreathed in smoke and choking clouds of dust. Raif heard the command to advance and he moved out of cover cautiously joining the group of *mujahideen* who had materialised from crumbling doorways and behind broken walls.

They progressed cautiously down the deserted street to where sounds of battle marked the Government position. Ahead of the main group, a fighter gestured urgently and, crouching low, ran towards an opening and disappeared into the heart of a gutted building. The group followed swiftly, aware now of the telltale rumble of an approaching tank. Seconds later it loomed out of the dust at the crossroad and swung into the street they had just vacated. It ground ponderously forward, its gun protruding like some alien proboscis, sniffing the surrounding buildings and resting for a hideous moment on their place of hiding. The tension was palpable; no one ventured a sound. The gun swung away and the tank rolled on.

"Allahu Akbar!" This time the words indicated a release of tension. There was some laughter as they stood up and slung their weapons over their shoulders. Farid Al-Balawi clapped Raif on the shoulder.

"The bastard missed a golden opportunity!"

Raif grinned. *"Insh' Allah."* They adjusted their chequered head-covering so that only their eyes were exposed to the dust. The action emboldened them as though the anonymity afforded by their covered faces somehow rendered them invisible to the enemy.

Although the streets were deserted, the men were on full alert for the possibility of soldiers stationed behind their defences. Fingers of sun touched the broken facades, highlighting incongruities; transforming motes of dust and dangling cables and turning shards of glass on the pavement before a deserted shop to gold. Nothing moved.

Through the slit in his face mask, Rafik saw, or felt the movement on their exposed flank and shouted a warning. It came a moment too late. They were raked with automatic gunfire and three men on the road just ahead of Raif went down instantly. He dropped behind the burnt-out shell of a vehicle, inhaling and exhaling hard in an attempt to steady himself. He could see nothing, but he knew where the firing had come from.

"Raif!" Farid crouched behind him, weapon at the ready. "Up there. We can take them!"

Raif nodded and raised himself up so that he could just see through the glassless side window of the car. Both men waited. There was another burst of fire from across the street and bullets raked the tarmac not far from where they lay.

"Now!"

They hoisted their weapons and fired, hearing the bite and rip of the bullets against the masonry. The return of fire slammed into the bodywork of the car.

Farid turned to a fighter who had taken shelter in a doorway parallel to where they were concealed. "Nabil, use the rocket!"

Nabil nodded, heaved the launcher onto his shoulder, and took aim. The explosion was deafening. Masonry tumbled into the street and a cloud of dust rose into the air marking the impact of the blast.

They waited. Four more IS militants crouched and ran, joining Raif behind the dubious protection of the vehicle. There was no response from the position across the road.

"It could be a trap. Better to wait," one murmured.

A few minutes passed. "There's a break in the building just ahead," Raif said quietly. "I'll go. You cover me."

Gripping his automatic rifle under his arm and bending low, Raif sprinted for the gap; he pressed his back to the raw brick, gasping for breath. The silence was unbroken. A plastic chair lay amid the rubble in the room and on the wall opposite, a sepia-toned wedding picture hung at a crazy angle, displaying a self-conscious young couple in old-fashioned dress. For a brief moment, Raif allowed himself to wonder who had lived here and where they were now. He waited until his breathing steadied and, keeping his back to the wall, glanced out to where the bodies of his fellow soldiers lay inert on the street. They had never stood a chance. He drew back without regret. Had they been wounded, they would have had to try to move them, to get them back to camp, an action fraught with danger.

One by one, the others made the dash along the street and joined Raif without any further attack on their position. They took a quick drink from their water bottles.

"The main contingent is a couple of streets to the south. We'd better regroup."

"What about that gun?"

"Almost certainly silenced, but we'll move individually and keep one another covered as before."

The speaker led the way, moving in short bursts of speed between available cover and the others followed.

They heard the pickups as they rounded the last corner. *Mujahideen* were leaping onto the back of the Toyotas and some were triumphantly waving black flags. Several bodies lay where they had fallen and those in IS uniform were being put in body bags and heaved onto the back of one of the other vehicles. Tonight they would count the cost and once more bury the dead as martyrs to their cause but, for now, Government forces had been pushed back; the area was secured in the hands of Islamic State, and there was a deep sense of triumph.

The Caliphate was established in June 2014, and the news was received with intense excitement by ISIS. Abu Bakr al-Baghdadi was declared Caliph and leader for Muslims everywhere. Under his headship, the intention was to establish a Sunni Caliphate over the Levant region of Syria, Lebanon, Jordan, Cyprus, Southern Turkey and of course, Israel. For hours that night, the militia fired guns into the air in celebration.

Caliph Abu Bakr al-Baghdadi, successor of the Prophet Muhammad and representative of God on earth to the Muslims, chose to make his first public appearance in Mosul at the Great Mosque of al-Nouri. The Mosque was built in 1172 by Noureddine Zangi who opened the way for an Islamic state between Iraq and

Syria and later expanded it into Egypt overthrowing the Fatimid Dynasty. Zangi had intended to liberate Jerusalem and fought several battles against the Crusaders. The destruction of Israel and the liberation of Palestine was the ultimate goal of anyone who took the trouble to read the intentions of the new Islamic State.

Not only was the subliminal message of the Caliph's emergence into the public arena carefully orchestrated, but technical details, and the filming of the television broadcast, were professionally handled. Media warfare was intended to perform a major role in the networking of terror.

In their initial thrust after the formation of the Caliphate, Islamic State forces, in a major offensive, captured Samarra, Mosul, and Tikrit. Iraqi government forces were compelled to retreat further south and ISIS gained control of the Syrian border with Jordan, celebrating the fall of yet another prize—Kirkuk.

"ISIS began in Camp Bucca," Majid Abu Ahmed told them. The recruits were assembled to hear this visiting Islamic State leader speak. They sat cross-legged in their rows on the floor of the hall. Although it was early evening, the concrete walls still exuded waves of desert heat and the atmosphere was stifling. A fan near the podium stirred the air offering no relief to those beyond its circle.

"Our Caliph Ibrahim, bless his name, was incarcerated with us in the camp, but the Americans treated him with favour. Perhaps they believed he was a peacemaker." This notion was received with general laughter from Majid Abu Ahmed's audience. "It worked well for us as he was permitted to move between camps. Ordinary prisoners could not do that. In Camp Bucca, we were only a few hundred metres from where the leadership of Al Qaeda was interned in the other prison. Ibrahim Al Baghdadi, our Caliph, bless his name, would meet with these men and bring back information. It built our ideology. In any other place, it would have been dangerous for us to have met like that, but in Bucca, we were safe— protected. All of us prisoners were Sunni and we came from various militias. Bucca was a factory; in there we became like Damascus steel beaten and hammered together into one sharp new instrument."

Abu Ahmed mopped the perspiration from his face with a handkerchief, folded it neatly and returned it to his hip pocket. He went on to outline the ideology that was birthed in the environment of the US prison camp and the way the movement had developed and grown from that point. Despite the discomfort, the men listened intently. Theirs was a new, proud militia and more than a militia—a Caliphate. It was the destiny of the Islamic State to restore the Sunni faith to the force that it had been under the Prophet Muhammad. They would strike terror once again into the souls of the unbelievers.

"When the U.S. commander released Abu Bakr al-Baghdadi from detention in 2009, he gave the Americans something to think about; they would call it his 'parting shot'. He turned to his captors and said, "I'll see you guys in New York!"

The room exploded with laughter and fists were raised and pumped in the air. As the men departed from the hall, that was the phrase on their tongues.

"See you guys in New York."

Chapter 6   Betrayal

"Faced with disconcerting episodes of violent fundamentalism, our respect for true followers of Islam should lead us to avoid hateful generalizations, for authentic Islam and the proper reading of the Qur'an are opposed to every form of violence." Pope Francis I

"You can't say Islam is a religion of peace because Islam does not mean peace. Islam means submission, so the Muslim is one who submits. There is a place for violence for Islam. There is a place for jihad in Islam." Anjem Choudary, British Islamist

Baasir Al-Safi had slipped away from the camp the night before and was reported missing the following morning. He had taken his handgun, his water bottle, and a few personal effects. Raif Ahmadi was part of the group sent out to hunt him down.

"Who knew about this?" The *raqib* was furious. "Someone must have known! Who are his friends?" Farid Al-Balawi stepped forward reluctantly and gestured to Jabal who billeted with him and Raif. "So, he must have spoken to you. Why did you not report to me?"

The two men denied vehemently having known anything. "He was very quiet for two days; we didn't think anything of it. Baasir is not a very talkative man," Farid said.

"Does he have family living in Syria?" the *raqib* snapped. They eyed one another uncertainly.

Jabal shuffled uneasily, "He did say his brother is supporting his parents," he offered.

"Where?"

"I'm not sure..."

"It was down-river from here," Farid chipped in suddenly. "I remember him once saying something about a village near Deir ez Zor."

The *raqib* barked some orders. "Two vehicles should be enough. You two!"

They snapped to attention.

"You will be part of the contingent that goes out." The *raqib* slammed the palm of his hand down on the table, "Find him and bring him in. There can be no defectors from the Islamic State."

Raif was sent out with the group. He prayed that somehow Baasir would escape, that he would get off the road into the countryside. Most of all he hoped that he had not made it home; if by some miracle he had got that far, the whole family would die.

They picked him up a little more than twenty kilometres south of Raqqa. Baasir Al Safi was on the road making no attempt at concealment but when he heard the pick-up's approach, he swung round and tried to run. The *mujahideen* leaped from the back of the vehicle and tackled Baasir to the ground just as he tugged his pistol from his belt and put it to his head. Jabal wrenched his right arm behind him forcing him to release his weapon while one of the others used cable ties to secure his hands and feet. They pulled a balaclava over his face and tossed him onto the back of the Toyota. Raif knew he was looking at a dead man.

There was a brief "trial" before they pronounced him guilty and dragged him off to the basement of the headquarters. For hours, the screams that emanated from there sickened Raif to his stomach. The sounds were less than human. He longed for it to be over for Baasir but there was little respite. At dawn, they dragged the broken shell of a man up the stairs. His hood had come off and Raif briefly met the eyes now sunken into the bloodied mask of his face. The expression was blank, as though a light had been extinguished. They laid him on the parade ground with a concrete block under his head and decapitated him with a knife. The *raqib* gripped the head by its hair and held the macabre trophy aloft.

"If anyone cares to leave the Islamic State, this will be your end!" he told the men who had gathered round for the entertainment. Laughing, he threw the head into the dust already stained with blood.

Farid Al-Balawi swaggered away from the grisly scene and met Raif's eyes.

"Whoever obeys his whims has sold his soul for worldly life." he quoted with a grin.

From Raif's point of view, the moment constituted the end of a
friendship. But the pretense had to go on, or his own life would
amount to as little as that of Baasir's.

The *raqib* glanced down at the slip of paper that had been handed to
him at the end of the morning's parade and then looked up at the
lines of men standing to attention before him.

"You," he said, pointing to Raif, "I have a new assignment for you
until further notice. A man is needed to oversee the bakery; do you
have any experience with bread making?"

"Yes sir, I do."

"Good," the *raqib* said with obvious disinterest. "Wait here and
you will be given instructions."

Raqqa's infrastructure, which had been virtually destroyed in the
fighting, was being rebuilt by the Caliphate. At present, this was to
serve as their capital. With money flowing into their coffers through
the captured oil fields in both Syria and Iraq, and looted money from
a bank in Mosul, the budding state was doing well. Funding and
armaments were also coming in from Arab sources sympathetic to
their cause. Bread was a necessity for the growing army and repairs
to the damage suffered by the larger bakeries had been a priority.
Local bakers were told to get back to work under the protection of
the Islamic State.

It had to be an answer to his prayer, Raif decided. Of course, the
only baking experience he had was watching his aunt and Amal at
work in the kitchen but that hardly seemed to be a problem. It was
obvious that the *raqib* had chosen him randomly from the assembly,
so experience was not paramount. For now, he was off the
battlefield and it was just possible that this new position was a step
closer to the freedom from the savagery of ISIS for which Raif now
yearned.

Encouraged by the temporary lull in fighting in and around Raqqa
now that the Caliphate was in control, other shop owners began to
repair and re-open their stores and cafés. *Sharia*[11] police chosen
from among the local population patrolled the city to maintain order.
There were no more freedoms. Women were compelled to wear the

---

[11] Islamic canonical law based on the Qu'ran

niqab and none were permitted onto the streets unaccompanied by a father or husband.

On his third day at the bakery, Raif walked into the kitchen in the morning to find a young woman flattening the dough into neat circles ready for the oven. She looked up defiantly from her work.

"Marhabba."

She ignored the greeting. "If you are wondering why I am not wearing the *niqab*," she said, "work it out for yourself!"

"I would have been surprised if you were trying to knead bread if you were," Raif replied. "It doesn't give you much freedom to move."

She tossed her head. "A neo-liberal under the Caliphate," she mocked. Her eyes were unsmiling and she returned to her work without further comment.

"I haven't seen you here before," he said. "But you obviously know your job."

She did not look up. "I am the daughter of Walid. He is the owner of this building."

Raif thought it wise not to remind her that the Caliphate now considered the bakery their property. He watched the adept hands at work for a moment longer before returning to the office.

He had experienced no freedom of movement since joining ISIS three months before and although Raif savoured his return to the streets; his uniform formed a barrier between himself and the people. Men crossed over to the other side to avoid him or found a shop window that caught their attention. Women dropped their eyes and some even cowed in fear as he passed them. Nevertheless, the milling crowd, the smells and the sounds brought a semblance of normality and added a new lightness to his step.

Raif Ahmadi found an unpretentious restaurant off a side street. He ordered *ful m'dames* and *araq* and sat down to wait at a bare table in front of the shop. His meal was pushed unceremoniously across to him by the proprietor, a large man with a surly expression and an off-white apron tied across his protruding stomach. He slapped a few rounds of bread onto the table top and returned to the fat bath where he was frying falafel. The small movement of air at the front of the shop fought with the heat and the over-bearing smell of hot oil, and lost.

Music pulsated from a bar across the road; some youths gathered on the pavement laughing and shouting encouragement as two of their number twisted the levers on an old football machine at a frenetic pace, moving the ball from one side to another towards the goals. Raif sighed and looked away. He knew that in the very near future all such entertainment would be banned under orders of the Islamic State.

A peasant leaned his stick against a pillar outside the shop, reached in and removed the water carafe from Raif's table. He tilted his head back allowing a long stream of liquid to pour unchecked down his throat. Replacing the carafe, he wiped his grey beard with the back of his hand and disappeared into the crowd. Raif smiled to himself. It was one of the few times since being back in Syria that he had felt a bond with his homeland. That simple gesture had ignited a small place of warmth that the araq was unable to spark. He finished his meal, tossed some coins onto the table, and called his thanks. The proprietor grunted his acknowledgement.

As he turned the corner towards the bakery, angry screams reached his ears. Raif ran towards the scene and pushed through the knot of onlookers. Two *sharia* policemen were mercilessly bludgeoning a woman with their truncheons.

"Stop!"

One of the men glanced back, his weapon still raised to strike. The woman was bent double against the wall shielding her head from the blows. It was the familiar black uniform that brought a halt to the beating.

"What is this about?" Raif demanded.

"She was in the street, alone!"

"And her ankles are exposed," the other added, gesturing with his head towards the sandaled feet.

"Leave her alone. Let her go!" Raif snapped.

The woman stood up gingerly hugging her arms to her body and gripping her shoulders. She glanced at Raif through the veil of her *niqab*.

"Are you able to walk?"

She nodded briefly, picked up her handbag from the pavement and slung it over her shoulder. She limped away slowly and the onlookers also moved on.

"In future, there is no need to use such force."

The two men scowled at Raif but said nothing. He waved them on, entered the bakery premises, and let himself into his office. The sense of well-being had left him and he was again disturbed and angry. His father had taught him to respect his sisters and his female relatives but his father did not represent Islam. Those who chose not to fully adhere to the tenets of Islam were branded heretics or, worse, apostates, worthy only of death. Moussa, Raif's father, would be rightly included in that class.

"Allah," he prayed, "please open my heart to the truth."

Chapter 7   Betrayal

Long after the event, Alexander Wesley-Smith decided it had been more than chance that led him to the cards. Destiny, perhaps; a guiding hand in the universe, something of that nature, but not chance.

He had been conducting some research on the internet when he stumbled across the information, and one thing led to another. It was a post on one of those typical conspiracy-type web pages, about a card game developed by a role-playing inventor in 1990, which he had dubbed "Illuminati New World Order". How the game worked was of little interest to Lex, but the cartoon-type images instantly caught his attention. A playing card headed, "Terrorist Nuke" depicted a massive, fiery blast as some object struck the upper storeys of twin towers. A second card in the suite, entitled "Pentagon" bore a graphic image of flame billowing from the heart of Arlington County's Headquarters of US Military Defense.

Lex was staggered. If this was genuine, the coincidence was nothing short of amazing. How had some game designer come up with images depicting the United States terror attacks eleven years before the event?

Someone had got wind of that game before it could be marketed, because at the beginning of March that year, the designer's premises were apparently raided by armed Secret Service agents who removed his computer equipment and printers.

Lex checked the other cards shown on the site. They portrayed the classic images any conspiracy theorist might have come up with in a game of that sort, global epidemics, destruction of books, and disasters. Down the page, his attention was drawn to a third card. In the foreground of the illustration, a tall black building dominated the skyline and the suggestion of a human skull was illustrated in dark, billowing clouds overshadowing the city. The heading read, "Goal—Population Reduction".

It was a random thought but it stayed with him. In the light of the World Trade Centre and the Pentagon images of the previous cards could it be possible that this building represented the One World Tower and, more important, was the One World Tower intended to convey some sort of message to the global community?

Lex was well aware that the cards and the story could be someone's idea of a clever hoax except that the company, S.J Games still existed, using the all-seeing eye within the pyramid as their personal logo. If, as it was said, they sued the state, ultimately won their case in court, and were awarded damages, these were facts that could presumably be checked. And if it were factual, the nature of this game suggested insider information rather than human intuition. Despite himself, Lex was intrigued.

It was still early enough in the day for the sun to enhance the silver of the olive trees and add a purple sheen to the clusters of ripening grapes clinging to the pergola over the entrance door below him. Spider's webs caught the rays and gleamed with iridescent light. Lex rested his arms on the balcony rail and gazed out to where the blue Mediterranean Sea met the azure sky in an intimate embrace. At present, the air was still and within an hour or so, the sun would beat down mercilessly on the Spanish coastline and people and plants would become limp with heat.

This was undoubtedly the best time of day, he thought. None of the usual irritations and tensions had yet managed to slip in and interfere with his well-being. The world was still a beautiful place unsullied by the planet's stark realities.

"I've brought you a cup of coffee," Adriana's voice cut across his thoughts. He turned to his wife as she set two steaming cups down on the painted wrought-iron table. From the wooden bench against the wall, she chose two of the bright cushions they had bought on their last trip to Morocco and tossed them onto the chairs.

Lex joined her at the table. "Thanks," he said. "I needed a bit of a kick-start."

"You were up during the night?"

"I worked on the book for a few hours."

She raised her eyebrows, "That's unusual for you. If you can't sleep, it's generally the TV that wins out, not work!"

He shrugged. "I just feel a sense of urgency with this one," he said. "Probably because it's so close to home."

Adriana frowned slightly and nodded, "I know what you mean."

"The research hasn't been difficult in one sense," he said. "A lot is being written about Islamic fundamentalism at the moment and the Islamic State is making sure they grab the headlines at every opportunity."

"Those beheadings!" She picked up her coffee cup absently and took a sip.

"I came across pictures taken in Iraq by their own men and proudly posted online," he said. "That shook me! Little kids— beheaded! A woman, photographed as they cut her throat!"

"I don't want to know, Lex!"

He smiled at her exaggerated shudder.

"I know. I'm sorry." He toyed with his cup. "I'll spare you the details. But you can see that I feel compelled to write this book. I see it as a warning. None of us want to know what's really happening. We want to preserve our life as it is. But when I see how it has affected Eugenia, I have to hope there's a way to stop things from going any further."

"You don't think she's put it behind her?"

Not for the first time in his marriage to Adriana, Lex was left wondering whether his wife ever fully empathised with other people. He chose his words carefully.

"I think it will take her some time."

"I'm sure she'll be fine once she's back at university and among friends," Adriana said brightly, glancing down at her hands. She picked up the empty coffee cups. "I must get on. I'm going to get my nails and hair done before the opening tonight."

Lex smiled. "I'm looking forward to it," he lied.

It was becoming obvious to Lex that the Palestinian problem and the frequent invasions of Gaza were not the prime reason for the exponential rise in anti-Semitism. It was certainly a strong motivation, but the imbalanced response of society to the atrocities occurring on the other side was glaring. Big things were going on in the world, things that could have far-reaching consequences, but attention seemed to be focused on one thing—Israel.

He spoke to Juan as they drove into Malaga for Adriana's exhibition that evening. When the children were young, the centre of his attention was usually Eugenia. With her natural girlish charm, he often complained that she had wrapped her father around her little finger and often succeeded in wheedling things out of him. Juan, on the other hand, had come in for a slightly tougher upbringing. Lex had justified this disparity neatly by telling himself that boys needed a stronger hand, but as the children grew into adulthood, he and Juan increasingly connected on a man-to-man level.

Juan was Spanish in every sense of the word. He had his mother's dark good looks and, left uncombed, his curly hair naturally fell into the spiky, dishevelled look that was high fashion among the youth; Adriana complained good-naturedly that her son did not even own a brush. His skin was slightly sallow; his eyes a long-lashed, liquid brown and, although his mouth was firm, it detracted only slightly from the puppy-dog look so captivating to the opposite sex.

"You know more about what's going on in Malaga than I do," Lex said. "What do you think? Is there an increase in radicalism among the Muslim youth?"

Juan shrugged. "No, not really," he said. "There have been some incidents. Muslims outside nightclubs calling for Sharia Law, that sort of thing. But nobody really takes much notice."

"Perhaps they need to start," Lex said grimly. "There are places in Germany where "Sharia police" are patrolling the streets at night. Residents are scared to move out of their homes."

"So, are the German police helpless? It's their country, why don't they lock these guys up?"

Lex shrugged slightly. He glanced in the rear-view mirror and indicated a left turn. "Beats me," he replied. "I would have thought that this thing should have been nipped in the bud ages ago, but the authorities across Europe and the States seem to have completely underestimated the threat. There are Muslim enclaves now where even the police prefer not to go." He glanced across at his son. "Research for this book is proving interesting. Did you know that the Qur'an says that Allah will make Islam victorious over all other ways of life even though disbelievers hate it?"

Juan shook his head. "No ways! The West would never accept Islamic rule."

A frown wrinkled Lex's brow. "I would have said the same a few weeks ago, but now I'm not so sure. The problem is far bigger and more entrenched than we realized but no one appears to be aware of it."

"What do you mean?"

Lex took a hand off the steering wheel and ran his fingers through his hair. "To be honest, Juan, I'm not sure. Everyone thinks jihad implies war, but I think jihad has crept up on us. The quiet settlement of Muslims across Europe and America has been accepted and even encouraged. Now we're seeing something none of us anticipated. An uprising from within."

"So, you're taking this threat against Andalucía seriously?"

"The intention is not just to take Andalucía. When Muslims speak of al-Andalus they are talking about the whole of Spain and Portugal. And if that isn't sufficient, they want the United States and Europe as well!"

"They can't do it, papa! There are just not enough Muslims in any of these countries to rise up against established armies. It's impossible."

Lex had already weighed up the possibilities in his own mind and reached the same conclusion, but he could not escape Captain Sergio Fernandez's intimation that Islam was being allowed to act with impunity. But why, what was the point of permitting a hostile force to threaten Western governments? It made no sense.

"You're right, Juan, I don't think there is a way it could happen in the immediate future." Lex scratched his head reflectively.

"So your book is developing along somewhat different lines?"

"At the moment, Juan," Lex said honestly, "it's almost out of my hands. I have absolutely no idea where it is going."

"Do you see the incident that Genie faced as a sign of a growing international radicalism?"

Lex found a parking place near the art gallery and switched off the ignition. "All I know is, that the more I read, the more disturbed I become," he said slowly, turning to face Juan. "I have a feeling something big is cooking and I need to put out a warning."

"Hence the book?"

Lex nodded. "But this time it needs to go out into the marketplace," he said. "I can't settle for selling just a few copies."

"Have you found a title?"

Lex shook his head. "Not yet. It will come to me as the story develops." He glanced at his watch, "We'd better go in. Your mother will kill me if we're late."

Juan grinned, "Bear up, pops, at least there will be drinks and snacks."

"And small talk and speeches…"

Juan clapped him on the back as they crossed the road, "You'll live to fight another day," he laughed.

Chapter 8   Betrayal

*I will cast fear into the hearts of unbelievers. Therefore behead them
and cut off all their fingertips. Hadith 8:12*
*"There's not a problem with Islam. For those of us who have
studied it, there's no doubt about its true and peaceful nature. Tony
Blair: British Prime Minister*

Moussa Ahmadi watched the news that came in from Syria with a
deep feeling of loss. Not a day went by without the accompanying
fear that he would hear of Raif's death, but the loss was on another
level. Jihad, the pinnacle of Islam, perhaps the highest tenet of the
faith, had captured his son. Surely Raif could see what was being
done in the name of Allah; the atrocities in Iraq and Syria, the
destruction of lives, and the hatred of anyone who did not choose to
share their beliefs: Raif, who had always been a gentle child, deeply
aware of the suffering of others. Until they moved to Spain, his
obedience was unquestioned. So, what had gone wrong? It could
only have been peer pressure and the influence of the imams.

A jarring commercial break penetrated his thoughts; Moussa
picked up the remote, turned off the television and sat for a long time
staring into the blank screen. It was true that Raif's death would
have been easier to bear than his defection to a militia whose deeds
were becoming more alarming by the day. Life in Syria during the
war had been a nightmare but, for a father, this burden was far
harder to bear. Since Raif's departure, there had been little
communication from him. A few text messages were sent when he
could find signal for his cell-phone, an email when he arrived safely
in Iraq, nothing more. Moussa missed his son and longed for his
return, but these were unspoken thoughts. Amal had begun to see
her brother as a liberator of Syria, a hero. Her head had also been
turned, or so it seemed. In all the years of their upbringing, the

possibility that they could have accepted a more radical stance than his was inconceivable and his failure weighed heavily on him.

* * *

The baker's daughter was there again the following morning. She had tied a maroon scarf over her head and knotted it at the nape of her neck so that her dark hair was gathered into a tumble of loose curls down her back.

He decided to risk another tongue-lashing, "*Marhabba.*"

She nodded briefly, dipped her hands into the flour bin and kneaded down one of dozens of balls of dough on the countertop in front of her. Raif caught sight of the bruised cheek and closed eye, and drew a sudden breath. He glanced at the blue jeans and sandaled feet.

"Was it you they were beating yesterday?"

"I suppose you think I should thank you," she retorted stiffly, "but it is you that have imposed this on us. So what do you care?"

Her words stunned Raif into silence. He turned and walked out of the kitchen. What she said was true. He had intended to join an armed struggle against an enemy of the people but, by wearing the ISIS uniform, he had become synonymous with all they stood for— and what he stood for stank in the eyes of the people. Increasingly, Raif was seeing Islam as deeply divided, not only into Sunni and Shia, but also into fundamentalists who chose Islam as a complete lifestyle, and modernists for whom the religion simply identified them as a people.

He was suddenly angry at her recklessness, and also that she judged him in such a self-righteous manner and he went back to tell her so.

"What did you think you were doing out there?" he demanded.

She straightened up and wiped her floury hands on her apron. Her expression challenged him and he noticed with quiet admiration that she was without fear.

"What do you mean?"

"You know what I mean! Why were you out there without your father?"

"My father was not available."

"And with your feet uncovered?"

She looked at him contemptuously. "And what is wrong with my feet?"

"There's nothing wrong, but you know the law!"

"These are petty, despicable rules made by misogynists who take out their repressed sexual frustrations on women!" she flung at him. "They enjoy belittling us, beating us, and lording it over us. You show me where the Qur'an says that women must be covered!"

Raif sat down. The anger had dissipated leaving him tired. "There is no such rule."

"Exactly!"

"What is your name?" he asked.

"Nour." Her face softened and a hint of a smile touched her lips. "And yours?"

"Raif Ahmadi."

"So, Raif. What are you doing with the Islamic State if you don't agree with it?"

He shrugged. "Confession could lose me my head."

"That statement would be amusing if it wasn't so true," she said.

He held out his hand, "Can we be friends? Try to overlook the uniform."

She ignored his gesture. "It will be difficult on both counts," she said but, as she turned back to her bread-making, Raif saw that she was smiling.

Nour placed the dough onto long metal sheets blackened by years of use and her father, Walid, came down from the office to help her slide them, by means of long handles, into the deep ovens. Once baked, the circular loaves, puffed with heat, were tipped off onto wooden trays. The first deliveries went to the kitchens of the Caliphate and anything that remained was sold to the townspeople.

There was one other worker besides Nour's father. Sherif Raad made sure the mixing machines and the ovens were in working order but he left the baking in the hands of Walid Zaky and his daughter. Raif took an almost instant dislike to Sherif Raad. The feeling was without a rational basis; on the surface, the man was polite and somewhat withdrawn, but Raif sensed the quiet arrogance behind his smooth exterior. The feeling was obviously reciprocated and, as far as possible, both men avoided one another.

Lengths of afternoon shadow lay quietly at the foot of every building by the time Raif returned to base for evening prayer and he was called to the office of the *raqib* when the usual rituals were over.

"You have a man working at the bakery," he said curtly. "Raad."

"Sherif Raad."

"Tell him to come in here tomorrow morning. I will meet him in this office at ten."

Raif looked at him curiously. "Is this to do with the bakery?" he asked.

"*La,* no. We have used him before. He will know what it's about." The *raqib* tugged on his beard, his dark eyes perusing Raif's face. "This is an intelligence matter. I ask you to speak of it to no one."

Raif delivered the message the following morning. Raad glanced at him with passing interest and nodded. He left the premises without a word at fifteen minutes to ten and returned before the lunch break.

Nour gave him a dark look and continued stacking bread onto trays.

"You don't seem to like him," Raif observed quietly when Sherif disappeared into the front of the shop where Walid Zaky was working.

"You could say that," she returned dryly.

"Why?"

She shot him a glance and he was gratified to see that she was not angry with him for asking.

"He wants to marry me," she said. "Or so my father tells me."

"And your father? Is he going to enforce the marriage?"

She laughed. "Fortunately my father is not like that," she said. "He says he will allow me to choose my partner for myself."

Raif was surprised to find that he was relieved. "You are fortunate," he said. "Most fathers still like to arrange a marriage for their daughters."

"Can you imagine me marrying a man like Sherif? He has no emotions, no intellect, no soul."

It was Raif's turn to laugh, "That's heavy judgment on the man," he said.

She tossed her head. "See for yourself. You will arrive at the same conclusion."

Walid came through a little later with the news that Sherif Raad would be taking the next few days off.

"Something's come up," he said. "He has to go through to Lebanon. Something to do with a sister who is ill."

Nour raised her eyebrows without comment. Raif Ahmadi, for his part, wondered what use the Islamic State had for a non-combatant, nominal Muslim such as Sherif Raad. Lebanon. The thought was intriguing.

Chapter 9   Betrayal

But what they do not know is that, once they allow us to vote, we will
all vote for Islamic parties because we do not believe in left and
right. This will make us win local councils and as we begin to
accumulate power in the Catalan autonomous region, Islam will
begin to be implemented.
Abdelwahab Huzi, Salafist – Lleida.

Sullen clouds gathered over the hills. The sea darkened, rippling and
bending under the growing intensity of the storm. Jagged arms of
lightning flashed over the mountains and the first rumbles of thunder
could be heard over the noise of the traffic. Palm trees bowed their
heads, their fronds clapping in the wind. Rain began to form large
wet pats on the pavement releasing from the city the lost fragrance of
the earth and, for a moment, it transcended the taste of exhaust
fumes. Eugenia Wesley-Smith tilted her umbrella against the
direction of the rain and ran across the street one step ahead of the
deluge. She shook her umbrella, closed it, and ran her fingers
through her damp hair as she entered the little shop.
    "You got caught, I see," Senor Espinosa said, stating the obvious.
    "I certainly did! It's coming down hard."
    "Well, I suppose that will be the end of our customers for the
afternoon," shrugged her employer pessimistically. He shuffled off
to his office and Eugenia took her place behind the counter. She had
been working for the past two months at this small photographic
outlet in Nerja. The job kept her from boredom during the long
summer break, brought an income, and went some way towards
paying her university fees. Apart from that, she enjoyed the work.
Cameras were her passion and comparing the technical particulars of
different brands came easily.
    As it happened, Senor Espinosa was right, there were few people
about during the afternoon and Eugenia passed the time cleaning
display shelves. At 4.00 pm the doorbell rang and one of their

regulars came in, hair plastered against his head and water dripping from his overcoat.

"Mr. Ahmadi, what brings you out in this weather?"

"I apologise for wetting your carpet. I have come to collect my photographs." He handed Eugenia the slip and she reached under the counter for the box containing prints ready for collection.

"I took a look at them," she said. "They are excellent, as usual."

He smiled. "You are very kind."

"Not at all. You are one of the few people I know who still choose not to go digital and you know how to get the best out of your camera."

"Apart from yourself, young lady."

She laughed, "I think we both like the challenge of real film."

"So, can you show me how they've turned out? I can't touch them myself."

Eugenia slipped the large prints out onto the counter and they poured over them discussing the lighting and composition. His subjects were generally people on the streets or at their work but he also had a good eye for landscapes.

"Have you ever exhibited?" she asked.

"No, no! This is just a hobby—for my own pleasure."

"You should, you know. You are gifted. I know a gallery in town that would happily take them. My mother exhibits there quite regularly."

He clapped a hand to his head. "Of course, how stupid of me! Adriana Wesley-Smith, the same surname as yours. So, Adriana is your mother!"

"You know her?"

"I own one of her paintings. Yes, we've met several times at her openings and I was introduced to your father recently. I'm afraid I don't remember his name."

"Alexander. Everyone calls him Lex though."

She slipped the photographs back into the envelope and Mr. Ahmadi took out his wallet.

"I should introduce you to my daughter, Amal," he said. "She's about your age and does not have many friends here. I think you would like her."

"Then perhaps I should invite you and your family to come to our home," Eugenia said. "I will speak to Mama and call you."

He bowed his head slightly and thanked her. "It would be our pleasure."

As Eugenia left the shop a little later, water still poured off canopies and down the gutters, and the smooth cobblestones tossed up reflections of red and yellow light. Although her brush with the jihadists had made her afraid for her life, it had also sparked an unexpected perversity of spirit. She was determined to discover more about Islam. A friendship with Mr. Ahmadi and his daughter would be one way of dealing with her fears and, at the same time, broadening her understanding.

"Yes, I do remember him," Adriana said when Eugenia mentioned the encounter to her mother that evening. "He's an engineer but very *simpático* when it comes to the arts. You say he is a photographer?"

"A very good one!"

"Well, let's invite them round. How about next weekend?"

Lex was less amenable until Eugenia mentioned that Ahmadi was a Muslim.

"I think it would be better, papa, if you didn't mention my encounter with ISIS."

Lex brightened noticeably, "I didn't realise they were Syrians," he said. "It would be a great opportunity to see what a moderate Muslim makes of these radicals. I'm sure he wouldn't be offended, it will be interesting to see where they stand, Genie."

Eugenia shrugged and smiled to herself. Her father was so predictable.

"Is there a Mrs. Ahmadi?" Adriana asked.

Eugenia looked thoughtful. "You know I don't think there is. He told me he has a daughter, but there was no mention of a wife. I'm sure you'll ferret the information out of him, Mamma, when you phone to confirm."

Adriana laughed. "Well, I'll have to know how many I'm to cater for, won't I?"

The almond trees had gone from white blossom to full leaf and now the budding fruit was starting to show among the twigs. Orange and white daisies formed a colourful carpet beside the pond. Miles below, the sea was a slab of brilliant blue.

They could see Ahmadi's white Mercedes as it climbed the winding road leading to the house and, as he parked under the lemon tree, Eugenia walked down the path to meet them.

Despite their diverse backgrounds, the two girls took to one another immediately. Eugenia soon came to realise that Amal's initial shyness covered a feisty nature and a lively sense of humour. She was an unspoiled beauty, petite, with shoulder-length dark hair and a captivating smile. Although not particularly artistic herself, Amal shared her father's interest in art and photography but declared herself to be a 'word' person.

"Mostly poetry," she confessed to Eugenia later. "But I have written some short stories."

"No novels?"

She laughed, "Oh no, not yet. Perhaps when I'm certain my writing has matured."

Over lunch, primed by his daughter, Lex probed more deeply and was interested to hear that Amal's poetry reflected the hurts caused by the devastation of Syria. He persuaded her to bring some of her work when she next visited.

"It's difficult for us to comprehend what it must be like over there," he said. "We need to get to know what you and your people have gone through."

A warm breeze flowed in off the sea and rustled through the leaves of the grapevine.

"This reminds me so much of home," Moussa Ahmadi confessed with a touch of sadness. "Do you remember, Amal? The whole family would come and we would eat at a long trestle table in the garden. We had a vine like this," he said to Lex, "but green grapes – very good, sweet."

Eugenia shot a glance at Amal and saw that she also remembered without her father's prompting. Amal smiled and nodded. "Those are the things we will always carry with us," she said reaching over to pat his hand. "Memories are bittersweet."

Adriana went indoors to fetch the dessert while Amal and Eugenia stacked the plates and took them through to the kitchen. Cicadas shrilled in the trees, a backdrop of sound.

"The battering Syria has taken must be very painful for you and your family," Lex said.

Moussa set his wine glass down on the table. "So much has been destroyed. It will take generations perhaps, to restore what has been lost."

"Lebanon recovered quickly," Lex reminded him, "Beirut is possibly even more beautiful than before."

Moussa nodded, "You're right of course, but our countries are so volatile, and peace is fragile. Even now, with the threats the Levant is facing, Lebanon could lose it all again."

"The threat from the Islamic State?" Lex asked.

Moussa nodded, "Also Israel," he said. "If Hezbollah decides to attack Israel, it will be war again." He sighed and pinched his fleshy nose between finger and thumb, a weary gesture. "You will laugh, but I would prefer to cast myself on Israel's mercy rather than these Muslim terrorists."

Lex looked down at his hands. "Adriana and I have always thrown our support behind the Arab nations," he said, "but lately we've had a bit of a change of heart. I don't think we like Israel any better, but we can see that they are almost holding back the radical forces of Islam," he glanced up at Moussa. "I hope you don't mind my frankness?"

"Not at all!"

"While the girls are away, let me tell you what happened to Eugenia recently," Lex said. He briefly recounted the story and the obstructive attitude of the police towards the occurrence.

Moussa listened in silence. "This is not an isolated incident," he said at length. "I thought when I brought my family to Spain that we were leaving that sort of fundamentalism behind us, but I was wrong. These groups have used the Israeli-Gaza war to justify their movements. The spores were already there just waiting for the right temperature to mushroom. We've both heard the warning voices— most people ignore them and believe it will all die down again."

"But it won't," Lex said.

Moussa gave a brief toss of the head and a click of the tongue to convey the negative, "Definitely not! As I see it, this is just the beginning. They want the black flag to fly over the White House and are quoted as saying they intend to make it a super-mosque when they overthrow the American government."

Lex grimaced. "I can see the disenchantment with the U.S.," he said. "But there's a universalism that is frightening—at least for us!"

Moussa grinned. "Don't imagine that you Westerners are on your own," he said. "Radical Islamists will have more mercy on the *Dhimmi* than on a non-practicing Muslim such as myself."

"*Dhimmi?*" Lex asked.

"People of the Book. The Prophet Muhammad assimilated many Jewish and Christian scriptures, with some deviations of course, into the Qur'an. In fact, Islam considers the Jewish faith closer to Islam than the Christian because belief in the Trinity suggests the worship of three gods and Islam is strictly monotheistic. The idea that God has a son is abhorrent to Islam."

"The radicals are not showing much tolerance of either religion at the moment."

"No, you're right. ISIS is slaughtering anyone that stands in their way. But it's also true that many Muslim countries have dropped the practice of *Dhimmi*. When they do allow other religions to remain in the country, they are very restricted and heavily taxed."

The three women reappeared with bowls of fresh fruit salad and frozen yoghurt, and the conversation turned to food. They parted later with promises of a return visit.

"Juan was with friends today," Eugenia said to Amal, "but you'll get to meet him next time. Are you an only child?"

Amal smiled, "Oh no, I have a younger sister who has stayed with a friend today and an older brother. But he's away at the moment." Something in Amal's eyes warned Eugenia not to pursue that line of conversation. Her curiosity was aroused but she said no more.

Chapter 10   Betrayal

Thinking back, it was difficult to pinpoint the moment when Eugenia had first decided to investigate the persecution of women and girl-children in the Middle East. She stumbled upon one case, the well-documented story of a Pakistani Christian woman, Asia Bibi. She had been accused of blasphemy against the Prophet by her Muslim neighbours after she drank from a communal water bowl thereby "polluting" it. A Christian Minority's minister and a Pakistani government politician were both killed after advocating on Bibi's behalf. She had already spent nearly five years in prison; her family was in hiding after receiving death threats and, despite petitions from many sources, the death sentence had been upheld by the courts. Eugenia was aghast at the injustice of the charge and began looking at other cases.

In a YouTube video, Nada Al-Ahdal, a bright, confident eleven-year-old girl from Yemen, addressed journalists explaining how she had run away from home and laid a complaint with the police against her mother who was forcing her into marriage.

"What about the innocence of childhood?" she asked earnestly. "What have the children done wrong; why do you marry them off like that? I'm not the only one; it can happen to any child. Some children throw themselves into the sea. They're dead now," she added matter-of-factly.

Eugenia wept as she watched the video knowing that despite Nada's confidence that she had "solved her problem", this vibrant young life was snatched away by an uncle soon afterwards. Her disobedience, and the sin of disgracing Islam, could not remain unpunished. Then there was the account of an eight-year-old that died on her wedding night after suffering internal injuries due to rape by a husband five times her age.

Adriana was still in bed early the following morning when Eugenia, still in shock, cuddled up beside her.

"Mama, it's awful! Did you know that over a quarter of Yemen's girls are married before they're fifteen? Some of them are still little children!"

Adriana sat up and plumped her pillows up behind her. She slipped an arm around Eugenia's shoulders. "I wish you wouldn't read those things," she said. "You only upset yourself!"

"The only thing necessary for evil to prevail…"

"Is if good men do nothing—I know. Surely it must be against the law?"

"What, doing nothing?" Eugenia teased. "Not that I know of."

Adriana laughed. "All right, I give up. Isn't there a law against these early marriages?"

"They did pass one in 2009 making the legal age seventeen but it was repealed as being un-Islamic."

Adriana raised her eyebrows. "Un-Islamic!"

"Muhammad was married to his second wife, Aisha when she was six-years-old and had intercourse with her when she was nine. The Prophet set the benchmark for men under Islam."

"Are you sure you want to pursue this?" her mother asked. "There's a lot of shocking things in the world that you are never going to be able to change."

Eugenia hugged her mother briefly and got up. "I don't really know yet what I'm going to do. Don't worry about me, if it gets too upsetting, I'll drop it."

But once the decision was made to create a website dedicated to women's plight under Islam it grew into something far larger than she could have anticipated. At first, the reports and photographs of the atrocities were so horrifying that she wondered whether she would have the strength to continue but, by then, it had developed into an obsessive desire to expose the cruelty these women laboured under and she knew she must go on. Soon she was posting cases daily and the interest grew exponentially.

Adriana looked in on Lex who was studying the latest reports from the Middle East on his laptop before starting work on his next chapter.

"I've just met with Moussa," she said. "I'm so pleased, Lex, the gallery is going to do an exhibition of his photographs. He's really good. You must come and see them when it opens."

Alexander Wesley-Smith turned away from the article he was reading. "I'd like to. I was hoping for an excuse for another get-together; I need to sound him out on a couple of issues. When did you say this exhibition will be opening?"

Adriana tossed her leather sling bag onto the chair and wound her arms around her husband's neck.

"I didn't," she said. "I have an idea it will be at the end of the month. I should hear from them tomorrow. But Moussa's made a booking at a Lebanese restaurant in Malaga for this weekend. I presumed you wouldn't say no."

"I'm happy with that," he said.

The restaurant was situated in a fairly dingy part of the old city, but Lex and Adriana, always adventurous, were intrigued rather than put off by the surroundings. As the door opened, their senses were assailed by the tantalizing smell of roast chicken, garlic and lemon, and it quickly became obvious that this 'discovery' was destined to become one of those delightful regular haunts. Moussa had already arrived and ordered the *mezza*. They chatted over a glass of wine as the array of small dishes was brought to the table.

"Adriana tells me you are about to make the Big Time," Lex said.

Moussa frowned. "I think you would have to admit it's only a tiny slice of success," he said. "But I'm grateful to your wife for forcing me to do something I would never otherwise have considered."

"The last time she did that to me, it was marriage!" Lex said.

Moussa laughed. "How's the book progressing?"

"Quite well," Lex said. "But the more I learn about this Islamic State the less I like it. I would appreciate it if I could use your knowledge of the culture to help me understand some of the issues."

Moussa fell silent, tapping his fingers thoughtfully on the edge of the table. Then as though a decision had been reached, he looked up. "I would like to help, Lex," he said at length, "but there's something I need to clear away first."

"Sure."

"My son, Raif, has joined ISIS and is fighting in Syria."

Both Lex and Adriana stared at him nonplussed and at a loss for words. Moussa spoke over their confusion.

"I understand your shock," he said. "And perhaps you can understand how deeply stunned I have been. I have faced some difficult things in my life, but nothing as painful as this."

"How did it happen?" Lex asked.

"It began with some deep hurt over his home country," Moussa replied. "I don't know exactly what happened after we arrived in Spain. He was still at school and seemed happy enough but there are a lot of Muslims in this area and many are radical in their beliefs. Someone got to him."

"What did he tell you?" Adriana asked.

"Very little. He knew I was angry." Moussa refilled their wine glasses, took a sip from his glass and set it back on the table. "Raif saw Assad as the problem. He believed that overthrowing him would free Syria."

"But why ISIS?"

"They were relatively unknown at that stage and I don't think he took the time to investigate. He'd set his mind on going and there was a group here who made the connections. I objected, obviously, but he wasn't prepared to listen."

"Have you heard from him since he went over?"

"Very little—almost nothing really."

Adriana reached over and gave Moussa's hand a squeeze. "I'm terribly sorry," she said. "It must be very tough."

"He was always a gentle boy," Moussa said. "If he is still alive, the things they are doing over there…" He shook his head, "They will destroy him."

He ripped off a piece of Arabic bread, leaned over and used it to scoop some *baba ganoush* from one of the dishes. "Please," he said, "help yourselves. *Sahtein.*"

"*Bon appétit,*" Lex replied with a smile.

They turned to a discussion of the various dishes of the *mezza*, some familiar to Adriana and Lex, some foreign. A waiter cleared away and took the order for the main course. Moussa drained his glass and set it down on the table. "I will help you as best I can, Lex. What do you need to know?"

Lex tapped his mouth lightly with finger and thumb as he gathered his thoughts. "I need to understand the purpose and intent of Islam in the West," he said. "Muslims have settled in England, the

Netherlands, and France, for example, and have demonstrated and threatened the host nations with death and holocaust. Why?"

Moussa nodded grimly. "All radical Muslims despise the West as weak. Islam is a triumphalist religion and what you see taking place is a form of *jihad*. They intend to conquer the enemy from within. It is a sort of wooden-horse invasion. If I'm not mistaken, their use of the word holocaust is intended to imply an alliance of the West with Israel." He tugged at his bottom lip. "At the moment, the numbers are small. If the governments act now and act decisively, they may bring the situation under control, but they don't seem to have the political will to stand up against what is happening."

Lex shook his head. "There appears to be a policy of hands-off," he agreed. "And I can't honestly understand the reasoning behind it. If people are blatantly threatening harm, surely the obvious thing is to send them back to where they came from?"

Moussa shrugged. "Ask countries like Saudi Arabia or the Emirates how they deal with troublesome ex-pats. I would say that either the host nations are weaker than I would have given them credit for, or they're being held to ransom."

Their waiter set steaming plates on the table and refilled their glasses. Lex reviewed in his mind the other questions he had wanted to pose, but in the light of the revelation about Raif, decided it was prudent to shelve them for the present.

"The food here is wonderful," Adriana commented.

"They have an excellent Lebanese chef," Moussa smiled. "If I want to eat the sort of dishes my mother used to produce, this is where I come."

As they left the restaurant later, he turned briefly to Lex, "Many people are living in a fool's paradise at the moment," he said. "I hope this book of yours will begin to wake them up."

Chapter 11   Betrayal

There's no such thing as moderate Muslims and radical Muslims. A Muslim is one who submits to the command of the creator. If he submits, he is a practicing Muslim – if he refuses to submit, he is not a Muslim. Anjem Choudary, British Islamist

Sherif Raad walked across the square to the main taxi rank carrying with him an overnight bag containing a change of shirt and underwear, shaving equipment, and a toothbrush. People elbowed their way onto packed buses, tossing heavy bundles up onto the roof racks and pushing light luggage up the steps before them like dung beetles.

An old man greeted him as he passed. He walked strongly under a heavy load betraying no sign of strain. His sunken mouth was lightly disguised under a soft moustache and flowing white beard. His face under a white turban was strong, darkened by the sun and moulded by the elements.

Babies howled. Over the revving engines of the buses, drivers chanted their destinations. Tyres screamed on the tarmac and horns blared. A dissonant wail of music arose from the open-fronted shops bounding the square, snatched and scattered by the breezes which also carried with them the cooking smells from several little bars. Red and white chequered *keffieh*, strings of black headbands, plastic flowers, and copper coffee pots, hung in profusion above the openings. Vendors hemmed in by bags of fruit and grain, barrels of olives, vegetables, and clothing, shouted their wares to anyone who would listen.

Sherif found the taxi he was looking for. The bald driver sat behind the steering-wheel baring his teeth in little dog-like grimaces as he waited for passengers. He greeted Sherif effusively, clasping his outstretched hand in both of his own.

"*Marhabba*." Sherif extricated himself delicately.

"*Marahapt'ein! Kifak?*"

"I am fine. You are going to Beirut?"

"Of course, of course!"

Sherif Raad paid the fare and settled into the back seat. A large woman, laden with packages, squeezed in beside him. She was perspiring freely causing darker rings under the armpits of her black dress and he moved further into the corner to avoid her.

Sherif Raad's father had been Syrian, his mother, Lebanese. During the civil war, they had left Lebanon and his mother died not long after that. He had scant recollection of her; his upbringing had been continued through a series of aunts in conjunction with his father and he remembered his childhood with distaste. His father was an ambitious man who had gained what he could despite his limited opportunities and had vicariously transferred his ambitions to his son. Sherif still remembered the fear with which he had faced every interrogation regarding his schoolwork and, later, his future. Gradually, he had gained certain cunning. He came to anticipate the answers required of him and covered his feelings of inadequacy with a cool façade. From there, it was a simple step to withdraw his emotions, to isolate and expunge them one by one. His veneer was composed of what he believed was expected of him and gradually this pretence became a reality.

Muhammad Mustapha Khalil needed two more passengers before he could leave. He leaned out of the window and yelled.

"Beyrouth?"

A man Sherif judged to be in his early thirties, ambled over and haggled over the fare.   The transaction settled he slid into the front seat shifting his buttocks slightly until he discovered a comfortable position. Reaching into the inner pocket of his checkered jacket, he retrieved a battered packet of cigarettes.

"*Cigarra?*" He swung around with an expansive gesture. Sherif gave a characteristic toss of the head in refusal; the man shrugged, drew a cigarette from the pack and cupped his hands protectively around it as he struck the match.

A fourth passenger crammed himself into the back seat and the Mustapha Khalil started the engine. He cleared his throat, spat onto the pavement, and swung out into the flow of traffic. The driver nudged the horn sporadically and accelerated as he gained the open road.

Muhammad Mustapha Khalil was proud of his taxi, a Mercedes Benz only ten years old, which he maintained in immaculate condition. He leaned out of the window as he drove, constantly alert for a change in the tone of the engine. He was a tall, sparse man with a dry, yellowed complexion and uneasy colourless eyes. What hair he still had was slicked back above small lobeless ears.

The road to Beirut through Raqqa province was dangerous. Various factions were at war with the Syrian army and with one another. Travelling any distance meant living by your wits and in the hope that Allah looked favourably upon your journey. Both Aleppo and Hama were cities in turmoil and armed *mujahideen* roamed the countryside. Taxi drivers relied on friends for reports en route. Taxis coming the other way were stopped with a flash of the headlights and the drivers grilled. Often, at the innumerable checkpoints, a hostile attitude was softened by the sharing of a packet of cigarettes, and Muhammad Mustapha Khalil kept a good supply in the boot of the car.

They arrived in Beirut late the following morning without incident, and Sherif Raad booked into a hotel. He changed into a clean, grey *thobe* and made his way on foot to the mosque. Entering the massive gates, he removed his shoes in the ablution room just as the call to prayer came from the minaret. He performed *wudu'*, the cleansing of the body, washing hands and feet in the prescribed manner but felt no need for *Niyat*, the cleansing of the mind. Religion was irrelevant to Sherif; his soul had no need of it.

In the cool interior of the building, robed figures squatted on their haunches in groups chatting quietly among themselves. Sherif entered the main prayer room and joined the rows of men on their prayer mats. He carried out the prayer ritual automatically, folding his hands across his chest, prostrating himself, and reciting the passages.

"*Allahu Akbar*, God hears those who call upon him. Oh Lord, praise be to you."

The men rose to sitting position and prostrated themselves once more. Rising and sitting, rising and prostrating, moving in unity like the waves flowing into the shore.

Sherif was known to his contact, Abdul-Basir, a bald man with a friendly smile and deep creases around his eyes. He sought him out when the prayers were concluded.

"*Marhabba,* M. Raad, the imam is waiting for you. Come."

Sherif followed him through the building and up a broad staircase to the offices located on the first floor. The imam was seated behind an oak desk. A generous white beard which alone, Sherif decided, would have afforded him a high position, flowed over an ample chest. Pudgy fingers were clasped together above the shelf of his stomach. As he straightened the folds of his head covering and indicated that Sherif should sit, his eyes reflected unveiled hostility. Sherif was well known to him by reputation. The interview was brief and the contempt of the imam was tangible. Even the people of the Book, those with *Dhimmi* status, were better than these infidels who would not submit themselves to the law of Allah. They were worthy only of death. There would be no drinks offered, no sweetmeats, it was better to cut this time short lest he take a sword to this man's throat himself in the name of Allah and his Prophet, blessed be his name.

"You understand the importance of what you will be carrying?"

"I was briefed in Syria," Sherif replied shortly.

"And you have been paid for your services?"

"I will receive the full amount when the parcel is safely delivered."

The imam felt his hackles rise further at the lack of reverence in Sherif's address. His eyes narrowed as he spoke. "If my contacts in Raqqa find that you have tampered in any way with what I am about to place in your hands, or if you lose it, you understand that the consequences will be extremely serious?"

Sherif nodded shortly. The threat was not lost on him. The imam leaned down over his stomach with some difficulty, retrieved something from a desk drawer and passed it across to Sherif. His eyes widened with surprise and he looked across at the imam questioningly.

"A Qur'an?"

"And this cell phone. Remember what I said. You will protect it with your life should that become necessary."

He nodded slightly. "If that is all…"

"When will you be back in Syria?"

"We will leave tomorrow night and all being well, we should be in Raqqa the following evening." The imam added a silent *insha Allah* to that statement and, with an imperious gesture, showed him the door.

Sherif Raad returned to his hotel room and slept with the Qur'an and the phone under his pillow. The following morning, he bought a needle and thread from one of the shops below the hotel and stitched the book crudely into the inner lining of his leather jacket. He observed to himself that this was the closest he had ever come to being religious. As he had expected, the cell phone was secured with a password. He removed his own phone from his belt pouch and replaced it with the one given by the imam.

There was some personal business to attend to in Beirut, and it was late afternoon on the following day when he settled his bill and made contact once more with Muhammad Mustapha Khalil. He paid for a seat in the taxi and left his bag in the care of the driver. Sherif crossed the road to a restaurant. It was an hour before a boy came to call him and three other passengers were already waiting in the car.

Chapter 12   Betrayal

"Papa, does Moussa Ahmadi know his son has crept into your book as a main character?" Eugenia asked innocently.

"Not really," Lex replied.

"So, don't you think you should tell him? How is he going to feel when he finally reads what you've written?"

Alexander Wesley-Smith looked up from his newspaper a trifle irritably. "I've used Raif's name," he said, "but I honestly don't know anything about him. The whole thing so far is a figment of my imagination."

"Except for the way his decision came about," his daughter persisted. "You told me yourself you wrote it as Moussa told it to you."

Lex folded the newspaper back so that he could read the editorial on Ebola. "Moussa won't mind," he said shortly. "But I'll let him know sometime—or perhaps I'll rename the guy."

Eugenia rolled her eyes and shook her head but Lex pretended not to notice. She changed her line of questioning.

"Have you found a working title yet?"

"I haven't. Titles are tricky; somewhere along the line, they evolve out of the story. It will come to me eventually. Now, don't you have something more important to do?"

Eugenia smiled good-naturedly and left the terrace.

Lex returned to the Ebola article. On one side there was ISIS and, on the other, the catastrophic increase of Ebola. Both were spreading with horrifying rapidity and both were deadly. He folded the newspaper, left it on the coffee table in the living room, and headed back to his office.

Half an hour later, Alexander Wesley-Smith whistled softly between his teeth and rolled back on his office chair. According to a source on the web, when the Bin Laden construction company under Minoru Yamasaki played their part in the construction and engineering of the first World Trade Centre back in 1966, one of the workers had actually asked where the demolition devices were to be placed in building seven. The report proved even more interesting. In a federal court RICO suit, it transpired that the army had been commissioned to outline a scenario in which the twin towers could be brought down using commercial airlines as weapons. McNiven, who was part of C-Battery 2/81st Field Artillery stationed in Germany in 1976, had been involved in the planning and had filed an affidavit after the 2001 attack followed—in precise detail—the scenario the army unit had prepared.

In '73, two months after the completion of the Rockefeller's World Trade Centre, David Rockefeller launched the Trilateralist Commission. According to McNiven, the attack was intended to have taken place in 1976; the Towers were built for demolition and were never designed to stand for as long as they did. Something had caused a change of plan.

If this was not damning enough, director and film maker, Aaron Russo, declared that eleven months prior to the 9-11 attacks, Nicholas Rockefeller had predicted that there would be an event that would trigger an invasion of Afghanistan and Iraq.

Lex sat back and swigged at his coffee. Whether it was the Illuminati, or whatever you chose to call it, these accounts from apparently credible sources testified to the presence of a powerful shadow group. Around the time Aaron Russo released his movie, America: From Freedom to Fascism, he had made it clear that Nicholas Rockefeller put forward reasons for the invasions which had nothing to do with the official Bush line of dealing with Al Qaeda.

"We're going into Afghanistan," he told Russo, "so we can run pipelines through the Caspian Sea." And the reason for hitting Iraq? "To take the oil and establish bases in the Middle East, making it part of the New World Order."

As far as Lex was concerned, there was a whole lot that continued to make little or no sense at all. Control over Middle Eastern oil reserves was one way of holding the world to ransom, of course. But why pulverise nations, raise the hatred of a plethora of militant groups, arm and finance them, and allow them virtually free access into the West to carry out acts of terror?

Lex shifted his chair forward, put his empty cup down on the desk beside his computer and turned back to the keyboard.

So, if you were some sort of insider and you wanted information, or misinformation for that matter, leaked to the public, how would you go about it? The answer was simple of course, you befriend a filmmaker. It was unlikely that Nicholas Rockefeller had anticipated confidentiality when he provided this tidbit to Aaron Russo in another of their friendly conversations: "The end goal is to get everybody chipped, to control the whole society and to have the bankers and the elite people control the world."

* * *

At forty-two, Nour's father was broad-shouldered, with a good head of black hair, a black moustache, and heavy eyebrows over fleshy features. Ever since Nour's brush with the Sharia police her father had walked her to and from work. He still strode out with a slight swagger left over from his macho younger days and his olive complexion sported a perpetual two-day growth of beard.

Nour insisted on wearing gum boots under her robe as a private act of rebellion against the list of laws under which she now had to live, but she carried her sandals in her bag to slip on once she arrived at the bakery.

"How can anyone be expected to walk in such stupid clothing," she fumed after tripping over rubble on the broken pavement. "I presume they invented the *niqab* as a form of punishment for the sin of being born female. I can hardly see where I am going!"

Walid turned to look at her. "It would help if you wore shoes!" he remarked with a grin. "No member of the Islamic State cares if you are wearing those things, but you'll end up on your nose if you're not careful."

"My nose is covered, *Baba*," she reminded him bitterly.

She disappeared into the toilet at the back of the shop and returned wearing jeans and a tee shirt with a dark blue *hijab*[12] tied stylishly over her hair.

---

[12] Islamic head scarf

Nour watched Raif Ahmadi surreptitiously. He interested her and if she had been honest with herself she would have had to admit that he attracted her. He arrived from the barracks each morning changed his uniform for a set of white overalls and worked with Nour until he knew almost as much about bread-making as she did. Despite herself, she began to look forward to seeing him. Over time, he told her about his background and his family, but it was when he spoke about the death of his grandparents that she began to see what had brought him back to Syria.

"Did you really think that joining these rebels could make amends for what happened to them?" she asked.

He met her eyes for a moment. "I honestly don't know what I was thinking," he said. "At the time I was convinced it was the will of God."

Nour raised her eyebrows. "You can't tell me that anything these savages are doing is the will of God. You are not like these men, Raif. So why do you stay?"

"I joined on the understanding that I would be free to leave after two years."

"In the meantime, just being with them means that you are contaminated by what they are doing. Is that what you want?"

He turned away. "I should not be talking to you like this, Nour."

"And why not? It's the first time you have begun to speak any sense!"

He grinned despite himself. "Because, knowing how you shoot your mouth off at every opportunity, what I am about to say could get us both into trouble."

"So, tell me then!"

"The only thing that has kept me from walking off into the desert so far is you."

Nour turned abruptly back to the task of shaping the dough and Raif could see that her face was flushed.

"And I suppose the thought of what the Islamic State might do if they caught you wouldn't discourage you at all?" she asked sarcastically.

"I would make sure that I would never fall into their hands," he replied without hesitation. "I have seen what they do to deserters. I would have to find a way to mingle with the refugees."

She shot him another glance. "Then go, Raif, get out while you can! There are so many leaving the city at the moment."

He took her by the shoulders and looked into her dark eyes. "Nour, I was serious just now, when I said I didn't want to leave you. If there is a way to get out, would you come with me?"

"How can you ask me that? We hardly know one another."

"I know you well enough to know that I want to be with you."

"My life is here in Syria."

"Syria is crumbling."

She shrugged, "Things will turn around eventually."

"And then, perhaps, you could settle down and marry Sherif Raad," he teased.

She laughed and threw a piece of dough at him which he caught deftly. "A fate worse than death!" she assured him.

That lunchtime, Nour's father was standing waiting for her with muscular arms folded over his chest. As always in the warmer weather, he wore brown slacks and a white vest that displayed his upper torso to perfection.

"We need to talk, Nour."

She looked up at him, startled. "Sure, *Baba*, what about?"

"I want you to reconsider Sherif's proposal."

"*Baba*, you can't be serious! I've told you, I don't even like him."

"With marriage, liking is not the point," he said. "Your mother and I hardly knew one another but, with time, we learned to love. It's about attitude."

"But why are you asking me again? You know I want to wait for marriage."

"Do you?" he asked pointedly. She blushed and dropped her eyes. "Do you think I don't see or hear?" His voice rose in anger. "This ISIS man has his eyes on you. Can I allow that to happen? You know what these men are like. If he takes you, Nour, you will become his slave. Later, when he becomes bored with you, there will be other wives."

"*La, Baba*. You're wrong about Raif," she said quietly. "He's not like the others."

"Don't be foolish, Nour! Use your head. Do not let me have to order you to follow my bidding. When Sherif returns from Lebanon, I want you to give me your answer."

"*Baba*, please don't do this!"

He turned away. "You are my daughter, Nour. Believe me; what I'm doing is for your protection!"

Chapter 13   Betrayal

There were two men and a youth in the car besides the driver,
Muhammad Mustapha Khalil. Sherif nodded a greeting to the front
seat passenger, Ahmed Samal. They had met before on this route.
Sherif was unacquainted with the third man, whom Khalil introduced
as Rashid, and sat well away from him as though the idea of human
contact was repulsive. A heavy moustache partially hid an old knife
wound that severed the corner of this passenger's mouth and
streaked back in a thin, white line across a face as pitted and pithy as
that of an old orange. The boy, who was dressed in a discoloured
robe, gazed vacantly at each of the men in turn before settling down
against the back door. In a few moments, his head lolled and he
dozed.

Samal was the most animated member of the party. He spoke
rapidly and often, in a guttural manner that made the words sound as
though they were coughed from the back of his throat. In moments
of silence, he would suddenly giggle to himself or burst into
unrestrained song. His pupils were dilated in eyes that appeared
black and agitated.

"How long before the border?"

Muhammad Mustapha shrugged without bothering to answer. His
headlights had picked out the inert body of a dog on the road and he
swung the wheel heavily to avoid it without lifting his foot from the
accelerator. Pulling his head in from the window, he inserted a CD
into the deck and the deep-throated voice of Fairuz filled the car.

At Batroun they stopped for a beer and Muhammad Mustapha
informed Sherif of a change of plan.

"These guys are going to join the Caliphate," he said. "We can't
take them through the border; they don't have the necessary
permits."

Sherif had travelled with Khalil on his alternate routes when he
carried contraband. The driver always assured him they were no
more dangerous than the border posts. It would be risky, of course,
but risks were there to be taken. The northern border post was the

only feasible route into the war-ravaged area north of the Euphrates but it remained tense and dangerous. Closures were endemic. The border itself was porous and regularly used by insurgents for smuggling arms and people. Muhammad Mustapha had developed his own routes since the war made crossings dangerous. Getting customers through was his specialty but the costs were high and everyone knew that detection on either side could be fatal.

Sherif Raad shrugged and nodded. "Which way will we be going in?"

"Hekr Ed Dahri. Can you get them across?"

Sherif scratched his head. "If I can keep Sammal quiet. It's possible."

There was an armed barricade before Tripoli; the Lebanese military was engaged in a routine check. Two soldiers cradling automatic rifles lounged against a makeshift guard hut and a third sauntered over and inspected each of the men slowly and deliberately before speaking.

"Where are you coming from?" he demanded. His tainted breath fanned the driver's cheek.

The man in the back seat nudged the boy awake with his foot and hissed at him to find his papers. The youth moaned slightly and blinked into consciousness, wiping a line of spittle from his mouth with the back of his hand. The spotlights were harsh and uncompromising diffused only by the motes of dust stirred up by the taxi. A second soldier lifted his back from the wall of the hut and approached the vehicle while the smaller of the two wearing an ill-fitting uniform leaned across the driver and tapped the panelling of the dashboard.

"Open the boot!"

Muhammad Mustapha Khalil took the keys from the ignition and walked around the back with the soldier. He cleared his throat and spat into the dirt. His hips were thrust forward in a self-assured pose but his mouth formed unconscious grimaces around his front teeth.

The second soldier opened the door on Sherif's side and inspected the door panels. Whimpering with fright, the youth pressed himself into the corner of the car.

"What's wrong with the boy?"

Sherif shrugged.

"What's wrong with you, boy?"

"*Ma fi shi*. Nothing. Don't shoot me! Don't shoot!" The boy was dragged from the taxi, fighting wildly. One of the soldiers adeptly ran his hands over the youth's robes and shook his head.

"Nothing."

"Get out! All of you!"

As he left the car, Rashid momentarily brought a hand up to his mouth to cover the scar, a habit as old as the scar itself. He retrieved a string of worry beads from the pocket of his jeans and clicked them over one by one.

"Whose luggage is this?"

The driver indicated the youth.

"Come! Open it up! Where are you going?"

"Tripoli." He fidgeted nervously.

They made him undo his bundle at the side of the road, scattering clothes and cooking pots and a small parcel of food wrapped in newspaper. They did not expect to find anything, but a little fun helped to while away the long and tedious hours.

"Where are the rest of you headed?" the short soldier asked as he examined their documents.

"Nahr al-Kabir."

"Good luck with the crossing. There have been hold-ups. Trucks have been waiting to get in for days since the last disturbances."

They dropped the boy off in Tripoli and continued on the north road.

Muhammad Mustapha Khalil left the coastal road at Cheikh Zennad Tahta. Few lights were now visible as they travelled through miles of farmland. It was 3.00 am when they passed through the small town of Knaisse.

"We are nearing the village of Hekr Ed Dahri," Muhammad said. "I will leave you nearby. There is an old bridge that crosses the Al Kabir River. Often there are patrols in that area so you will need to be careful. Once you are over the river you are in Syrian territory."

Samal's face twitched nervously. "You are just leaving us?"

"There's no way of getting the taxi across," he replied irritably. I will return to the crossing at Nahr al-Kabir."

"There's a goat path on the other side," Sherif cut in. "It leads to a farm road. We are to wait at the mosque where the imam is expecting us. Someone will take us to Homs."

"I will pick you up there, *insh'Allah*," Muhammad Mustapha said. "Sherif knows the connection. He also knows what to do if I don't arrive."

Samal handed out cigarettes and put the packet back in his pocket. They smoked quietly, reflectively, their inhalations causing red tips to glow brightly in the darkness of the cab, and their exhalations to fill the car with smoke. Then, until they reached Hekr Ed Dahri the only sound was the steady click click of Rashid's worry beads.

All of them knew that the night had just begun.

Chapter 14   Betrayal

For the first time in her life, Nour felt trapped and there seemed to be no way out of the mess she was in. The thought of marriage to Sherif Raad was repugnant but her father had become intractable, refusing even to discuss the situation further and her mother simply advised her to obey.

"Sherif's older than me," she pleaded.

"Not so much," her mother replied, "Your father says he is only thirty-three."

"And I am eighteen! To me he is old. And anyway," Nour added pressing her case, "I don't trust him. There's something missing from his psyche!"

Her mother laughed. "Now you are being silly, Nour. He's quiet, and a little inhibited, but we have known his father for years. He's a good man, a businessman, and Sherif is likely to continue in his footsteps when Syria returns to normal."

"I'm not interested in marrying for money," Nour said defiantly, "but I do want to marry a man who will make me happy. He is not that person."

She saw the sympathy expressed in her mother's eyes, but both women knew there was little they could do to change Walid's mind. Nour put her head in her hands and wept. She wept for what she was about to lose knowing now that the decision had been made for her. And she cried for the growing feeling within her for Raif, which might if it were allowed, become love.

"I hope he never comes back," she said angrily through her tears. "I really pray he never comes back."

In the days which followed, Nour treated Raif like a stranger again. He had no idea what he might have done to deserve the sudden chill that had developed between them.

He waited until Walid had left the shop before challenging her to tell him and was startled by the sudden flood of tears. He reached out a hand awkwardly and placed it on her shoulder.

"*Shu beki inti?* Tell me what's wrong."

The story came out between sobs. "I never thought he would force me to do this. He has always understood how I feel."

"But why now?" he asked.

Nour looked up, her eyes were red-rimmed. "He wants to protect me."

"I don't understand, wants to protect you from what? "

Her glance was almost pitying as though she could not believe he could be so obtuse.

"Raif, he is afraid of you…" her voice tailed off and Raif stared at her with growing comprehension. He was amazed at the strength of his emotions.

"I can't let him do this!" he said. "You can't marry a man you don't like; it will ruin your life." He ran his hands through his hair. "I must leave here," he said. "If I get out of the picture he will change his mind."

She reached up and touched his face. "Raif, if you go the Islamic State will hunt you down and kill you. I could not bear that."

Their eyes met and, as they locked glances, there was a conjugation of spirit that went beyond the physical attraction he felt for her. He took the small oval face between his hands and kissed her softly. She drew back, confused, and looked round, fearful that they may have been observed but they were still alone.

"You shouldn't have done that."

"I know, I'm sorry." They both recognised the lie.

She was awkward under his regard; a tension had developed between them. The question had no answer; the problem remained unresolved. They returned to work each consumed with the proximity of the other and the turbulence of their own thoughts.

"There must be an answer," he said. "We just have to find it.

* * *

As they approached the little village Muhammad Mustapha Khalil switched off his lights and then his engine. The taxi rolled to a stop, its wheels crunching the small stone on the verge. There was silence in the vehicle.

"The bridge is straight ahead, about half a kilometre down the road," Muhammad said softly. "Hekr ed Dahri is further up on our left. As you come to the bottom of this road, there are buildings against the road on your right-hand side. I don't need to tell you to be very quiet."

"Military?" Rashid asked the question.

"It's a while since I've been this way. It's an obvious illegitimate crossing point, so it is possible."

Sherif took his overnight bag and stepped out into the darkness. A waxing moon cast a little light. Once their eyes had adjusted, they should be able to see their way without too much difficulty. There was tree growth on the other bank of the river that would limit their visibility, but by then they should be out of immediate danger.

The two men joined him and saluted silently to Khalil. He started his vehicle and without using his headlights, he swung round in the road and headed back the way he came.

Samal raised his hands angrily. "*Yihrib-dinak*! We paid him good money to get us across the border and he dumps us on the road and tells us to find our own way!"

"Shut up!" Sherif snapped. "I don't want to hear another word from you until we're on Syrian soil—do you understand?"

Samal spat into the dirt. "Who the hell do you think you are?" he growled but he lapsed into silence nonetheless.

Sherif set out at a steady pace until he became aware of the buildings looming black against the skyline. He turned to make sure that Samal and Rashid had seen them. There was a plantation on their left and Sherif moved onto the verge against the shadow cast by the trees and beckoned the others to follow. They walked slowly, watching for any sign of movement, straining against the silence of the night for any unusual sound.

The shrill, pulsating cry of frogs signalled the closeness of the river. Somewhere an owl called and another answered. The men reached the corner of the road where it made a wide sweep to the left. Opposite, beyond a group of trees, the ground banked away towards the water. The three men waited and watched. A cat, crouching low, crossed the road ahead of them and disappeared into the undergrowth. Samal whistled between his teeth and laughed softly.

"Let's go," Sherif whispered and, as he led the way across the road and down the shallow bank, the eerie chant of the frogs ceased. The men could make out two concrete structures at the entrance to the bridge, pale in the uneasy light of the moon. As they drew closer Sherif saw that they were heavily pock-marked by gunfire.

Another fifty meters would see them on Syrian soil. They were unprepared for the infrared beam that was triggered the moment they stepped onto the bridge. In an instant, they were held in the naked glare of spotlights and the persistent wail of a siren shattered the silence. There was the urgent sound of running feet and someone shouted a command.

"Stop or we will shoot!"

"Run!" Sherif was already halfway across the bridge with Rashid hot on his heels. Samal was some distance behind them. Bullets slammed into concrete as the two men flung themselves into the bushes at the far end. Samal never made it. His body lay as it had fallen at the centre of the bridge over the Al Kabir River, head and shoulders into Syria.

The two men lay panting, not daring to move in case the soldiers would violate the rules and cross over into Syrian territory. They could hear the clamour of angry voices only meters away and the thud and scrape of Sammal's body being dragged back without ceremony across the bridge. Someone shouted for their benefit no doubt, that it should be tossed into the river and fed to the fish. Eventually, the siren stopped, the voices retreated, and the frogs began their chorus afresh. Sherif tapped Rashid on the shoulder. They crouched low and made their way slowly through the sparse undergrowth until a more defined path became visible. Several of the local people, alerted by the noise, were waiting for them outside one of the houses.

"*Kisimek, yani*, we thought you were all dead!"

"We left one behind on the bridge," Sherif said. "We were lucky to make it."

"Come in, come in! We will drink tea before we find you a place to rest."

The siren, they were told by the eager group of men, was new. One previous crossing had been attempted but none had made it through.

"Allah was with you, blessed be his name!" He was a short, stocky individual with a broken nose and greasy sideburns that oozed down the angle of his jaw. His wife, wearing a pink *hijab* over her head and a blanket wrapped around her nightgown, brought a steaming kettle and a tray of small glasses. She set them on the floor without a word and went back to her bed. The men sat cross-legged and over their glasses of sweet tea, and discussed with great animation the events of the night. No one seemed to mind that neither Sherif nor Rashid added much to the conversation. Much later, they were given a blanket and basin of water in which to wash. They rolled themselves up and soon a gentle snoring from the other side of the room told Sherif that Rashid was asleep. He lit a cigarette and waited for the dawn to come.

The men arose at 4.00 am for morning prayer and then slept again till daybreak. There was the smell of the cooking fires, the tinkling of bracelets on the arms of the girls who brought water from the river. Sherif and Rashid were served freshly baked bread, creamy *laban,* and salty black olives before a youth directed them to the mosque.

It was a small cubist building with only a central dome on the roof relieving its uniformity. The door was painted in a cobalt blue with chips in the paintwork revealing numerous layers of colour underneath. The imam greeted them cordially.

"*Marhabba. Shu al-akhbar?*"

"*Marahabt'ein.*"

Sherif updated him with news from the previous night, of which he suspected the imam had already been apprised. Rashid hung back looking even more ill at ease in the religious setting than he had since entering the taxi the day before.

"There is a man here with a car," the imam said. "He will take you to Homs. Muhammad Mustapha Khalil has told me you will pay."

"He said nothing to us," Sherif replied shortly.

The imam raised his hands and dropped them. "Carrying passengers is a very dangerous and expensive business these days. Without money, no one can move."

"How much does this man want?"

The imam named his price and Sherif and Rashid exchanged glances. Some bargaining took place and eventually a more realistic figure was agreed upon.

The vehicle, a pick-up truck with a canopy, was in dubious condition. The front bumper was roped in place, the passenger door deeply dented and the windscreen cracked, but their driver, whom they recognised from the previous night, assured them it would reach Homs without any trouble. He shook hands enthusiastically with both men and introduced himself.

"I am Hafez al-Khatieb," he said proudly. "I am, without doubt, the best driver in Syria. With me, you need fear nothing!"

Before they were halfway to their destination, Sherif decided that facing bullets on the bridge over the Al Kabir River was preferable to being a passenger in the vehicle of Hafez al-Khatieb.

They avoided the old section of Homs where grey, derelict buildings gaped like heaped skulls picked clean in a desert land. Bashar al-Assad's government forces had fought for control of Homs for two years and finally succeeded in ousting the rebel army in May. Since then, the city had enjoyed a period of relative peace and normality.

Hafez overshot the taxi rank in Deir Baalbah, threw his pickup into reverse, narrowly missing a motor cyclist, and skidded to a halt. He grinned at Sherif and Rashid.

"This is the place. What did I say? You are here safely, I have an excellent record."

Sherif paid him and wished him a safe journey home. Hafez made a quick u-turn, heedless of the blaring horns of the oncoming traffic, and sped off in the opposite direction.

Chapter 15   Betrayal

It was another two days before Muhammad Mustapha Khalil arrived
to collect the two men. In the meantime, they had found a room in a
cheap hotel nearby and paid the son of a taxi owner to report to them
the moment Khalil arrived at the rank.

Sherif paced the streets irritably as they waited for news. Rashid
lay on his bed with his eyes half-shut and chain-smoked while
listening to war reports on a bedside radio. When Muhammad
Mustapha Khalil finally arrived, they were in a state of high tension.

"Where have you been, *yani*?" Sherif demanded.

Khalil picked his teeth with a sharpened matchstick and shrugged.
"The border was slow, thirty hours of waiting on that side. And of
course, after that, I visited my sister."

Sherif steadied himself. "You heard the news about Samal?"

"*La*," the slight backward toss of the head denoted the negative.
"He didn't make it?"

"He was shot on the bridge."

"He was a little crazy," Khalil said lifting his hands and dropping
them as though that was a worthy explanation of Samal's death.
"So, next time we must use another crossing. There is a farmer I
know with a boat. It's a pity, the bridge was useful."

Sherif took the front seat and he and Rashid waited while another
couple of passengers were found before they headed north on the
road to Hama. The Syrian Military had recaptured most of the
villages and towns on the road to Hama from al Nusra, but signs of
devastation were everywhere. Shattered buildings, burned-out
vehicles, traumatised women and children, all bore testimony to the
futility of war. There could be no victors in this conflict and the
scars, if they were allowed to heal, would take many, many years to
erase.

There were still contested areas and the possibility of rocket fire or
a stray bullet. But the men had grown accustomed to the risk of
death. Rashid slept, Sherif watched, and conversation was minimal.

They passed through Hama, dropped off the passengers, and took on a man, his wife, and a young child who were bound for Aleppo. The young woman was elegantly dressed in a long grey skirt and matching jacket. She wore a lighter grey *hijab* over her head and twisted over one shoulder. Her face was intelligent and expressed a quiet dignity, and she held her young son protectively against her for much of the journey. Her husband's face was tired and drawn with sorrow that deeply touched his eyes. He gazed wordlessly at the scenery, the scrubby trees, the land left untended, crumbling rocky walls the same buff colour as the endless sand. The villages had been broken by the power of the guns, by the arrogance and the fury of man; their scars bore testimony to the noise and smoke, to blood spilled and bodies broken, the final tally of which lay beneath the wordless undulations of the sand. And the men with the guns were thirsty still; not yet satiated by the destruction, the maiming and the killing, by the bleak eyes of a million children and the tears of a nation.

"Are you going to stay in Aleppo?" Muhammad asked the man conversationally.

He shrugged. "We are hoping to get over the border into Turkey."

"There is fighting in the area between Aleppo and the Turkish border at the moment," Khalil said. "You would do better to try Lebanon. If you have money, I could get you across."

The woman gazed uncertainly at her husband, but he was looking out of the window once more.

"We are refugees," she said at length, speaking over the silence. "We no longer have money. Perhaps at the Turkish border the international community will help us."

"Perhaps," Muhammad replied and then he too lapsed into silence. They were approaching the outskirts of Aleppo.

Suhail al-Hassan, a strong, strategic commander of Bashar al-Assad's army, known by his men as the Tiger, had managed to bring a level of calm to the city. Young, charismatic, long-haired, and heavily bearded, the Tiger's role was to infiltrate and work with al-Qaeda to undermine the revolution. There were still skirmishes and exchanges of gunfire between armed groups and the Syrian army, but the focus had shifted to rural areas around Hama and the city was licking its wounds. Many factories had begun working once more as the army cut off the supply routes of the rebels and the siege on the industrial area was lifted.

The drive downriver from Aleppo to Raqqa was a short but dangerous journey. No one could be certain at any time which army, or faction, was in control of the area. Sherif and Muhammad Mustapha Khalil held passes from the Islamic State and Al-Nusra, as well as their identification documents, which could be produced if they met up with blockades by the Syrian Army. The difficulty was in knowing which to produce at any one time. Uniforms were seldom a giveaway. Rashid carried no local identification and he was an obvious danger to the others. Muhammad, who had done all this before, carried documents he had picked up on the black market for these smuggling trips. The previous owners of the papers were all deceased, so he considered his possession of them to be quite within the bounds of legality. He had provided Rashid with a set of identity documents that would satisfy all but the most thorough scrutiny.

They were stopped several times at roadblocks along the way and Muhammad Mustapha's cool head and familiarity with the circumstances enabled them to produce the right documents at the right moment. The atmosphere in the taxi remained tense and Rashid's worry beads clicked over the worn leather thong slowly and systematically as they reached the second ISIS checkpoint a few miles from Raqqa.

The soldiers wore camouflage against the desert conditions but had not abandoned their ominous black head covering. They approached the vehicle with automatic rifles at the ready and ordered the men from the vehicle. Muhammad Mustapha Khalil's confidence never seemed to flag under a challenge and he greeted them cheerfully.

"*Marhabba*! How are things going here? Are things still quiet in Raqqa?"

They gave the identification papers a cursory check and handed them back. Sherif kept an eye on them as he lit a cigarette. Their behaviour was edgy, which he recognised as a sure sign of danger. He stood with Rashid and Muhammad as a couple of soldiers searched the vehicle.

Muhammad tried again. "*Shu al-akhbar*? What news?" he asked.

"There's a lot of talk from the Americans, many people are leaving Raqqa."

Muhammad showed his teeth in a characteristic grimace. "They've been talking for weeks about attacking, *yani*. Obama is all talk!"

The soldier shrugged, "You're right, maybe it's nothing."

Muhammad glanced swiftly at Sherif who dragged on his cigarette, dropped the butt, and ground it with his heel.

"So, can we go?" Khalil asked.

"Sure. Go! *Allahu Akbar.*"

"*Allahu al-Akhbar*," Muhammad Mustapha reiterated absently. One of the soldiers raised a hand as the taxi sped away.

The sun was already lying low over the horizon as they left; a fiery ball magnified many times by the dust haze. The sky was blood red across the horizon; an annunciation of things to come.

It was after 8.00 pm when they arrived. Sherif made his way to his room above the bakery and emptied his overnight bag. He slept, as he had since leaving Beirut, with his jacket on and the reassuring weight of the Qur'an on his chest. There was good money to come from this delivery, but it would have to wait for morning.

Chapter 16   Betrayal

"Faced with disconcerting episodes of violent fundamentalism, our respect for true followers of Islam should lead us to avoid hateful generalizations, for authentic Islam and the proper reading of the Qur'an are opposed to every form of violence." Pope Francis I

"You can't say Islam is a religion of peace because Islam does not mean peace. Islam means submission, so the Muslim is one who submits. There is a place for violence for Islam. There is a place for jihad in Islam." Anjem Choudary, British Islamist.

As the merest hint of light announced the coming dawn, the first U.S. air strikes were made against Raqqa. At the time of the call to early morning prayer, brilliant flashes illuminated the city turning the sky crimson and shaking the earth with the force of the explosions. Aircraft rolled in from the north as the U.S and its allies, Saudi Arabia, Jordan, the United Arab Emirates, Bahrain, and Qatar, launched against the city.

Sherif Raad stood at his window and watched the bombs fall. ISIS used Raqqa as a weapon distribution center but they had had ample warning to move their arsenals. Everyone knew the attacks were imminent; the U.S. had been promising to launch against them for weeks. Hundreds of civilians had already left Raqqa for the Turkish border and, at the same time, the Islamic State had begun to disperse their fighters among the civilian population.

Naturally, Sherif was curious about the information he had brought in from Lebanon. He had checked the Qur'an carefully to see whether it was coded in some way, but his eye could discern nothing unusual. They probably would not sustain the offensive for long and he decided to wait for daylight before making the drop-off. It would be necessary to deliver the book to the right hands as soon as possible. Sherif was not overly disturbed by the bombing. He had survived many attacks on Beirut as a child. Neither the noise, nor the suffering of others affected him to any great extent: you feared, or you overcame fear; you felt, or you conquered feeling, it was as simple as that.

He dressed and waited until the noise abated as suddenly as it had begun and the aircraft headed back for base. The silence at first was eerie, but then the sirens blared as the rescue vehicles and ambulances appeared, apparently from nowhere, and sped towards those areas that had come under fire.

The pre-arranged place for Sherif's meeting was fortunately not the military headquarters, which had taken several direct hits, but a nearby mosque. Again, he was amused by the irony that he had spent more time in mosques in a few days than in the past several years.

"*Marhabba.*" The imam in the small side office returned the greeting and gestured to an armchair loosely covered in a faded green fabric.

"Please, sit."

Sherif lowered himself into the chair, retrieved the cell phone from an inside pocket, and placed it, with the Quran in its cloth bag, on the low table.

"Coffee?"

"*Shokran.*"

A few minutes later, a boy brought in a tray with a pot of Turkish coffee and two small cups. The imam waited for the foam on the coffee to settle before pouring it.

"So, the Americans were bombing this morning," the imam said stating the obvious.

Sherif nodded.

"Was there much damage?"

"I didn't see much in this area, only smoke from military HQ."

"And this has come from Beirut," the imam said as Sherif passed the Qur'an and the cell phone across the table. He slid the book from the bag and flipped through the pages. His finger rested on a verse in the *Surah* of the Bee. "'Gabriel hath revealed it from thy Lord with truth,'" he read aloud, sliding his finger along the words to detect the fine pin-prick inserted as a code, "'that it may confirm those who believe, and as guidance and good tidings for those that have surrendered.'" He looked up and smiled from behind his ragged beard at Sherif's blank look. "You will excuse me, M Raad, but it was necessary to check if you had tampered with the holy book or, Allah forbid, exchanged it for another." Switching on the phone, he waited for a moment before keying in a password. He nodded his satisfaction, took a fat envelope from the desk drawer, and passed it to Sherif. "It's all there," he said, "but you must feel free to check it, even as I have checked on you."

Sherif murmured his thanks and slipped the envelope into his jacket pocket without comment. He finished his coffee, stood up, and the boy saw him to the door. A discordant chorus of sirens still wailed across the city like mourners who trailed behind the coffin at a funeral.

* * *

"We have received important information with instructions from headquarters," Muhammad Hamid al-Duleimi told the meeting of Syrian governors and the *Shura*[13] Council. Al-Duleimi, whose code name was Abu Hajar al-Assafi, was one of the Cabinet Advisors and the co-ordinator of information across the territories under ISIS rule. "I would like each one of you to copy this to your laptops and make a careful study of the material. It is from Caliph Ibrahim himself. The information was brought in from Beirut."

He flashed the first document up on his screen.

"How did it come in?" There was always interest in Muhammad Hamid al-Duleimi's methods and he was never opposed to showing them off.

"A courier delivered it this morning. The information was brought in using a cell phone and the password was encrypted into a copy of the Holy Qur'an. It is never difficult to bring a Qur'an into Syria." There was laughter from the assembled company. There were twelve men present at the meeting, each of them senior in the Islamic State's chain of command.

"If I may ask, was that not a dangerous method of relaying sensitive information?" one of them asked.

Al-Duleimi was anticipating the question and it pleased him to provide the answer. "Not at all," he replied affably. "The courier

---

[13] Advisory Council or Assembly

carried it as his own phone and the documents were encrypted into a video and three photographs by a process known as steganography." As he had expected, there was an immediate rush of questions. He held up a hand for silence. "I will briefly explain how the system works," he said. "Steganography can be used to hide files very securely by embedding them into a vessel data file, which acts as a cover. Generally, true colour images are used as dummy files and the complex areas are used to hide the confidential data."

One of the men raised a hand, "How much data can you hide in a file of that sort?"

"Under normal circumstances, only about an eighth of the carrier document can be used before there is any degradation of the image," Muhammad Hamid al-Duleimi replied, "but that can be greatly increased by using multiple bit-planes. We have steganographers who are experts in the field working with our Caliph, blessed be his name." He silenced any further questions. "*Shebab,* let us move on."

He checked his notes and looked up at the gathering. "Before we get to the main purpose of this meeting there are some points I want to make. Islamic scholars have called for a manifesto on repulse jihad[14] to be put out by Nasr Al-Fahd against the West. We all know that the command is to kill any American or European who is not a believer and this includes those countries that have entered into a coalition against the Islamic State." He scrubbed the dark stubble on his chin between finger and thumb. "The *kafur* must discover that nowhere is safe, even in their own bed as they sleep. They are to experience the terror of the day and of the night." He paused for effect and looked around the room. "I am going to call our Deputy to instruct you further. He has the mind of the Caliph on these things." The Deputy got to his feet slowly and, taking the speaker by the shoulders, he kissed him on both cheeks. He was a sallow man in his late forties and held the highest position in the Syrian branch of the Caliphate. He indeed had the ear of the Caliph Ibrahim.

---

[14] Using weapons of mass destruction against an enemy to silence him permanently

"Nasr al-Fahd's *fatwa*[15] on the issue of weapons of mass destruction is ultimately intended to destroy the enemy for once and for all," he said.

There were cries of, "*Allahu Akbar*, God is great!"

"We also know that the first lesson in such killing is *Ihsan,* to kill with kindness and charity. For this, your weapon must be sharp and the death should be quick. This is the way we have killed women and children so far. In *Hadith*[16] 107/13 the Prophet, Blessed be his name, says that you are to 'sharpen your blade and comfort your sacrifice'. We are all familiar with this sort of killing when their necks are tender and the death is not prolonged. We are in effect, making sacrifice to Allah." He fingered his bottom lip with his index finger.

"Nasr al-Fahd's *fatwa* brings a stronger emphasis. Again, we have applied such methods to those Syrians and Iraqis who have proved to be our enemies. By fighting against us, they are warring against Allah himself. These men we have shot without compunction. We have slaughtered the *Dhimmi* who have not chosen to submit to Allah and some we have hung on crosses as a warning to those who will not choose to do right."

"Now we are faced with a greater mission. America and her allies, including some countries that say they are Muslim and are not, have bombed us. They have bombarded our people. No one but Allah can enumerate the loss to Iraq, Syria, and Afghanistan. So many deaths, so much homelessness! The *fatwa* against America, Europe, and these other nations, means we can kill them by any means including weapons of mass destruction." He smiled as he pronounced the judgment made by Nasr al-Fahd. "Therefore, if a bomb is launched at them that will kill ten million, and it will burn their land as they burned Muslim lands, this is permissible without the need to mention any other evidence. Only when we have destroyed ten million will there possibly be a need for another fatwa to be written."

In a few months, the Saudi theologian would renounce his *fatwa* under pressure from his government and be incarcerated in a Saudi

---

[15] An Islamic legal pronouncement issued by an expert in religious law

[16] Prophetic traditions - teachings, deeds, and sayings of the Prophet Muhammed

Arabian prison. However, the declaration was deemed binding to those who chose to adhere to the teachings of such a scholar, and Nasr al-Fahd resonated well with the Islamic State.

The Deputy waited until silence fell once again. "Of course, the teaching says it is permissible to kill using whatever method is at hand whether fire, scorpions, snakes, or water. You are permitted to bring their buildings down upon them, to poison their source of water. Whatever method you use it must be done well."

He handed over to al-Duleimi once more and the co-ordinator of information began to outline the intelligence that had come in from the Caliph. This detailed a wholly different perspective of co-operation with Western leadership at the highest level; these were insiders with an agenda predisposed to the creation of foment. The provision of arms supplies to the different factions was minutely specified. Added to this were intelligence reports from top Islamists embedded in Europe and America, not only giving details of the activities of the jihadi sleeper cells but also specifying strategic installations which, in the hands of the Caliphate, could be counted upon at some future point, to cripple the host countries.

"I will tell you that among these documents received today," Duleimi said, "is one that gives us the time and method of the operation. We are instructed to infiltrate men and women, properly trained, into the mass of refugees seeking to leave Syria and Iraq. Already there has been an influx into Europe and this will soon grow exponentially as further pressure is placed on the refugee camps. This is our opportunity to expand the Salafist movement and bring holy war to bear on every nation on the face of the earth. We are to seek volunteers, fearless and ruthless *mujahideen*, from among our ranks to become involved in this project."

There was a roar of approval from the gathering and Duleimi waited patiently for the hubbub to die down.

"I am not yet at liberty to reveal the contents to anyone but suffice to say in time there will be an event that will set every true Muslim at the throat of the *kafur*. In the meantime, there is still much work to be done in Syria. In a few days, *insha Allah*, we will launch an attack on Kobane on the Turkish border and begin to rid ourselves of the Kurds. The next step, *shebab,* is Turkey!"

* * *

The reason for the call to Walid Zaky's office was unexpected. The baker appeared agitated and uncomfortable. Sherif sat down and drank the small glass of sweet tea that was offered, holding it awkwardly between finger and thumb, and waited to hear what was on his employer's mind. Perhaps, having returned from Lebanon later than expected, he was in trouble, but the questions about the trip and his sister's health were cordial.

"I have an answer to your proposal," Walid said when the usual social niceties were out of the way. "Nour will accept you as her husband."

For a brief moment, Sherif Raad was shocked. He had made the offer lightly. At his age, it was right that he should marry, but the proposal had not come out of any deep feelings for the daughter of the baker.

"She has given her consent?" he asked, surprised.

"I have asked her to accept you," Walid replied stiffly, "therefore the marriage will go ahead if you are still willing."

"Of course."

"Then I suggest we don't delay too long," the baker said. "I am anxious that my daughter comes under the protection of a good husband. Present events in Syria are a cause for concern."

Sherif nodded slowly. "When do you suggest?"

Walid took a deep breath. "We will say two weeks from now. That will give the women time to prepare."

The matter was settled. Walid took him by the shoulders and kissed the cheeks of his future son-in-law and braced himself for the fury of his daughter.

Even as a little child, Nour had never proved submissive. She had been a strong-willed toddler, an independent child, and a somewhat rebellious teenager but in all that, she had enchanted her father from the moment the dark baby curls appeared in the nape of her neck and the first tooth enhanced her grin. Walid was besotted with Nour and until now, even her anger had been a source of amusement to him. He braced himself for the battle ahead, knowing full well that he was sailing into a storm. Nour's response was worse than Walid anticipated. She shut herself in her room for hours on end and treated him as though he was a stranger; the punishment was almost greater than he could bear.

It was several days before Nour could bring herself to tell Raif what was happening. She waited until both her father and Sherif were out before breaking the news.

"My family is preparing for my wedding," she said bluntly. "I have been informed that I am to marry Raad the Saturday after next."

Raif stopped in his tracks, looked at her almost defiant expression, and recognised the pain that was written there. He slammed the tray of bread into the oven with undue force.

"No! They can't do this to you!"

"There's nothing I can do, Raif."

"There are still refugees leaving Raqqa, we could join them. Please, Nour, don't subject yourself to a lifetime of misery with a man you don't love."

"My family is here, Raif. Believe me, I have thought of nothing else but running away since I heard this news from my father but I still love them. I know they want what is best for me."

"So they force you into an unwanted marriage with a man they know you don't even like or trust!"

She reached up and placed her finger on his lips, "Don't, Raif. I've spoken all these words to myself this week and I still know that I can't leave."

He turned away from her, afraid at the extent of his anger. It seemed he was forced to become an unwelcome spectator to an event he knew would destroy Nour. And anything that hurt her would inevitably wound him.

Chapter 17   Betrayal

Raif was called away from the bakery by a curt summons from headquarters. As fighting intensified, he was needed in the militia; the
bakery was running smoothly enough, he was informed, his
oversight was no longer required. That his non-combative position
in the bakery had suddenly been whipped away at almost the precise
moment of Nour's marriage, proved a huge relief to Raif. The idea
of working alongside her now was painful. At the same time, being
thrust back into the horrifying reality of daily life in the Caliphate
was almost more than he could stomach. He was desperately
homesick and longed to turn back the clock. To undo all that could
no longer be undone.

"Now then," the cleric said congenially to the group seated on
rugs around the room.[17] "Let's talk about what it means to perfect
your killing."

"Does it mean we are supposed to give them an anaesthetic?"
asked one student hopefully.

"No, no, not in this case," the imam waved a hand in negation. He
sat cross-legged with his laptop open on the floor in front of him.
"Not in the commandment to slaughter. No, no. What Nasr al-
Fahd's *fatwa* means is you get your sword and you take his head like
this," he pushed an imaginary head down under his hand. Sensual
lips drew back off his teeth in a merciless smile. "And then you
begin to have all the fun!"

Several men in the group fingered their throats uneasily as,
without getting up, the imam picked up a curved sword from the
carpet next to him. "You go like this," he said using a high-pitched
whine to give the desired sound effect. "Eeeeh, forward, but it hasn't

---

[17] Wahhabi cleric explains the correct method of beheading.
https://www.youtube.com/watch?v=yHt-erqLEOY
the video is no longer available.

cut all the way through. And again, eeeeh, it's still not through."
His thin beard waggled over his white robes. "Eeeeeh! You try
again!" The exaggerated demonstration drew nervous laughter from
the men. He placed the sword on the floor next to him, "And so you
slice and you slice until the head is completely removed."

The imam drew his right-hand time and again in great strokes
across his own throat. "You slice," he hissed. "*Slice!*"

Raif watched hypnotized, sickened to his stomach. He wanted to
run, to hide, but self-preservation kept him rooted to the spot.

"Slice," the imam enunciated once more. "And enjoy!" He
exhaled as one who took pleasure in a gentle sea breeze or delighted
in the mountain air.

Raif left the room with his fellow mujahideen shut himself in one
of the toilet stalls and vomited. It was that final word that finished
forever, his brief flirtation with jihad. "Enjoy!"

* * *

Sherif Raad lunched with the Zaky family two days before the
wedding. Nour and her mother carried dishes of stuffed aubergine
and boned chicken to the table filling the atmosphere with a
fragrance of lemon and garlic. Nour ate in the kitchen with her
mother. She was sullen and resentful and made no effort to engage
her future husband in conversation. Sherif, in his turn, more
congenial than she had ever seen him, appeared not to notice.

They took coffee together in the living room, a room decorated
predominantly in dark wood and shiny blue cloth edged with lace
that had turned coffee-coloured with age. The ball-and-claw lounge
suite was firm and uninviting and the blue roses on the carpet were
faded and, in several places, quite worn away. Dozens of small
ornaments and a maroon and gold coffee service were displayed in a
glass-fronted cabinet and an assortment of cigarettes was hospitably
displayed on the coffee table.

Nour was informed that following the marriage she and Sherif
would be moving into a furnished apartment within walking distance
of her parents' home.

"The owners are friends of my father. They left Raqqa last week
and have gone back to Lebanon," he said. "They are happy to have
someone stay in their home until things return to normal."

Nour said she wondered if anything would ever return to normal and left the room.

"I apologise for my daughter," Walid said uneasily. "She is not herself at the moment."

"It is nerves," Raad replied solicitously. "I understand that in arranged marriages, such feelings are quite common." He could not fail to recognise the increase of Nour's hostility towards him but he was unconcerned. Once they were married he was certain the barriers would be overcome. She was intelligent, which pleased him, he could not tolerate stupidity in a woman, but it would be necessary to build in her an awareness of her station so that her brain did not become an encumbrance. As an only child, she had been spoilt and that would not be allowed to continue under his roof.

It was not true to say he lusted after her; lust was an emotion foreign to Sherif Raad. All his emotions were thin washes. He had learned early in life that keeping a rein on his feelings meant his head was clear for more important issues. Nour interested him, however, and she had the potential to become a good wife.

He joined Walid in the courtyard in the late afternoon and the two men chatted amicably in the sun that fell in patches between the leaves of the grapevine which spread over the pergola. Sherif leaned against a pillar stroking his dark moustache with long slender fingers. Walid sat back in a garden chair uncomfortable in the jacket he had worn for the occasion. They did not speak of the wedding, preferring to leave women's talk to the women. They skirted around the weather, which was beginning to cool with the onset of autumn, and about the deep things affecting their country. They discussed the recent bombardment and the possibility of more to come, and of the control of the Islamic State over Raqqa, but this was discussed cautiously because even those you thought you knew well could prove to be the enemy.

The war ensured that wedding traditions were cut to the bone. Nour was relieved that a fashion parade of several lavish outfits would be reduced to two and she would not be required to change every hour for the pleasure of the women who were to celebrate with her. The marriage would be conducted separately in accordance with Islamic rites. There was no possibility in Raqqa of a Western-style occasion, such as had become quite popular before the Islamic State took over.

At five in the afternoon, young male relatives of Nour's family and a handful of Sherif's friends, arrived at his apartment to take him to his wedding bath where he was shaved, and his hair neatly trimmed. He endured the horseplay and the pricking of needles, which was intended to bring luck to his bachelor friends, and the general good humour that accompanied the sword-play and songs of the *arada*[18] band. The band was reduced to four men from the usual twelve, but they were traditionally dressed for the event in embroidered vests, white cotton shirts and loose black trousers, and their skill in handling their swords delighted the men.

The women that gathered in the Zaky's living room spilled over into the courtyard where long tables had been laid and white cloths came to life in the wind. There were relatives and neighbours, shy girls giggling behind their hands, old women dressed in black. Children ran in and out, and babies howled. After a brief ceremony by the local imam, platters of food were brought to the tables, a stuffed lamb and yellow rice with all-spice and pine nuts. They all looked critically at Nour and found her dress beyond reproach in such difficult times and her complexion too pale and, afterwards, everyone commented on what a good-looking bride she had made. Only those closest to Nour recognised the anger in her eyes, and they chose not to see.

The *arada* announced Sherif's arrival later that evening with much singing and beating of drums in the street. The men waited outside while he went in to claim Nour as his bride, speaking for a while to the women. When he chose, Sherif could be charming; it was difficult to assess his character from his outward appearance. His features were average, as lean as his physique, with a narrow, rather prominent nose, thin mouth, and small ears set neatly back against his skull. He was enigmatic, giving nothing of himself, and this was recorded in the reticence in his eyes and the absence of expression. There was a lot hidden within the man that gained no access to his face. He played the part of a polite and thoughtful groom towards Nour pretending not to notice her blank withdrawal; greeted friends and neighbours cordially, and was pleasant and polite to her parents.

---

[18] Traditional music group

The newly married couple was seen back to their apartment by a group of well-wishers. Nour had shrunk back into herself and hardly noticed who was with her but she wanted them to stay. Even more, she wanted to be alone, to have time to weep and get to grips with what had been forced upon her. She endured the ribald laughter of the men, the curious glances of her friends, and the sly innuendos. And then they were gone and the house was unnaturally silent.

"It's alright little one," he comforted, "there's a lot of time ahead of us. It's natural that you should be afraid."

Sherif reached for his cigarette packet. He had switched off the bedside lamp and the flare as the match was struck briefly illuminated Nour's huddled body. She lay away from him on the bed, her legs drawn up into her stomach and her hands clenched against ragged, angry sobs. He could not see her face and her tousled hair completed the barrier between them. The tip of his cigarette glowed and dulled in the dark. He felt no anger towards her, his passions were seldom overwhelming. On the contrary, the prospect of a slow, teasing build-up towards the final act of consummation pleased him.

Nour was glad that the dark concealed her rage. The turbulence of her emotions frightened her. They had thrown her together with this man, a virtual stranger, and, as the result of a ceremony, expected her to submit to his body. She felt degraded, as though her father had sold her to Sherif as an object. Like a trapped animal, her mind veered this way and that as she desperately sought a way out, but the time to fight was passed. By giving way, she had empowered them. Now, the only way forward was to submit. The inevitability of what must follow swamped her then and she lay with the steady tides of her future washing over her until at last she slept.

It was a week before she returned to her work at the bakery. Sherif had insisted that the jeans and tee shirts must no longer be worn beneath the *niqab*.

"Now that you are married, I expect you to dress properly. The clothes you were wearing shamed you before men. Get rid of them."

She obeyed out of fear. From the beginning, some instinct told her he was dangerous and his courteousness to this point had done nothing to change her mind. For the hundredth time, she wondered how she would face Raif Ahmadi. Nour took off her *niqab* in the small toilet at the back of the shop, hung it behind the door and smoothed down the folds of her long skirt. She wound a white scarf around her head and throat and tied it behind her neck. It was only as she began work that she realised Raif was not there. It was two days later when she finally plucked up the courage to ask Sherif where he was.

"He left," he said shortly. "They have sent someone else in on a couple of occasions to make sure we are operating under their requirements!" He spoke the words sarcastically. "Apparently we must be as they're not keeping us under full-time surveillance anymore." He glanced at Nour astutely, "Pity you've lost your partner," he said. "I'm sure he was good company."

The colour in Nour's cheeks heightened but she said nothing. She missed Raif with every fibre of her being but she hoped beyond hope that he had found a way to return home.

Chapter 18   Betrayal

They drove before dawn in a convoy of identical desert-beige Toyota trucks into villages in the vicinity of the Taqba airbase where fighting had already been raging for several days.

This last stronghold of the Syrian government in Raqqa Province was twenty-five miles southwest of Raqqa city. Syrian troops and airmen had held out there for the past two years, using the facility to launch attacks against various rebel factions in the north. The Islamic State pushed their most seasoned fighters into the air base assault while those less experienced were to capture the surrounding villages as they tightened the noose on the Syrian stronghold.

As their pick-ups skidded to a halt in the town square raising a billowing cloud of dust, fighters leapt from the back of their vehicles. The sound of their arrival brought the townsfolk to their windows. One of the *mujahideen* shouted.

"Down there! By the river!" He raised his weapon to his shoulder and delivered a burst of gunfire towards the water. Several men from the village had slipped around the back of the buildings in an attempt to escape. They skidded down the sandy banks, ran through the shallows, and swiftly struck out into deeper water. The *daabit*[19] yelled a command, and gunfire raked the surface of the river. Raif heard the men's screams as bullets met flesh; he witnessed their frantic threshing. The firing ceased. More than a dozen corpses drifted face-down on the water turning it to crimson and forming ribbons which faded as they caught the flow of the current. The *daabit* summoned his men and, with a wide gesture, directed them towards the settlement.

Dressed in uniform black, the ISIS insurgents were a formidable sight. Chickens squawked and scattered between the silent

---

[19] A Military Officer

buildings. The militia fanned out; their orders were to find anyone affiliated to Assad's regime and arrest or kill them.

As Farid Al-Balawi, weapon at the ready kicked the doors open and forced his way into the houses ahead of him, Raif smelt the terror of the people. It showed in the slowness of a man's movements and, in the rare instances when their eyes met his, in the raw panic or dull surrender he saw reflected there. These were not the people Raif had come to fight; they were families like his own. Children clung in mute fear to their mothers and fathers, and babies screamed. Women wept as their men were dragged into the streets, hands tied behind them. At an order, they were marched into the desert a few hundred meters from the village, and Raif watched in mute disbelief as about twenty men, young and old, were forced to kneel. It took four soldiers armed with Kalashnikovs to mow them down and their bodies were left for the villagers to bury.

On the ride back to base, many of the men laughed and joked as they recounted the events of the raid. There was an atmosphere of celebration, as though a battle had been fought and won. Raif gazed out on the wide expanse of semi-desert feeling sick to the stomach. If Farid suspected how Raif felt, he said nothing. It was as though the incident had never happened.

On 19th August 2014, the Islamic State renewed its attack against Taqba airbase with a double suicide bombing near the entrance. Two hundred *mujahideen* armed with heavy weapons looted from abandoned bases in Iraq, followed up on the suicide bombing with an unrelenting ground assault. The trapped airmen retaliated with heavy shelling. Syrian jet fighters screamed overhead, strafing the fighters on the ground. The *mujahideen* pulled back the following morning after several men went down with horrifying injuries as they encountered a minefield. A second wave attacked in the afternoon. In the meantime, the Syrian army and Air Force rushed to the defence of their trapped men. Reinforcements strengthened the fortifications within, bringing much-needed supplies of ammunition and food.

At night Raqqa reeled under a massive air assault launched by Syrian Government forces. Sudden flashes of blinding light pinpointed the strikes against known ISIS positions. The explosions were terrifying. One direct hit destroyed the water plant and cut off the water supply to the city adding to the misery of its inhabitants.

Undeterred, the Islamic State surrounded and advanced steadily on Taqba. Towards the end of August another suicide bomber blew himself up in a vehicle against the entrance gate. The fighters renewed their shelling of the position as they made a further attempt at breaching the fences. Again the attack was repulsed and the Air Force pounded ISIS positions, this time in nearby Taqba city. Two days later, as the defeated Syrian Army staged a retreat; a way was finally made into the air base. The Air Force had managed to escape with all its helicopters, fifteen MIG-21B fighter jets, and to evacuate seven hundred men. The small garrison left behind to hold the position fell later that day and one hundred-and-seventy soldiers died in the final assault. Islamic State fighters proudly posed with the heads of their enemy; gruesome trophies of their victory, before posting the pictures on the web as a warning to the West. ISIS transcendent was intent on imposing terror upon the world.

The last pockets of resistance around Taqba were quashed in the days that followed. The Islamic State had opened up three fronts in the fighting in Syria and had become the most capable fighting force in the Middle East, surpassed in power only by Israel. ISIS had moved across Syria at lightning speed taking back areas lost to it earlier in the year and establishing a power base over an area close to that of the United Kingdom in extent.

To Raif, the whole thing was a nightmare. The new recruits completed the mop-up of the villages and the scenes of horror were replayed like a recurring nightmare. Then in the days that followed, their trucks rolled into one ghost town after another. He and Farid were not the only Syrians among the recruits and all of them were shaken by the devastation. Buildings in most places were reduced to rubble and roads had been ground to dust under the wheels of tanks. The remaining inhabitants were desperate for food. There was no sanitation, no running water, no electricity, and communications were almost non-existent.

"That bastard, Assad! When we get him, we will deal with him!" they promised one another darkly.

People moved between buildings like specters. For the most part, they gave ISIS a wide berth and in those moments when individuals were forced to come face to face with the militia, they were effusive or quietly deferential. Raif had naïvely believed the Islamic State would release Syria from bondage, but what he saw was the perpetuation of the country's suffering. Again Raif was struck by the fact that he was not an objective witness; he had chosen to be part of the militia and, in the unlikely case he could escape, the taint of their deeds would be part of him forever.

* * *

The Islamic State made a thrust for the strategic prize of Iraq's capital, Baghdad, while their goal on the Syrian front was Kobane on the Turkish border. A group of reporters stood on the bare hillside overlooking the sprawling town where billows of black smoke rose slowly into the air. With them was a young Peshmerga fighter, a Kurdish woman, whose *nom de guerre* was Narin Afrin.

"If you don't help us against ISIS, they will come for you one day," she informed them bluntly.

Ain al-Arab, better known by its Kurdish name, Kobane, lay cupped in the palm of the surrounding desert and, in colour, was almost indistinct from it. After a month of fierce fighting, the embattled town appeared set to fall into the hands of the Caliphate. Their American tanks, seized from bases in Iraq had, so far, proved more than a match for the weapons of the Kurdish Peshmerga troops.

This plea from the Peshmerga Commander of the battle against the Islamic State stated a simple truth but her cry for help was spoken into the wind. The Turks among the group were well aware that Turkish aid had proved an empty promise and air support from the NATO Allies was inflicting a great deal of damage without appearing to push back the advance.

"Thousands of civilians are still inside the town," Narin said, weariness showing in the lines around her eyes. "They have nowhere to go; everywhere is blocked."

The Kurdish goals of independence, their moderate cultural, civil and political leanings, and the emancipation of their women, automatically put them on Ba'athist and ISIS hit lists. What was once known as Kurdistan now falls within the borders of three nations. War is an integral part of Kurdish survival and, after three decades of fighting their Persian, Turkish and Arab neighbours, women were considered a major part of the defence of their embattled people. The Second Battalion of Unit 106 was an all-female fighting force; women, young and middle-aged, beautiful and plain, educated or peasant, stood together as a formidable entity.

For the Caliphate, the fear of fighting against women was twofold. Defeat by a fighting unit commanded by a female would mean the deepest humiliation. Worse, death at the hands of a woman fighter meant that a jihadi could not enter paradise. A few days before Raif's fighting force moved into the area, a Kurdish woman fighter blew herself up in an attack outside Kobane, killing dozens of militants. The ultimate expectation of jihadi existence, the very essence of his being, was the final reward of life after death. In an instant such as this, all that he stood for was lost and his only expectation was an eternity in hell.

Narin Afrin's message was simple. Destroy this scourge while there is still a possibility of doing it, or you will be next in line.

* * *

If Sherif Raad had had his way, Nour would not have been allowed to continue work at the bakery. Only the fact that her father, Walid, insisted that she was needed, kept Nour from being held a virtual prisoner in their apartment. Her anger with her father for having allowed this marriage and with her mother for failing to stand with her had deeply wounded Nour. She punished them by refusing to visit and spoke only to her father when it concerned business.

Walid was devastated. It was not long before he realised what he had inflicted on his daughter was just that from which he had intended to protect her. His relationship with Nour lay in ashes and he was at a loss as to how it could ever be restored. Legally, she was now in Sherif's hands and there was nothing to be done to alter the circumstances.

Whereas she had never been given reason to fear her father, Nour intuitively feared Sherif from the outset without really understanding why. His controlling nature soon began to surface. For the first week or two of their marriage, Sherif had shown understanding when Nour tried to deflect his advances, but she knew with deadly certainty that she could not continue on that path. She gave way reluctantly but made no attempt to please him. A few days later, when Nour again attempted to reject him, she elicited a different response. Sherif gripped her by the hair and dragged her head back onto the pillow exposing her throat in an unnatural arc.

"Woman," he hissed. "In this marriage, you will do what I tell you to do. You are not here to please yourself anymore; you are my wife! If you ever do that again, you will be given a lesson you will never forget!" With that, he forced himself on her.

Nour felt defiled, degraded and humiliated. Most of all she was afraid. When at last she knew he was asleep, she crept from the bed, curled up in an armchair in the adjacent room, and wept bitter tears for all that she had lost.

Although he professed no adherence to Islam, Sherif's attitude towards women differed little from that of the Caliphate. Apart from his expectation that she cook, clean, and meet his physical needs, Nour found herself largely ignored after the first month of marriage. She felt stifled, with no real vent for her anger. Worse, she began to experience feelings of worthlessness; a void had developed in her soul that, perversely, she longed for Raif to fill.

A month after the fall of Taqba, Raif Ahmadi was on the back of a transport lorry that formed part of a convoy heading north towards the Turkish border. His one consolation was that Farid Al-Balawi had been transferred to another area and he had no need to make any further pretense of friendship with him or any other fighter.

A seventeen-year old boy had been caught filming the Islamic State headquarters in al-Bab. He was tortured and killed and his body crudely crucified for all to see, with a board hung over his chest proclaiming his sin of apostasy. Raif saw the body as the troops passed through from Aleppo on their way to the Turkish border. Some of the men jeered and laughed as they passed, and craned their necks to see the spectacle for themselves.

"*Yihrib-dinak*[20] for five hundred Turkish *lira* the stupid kid takes on the Islamic State!" one shouted belligerently as he read the notice. "That will teach those journalist bastards who are too scared to come here and do their own dirty work!" He cleared his throat volubly and spat over the side of the pickup.

---

[20] A curse on an individual's religion

A fighter stubbed out his cigarette and flicked it contemptuously in the direction of the corpse. Then, as they moved on, the conversation switched to women, and the scene was forgotten.

It was just a foretaste of the carnage to come. When Kobane was breached Raif witnessed the horrors that those on the front lines had perpetrated against the civilians; the headless corpses that littered the streets bore stark testimony to the savagery of ISIS fighters.

He no longer cared what happened to him. At this point, death would have been welcome. His faith was in tatters, and life had boiled down to one thing—getting through another day. Nour had given him hope and even that had been snatched from him. His future was not that different from the bleak picture of Kobane with its broken monochromatic walls, leafless surroundings, and death.

Day and night, the city was rocked by explosions as ISIS ploughed forward, often street by street in an attempt to improve its position. Both sides fought on under a cloud of smoke and dust with a fanatical determination to win. For the Kurds, this victory was vital. Despite Turkey's claim to being part of the coalition against the Islamic State, it was becoming increasingly clear that the livelihood of the Kurds was still of no concern to them. Any Islamic State victory over this Turkish thorn in the flesh would be welcomed.

Chapter 19   Betrayal

"To undermine Iran, which is predominantly Shiite, the Bush Administration has decided, in effect, to reconfigure its priorities in the Middle East. In Lebanon, the Administration has cooperated with Saudi Arabia's government, which is Sunni, in clandestine operations that are intended to weaken Hezbollah, the Shiite organization that is backed by Iran. The U.S. has also taken part in clandestine operations aimed at Iran and its ally Syria. ***A by-product of these activities has been the bolstering of Sunni extremist groups that espouse a militant vision of Islam and are hostile to America and sympathetic to Al Qaeda.***" *(Emphasis added)*
Seymour Hersh's 9 page report 'The Redirection' 2007

"What the Islamic State is doing in Syria and Iraq is horrible," Amal said. "I know that Raif would have nothing to do with such things. He is not a violent person."

Moussa put down the book he was reading. "I know what you mean, Amal," he massaged his forehead between finger and thumb, "Raif was the most harmless of children. I can't imagine him participating in the sort of things that are taking place. But you must remember that people change, especially under the sort of brainwashing of the radical imams. Jihad is a potent concept and a man awakened to a cause can become dangerous."

"But not Raif!" Amal said unhesitatingly. "Nothing would make him brutal."

"Perhaps you're right, *habibti*[21]."

"Why beheadings?" she asked. "And crucifixions—are they in some way aimed at Christian beliefs?"

---

[21] An endearment

He shrugged. "There might be something in that," he replied, "but these practices have been part of our background for hundreds of years under Sharia law."

Amal threw a startled glance at her father. "I know that in Saudi Arabia hands are cut off for theft," she said slowly.

"*Habibti*, I can see I have sheltered you far too much," he smiled. "In Saudi Arabia, hundreds die by what they call "punishment by the sword". For the average person over there it's a form of entertainment."

"They do it in public?" She looked shocked.

"In Riyadh, there's a place the locals call Chop Chop square. They cordon it off to prevent people from crowding in on the scene, but it's a public event."

"But they don't crucify people like Islamic State are doing!"

"In some cases they do. Some time ago, seven Yemenis were beheaded. If I remember correctly it was for drug smuggling. The corpses were crucified for several days as a warning to others."

"Without their heads?" despite her horror Amal was determined to know the details.

"They wrapped the heads in plastic and hung them over the bodies."

She shuddered. "That's so barbaric."

Moussa nodded. "In our thinking it is," he said. "This year the number of beheadings in Saudi has been on the increase. Typically, the West applies one of its double standards. It maintains ties with the country and a policy of hands-off, yet Iran is labelled the "axis of evil" for doing the same sort of thing."

By sheer coincidence, in Moussa's inbox that evening was another article on beheading, this time from the United States of America where a federal judge had added his voice to the proposal that guillotines and firing squads be used as the preferred form of capital punishment nationwide. Moussa forwarded the email to Lex and minutes later his cell phone rang.

"They've already passed that law in Georgia," Lex elucidated when the usual formalities were out of the way, "but that was years back and it's never been implemented.

"This was the first I had heard of it," Moussa replied. "Surely it has to be more than coincidence, Lex! We've got ISIS on the rampage in the Middle East beheading not only their enemies in battle, but even their own people for minor transgressions. And just at this time, some guy promotes it as a merciful form of killing for prisoners."

"There have been rumours doing the rounds for years regarding the purchase of a huge number of guillotines for use in the U.S. but no one has come forward to offer proof. It's interesting and a little chilling. Considering the Guidestones protocol of population reduction though, could it be coinicidence that the guillotine law was first passed in Georgia?"

Moussa leaned back against the cushions on his armchair and rested his feet on the coffee table. "You do think something's on the go or you wouldn't have phoned me."

Lex laughed. "You probably read that Senator John McCain met with the FSA commander, Salim Idriss last year."

"I saw a couple of photos that have been doing the rounds," Moussa said. "They showed him with a man who looked a lot like Ibrahim al-Badri."

"That's right, the guy who's now Caliph of the Islamic State." Lex picked up his beer, swigged a mouthful, and set it down on the table beside his armchair. "Yesterday, United States Congress passed legislation authorising the payment of four billion dollars to train and equip Free Syrian Army militants."

Moussa whistled softly. "There is no chance that that money will stay with the FSA," he said.

"Exactly! I've just picked up a couple of quotes from The Daily Star in Lebanon. One of their brigade commanders says his forces are working with Jabhat al-Nusra and Islamic State near the Syrian/Lebanese border."

"These guys are all jihadists," Moussa said bitterly. "They will accept whatever the West has to offer and use it for their own purposes—even if it's to blow off the hand of the giver."

"You're absolutely right, Moussa. The U.S. is pumping money, training, and weapons into Syria and they don't give a damn about where it's going just as long as it brings down Bashar al-Assad. My question is why? What is the driving force behind this?"

Moussa scratched his head. "It boils down to Sunni versus Shiite," he said. "As far as I know, Assad has done nothing to match the atrocities by the Islamic State, or even the Free Syrian Army, for that matter. But he's a Shiite and therefore aligned with Iran. They will oust him on that basis, no matter what!"

"Am I right in thinking that Hezbollah in Lebanon could be next on their hit list?" Lex asked.

Moussa paused. "It's possible," he replied, "but the prime target has to be Israel—hence ISIL, the Levant. Any Muslim army that can do the unthinkable and conquer Islam's arch-enemy will be hailed by the whole Middle East as saviour."

"Israel's too strong for ISIS."

"Absolutely, and they know that. But if Caliph Ibrahim can prove by conquest that he's Islam's equivalent of pope, God's minister on earth, most of the Islamic States would rally behind him to aid in the taking of Israel. You can see the Islamic State's tactics. On a couple of occasions, there have been rumours of the Caliph's death, after which he miraculously reappears. It all goes to build his reputation of invincibility."

Lex was silent for a moment as he absorbed what Moussa was saying. "You know, Moussa, if Israel was overrun by Islam, I think the West would largely cheer them on. The anti-Semitic sentiment is so high at the moment that I wouldn't be surprised if another Jewish genocide was on its way."

"My turn to ask why," Moussa said. "What is it about the Jews that cause the nations to hate them so much?"

Lex was thoughtful. "As I see it, two things. Firstly, it's their belief that God chose them as a nation, which sets them apart and intimates that they are somehow better than others. You could put it down to jealousy—or hatred of God."

"Certainly from the Islamic point of view, it is believed that Muhammad is the last of the prophets and that God has finished with Israel. For that reason alone, Israel has to be destroyed to prove Islam right," Moussa said. "But from a Western standpoint, you said there was a second reason."

"A bit more complicated. Israel seems to be deliberately discredited by a powerful few of their own people, so the nation as a whole suffers. It's a continual stigma that surrounds them perpetuated during the Second World War by the Nazi use of the Protocols of Zion."

"I know of it. The document was supposed to be a fabrication. Do you think it has a factual basis?"

"I have no idea," Lex replied. "Except that the world is moving neatly into line with each protocol as it was laid down, but most people today wouldn't dare suggest it has any validity." He pushed his fingers through his hair irritably. "As I've researched this book, another thought has struck me."

Moussa removed his feet from the coffee table as Amal came through with a tray. "Yes?"

"The writers of the Protocols declared their intention to create a reign of terror. This *fatwa* put out by ISIS is in its early stages but it's doing exactly that! Already in the States, there's this feeling that if the guy next to you looks Middle Eastern he might be packing a knife."

"I know, I've experienced that kind of reaction from Westerners at airports myself," Moussa said, smiling ruefully. "But America and Europe have allowed these jihadis in, often knowingly, let them build their mosques, and turned a blind eye to their radical messages. They've virtually opened a freeway for the traffic of Salafist ideologies. The only thing that will stop them now is wholesale repatriation."

"And that's not going to happen!"

"Definitely not!" Moussa agreed. "In fact, they're going to the opposite extreme in assuring everybody that these Muslims are peace-loving and have nothing to do with extremists such as those waging war in the Middle East. Obama is inviting the Muslim Brotherhood into the White House and elevating them to high places, even in security. I wouldn't be surprised to see the dam burst in the not-too-distant future."

Lex nodded. It was becoming abundantly obvious that something was about to give way as Moussa said. A dam burst was a pretty good description of what was a potentially disastrous situation.

Chapter 20   Betrayal

"Faced with disconcerting episodes of violent fundamentalism, our respect for true followers of Islam should lead us to avoid hateful generalizations, for authentic Islam and the proper reading of the Qur'an are opposed to every form of violence." Pope Francis I

"You can't say Islam is a religion of peace because Islam does not mean peace. Islam means submission, so the Muslim is one who submits. There is a place for violence for Islam. There is a place for jihad in Islam." Anjem Choudary, British Islamist.

Sherif Raad sat opposite the *raqib* in the Islamic State military headquarters in Raqqa. It was the first overcast day in a long while and the sullen cloud cover came as a relief as the relentless summer turned to autumn. Nevertheless, the ceiling fan rotated monotonously over the battered desk that lay between the men.

"You are to go as before," the *raqib* instructed.

"The same mosque?"

"Exactly. Follow the same procedure."

"I will be asking for payment in Jordanian lira, and my fee will be higher this time," Sherif said. He tugged at his ear lobe as he named his price.

The *raqib* looked deeply shocked and a little hurt. "*Yirab-dinak,* M Raad. My superiors will never agree."

"The route is becoming increasingly dangerous, and I now have a wife to consider," Sherif replied, his expression unwavering.

"Yes, yes..." the *raqib* waved a plump hand airily. "But you must realise that we are fighting a war, we cannot simply double a man's fee for doing a simple enough duty!"

Sherif frowned. "I am not a fighting man," he replied. "I don't consider such work a duty; for me, it is a business. I will help your cause as long as you meet my requirements. There are not many trustworthy men who would be prepared to make such a journey, and they certainly would not do it for less than I am asking."

The *raqib* muttered something under his breath and shuffled a pile of papers. When he looked up it was with annoyance. "How do I know that you will come back if I am paying you in Jordanian money?" he snapped.

"I will be back for the other half of the payment." It was a statement of fact.

The *raqib* weighed the proposal and capitulated. "Return this evening. Jordanian lira will be more difficult to organise."

Sherif had arranged for Nour to return to her parent's home for the time he was away. Knowing how she chafed under his restrictions, he did not trust her to remain in the apartment alone. Walid was delighted to have his daughter back under his own roof for a few days, but as much as it was a pleasure to have her physical presence among them once more, the old Nour was still not with them. She was quiet, withdrawn and, Walid knew, angry with him for betraying her trust in his fatherhood.

Nour was relieved to no longer have to submit to her husband. She despised Sherif's rule over her; his expectation that she should serve him, perform for him. She loathed his sexual demands; even the smell of his manliness revolted her. Now that she was at home she longed, above all else, to weep in her father's arms and beg him not to send her back, but the divide was just too great between them. Instead, she was passive, unnaturally compliant, and sought her own company in the silence of her familiar bedroom.

Having made a prior arrangement with Muhammad Mustapha Khalil, Sherif Raad found the taxi at its usual spot on the rank. Khalil was sitting on the bonnet of the car kicking rhythmically at the front tyre with the heel of his shoe. In the taxi, three passengers waited and the driver was anxious to leave. Within minutes, they were out of Raqqa and on the road to Aleppo. The occupants of the vehicle were silent and, after a couple of attempts at engaging them in conversation, Muhammad Mustapha Khalil slipped a CD into the player, listened to Sabah, and resigned himself to a dull journey.

The passengers got off in Aleppo and Sherif and Muhammad Mustapha stopped for a meal of bread and *ful m'dames* at one of the small eating places that hung on tenaciously amid the surrounding devastation. An hour later they picked up a new group of passengers and continued their journey through El Bab towards the northern border post. The black flag of the Islamic State hung everywhere and the fighters, some with their faces partially covered under their black head scarves, strutted down the streets with weapons on display and heads held high. On the roundabout in El Bab, another crucified body hung for all to see. The passengers were heard to mutter among themselves, but neither Sherif nor the taxi driver gave the ghoulish corpse a second glance. They reached the border post without incident; their identification cards were cleared, the taxi searched and, in two hours, they were back on the road. Everyone breathed a sigh of relief as they entered Lebanon.

Everything was accomplished with incredible smoothness. Even the meeting at the mosque was a trifle less hostile than before. Again, Sherif was shown to the imam's office by his contact, Abdul-Basir, and was handed a cell phone, and a cloth bag containing a Qur'an which he slipped into the lining of his jacket.

Only one man showed any interest in Sherif Raad as he left the building. He crouched like a bundle of rags at the foot of a brightly lit column and he kept his eyes on him as he retrieved his shoes from the racks in the ablution room. Moments later, he padded behind Sherif through the narrow crowded alleyways, past groups of soldiers, barrow bearers, shop-keepers, and pickpockets.

He waited at a discreet distance when Sherif stopped at the taxi rank and spoke for a few moments to a driver. Wadih Hashim followed him to the front entrance of the hotel and called Abdul-Basir on his cell phone.   He crossed the road, drew the folds of his *keffieh*[22] more closely around his face, and squatted on his haunches with his back to a lamp-post. He was still there when Sherif emerged hours later, into the late afternoon sunlight carrying his overnight bag as he headed once more for the taxi rank. Wadih Hashim sauntered down the street some distance behind him and, as he slipped into the front seat of the taxi, he made a second call.

---

[22] Chequered headscarf

This time, only two other passengers travelled with them and both men got off near Tripoli. It was late as they approached the northern border post of Nahr al-Kabir. The night was humid and screaming with insect noise after a shower of rain. Traffic was heavy but no one seemed in much of a hurry. The driver sweated with impatience. His shirt clung to his back where it had made contact with the leather seat of the Mercedes and showed damp almost to his waist where rivulets of perspiration had trickled from his armpits.

A customs official, his face reddened with heat, stood on the open veranda of the Duane. Moths and beetles performed suicidal dances under the lights, battering themselves between corrugated roof and the concrete floor. Sherif offered his packet of cigarettes to Muhammad Mustapha Khalil, struck a match and held it out to him in the shelter of his cupped palm.

"*Marhabba, shu al-akhbar*[23]*?*"

"There's a blockade a kilometre up the road. Good luck."

"*Shokran*[24]."

The officer nodded and moved back into the building. Once their documents were perused and stamped, he followed them out and instructed the removal of all luggage from the boot. Everything was carefully and systematically checked. When he nodded them on, the gesture was curt and officious.

Sherif lit another cigarette from the butt of the one he was smoking. He betrayed no other sign of tension. His slim hands were controlled and almost unnaturally still. Darkness closed in around the taxi as they left the border post behind. Trees formed tall silent shadows and the road lay between them, river black.

No one spoke. A small twitch had developed below Muhammad Mustapha's right eye. The steady beam of the headlights methodically picked out the broken line in the centre of the road tossing lengths of it behind the vehicle like a sailor hauling rope. Khalil, gesturing briefly with his head in the direction of the lights that appeared in the distance, slowed the Mercedes. Soldiers, thrown into relief by the glow of the headlights, were strung out across the road. As they approached, details of guns and uniforms

---

[23] Hello, what news?

[24] Thank-you

sprang to life although the faces remained in darkness. The green headbands identified them instantly.

Muhammad Mustapha swore volubly. "Hezbollah!"

Sherif stiffened at they drew to a halt at the wooden barrier. A Jeep was parked on their left and a man loomed out of the shadow and into the circle of light. Muhammad Mustapha Khalil switched off the engine and doused the headlights. One lamp hung over the small guard hut and another two red warning lights had been placed in the road. Lit as they were from the feet, the soldiers took on a demonic appearance.

"Get out!"

The driver protested, lifting his hands and dropping them again onto the steering wheel.

"I said, get out!" The officer gesticulated with his automatic rifle. His face was sallow in the poor light and the pouches of skin beneath his eyes showed almost black. The eyes appeared dull and expressionless.

Muhammad Mustapha left his seat with his hands slightly raised in a gesture of goodwill. Sherif moved indolently, stopping before he closed the door to light another cigarette. A soldier moved swiftly out of the circle of red light, covering him with his weapon and urging him on with an impatient movement. He followed Sherif to where the taxi driver stood at the roadside and stood over them, rifle at the ready. While his attitude was studiously casual, a malicious smile curled his lips off his teeth and his expression was mocking.

Sherif watched the men impassively, drawing quietly on his cigarette as they conducted their search of the car. He was confident that there was nothing to find.

The officer turned from the taxi and barked an order to his men. "Search them."

The Qur'an was retrieved immediately from its hiding place in Sherif's jacket.

"What's this?"

He shrugged, "You can see, *yani*. I'm a religious man; I like to keep the book close to my heart."

The officer flipped the pages. "The Prophet, bless his name, would commend you for your zeal, but this Qur'an has never been read."

"It is new. It was bought in Beirut today."

The officer ignored him. "Cell phones!"

Sherif Raad retrieved his phone from his pocket and handed it over. The officer indicated the second cell with a deliberate nod in the direction of Sherif's belt. He unclipped the pouch without comment. There was only one question in his mind—where had the breach come in?

"Take them in," he said. Placing the Qur'an and both cell phones on the front seat of the Jeep, he started the engine. Sherif was pushed into the passenger seat and Muhammad Mustapha Khalil into the back. A soldier took the seat beside the taxi driver and trained his gun on them, while the one who had conducted the body search, eased his bulk into the driver's seat of the Mercedes and gunned the engine. He reversed, swung the wheel hard, and, slamming it into second gear, sped off behind the military vehicle in the direction of the border post.

Sherif caught a brief glimpse of the customs cfficer's tense face as they were manhandled into the building, but no sign of recognition passed between them.

Khalil and Sherif stood waiting while the Hezbollah officer engaged officials from the Duane in animated conversation. Muhammad Mustapha Khalil clenched and unclenched his jaw. His face was taut and glistening with sweat; his eyes moved nervously around the room. Sherif leaned against the wall, one hand thrust deep in the pocket of his trousers while he carefully examined the fingernails of the other.

Their papers were closely scrutinised and questions were fired at them about their movements in and out of Lebanon. There was a brief confab between the officials and, as the Hezbollah officer approached him from across the room, Sherif felt the first real burgeoning of unease and fought to suppress it.

"You," he rapped at Sherif, "you come with us! Let's get moving."

He was grabbed roughly by the arm and shoved towards the door; his face appeared calm, almost deadpan. As the officer passed the silent form of Muhammad Mustapha Khalil, he slammed the butt of his rifle into the taxi driver's shoulder. Khalil gasped with pain and slumped, white-faced, down the wall. He moaned and clutched at himself.

"You, my friend, we will be watching you! Perhaps you should open another business."

Chapter 21   Betrayal

"Faced with disconcerting episodes of violent fundamentalism, our respect for true followers of Islam should lead us to avoid hateful generalizations, for authentic Islam and the proper reading of the Qur'an are opposed to every form of violence." Pope Francis I

"You can't say Islam is a religion of peace because Islam does not mean peace. Islam means submission, so the Muslim is one who submits. There is a place for violence for Islam. There is a place for jihad in Islam." Anjem Choudary, British Islamist.

Lex, Moussa, and the girls walked together between the silver-leafed olive trees heavy with ripening fruit. Even with a relatively small crop each year, Lex became edgy about when to harvest and watched the weather conditions with all the anxiety of the local subsistence farmers. The flavour of the oil was the prime factor rather than the yield and harvesting too soon meant the oil would be greener and somewhat bitter; harvesting too late could result in a crop ruined by frost or storm damage. This year's warmer autumn was causing the crop to turn faster than usual.

"We'll try for next week," he said to Moussa. "I'll see what the neighbours are doing about theirs; we generally share labour."

"I would love to help with the picking," Amal offered.

"What about Layla?" Moussa asked, glancing down at his younger daughter.

"I can come with her," Layla said quickly. "I don't have classes next week."

"They would both be a great help," Lex assured him. "I'll let you know when we will do it and Juan could pick them up. As far as I know, we shouldn't have rain next week."

Moussa and his daughters had become regular visitors at the lime-washed *cortiga*[25] in the hills outside Frigiliana. It was a while before

Adriana and Lex had noticed that Juan contrived to be home for those visits and that Amal was the reason. They watched the developing relationship with interest.

"I'll be around most days," he said casually. "It would be no problem to fetch the girls."

Juan had finished his masters at the University of Granada earlier in the year and was toying with the idea of doing a doctorate and, while Lex was not keen for his son to settle down too soon, he secretly hoped that he would choose to find a job rather than continue his studies.

Amal had brought homemade *tabbuleh*, *humous*, and Arabic bread to add to the picnic lunch by the pool. It was still warm enough to swim and the men joined the youngsters for a while before returning to their towels on the grass to sunbathe.

"I have had word from Raif," Moussa said.

Lex sat up and searched his friend's face, "Good news?"

"I think so. It was just a text message, but he says he is working in a bakery in Raqqa."

"A bakery!"

"I was just as surprised. But I hope it means he has found a way to be free of ISIS."

"Any thought that he might come home?"

Moussa shrugged, "For Raif, it may be that Syria *is* home."

Lex stood up and picked up his towel, "Don't discount the pull of family," he said. "I reckon he'll come back. I'm ready for a cup of coffee. Would you like one?"

Amal sat down in a deck chair next to Eugenia and surveyed the view. She had slipped a cornflower-blue skirt on over her costume which looked good against the deep tan of her legs.

"I love the view of the mountains from here," she said. "This is such a perfect spot."

"You're right, it is lovely."

"I've been following the posts on your website," Amal said cautiously.

Eugenia glanced across at her, "I hope you don't find them offensive."

---

[25] Cottage

"I have to agree with most of what you write," Amal admitted sadly. "There's a lot wrong with the society I come from," she paused, her eyes on the horizon, but she was no longer taking in what she saw. "I notice many comments are from young Saudi Arabian women. They seem determinedly happy with their lives. Their main complaint seems to be that they aren't allowed to drive."

Eugenia smiled. "It must be a frustration when they see that other Islamic countries permit it." She waited, knowing that her friend had something else besides driving restrictions on her mind.

"I saw one comment reminding you that Islam is a religion of love and peace and that murders, rapes, and kidnappings take place just as often in the West."

"Which is possibly true," Eugenia acknowledged, "but there's a difference, Amal. Our law doesn't uphold honour killings by family members; neither does it allow child marriage, or the stoning to death of rape victims. We have an imperfect judicial system but it does allow people a hearing and it supports the rights of women."

"You have to admit that western morals have been weakened by the excessive freedoms that you have been given," Amal ventured.

Eugenia was quiet for a moment, "They have damaged morality," she said at length. "Our liberty has caused Western society to rot from the inside out. We don't have it right but there's something deeply disturbing in the Middle Eastern need to police every aspect of human behaviour. Chopping a person's hand off for stealing does result in a reduction in crime, but is it right? I know of a woman who had her feet amputated for the sin of running away from her husband who was probably abusing her anyway."

Amal looked down at her hands which lay quietly in her lap. She knew that Sharia law supported such things, and more, in the name of Allah. "So," she said at length, "does any culture have the balance right?"

Eugenia sighed. "You know, I don't think so," she admitted. "There are no perfect solutions because there are no perfect human beings."

* * *

He needed a cigarette. Sherif Raad took the empty Marlboro packet from his pocket, checked it for the dozenth time and with an angry gesture, crumpled it and flung it across the room.

They had arrived in Beirut at first light and driven through the slowly awakening city to the familiar Hezbollah headquarters in the southern suburbs. Guards standing in front of the building saluted the officer and glanced, without much interest, at the prisoner as he was urged out of the Jeep with the muzzle of a rifle pressed to his ribs.

Hezbollah, Party of Allah, was conceived and funded by Iranian clerics following the invasion of Lebanon by Israel in 1982. With the blessing of Syria, Hezbollah's forces were trained by members of the Iranian National Guard as a force intended to resist the Israeli occupation. The Party grew into a state within a state and now deployed fighters beyond Lebanon's borders. Despite positive social work carried out in the community by the organisation, Hezbollah's support of Bashar al-Assad of Syria during the Syrian civil war had deeply tarnished their image. Suicide bombers had blown-up vehicles against the headquarters on several different occasions resulting in damage and many deaths. Deep rifts existed between the various militant factions. Hezbollah was Shiite, the Islamic State, Sunni; the religious distinctions between the two groups represented insurmountable odds.

Sherif's watch had been confiscated and without his cell phone, it was difficult to tell how long it was since they had arrived. From the light penetrating the grime of the barred window high in one wall, he estimated it to be around midday. He had seen no one since his arrival and was desperately thirsty, but although hunger had begun to explore his gut with small unexpected pangs, he had no desire for food.

He used his mental neatening process to order his thoughts. In all the time he had acted as a courier, Sherif's anticipation of capture had been purely academic. Now, he was under no illusions. From the moment he was taken into custody he knew that his chance of survival was very slim. It was obvious they had acted on a tip-off. Therefore, if they knew he operated as a courier for the Islamic State, that in itself made him valuable to Hezbollah.

Presumably, they already had men working on the Qur'an and the cell phone. If they were able to crack whatever passwords or codes had been used, it would be a major feather in their cap against ISIS. It also followed logically that he was unlikely to leave the building alive. Sherif Raad had no idea what sort of information he was carrying, only that it was important enough not to risk sending in any other way.

He paced the small yellowed room with its pervading stench of urine from a slop bucket until exhaustion and strain caused his legs to shake. He sat down with his back against the wall and faced the window with its receding light.

The unlocking of the door penetrated his dreams and he was on his feet in one fluid movement. Momentarily, the eyes of the guard registered a flash of fear and his hand dropped to the gun at his belt. He relaxed as he perceived in the prisoner's face the confusion of one who has slept deeply.

"Get out," he ordered roughly. "*Yella!*"

Sherif stumbled towards the door and the guard aided his progress with a shove of his boot. It was the action of a man accustomed to following orders now enjoying a brief moment of clout. They walked the length of the corridor followed by the echo of their footsteps. The guard knocked briefly on a door marked 102 and entered shoving Sherif Raad ahead of him.

There were two men in the room seated behind a wide oak desk. The guard pushed Sherif in the direction of a straight-backed chair and ordered him to sit.

"Your name?" The man had the well-fleshed, red-veined look of one who drank excessively. His thick-fingered hand toyed with the edge of a file lying on the otherwise uncluttered surface.

"Sherif Raad."

For the first time, the second man looked up and fixed cold eyes on Sherif's face. He was in his mid-forties, with a square, high cheek-boned countenance over which the skin stretched thin and dry. Sherif noted the thick vein that snaked down the centre of his forehead and knew the man was dangerous.

"Age?"

"Thirty-three."

"Occupation?"

Sherif noted the way the interrogator's eyes travelled back to the file on the desk as he asked question upon mundane question, that he was already in possession of the answers. He watched the thick face of his interrogator, seeking any nuance of expression, any change in tone that would indicate which direction the questioning might take.

"How long have you been a courier for Islamic State?"

"I don't know what you mean."

"How long?'

"I came to Lebanon for a short break. I was returning to my home in Syria."

"You came just to purchase a new copy of the Qur'an?"

"I did buy a copy when I was in Beirut, yes."

"From which shop?"

He was prepared for the question. "It was one of the small bookshops near the taxi rank."

"The name?"

"I did not take note of the name."

"Do you have the purchase slip?"

"I don't think they gave me one." Sherif licked his dry lips. "I have had nothing to drink since I came here. Could I have some water?"

The fat man's lips parted in a seraphic smile. He nodded to the guard. "Pass him the carafe."

Sherif tilted the spout towards his mouth, gulping down the cool water until he was satisfied.

"Now that we have had our little joke," the fat man said, "I will tell you where the Qur'an and the cell phone you were carrying came from. I can see you have forgotten." He named the mosque and the imam who had met with Sherif the previous morning.

The other man interjected and his words were directed at the guard. "Take him down!"

Sherif felt as though his skin had suddenly become too tight. The guard gripped his arm and ordered him to stand. There was no further word from the interrogators as he was led from the room.

The guard marched him down three flights of stairs to the basement of the building. Sherif did not need an explanation; one glance around the room confirmed what he already knew. He took in the machines used to electrocute, the metal implements, the bloodstained walls, and the manacles chained to the ceiling that would hang a victim by his arms for hours.

For the heroic, torture could endure for weeks, or even months, but such scruples were completely foreign to Sherif Raad. He had no desire to protect anyone apart from himself. Whatever they wanted he would give to make torture short and allow death to follow as swiftly as possible.

Muhammad Mustapha Khalil drove through Syria as quickly as good sense and self-preservation would allow. He took passengers because an empty vehicle would provoke questions. At one point, after seeing no vehicles coming in his direction for almost fifteen minutes, he swung the taxi around and took another route knowing that some sort of major blockade lay up ahead. He reached Raqqa by mid-morning and reported immediately to Islamic State headquarters.

Muhammad Hamid al-Duleimi, Cabinet Advisor to Caliph Ibrahim, and co-ordinator of information across the territories under the rule of Islamic State addressed the meeting at headquarters later that day. He was unshaven, and his heavy brows were drawn together in repressed anger.

"Our courier, Sherif Raad, was arrested by Hezbollah on the Lebanese border last night," he said. "He was taken into custody."

"How did we hear?" The question came from one who worked in the office of the Deputy.

"He works with a certain taxi driver, Muhammad Mustapha Khalil," al-Duleimi replied. "He reported the matter when he arrived, a few hours ago."

"Was Raad carrying information?"

"Of course he was carrying information!" he snapped. "We used the same method as before. A Qur'an generally draws no attention but the taxi driver seemed to think they searched for it specifically." He rubbed the black stubble on his chin with the palm of his hand. "The Qur'an held the password to the cell phone but *insha' Allah*[26], they won't find it." *Insha' Allah*, he added silently, Hezbollah's steganographers were not as good as those working within the Caliphate!

"How about the courier? Would he be of any use to Hezbollah?"

"He knew nothing," he said shortly. "I made sure he was told nothing. His only interest was money."

---

[26] By God's will

"Could he have sold us out?"

"It's possible, but I don't think so. The leak seemed to come from somewhere in the mosque we used as a collection point."

This was another sore point for al-Duleimi. If Syria's Deputy suspected that their use of Sherif Raad was in any way compromised, it would worsen his own situation. The Deputy was currently in Iraq for meetings with the Caliph and he dreaded his return. An incident such as this could signal not only the end of Muhammad Hamid al-Duleimi's career but also his life. His only hope now was that the code would hold.

Chapter 22   Betrayal

Walid handed the woman her bread in a brown paper packet and looked across the bakery counter to his next customer. Muhammad Mustapha Khalil was a regular and Walid knew him well by sight. He looked dishevelled and his eyes were red-rimmed.

"Marhabba," Walid greeted, "You look as though you have been driving all night."

Khalil returned the greeting briefly. "I have," he said. "There was trouble at the border."

"Fighting?"

"No, no. Look, can I speak to you privately somewhere?"

"Of course, come to my office. My daughter can take over here." Walid called Nour from the back of the shop and Muhammad Mustapha shot her a curious glance.

The baker drew up two chairs and offered Muhammad coffee. He shook his head. "I have disturbing news," he said. "Sherif Raad travelled with me last night," he cleared his throat, uncertain as to how to proceed. Death was simple to convey; arrest a little more complicated.

"Go on."

"Just after the Lebanese border post, we were stopped by Hezbollah militia and Raad was taken in."

The baker swore softly. *"Yikrab dinek,* why?"

"I'm not sure," Khalil said uncomfortably. "He was carrying some contraband."

"Contraband! What sort of contraband?"

Muhammad Mustapha Khalil leaned forward confidentially, "He was working for the Islamic State," he said in a stage whisper. "He was carrying a Qur'an."

"Islamic State... A Qur'an!" Walid became aware that he was parroting the taxi driver's words. "Why would Hezbollah arrest him for carrying a Qur'an? Sherif is not a religious man," he said. "And not political either. What you are telling me does not make sense."

Muhammad sat back and nodded his agreement. He grimaced twice in quick succession, a dog-like draw-back of lips from teeth. "You are right; Raad is none of those things. Perhaps the book had something concealed inside. This was not the first time I took him to Lebanon on some sort of mission. ISIS used him and they paid him well."

"Do you know any more than this?" Walid asked.

"*La*. But I have contacts in Beirut. I will let you know if I hear anything. Please, pass my sadness at what happened on to your daughter."

Walid thought of Nour for the first time. He knew without saying that she would not be grieved if her husband failed to return.

There was no way of knowing whether Sherif Raad was dead or alive. Nour displayed no outward emotion. She returned to the apartment Sherif had rented and resumed her life; inwardly she waited, not daring to hope that she had been set free. She was sorry that she was unable to mourn the man she had married but refused to suffer guilt. She only feared his sudden return and that the nightmare would begin again.

Days turned into weeks and there was no further word. Nour enjoyed the degree of freedom she had gained in Sherif's absence. Although Raqqa laboured under the restraints imposed by the Islamic State the city was now relatively peaceful. What was once a Westernised city had reverted suddenly, and painfully, to its Islamic root. Merchants hawked their wares from tables or mobile barrows on the pavements. There were fewer women on the streets; they moved with their heads down when they walked alone, and they were subdued in their interaction with the shopkeepers. No one openly sold alcohol and even those who brought liquor into the country and kept it in their homes were in danger of being reported to the Sharia Counsel by informants. Drug dealers and those found in possession of drugs could expect to die without recourse to appeal. Most prisoners under the Islamic State soon willingly, even effusively, declared their guilt and converted suddenly to a form of Islam more in line with the belief of their jailers.

Schoolchildren were now required to wear Islamic dress. The start of the new school year reflected both the cultural and the religious changes that were taking place in the country, and educational reform lay at the heart of the regime. Under the newly introduced Sharia-based curriculum the aim of the Caliph, prince of the faithful, was to eliminate all historical and scientific teaching that was not in line with his religious vision. Education in schools and universities was to be brought into line with the Islamic State's *Salafist* ideology and all university research work was stopped. Teachers had no way of protesting the new regulations; quite simply, those who did not conform would be expelled.

Businesses continued under the watchful eye of the *Hisbah* armed men who patrolled the city ensuring that every aspect of the Sharia law was enforced, whether of religious practice, dress, civil obedience, and even diet and personal behaviour. Their one intention was to establish a Caliphate that, in its outworking, would honour the Prophet Muhammad. Dressed in a simple white robe, black turban and a loose black waistcoat, they approached the people of Raqqa affably while slowly eliminating every aspect of Western influence upon the city. When the *Hisbah* walked through shops and questioned the prices they were met with good-natured co-operation and a barely disguised undercurrent of fear.

Nour chafed under the restraints but complied. There was little choice. She hated the unforgiving black covering she was forced to wear outside her home; she had chosen the thinnest veil which still darkened the sky and impaired her vision. And this slight deviation caused a vehicle to pull up beside them one morning on their walk to the bakery and a challenge was put to her father.

"Peace, my brother," Walid was given a friendly handshake. "Is that your wife?" The *Hisbah* nodded in the direction of the swathed black figure of Nour.

"Peace be with you. It is my daughter, *insh' Allah*."

"Tell her to change the fabric of her veil, it is too thin, her face can be seen. And she must not lift the hem of her gown so that we see what she is wearing underneath. It is your duty to protect your daughter."

All was done with a pleasant smile while his automatic rifle rested between his knees. Nour stood rock-still gazing in the opposite direction until the vehicle drove off.

"*Yikrab dinek*," she swore quietly. "May his religion be burned!"

"Nour, I heard that," Walid said, glancing around nervously. "Be careful what you say!"

Nour raised her eyebrows and continued walking. "I am not changing my veil," she called behind her. "Do they want me to be totally blind?"

"Nour, don't lift your hem!"

"So, for the Islamic State I must get my clothes covered in dust!" she snapped but she let the fabric trail.

She surprised herself nowadays on her ability to walk gracefully under the covering of the *niqab* and she had long ago abandoned the gum boots for more feminine footwear. There was little else a woman could indulge in.

That afternoon, Muhammad Mustapha Khalil visited the bakery and asked to see the baker. Walid Zaky came down from his office, took the taxi driver by the shoulders, and kissed his cheeks in greeting.

"Come in, come in! *Shu al-akhbar, yani?*"

"I have news from Beirut."

Walid searched his face for an answer and dropped his hands. "Come through to my office," he said quietly.

They sat down and Walid called for coffee. "So," he said. "The news is not good?"

The taxi driver tossed his head in negation. "*La!* I traced a cousin of Sherif's," he replied. "I could not go to the offices of Hezbollah personally, they would have told me nothing. But a relative can usually find information."

The youth Walid had employed to serve at the counter brought a carafe of water and a foaming copper pot of Turkish coffee. He held the handle awkwardly, poured the liquid into two cups, and left the room.

"What did he find out, this man?" Walid asked.

"They admitted they had taken Raad into custody but said he was shot when he tried to escape. They knew of no next-of-kin, so he was buried."

Walid whistled between clenched teeth. He picked up a tiny cup abstractedly between finger and thumb and sipped his coffee. "Was the cousin distressed?"

Muhammad Mustapha shook his head. "He said he expected such an end."

Walid raised his eyebrows. "Why?"

The taxi driver shrugged. "The cousin said he was too quiet and such a man knew trouble. He said the devil works in silent men."

Walid massaged his head with his fingertips. "And now I must tell my daughter she is a widow," he said. "They were married only a short time, you know."

Muhammad Mustapha nodded sympathetically. "A sad business," he replied. "You must give her my condolences."

Chapter 23   Betrayal

Juan knocked at the door of the apartment and stood in the corridor feeling the cool breeze as it rolled in off the sea. It was a sparkling autumn day with just a hint of a chill in the air. Layla opened the door and greeted him with an excited hug.

"Amal's nearly ready. She said I must ask you to come in."

The apartment on the hillside was one of Malaga's recently modernised older buildings. From the living room, expansive windows took in the spectacular view of the city which wrapped a protective elbow around the harbour. Where it relinquished its hold to the open sea, cranes rose above the water like the feelers of some gigantic sea creature. Neat rows of berthed yachts gave the impression of a frayed edge to the quayside; two ships were docked across the bay, one a sleek, white cruise vessel, the other a darker, more matronly hull. The sky was a clear blue, softening to peach where it united with the sea at the horizon.

The living room was furnished with deep brown leather sofas, a low glass coffee table and in an alcove off the main room, a glass-topped dining-room table. Woven rugs in rich colours adorned the white tiled floor and several of Moussa's framed black-and-white photographs hung on the walls. Layla led the way out onto the terrace.

"Come and sit down," she said importantly. "I can get you a drink if you like."

Juan shook his head, "I'm fine, thanks, Layla."

Blue-and-white striped cushions were piled onto the chunky outdoor chairs. Juan sat back and imagined how Amal might look seated here with her long hair loose around her shoulders and her legs stretched out in the sunlight. Layla chattered away and he answered her absently. His thoughts focused on Amal a great deal lately and he looked forward to spending this day with her.

She called a greeting, "Morning, Juan. Sorry for keeping you waiting."

"Not at all, Layla's been looking after me."

His warm appraisal as she met his eyes caused her to blush and turn quickly away.

"Let me take that," Juan smiled down at her as he took the picnic basket. She was dressed casually in jeans and a well-worn deep-red sweater in anticipation of the day's work. Setting her handbag down on the floor of the elevator, she drew her hair back off her face and secured it adeptly with a band from around her wrist. Juan's car was parked across the road and Layla clambered happily into the back seat. As they drove along the freeway towards Nerja, she plied him with innumerable questions about olive picking.

"Layla, that's enough now. You're going to exhaust Juan!"

He grinned and shook his head.

"You see, Amal, Juan doesn't mind," she said accusingly, but she sank back on the seat obediently and limited her chatter.

They left the main road and began the climb up into the hills towards the tumble of white dwellings that announced the village of Frigiliana and then beyond, along the winding track towards the Wesley-Smith farm.

Lex was already in the orchard, surveying his eight trees with satisfaction.

"The olives are just right," he pronounced. "They haven't begun to drop and the colour is perfect!" The branches were heavy with clusters of deep purple fruit which assumed a pleasing lustre in the sunlight. Lex and Juan erected a catch-net around the base of the first tree, gave each of the girls a long-handled fork, and demonstrated the way the fruit was combed gently off the twigs. Soon Amal was hard at work on the lower branches while Juan on a step-ladder combed the upper part of the tree. Adriana came up from the house to help Lex wash and pack the heaps of olives that were gathering into the net. Layla persevered for a while and eventually retired to the picnic blanket with her sketch pad and crayons to draw the scene instead.

They picnicked up there in the grove in the partial shade cast by the silvery leaves of the trees. Amal had packed cheeses and her home-baked bread; Adriana provided drinks and a fresh salad picked, as she proudly announced, from her vegetable garden that morning.

"So, Amal, have you brought some of your writing to show me?" Lex asked. Amal nodded and blushed as she brought a thin manuscript of her poetry from the basket and presented it to Lex. He settled back on the blanket and, much to Amal's embarrassment, read sections aloud for the others to hear as he paged through.

"This one is a powerful expression of what you have been through, Amal," he commented.

> *"Roofed marksmen watch*
> *The robot soldiers' slow advance*
> *Then split them red as pomegranate*
> *In the dust.*
> *Children's screams pave*
> *A blood path to freedom."*

Lex sat up. "I'm impressed with the way you write," he said. "The imagery is strong, hard-hitting and there are other poems that show a gentle sensitivity to the world around you. Keep it up, Amal! May I keep these for a while to have a closer look?"

"Of course, Lex. Thank you for taking the time."

Juan glanced across at her and there was a warmth to his expression that Amal did not miss. She covered her embarrassment by gathering the picnic things and repacking the basket.

It was late afternoon when Moussa arrived from work to take the girls home, by which time all the trees were stripped. They had a final 'sun-downer' on the terrace overlooking the mountains on the left and the Mediterranean lying quietly below until the scene was entirely sapped of colour, and pricks of light from the neighbouring homes began to appear in the dusk.

Within minutes, Layla was asleep in the back of Moussa's car. Once they were on the freeway, he reached out a hand and briefly patted the knee of his older daughter.

"You seem to have enjoyed your day," he said.

"It was hard work," she confessed, "but I did enjoy it."

"They are a lovely family," Moussa spoke slowly, measuring his words, "but you must be careful Amal, not to lose your heart to Juan."

She glanced at his face in the light from the dashboard. "Why do you say that, *Baba*? Don't you like him?"

"I like him very much," he replied. "But these are Westerners. For young people, casual relationships form part of their way of life. That's not what I want for you, Amal. I don't want you to be hurt."

She was silent as she absorbed his words. Her father was never dictatorial as some of her Syrian friends' fathers were and she had never wanted to disobey him but his words impacted her deeply. She looked down to where her hands lay quietly in her lap and tried to still the confusion of her heart. Was Juan like that, she wondered. Had his eyes spoken as intimately to other girls as they had whispered a promise to her several times that day?

"I don't think Juan's like that," she ventured at last.

Moussa's face was lit intermittently by the traffic on the opposite side of the freeway, he moved into the left lane in preparation for taking the turn into Malaga. Some way ahead, the city lights reflected richly onto the dark surface of the water.

"Perhaps not," he said gently, "but this is not Syria where there is chaperoning and protection. There's a freedom in relationships that you have not grown up with and often it leads to carelessness. As a father, I must warn you to be very cautious."

Amal turned her head away and looked sightlessly out at the bright city lights. She felt chilled. Moussa's words pushed aside all the pleasure of those hours spent with Juan and replaced it with doubt. She was so naïve; she had been a fool in thinking that he cared about her, while in Juan's mind she was probably just another prospective conquest. Well, Amal decided, she would not give him the satisfaction of thinking she was a pushover. She took the elevator to the apartment without speaking, said a brief goodnight to her father who had Layla over one shoulder and went straight to her room. Moussa took off Layla's shoes and put her to bed without bothering to change her clothes. Then he poured himself a drink and sat in the darkness of the terrace. He still had Layla's teenage years ahead. Who was he, a man, to bring up girls alone? It was not going to be an easy task.

"For years now, Muslims have been urged to work towards imposing Sharia law in their adopted countries," Moussa said.

"They bring people in, create enclaves, make them more Muslim than they were in their own countries, and then create discontent and rebellion."

They were sitting at a pavement café which they often frequented for lunch when Lex was in Malaga. Bright yellow sunshades reflected on the cobblestones, which were still wet in places from an early morning rain shower.

"There's that British activist, what's his name?"

"Anjem Choudary."

"That's him. Didn't he attempt to get Muslims to rally outside the White House some time ago?"

Moussa nodded. "They cancelled at the last minute," he replied. "Perhaps they rightly decided that it would have been too provocative. But I guarantee they'll be back. Radical Islam is getting bolder by the hour."

"And the intention is a worldwide revolution?"

"In their own words, '*insha Allah,* God willing, very, very soon'."

"Moussa, the more I research for this book, the more I see that the world is a tinder-box. It's all just waiting for a single event to blow it sky high."

"How's the book going?"

"The story is developing well," he paused and Moussa looked at him questioningly. "There's a whole lot more to it than meets the eye," Lex said.

"Such as?"

"You probably know some of it already, but it's new to me. Did you know that the American CIA funded and armed the *mujahideen* in Afghanistan to overthrow the Soviets?"

Moussa nodded. "I'd heard, but I don't know the details."

"It was back in '79 and code-named Operation Cyclone. They fed billions of dollars into the project over a ten-year period. Saudi agreed to match the money put up by America, dollar for dollar. Jimmy Carter initially authorised funding. He saw the Soviets as a real threat to world peace and decided that no outside force would be allowed to control the Persian Gulf. Reagan expanded that policy and went all-out to improve the prospects of the guerrilla war against the Soviets. The US avoided putting men on the ground not wanting their assistance to be recognised."

"In one sense it was justified. They succeeded in creating a fighting force which ousted the Soviets."

Lex nodded. "But it wasn't all happily ever after. Al Qaeda was one of the Islamic fundamentalist movements spawned from that interference, and ISIS is just another off-shoot of Al-Qaeda." Lex absently held his glass up allowing the sunlight to set the burgundy liquid aglow before taking a sip. "They're still at it, Moussa," he said.

"Meaning?"

"The United States continues to nurture and support radical Islamic groups to their own ends as you know. They fund them knowing they intend to establish Sharia over the nations."

Moussa nodded. "Their reasoning doesn't make sense," he agreed, "unless providing arms and training for their enemies serves their purpose in some obscure way."

Lex grimaced, "In the U.S's determination to destroy Assad they've only succeeded in splintering the rebel groups further. Surely they didn't imagine they could control them. Syria's in the same state as Libya now, it's a country tearing itself apart."

"I don't think any of it has been done naively," Moussa replied. "I'm pretty certain they're following carefully mapped-out policies."

Lex looked quizzical. "In what way?"

"Think about the Georgia Guidestones in the US. The stated intention is to bring the world population to under five hundred million and keep it there."

"Minor wars and skirmishes between factions wouldn't have any real impact on the world population!' Lex said.

"Unless the intention was to create a scenario for a Third World War..."

"Anyway, weren't the Freemasons supposed to have had something to do with that monument?" Lex protested. He poured himself another glass of wine. "Come on, Moussa, hardly anyone has heard of the Guidestones, and reduction of the population by six-and-a-half billion people is inconceivable!"

"Someone believed in it enough to put those stones there, to align them astronomically and to inscribe the message in four ancient languages and eight modern."

"It's a remarkable structure," Lex admitted, "but put there by some crank—or eccentric millionaire!"

"I don't think the Islamic State would have a problem with such a radical reduction," Moussa remarked with a wry smile, "so there's probably a host of others with the same mindset. And, of course, the guidelines could be intended for a population decimated by nuclear war." He finished his drink and put the glass down on the table. "I must go," he said. "I need to get back to work. I'll settle the bill this time. Give my best regards to Adriana."

Lex ordered another coffee and opened Georgia Guidestones on his laptop. Various sites reported that a cube of granite bearing the numbers 20 and 14 on the two visible sides had been inserted into one of the monument's stone slabs. The Guidestones had recently been vandalised. Gratuitously scrawled across them in red paint were slogans such as, 'Death to the New World Order'. Something else caught Lex's eye and he felt the prickling of his spine. It was the words, 'I Am Isis, goddess of love'.

Despite himself, Lex was intrigued. But it was only as he drove back to Frigiliana that his thoughts returned to the projections of the card game—was population reduction and control really the end game? He pondered the emblematic use of a cube in Freemasonry and wondered if there was any connection between the Masons and the protocols laid down on the Guidestones. His father had been a Mason for several years but after some sort of quarrel had left the local lodge and never returned. Purely out of curiosity, Lex had read a bit about it and even brought the Craft into one of his novels. He knew, for example, the Masonic apron represented the 'veil of flesh' which was a Biblical phrase meaning the body. Symbolically, the cube exemplified moral rectitude, the struggle for perfection and purity, and the discovery of the god within. And of course, the cube also played an important role in Islam.

Later that evening he researched the cube-shaped Ka'abah on the internet. According to Islam, the Ka'abah was first built by Adam and later rebuilt by the prophet Abraham who smashed the pagan idols and cleansed it. Muhammad had followed Abraham's lead when he again restored the Ka'abah retaining only a rock from among the pagan gods, a black meteorite which, according to Islamic tradition, fell from heaven to show Adam and Eve where an altar must be erected.

"And now," Lex said to himself thoughtfully, "we have a Caliph Ibrahim bringing his form of cleansing through ISIS." Of course, it was coincidence. The Islamic State could have absolutely nothing to do with Freemasonry, the goddess Isis, or the cube placed in the Georgia Guidestones. Or could it?

Chapter 24   Betrayal

Nour stood transfixed, for once thankful that her *niqab* made her invisible. Raif was walking down the steps of the Sharia court into the sunshine. He was wearing black jeans and an open-necked white shirt and his thick dark hair was tousled by the wind. Her spirit lifted within her; Raif was alive and, by some miracle, he was not out there fighting with the militants of the Islamic State.

She walked slowly up the steps into the large hall where Walid was waiting and made their report at one of the desks. The thin-faced official listened to Walid's account of Sherif's capture by Hezbollah and the subsequent news of his death and slowly wrote down the details. Officially, Nour was free. In reality, she was a non-person made captive by the restraints and restrictions of the Islamic State Caliphate and their application of Sharia law. As a woman under Sharia, she had few rights, little worth, and an uncertain future. But seeing Raif had given her an unreasonable flicker of hope.

Unable to pay the rent on the apartment, Nour was forced to return home and her parents were overjoyed to have her back. Although Walid could not bring himself to say he was sorry for enforcing the marriage on her, he performed little acts of contrition instead, and Nour's determination to remain permanently unforgiving was gradually worn down. She had always loved her father and appreciated his care of her. Many men adored their sons and despised their daughters; Walid loved his only child, never harbouring any bitterness that her life had deprived him of a son. A bungled delivery in childbirth had left Nour's mother unable to bear more children and with Sherif's death, it seemed they were to be deprived of grandchildren as well.

"If they hadn't declared a Caliphate," Walid observed to Nour as they walked to work one morning, "they would have been able to put more effort into their fight against al-Assad and Iraq. If you ask me, they shot themselves in the foot! Now they're forced to rule over the areas they've captured. That takes money and manpower."

Nour stopped to adjust the strap of her shoe. "Why do you think they did that?" she asked. "The Caliphate, I mean. Was it to give them some advantage over the Shiites?"

Walid glanced at her sharply. He enjoyed his discussions with Nour as much, or more, than with any of the men he knew. "It's possible," he said. "Because of course, there's that Shiite prophecy about Damascus and the coming of the *al-Mahdi*."

"That the Twelfth Imam would arise when Damascus is destroyed?"

"Exactly!"

"So, with Damascus almost in ruin and Iran looking towards the coming of the *al-Mahdi*, the Sunnis needed to prevent the fulfillment of the prophecy."

"Or to get in before them with a Caliph."

"Stop for a moment, papa!" Nour put a hand on her father's shoulder to steady herself. "This stupid shoe! The strap keeps slipping."

Walid rolled his eyes and thanked God that the *Hisbah* were nowhere in sight.

"Certainly," Nour said when her shoe was properly buckled and she could walk again, "ISIS could never allow a Shiite minority leader to dominate the Sunni. That would be a direct admission that the Sunni had been wrong all these centuries!"

Walid looked thoughtful, "Never let these thoughts go any further than this," he warned his daughter, "but it is certainly why every faction is determined to wipe out Bashar al-Assad. They want Syria cleared of Shiite rule."

"Which leaves Iran and Hezbollah in Lebanon," Nour said. "At the moment, the Islamic State is too small to deal with them, but perhaps the international community will step in after all."

* * *

"Juan, can we talk?" Lex asked as his son came up the pathway towards the veranda.

Juan raised his eyebrows. "So, what have I done this time, Papa?"

Lex grinned and shook his head. "Nothing, I hope."

Juan dropped into the wicker chair alongside his father.

"Okay, shoot!"

"I need to chat with you about Amal."

Juan sighed, "I thought so. What's the problem?"

Lex stretched his legs out and linked his hands behind his head. "There isn't a problem at the moment," he replied, "but you need to tread very carefully. Amal's been brought up in a conservative society. If a relationship develops, she and Moussa will treat it as serious."

"As in commitment?"

"Exactly!"

Juan was thoughtful. "I like her," he said at length. "Amal is different from all the other girls I've met and we get on well together. But it's too early to think of marriage."

"Then I would advise you to cool it until you're sure of where it's going," Lex said. "It wouldn't be good to mislead her."

"So you don't think I should take her out?"

"Not as in dating," Lex replied. "But you could invite her to go out with a group of friends, now and then, and keep it light."

Juan looked crestfallen. "I see what you are saying, Papa. Perhaps it's best if I talk to her first."

"If you did decide to marry Amal at any time, we wouldn't stand in your way," Lex added. "But you would need to understand her culture and her background better. Moussa is an exceptional guy, and likeable. But there are other things to be taken into consideration."

"Such as Raif?"

"Raif, certainly! He could cause trouble for his whole family, depending on the course he takes if, and when, he comes home. Amal thinks he's wonderful—that in itself is a problem!"

Juan nodded. "Alright, I'll think over what you've said. It's not a simple decision, Amal and I have a kind of understanding, but don't worry, Pops, it hasn't gone beyond that." He stood up and gave his father a high-five.

Chapter 25   Betrayal

"Cover up," was the terse order. "God loves a woman who is covered up."

Nour resisted the impulse to invite a bullet by spitting and, instead, walked meekly on. She was stopped regularly by the *Hisbah* but had never changed the fabric of her veil.

"Let them try walking around in a black haze for a while," she said to Walid when he implored her to buy another, "They can't identify me anyway, so let them complain if that makes them happy! I am not going to make myself completely blind for their sake."

Summer was slow in releasing its hold this year. Even under the high ceilings, the bakery was hot. Square columns swept upwards into barrel vaults on either side of the deep ovens but, despite the ceiling fans, there was not much natural ventilation. Scarves and long skirts added to the discomfort but, should the *Hisbah* decide to make one of its inspections, it was as well to be prepared.

Nour was irritated when the youth who served at the counter called her to the front.

"There's someone who wants to see you," the boy said.

"A woman?"

"*La.*"

She dusted the flour from her hands, retrieved her *niqab* from the hook behind the bathroom door, slipped it over her head, and adjusted the veil.

"Nour?"

"Raif!" She gripped the edge of the counter startled at the intensity of her feelings. She could feel the blood rising in her face cloistered behind the fine fabric of the veil.

"I heard about your husband."

Nour cast a glance towards the youth who was watching them with interest.

"You can go to the back," Nour said. "The next batch of bread will be ready in three minutes."

"Where did you hear about Sherif?" Nour asked as the young man reluctantly left his post.

"It was one of those strange coincidences," he replied shaking his head. "I am working at the Sharia Court as an interpreter and a clerk. A few days ago, I was asked to file some documents and yours was among them. Should I offer my condolences?"

"Hardly," she replied bitterly. "I'm afraid it was a relief."

Even through the dark cloth, she could see the gentleness of his expression.

"Poor Nour, I thought it might be. What do you know of his death?"

Nour briefly recounted the story as she knew it. "I am home with my parents again now. The marriage seems like a bad dream and I am so thankful it is over."

"I never stopped thinking about you," Raif said. He wanted to see her familiar face, to touch her, to hold her as he had so briefly before, and to heal the pain of the preceding months with her closeness. The distance between them was exemplified by the literal meaning of the *niqab*; a partition separated them from one another – a black curtain that cut him off even from the expression in her eyes.

"Is there any possibility that your father would allow me to see you?"

Nour looked dubious. "I don't know, but I could speak to him."

"I waited across the road until he went out," he confessed with a smile. "I was not going to lose this opportunity of seeing you again."

A man entered the shop with his veiled wife trailing behind him like a shadow. Nour thrust two loaves into a packet and handed them to Raif. She served the new customers as Raif deliberately fumbled in his pockets for change.

As they left, he handed Nour the money, and, for a brief moment, he held her hand in his own.

"Would you want to see me, Nour?" he asked quietly.

She nodded. "You know I would."

"Then we will move heaven and earth to make it happen," he said simply and turned and left the shop.

Nour watched him as he crossed the crowded street with a rising sense of joy and anticipation. She glanced down at the money in her hand; with it was a slip of paper on which he had written his cell number. For the first time since the war began in Syria, life seemed full of promise.

"*Baba*, Raif Ahmadi came to the shop this morning."

"He's still in Raqqa?" Her father looked up sharply from under his heavy eyebrows.

Nour nodded. "He works at the Sharia court as an interpreter. He saw the report we made of Sherif's death."

"So he came to see you." Walid's voice was gruff.

"To offer his condolences."

"Of course." Walid glanced at his daughter's face and he knew what was coming, he also knew he would be a fool to damage the relationship with his daughter a second time. "And so?"

"He would like to visit us here, if you would give your permission, *Baba*."

Walid played for time just a little longer while he attempted to deal with his jumbled thoughts. He had arranged a marriage for Nour and, in the process, nearly lost the love of his daughter forever. He could not, would not, dare to stand in the way of her happiness again.

"Do you want to see him?"

"Yes, *Baba*."

"He has a respectable job," Walid said, almost to himself. "And I suppose we need to recognise that the Islamic State is here to stay, whether we like it or not." He sighed. "Tell him he can come. Speak to your mother to set a time."

Nour leaned over the back of his chair and rested her head against his hair.

"There's just one more thing, *Baba*."

"What now?" he asked irritably.

"In case you wondered, I will not be wearing the *niqab*."

"I never doubted it, *habibti*," Walid replied. He dismissed her with a wave of the hand and smiled to himself. It pleased him that she was not subservient like her mother. He had mellowed too much with age and lost that rebellious spark that once was capable of igniting the world around him. It was good that Nour had inherited his old nature; in many ways, she had proved herself equal to any son.

* * *

It was two weeks before Amal heard from Juan again. Despite her resolutions, her heart skipped a beat when she saw who was calling.

"Amal, I'm in Malaga; if you are free can we meet for coffee?"

She hesitated for just a moment. Layla was at school and her father was working, there was nothing to stop her. She took a deep breath.

"Sure. Where?"

"There's that little café just down the road from you, what's it called?"

"The Alba."

"That's the one. Let me pick you up."

"It's fine, I can walk down," she said shortly.

"Fifteen minutes?"

Amal checked her appearance critically in the full-length mirror in her bedroom. She was wearing a long white sweater over black ski pants; she pulled on her boots, added a bright green scarf and a white beret, collected her handbag, and let herself out of the apartment.

Autumn leaves in russet and ochre crunched underfoot as she walked: the sun was warm but there was a cool breeze and Amal wished she had brought her jacket. The Alba was tucked away in a side street two blocks from where she lived. Juan had already arrived and was seated at one of the tables set out on the pavement for those who wished to enjoy the sunshine. The corners of the red and white checked cloths, anchored at the edges to prevent them from blowing away, fretted in the wind.

Juan stood up to greet her, "I think we would be more comfortable inside," he said. He opened the door and stood back for Amal. A gas fire flickered over convincing-looking coals in a corner fireplace making the room warm and inviting; they took a table close by and ordered cappuccinos.

"I must thank you and Layla again for your help with the olives."

"We enjoyed our day out. It was a new experience for us. Layla loved your dogs, the puppy is adorable."

"She is," he agreed readily. "And already she's a handful!"

"Handful?" Amal asked, confused by the unfamiliar turn of phrase. "What do you mean?"

He laughed. "She's mischievous. A bundle of laughs, but into everything, we have to watch her now because she's started chewing things—shoes, furniture—everything is fair game."

She smiled, "You will have to begin training her. I know so little about dogs; we never had one in Syria."

The coffees arrived and a silence fell between them. She watched his hands as he stirred his cup; his movements were gentle as though he had conquered a clumsier persona by quiet control. She dared to imagine his touch and trembled at the thought. Was her father right; were there women in his life that had known him in that way? Amal stifled the pang of jealous anxiety and looked up to find he was watching her. She blushed, afraid he had somehow read her thoughts but when he spoke his words were reassuringly neutral.

"Your father's exhibition is coming up in a couple of weeks," Juan said, "he must be excited."

"Perhaps," Amal replied. "He doesn't express things like that, but he has done a lot of preparation."

"His work is excellent judging by the prints you have on your walls. Has he photographed you?"

She nodded, "He will be including a portrait of Layla and one of me."

"I look forward to seeing them." Juan reached across the table and took her hand. Amal looked at him cautiously but did not draw away.

"I needed to meet you today to talk," he said. "It's difficult when there are others around. You know I am deeply attracted to you, Amal?" He looked into her eyes, willing her to speak but she was silent and her expression betrayed nothing. He blundered on. "Unfortunately, the timing is wrong for me. I'm still studying part-time and just setting out on a career. I wanted to let you know I am not ready for a committed relationship…" Even as he said them, he knew the words were clumsy and sensed that anything else he might add would probably make things worse.

Amal pulled her hand away. Her face was flushed and there was a spark in her eyes that he had not seen before.

"I am sure you are not," she replied tersely. "And neither am I! I think you may have misunderstood me, Juan. I have made no demands on you, and I never intend to!"

"That's not really what I meant," he said.

"You suggested that I was looking for marriage—what have I done to give you that impression?"

He shook his head. "You haven't, Amal. I thought I may have given you the wrong signals."

"By what, allowing me to come and pick olives?" she remembered the way he had looked into her eyes that day and blushed to know he was right. She had thought every day about the possibility of a life with Juan. She lashed out with words intending to hurt him.

"Do you think I know nothing about relationships in this part of the world?" she asked. "I am quite aware that men have a different approach to women here."

"Amal, I'm sorry. Please let me try and explain what I mean."

"Don't bother," she said. She pushed her chair back and gathered up her handbag and beret.

Juan stood up and caught her elbow, "Amal, don't just walk away," he pleaded. "I really want to be friends with you."

She lifted her chin defiantly, "It doesn't need any further explanation," she said. "I realise that we think differently. Western men don't appeal to me at all. Your values are different to ours and when I came here today it was that message that I wanted to give you." And with that, she turned and left the restaurant.

Perversely, as she walked up the street towards home, she hoped Juan would follow. The breeze was stronger now and it cut through her, chilling her body even as her heart was chilled. It was the wind that stung her eyes to tears.

Chapter 26   Betrayal

*'The decades of Western-backed oppression that have violated the
sanctity of Allah and plundered Muslim resources is coming to an
end and the dawn of a new age is indeed beginning. In light of this,
sincere Muslims have come together from different parts of the
world to orchestrate an unprecedented event of 3ʳᵈ March 2011 that
will undoubtedly add a new dimension to this intensifying conflict
and send shockwaves across the world. Allah is our objective, the
prophet is our leader, the Qur'an is our law, jihad is our way and
dying in the way of Allah is our highest hope. Allahu akhbar.'*
'Shariah4America' Intended march on the White House.

"They'd packed a lot of stuff on the cell phone," the steganographer
announced to the Hezbollah chief, "but only a video and four photos
contained a payload. They were good. We wasted a lot of time
checking decoys. They used multiple bit-planes and encoded verbal
messages in a lot of random data and white noise to cover it and we
were forced to check these decoys before we could progress."

"And the payload was encrypted?"

He nodded, "That was a real problem! Without the private key,
we had no chance of decoding the documents but our cryptologists
discovered it micro-dotted in the Qur'an." He chuckled. "It took
weeks; none of them had ever studied the Holy Book so diligently!
They found what they were looking for in the end under the *Kaf* in
the Surah Miriam."

It was three weeks since Sherif Raad had been brought into the
headquarters and men had worked on the project constantly. If
information was being smuggled over the border to ISIS in such a
way, the contents would have to be of vital importance. Hezbollah
was under no misapprehension, they were fully aware that their time
to do battle against the Islamic State would come, but while ISIS
was occupied with Baghdad and Kobane, Hezbollah was preparing
itself as a fighting force for the war ahead.

"Let me see the report." The steganographer handed a file and a disc over the desk. The chief was a big man, nearly two meters in height with a rounded belly and flabby arms. His facial features were fleshy, the skin under his eyes sagged, and his face had an unhealthy pallor but, for a man in his early seventies, he still had a remarkably thick head of hair. In his younger days, during the invasion of Lebanon by Israel, Kamil Ghassan had proven himself a fearless fighter. Later his skills as a strategist moved him from the war front to a desk where he had been ever since.

He speed-read the six-page document and looked up at Suleiman Mansour.

"Fantastic work!" he said. "This is one of those once-in-a-lifetime breaks that we only dream about. And everything else is on the disc?"

He patted the hardware fondly. "It's all there, sir."

"*Shokran*. You guys deserve a couple of days off."

"Thanks, chief. We could do with it."

"I don't need to remind you that not one word of this goes beyond our circle."

"Of course."

Mansour pushed his chair back and stood up. "What do you think chief, can they do it?"

Ghassan pushed his fingers through his hair and shook his head slowly, "Damned if I know," he admitted. "From what I've seen so far, the *mutawah*[27] in Saudi are looking for a leadership they can trust."

"But to ask the Islamic State to take out the House of Al Sa'ud and bring the holy places of Makkah and Madina under the Caliphate…"

Kamil Ghassan shook his head again, "Incredible, I know. But the Saudi royal house lives a lifestyle that offends the religious leaders. Their wealth and possessions have caused them to make huge compromises. The *mutawah* know these people live double lives and as god-fearing men they are offended." He picked up the file and leaned back in his seat. "Give me a chance to study this further, Suleiman. We must find a way to use this information to our advantage."

---

[27] Saudi Arabian religious police

* * *

Outside the rain fell monotonously and continually, deepening the autumn chill. The family was gathered around the fireplace in the small living room with blankets over their knees. Adriana was deeply absorbed in the novel she was reading, Lex was going through his emails, and Juan and Eugenia were playing chess.

"Genie, listen to this!" Lex said. "I don't know how widespread this is in the States, but school children now have to repeat the *shahada* as part of their Islamic studies."

Juan looked up confused. "What's that?"

Eugenia frowned, "It's the lettering on the ISIS flag," she replied. "The Islamic declaration of faith—there is no god but God, Muhammad the messenger of God. The word means testimony, or witness."

"To force a conversion to Islam, a Christian, or anyone of another faith, must repeat the *shahada,*" Lex added. "Apparently, these kids are being given a deep grounding in Islam while other religions are glossed over. But get this, in their curriculum, Spain is called Muslim Spain!"

Eugenia sat up, her chess game forgotten. "Is this just one school, or is it widespread?"

"I'm not sure. The school principal said it was core material, "state standard". It's pretty obvious that there's not just a minor bias in religious education reflected here. When the textbook proclaims that Muhammad is the final prophet and has the most complete version of God's truth, it is pure indoctrination."

"I'm going to look into it," Eugenia said determinedly. "I'd like to know just how widespread this is, especially when they have the temerity to call us Muslim Spain!"

Adriana set her book down on the arm of the chair. "I'm going to make a pot of tea," she announced. "Eugenia has baked some biscuits. Anyone interested?"

She left the room amid an enthusiastic chorus of assent. Juan made his chess move and Eugenia studied the board with renewed concentration. Lex followed his wife into the kitchen.

"Do you need a hand?" he asked.

"You could set the tray for me," she said. She turned to him and put her hands on his shoulders. "Lex, I worry about Eugenia. This study she's doing could turn dangerous."

"In what way?"

"Well, you know what the internet is like and now she has this website. The word gets around. Any sort of activism is risky, but especially so when we're facing a rising tide of Islamic anger."

Lex put his arms around her and kissed the top of her head affectionately. "Eugenia's a big girl," he said. "I believe she's using her negative experience positively. She could have chosen to hide away and live in fear but she knows what she's doing."

"Nobody ever gains much from ducking life's issues," Adriana agreed, "but I don't want anything bad to happen to her."

"Neither of us does, but she has to choose her way, even as we chose ours. She's chosen to become a voice for the voiceless—I like that."

Adriana smiled wryly, "I do too," she admitted, "but I'm still scared."

Lex held her, quietly looking over her head to the darkness of the day and the rain that still dripped over the eaves. He was equally concerned for Eugenia but knew that any interference would be wrong. The things she was uncovering were frightening. A fourteen-year-old Saudi Arabian girl sentenced to a hundred lashes after having been raped died at the seventieth stroke. There were those dying in agony under torture and crucifixion, and Eugenia had shown him a photograph online earlier that morning, of the deliberate lacerations of a woman's hand, sliced neatly to the bone as one would carve a roast. Her sin was being caught reading the Bible. Lex had never cared much for religion, but he could not help but notice the deep contrasts between the Christianity he had been taught from his youth, and the outworking of Islam in its fundamental form. Genie was doing a good job of opening the eyes of those who were unaware of the horrors perpetrated on women in the Middle East. *It could happen here,* he thought, *in 'Muslim' Spain. Our own women could come under the yoke even as those in Raqqa or Saudi Arabia*—and that was a frightening notion.

* * *

On this, their third meeting, Nour and Raif were sitting cross-legged opposite one another on the grass at the back of the house. Above them, the silvery leaves of an olive tree moved in the hint of a breeze.

Nour related her indignation at the *Hisbah's* insistence that she change her veil.

"If they think I am going to take all their stupid rules seriously, they can forget it!" she announced. "Let them show me where it says in the Qu'ran that I must not be allowed to see where I'm walking!"

Raif secretly approved of Nour's small acts of defiance against the Islamic State but warned her to be cautious.

"You know they won't hesitate to kill anyone who deliberately defies them," he said. "Their zeal makes them dangerous. If you are with your father, wear the heavier veil, Walid is recognisable even if you are anonymous. The rules are stupid but don't allow your anger to endanger your father's life or your own."

Nour picked absently at the grass stems; both knew that, at this moment, any conversation was inconsequential; though she was scarcely listening, she nodded obediently. He touched her hand and her gaze moved to his face. Raif's eyes locked on to hers. Her lips parted and her breath quickened.

"You are beautiful, Nour."

"Don't, Raif. They will be watching us."

"I know. The house has eyes." He longed to reach out and draw her to himself, to feel that small pliant body against his own. Raif touched the tips of her fingers and kissed her with his eyes. Nour looked down to where their fingers met. His hands were strong; with her index finger she stroked each nail, the gesture was simple but intimate.

He drank in her features, the well-shaped nose, expressive mouth, and the slight dimple in her left cheek. The essence of her being, vitality, passion, and humour, was expressed in her dark eyes. Freed from the veil that attempted to restrain and sap her as a woman, she was vibrant. He imagined what it would be like to lay his head in her lap and gaze up into that face, to feel the tracery of her fingers on his skin; for her lips to brush his cheek and come to rest on his mouth.

There had been time to test the reality of his feelings for Nour. He never again wanted to experience the pain of those months of separation. Knowing she was held captive in marriage to a man she despised had broken Raif to the point of despair. He had prayed for her release and received an answer; he never wanted to let her go again. He took hold of her hand and traced the palm with his finger.

"It may be too soon to ask you, Nour," he said, "but I want to marry you."

"I am already yours, Raif," she said simply, "body and soul."

"Then let me speak to your parents today."

"My father will let us marry," she said. "He knows it is what I want."

Raif stood up and reached out a hand to Nour pulling her to her feet. "Come," he said. "There is no reason to delay any longer. Let's go and ask."

Walid Zaky stood a little back from the window and watched them walk up towards the house deep in conversation. He attempted to prepare his answer to the question Raif would ask. It was obvious that Nour was happy with this young man and that pleased him, but it was so soon after Sherif's death. Walid shut his eyes wearily. No matter. If family and neighbours talked, he would have to tell them that that marriage had been forced on Nour against her will. In a country at war, when every Syrian knew that today could spell their death, it was unfair to tell them to wait. He lingered until he could hear them at the kitchen door before returning to his armchair. Walid looked up as his wife came into the room.

"There is to be another marriage," he said with a smile, "this time, God willing, it will last."

Chapter 27   Betrayal

The opening of the One World Trade Centre had taken place on 3 November 2014. Symbolically, a phoenix arose, at that point, from the ashes of the old: two ideologies exemplified by the grand Eleven of the Twin Towers had merged into one. This event signalled a countdown to the New Order but the unveiling was yet incomplete. The foreshadowing of the intention to withhold the moment of climax was subtly demonstrated by the creators of the Grand Mystery. The 120,000 square foot Observation Deck on the 102nd floor was to be opened later, in spring 2015, making the spectacular views of New York accessible to the public. At the same time, the world would begin to view the Master Plan of the highest orders of Freemasonry and discover that the net, which had been draped gently over their unsuspecting heads was about to tighten irrevocably.

In numerology, which is woven into the fibre, fabric, and design of the New World Order and equally so into the structure of the One World Tower, twelve figures as the number that corresponds to completion and integration. It is deemed to be a cosmic number, reflecting the notion of the wholeness of the universe and the manifestation of this unholy trinity to all corners of the earth. This is perfectly expressed in the four sides and three equilateral triangles of the pyramid. Each triangle encompasses three sixty-degree angles representing, in occultic terms, the trinity of father, mother, and son, with the numerical value of 666. The number twelve signifies both world government and the number of the hierarchy of Hidden Masters who uphold the One at the apex—the Observer revealed in the all-seeing eye of Horus.

The preparations had been long, intricate and costly. Multiple generations of men, architects of the 'New' Order, had come and gone without any expectation that they would live to see the fruit of their labour. As 2014 drew to an end, the beast was exposing itself with the full knowledge that nothing could prevent the plan from being implemented.

The initiators, known as the Illuminated Ones, emanated from the roots of Babylon an Order as old as Nimrod himself. A covenant between the Knights Templar and their Muslim brothers in the Holy Land more than a thousand years before reached its culmination in this massive edifice. Here was the melding together of East and West in an unholy union. The unthinkable had taken place—a subtle Islamisation of the West from within.

The system remained true to its Babylonian root, it was never anything but Middle Eastern, and always against God's Chosen people, Israel. The mask was soon to be torn away, the masquerade was almost over: Sharia law, under a different guise, was the obvious form of slavery under which to place the West.

* * *

Moussa Ahmadi's photographic exhibition ran in Malaga during the last week of October and received some excellent press reviews. The two families celebrated the opening night with supper at the Lebanese restaurant but Juan was not with them. Amal had practiced the disdain with which she would treat him and was deeply shaken by his absence. For her father's sake and for fear Eugenia would convey any negative behaviour to her brother, Amal determined to put on a brave front. She deeply missed Juan's presence and she could not, for a moment, rid him from her thoughts. Would he have liked her portrait, she wondered? Her father had captured something extraordinary in her expression; it was wistful, poignant, a little esoteric, and he had used his technical ability to soften and deepen the background with remarkable effect. She was aware that she desired Juan more than ever while determining with all her being to punish him.

"I've heard some news from Raif," Moussa said, "which makes this a double celebration."

"Did he phone?" Adriana asked.

"He emailed," Amal answered for her father. "It was so good to hear from him."

Lex raised his wine glass in Moussa's direction. "That's great news," he said. "What did he say?"

"He's still in Raqqa, but they've put him in a non-combatant position. He seems to be working in the city in some sort of peace-keeping role. Reading between the lines, I think he's relieved."

"He said he hopes to see us soon," Amal said. "I really hope he will be home next year."

Moussa smiled but said nothing. Lex took a sip of wine and set his glass down on the table. He knew what Moussa was thinking. Would the Spanish government allow Raif to return knowing that he had been affiliated with the Islamic State? Many of these militants were coming back to their surrogate countries, but once they tasted jihad, they were a danger to society. Was there any guarantee that Raif would be any different? Moussa faced a difficult time ahead and it would be better for the whole family if he stayed where he was.

"The Islamic State doesn't seem to have made much advance against Baghdad or Kobane lately," Lex commented.

Moussa shook his head. "They seem to have stalled," he said. "A month or so ago, everyone thought they were unstoppable but now they make advances in one area and lose ground in another. They suffered a major defeat when the Iraqi government forces took Jurf al-Sakhar. It was one of their strongholds; losing it means they will probably be prevented from getting closer to Baghdad."

"Kobane hasn't done them much good either," Eugenia said picking up on the conversation. "It's gone on too long and I think it's dented their image."

"It has," Moussa agreed. "They've lost a lot of men and now they're conscripting Syrians to fight."

"What effect have the airstrikes had?" she asked.

"It's made a difference. ISIS can't fight in large numbers the way they're used to and the Kurds are finding it easier to adapt their methods to work with the air bombardments. I think the Islamic State might have to pull out of Kobane and it will be a massive defeat for them."

"Enough to set them back permanently?" Lex asked.

"Don't write them off yet," Moussa replied. "They are still strong. Perhaps stronger than we realise."

The doorbell jangled and Adriana watched as a new group of men and women entered the restaurant. Under this roof, people from various Arabic countries gathered together without any sign of animosity. She and Lex had always loved the idea that Malaga was almost as Middle Eastern as it was Spanish. Listening to the talk around their own table, it was difficult to imagine that Moussa's son was involved in this war. The influence of ISIS was beginning to be felt on the West, and Eugenia's incident had brought the threat of terrorism so much closer to home. Interestingly, Lex had remarked recently that the more time and effort Eugenia put into her website, the more her fears appeared to diminish. He was right, Adriana thought. Genie no longer appeared edgy or nervous in the street, or even in a restaurant like this one where their family was in the minority. She smiled and deliberately changed the subject. This, after all, was a celebration.

Turning to Moussa Adriana began to discuss the response of the public to his photographs and the favourable write-up he had received in the local newspaper.

* * *

The villagers of Zauiyat Albu Nimr had fought valiantly against the greater forces of the Islamic State for weeks, but in the end, with no help from Iraqi government troops, their defeat was inevitable. They ran low on ammunition and food, and ISIS militants closed in like a wolf-pack to the kill.

"I can only imagine how they must have felt," Lex said. "These were men who had helped the American Marines defeat al-Qaeda. Central government ignored their repeated calls for help. They were just abandoned! It's the worst instance of systematic killings since ISIS first began to rampage through Iraq.

"Was this a Shiite village?" Juan asked.

Lex shook his head, "Sunni. But they had no intention of joining forces with al-Baghdadi's men."

Eugenia glanced at the report over her father's shoulder. "They are savages!" she said. "Three-hundred-and-twenty-two slaughtered including fifty women and children whose bodies were dumped down a well!"

"It must have been a terrifying end," Lex agreed. "But that's ISIS strategy, they conquer by terror. That way, many weaker enemies choose to join them rather than risk the fight."

"So, they've taken another step towards their main target!"

Lex nodded soberly. "They do seem to be making some headway towards taking Baghdad. For a while it was stalemate but now the Iraqi government has every reason to be worried. If the Islamic State succeeds in taking the city, the Shiite population will be shown no mercy."

"Baghdad's not likely to fall," Juan commented. "ISIS has some heavy weapons, but they don't have the air power."

"That is their weakness," Lex admitted. "If they did, the Islamic State would be virtually unstoppable. But if Iraq and the U.S. keep holding back and don't use their air advantage against ISIS strategically, they may lose this war."

"Have you heard any more about the Caliph?"

Lex shook his head. "There's a host of rumours but no confirmation."

"But he was injured in that U.S. attack?" Eugenia asked.

"That was the word from Iraq initially, but now the Americans are saying they doubt it."

The air attack had taken place two days before in al-Qaim, a town near the Iraqi border with Syria. Senior Islamic State leaders were gathering for a meeting when an ISIS convoy was struck, as well as buildings within the town itself. Fighters scrambled to ferry the injured to the hospital, which was cleared of patients to make way for their men. Others drove through the streets with loudhailers calling on residents to donate blood. Since then a veil of silence had fallen.

"A caliphate is not a caliphate without a Caliph," Juan said. "If he was critically injured they would probably want to keep it quiet for as long as possible while they waited to see the outcome."

Lex glanced back at his laptop. "You're right," he said. "But if Al-Baghdadi does die, there will be a backlash against the West. It may be better if he makes it."

The attacks were isolated, apparently disconnected; London, Quebec, New York, Jerusalem—especially Jerusalem; a crazed gunman, a stabbing, an attempted beheading, a car used as a weapon. Some reports would carry the addendum; the assailant was a radicalized Islamist, a jihadist, Salafist. Terror was putting out feelers into the West: the Hunter of the Blood Moon was extending his territory.

There was increasing fear of a new intifada in Jerusalem. Gradually the temperature was rising especially in the area of the Temple Mount. Once again the Al-Aqsa Mosque promised to become a flash-point.

As far back as June 2014, after Israeli troops, in their search for three kidnapped teenagers rounded up several hundred suspected Hamas members, Hamas declared that a new intifada against Israel had begun. A chief Rabbi urged Jews to stay away from the Temple Mount to stop the incitement. The European Union called for the formation of a Palestinian State. Accusations flew, but no matter how irrational the allegations were, the blame stopped with Israel. The wave of hatred was growing within the country and outside, and there seemed to be nothing to hold it back.

* * *

Hezbollah's Kamil Ghassan had formulated a plan based on information received from Sherif Raad. There was no doubt in his mind, or in the mind of other Hezbollah leadership, of the ultimate strategy of ISIL. The Levant, the place of the rising sun, which was included in the Islamic State's alternate acronym, demonstrated their intention to seize Southern Turkey, Jordan, Lebanon, Cyprus and, of course, Israel; all territories known as Al-Sham. The desire for ultimate power would not allow them to stop there, of course. The proof of that lay in his hands. In order to exercise complete control over the religious heartland of the Middle East, Jerusalem, Medina and Mecca, ISIS needed Saudi Arabia. Then, as their power base increased, the Caliphate intended to take Iran and cripple Shia Islam once and for all.

The parallel fomenting of Salafist Islam in Europe and the United States was intended to break the Western Nations from within. The establishment of the infrastructure was achieved by a process of gradualism with the knowledge and acquiescence of the hidden inner circle of Western government. In the fullness of time, it seemed, the chocks would be moved away from the wheels, and the vehicle of domination would roll forward and consume an unsuspecting world.

What Kamil Ghassan had proposed to the General Secretary and the Shura council was a gamble they all concurred might be to

Hezbollah's ultimate advantage. The meeting with two Ministers of the house of Saud was scheduled for this afternoon and the proposal would be delivered privately to King Abdullah, custodian of the Two Holy Mosques.

The Ministers were received under conditions of complete secrecy in a private residence in Beirut. There could be absolutely no leak of any collaboration between Shiite Hezbollah and the Sunni House of Saud. The royal Ministers were received with a courtesy that thinly disguised the hostility between the two disparate groups. Superficial smiles and socially accepted pleasantries were exchanged over tea and sweetmeats. With these formalities behind them, the servants were dismissed.

The Saudi Ministers were cool but curious at the invitation that had been extended. Before the meeting, discussion had taken place regarding the presence of bodyguards during the conference, but ultimately it was decided that Hezbollah would not lightly risk war with Saudi Arabia by doing them physical harm, and their men were instructed to remain in the ante-room.

"Some information has fallen into our hands which compromises the security of Saudi Arabia," Hezbollah's Secretary General said when they finally settled down to business. "We arrested a man at the Syrian border who proved to be a courier for the Islamic State." Ministers al Ajman and ibn Faisal waited in polite silence for him to continue. "We have decoded the information he was carrying. It directly affects the house of Saud."

Minister al Ajman's eyes narrowed, "What sort of information?" he asked.

The Secretary glanced at Kamil Ghassan and he continued.

"Of course, we would like to divulge the full nature of what we have gathered, as the Land of Two Holy Mosques is under the protection of King Abdullah bin Abdulaziz," Ghassan replied cagily, "therefore any action that takes place against Saudi Arabia has a direct bearing upon every believing Muslim, whatever their persuasion."

"Of course, that is true, may Allah be praised. The Royal Family of Al Saud has been given a great honour and responsibility."

"Therefore," Kamil Ghassan continued with equal caution, "when we see that there is a threat to the King and the whole House of Saud, we feel obligated to offer a warning."

"We are aware that the Islamic State perceives us as an enemy," Minister ibn Faisal commented frostily.

"But are you aware Minister ibn Faisal that the Islamic State is working directly with certain high-ranking *mutaween* to massacre the Royal family?"

Both Ministers stiffened perceptibly.

"Is the source of this information credible?" Minister Al Ajman asked.

"We believe so."

"It is impossible; the *mutaween*[28] would never conspire to bring down the House of Saud!" Minister ibn Faisal snapped.

"Your religious leaders have often found themselves in conflict with the Royal Family," Kamil Ghassan contradicted smoothly. "It is well-known that their association with the Western powers has been contentious, not to mention the conflict between the religious beliefs of the princes at home and the conduct of many such high personages abroad."

Ibn Faisal's eyes flashed angrily at the slight, but neither of the Ministers could deny the truth of Ghassan's observations.

"So, why are you divulging this to us," Minister Al Ajman asked petulantly, "it is obviously not for altruistic reasons."

Ghassan managed to look hurt. "We are all Muslims," he protested. "In certain instances, we must work together. When it comes to the machinations of the Islamic State, I think we all agree that we are fighting a common enemy."

The two men were silent in their acquiescence.

"Hezbollah is willing to offer the Saudi Royal Family military protection against any threat, either from within the country or from the Islamic State should it decide to attack," the Secretary-General proffered.

"Saudi Arabia has its own army," Minister ibn Faisal reminded him curtly.

"Of course, but you will forgive me for reminding you, in the past, your forces have not been known for their military prowess."

---

[28] Literally volunteers. Saudi religious police responsible for the enforcement of Sharia law.

The Ministers prickled. "Their strength has been greatly improved."

"Can the military forces be trusted to stand with the Royal Family should the *mutaween* allow ISIS a foothold in the country?"

Both ministers knew that there were possibilities of defection. Discontent festered just beneath the pride of many in their country and its history. The totalitarian rule of the House of Saud, the lack of reform and constant rumours of corruption plagued the country. Faced with an outside threat, it was not certain which way the army might fall. There could be no possibility of intimating such doubts to Hezbollah.

"What you are saying is simply not possible!" Minister ibn Faisal burst out angrily. "The *mutaween* would never work with the Islamic State."

"Are you certain of that? Islamic State's application of the faith is very close to Wahhabi Islam and that of the Muslim Brotherhood."

The two Saudi Ministers were again forced into retreat by what they knew to be the truth. Minister Al Ajman's heavy brows were drawn together over his spectacles. He sipped his tea in silence.

"We will convey this information to King Abdullah bin Abdulaziz," Minister ibn Faisal declared at length. "But there are two things. First, you need to offer us proof of this conspiracy and secondly, you need to state clearly what you want. While we appreciate the offer of protection, there is no love lost between Hezbollah and the Kingdom of Al Saud. What are your demands?"

The Secretary-General stroked his beard. "As we have stated, we have a common and cunning enemy. The Islamic State is well-armed; it grows fatter with every conquest. Before many months are out, Lebanon is likely to come under attack and if Hezbollah is to fight it will need to meet *Daesh*[29] on an equal basis."

"Your army is well provided for by Iran."

"Sanctions have affected Iran's ability to provide more modern weapons."

---

[29] Daesh is an acronym for the Arab name of Islamic State: al-Dawla al-Islamiya fi al-Iraq wa al-Sham. The word has a derogatory connotation and, depending on how it is conjugated in Arabic, can mean 'to trample down and crush', or 'a bigot who imposes his view on others'.

"We cannot be seen to be arming a Shiite militia," Minister ibn Faisal stated categorically.

The Secretary General's lips drew back over his teeth in the semblance of a smile. "Hezbollah is able to source its own weapons. We will need oil and money in exchange for our services. Your King is well-positioned to provide those needs."

Chapter 28   Betrayal

For Nour, the wedding to Raif differed in every way from that to Sherif Raad. There were few well-wishers, no bands, changes of dress, or large quantities of food; most of all, her heart was changed. This was a true celebration, the culmination of all she had longed for in months past. The man who came to take her home was the one with whom she wanted to live her life.

When they were finally alone, Raif was able to hold Nour in his arms and at that moment she felt content to stay there with her head resting just below his shoulder, forever.

It was the first time Nour had seen her new home. Raif had a small apartment above a shop in the central city area not far from the Sharia Court. The kitchen sink and two-plate stove were crammed into a corner of the living room which boasted a tiny balcony overlooking the noisy street, and the bedroom took the new double bed at a squeeze. Nour looked around her with unfeigned pleasure.

"It's perfect," she said.

"I wish it could have been a palace."

Nour laughed. "I am no princess!" she declared. "This is all we need when we have each other."

Later that night they lay wrapped in one another's arms listening to the passing vehicles on the street, the occasional shout, and the squabble of stray cats. It seemed too soon for the act of consummation; they hardly knew one another. Lights flashed against the opposite wall and faded. When dawn came Raif leaned on one elbow and watched the gentle touch of the light on Nour's face. He examined the contours, the softness of her lashes beneath the closed eyelids, her lips slightly parted and the flush over the cheeks. Her eyes flickered open as a ray of sunlight fell across her face and she smiled and reached out her arms.

Raif wondered what his father would say if he knew he was married; and Amal and Layla, would they be shocked, disappointed?

Nour had begun unpacking her few things; the curtains given to her by her mother, some bright cushions from her bedroom at home; three soft toys from her childhood, including a teddy bear, none of which had gone with her when she married Sherif. She re-arranged things and tested them in new places. Raif helped her to hang the curtains in the bedroom and Nour stood back and examined them with satisfaction.

"We can block the lights out tonight," she said. "The curtains are quite heavy, so they might dim the noise a bit too."

They boiled the kettle and made small glasses of tea and sat close beside one another on Raif's old sofa, which Nour said would look fine if they could find a throw to cover it.

Time slipped quietly away; they were together and for today life was perfect.

* * *

King Abdullah bin Abdulaziz of Saudi Arabia, custodian of the Two Holy Mosques, was concerned by the news that the Islamic State intended to destroy the House of Saud, but not unduly disturbed. Such threats had rippled the pond before but were long forgotten. ISIS had enough to preoccupy it at present without going off on a tangent to attack Saudi Arabia. What was more worrying was the *Haia*[30], the government agency that employed the *mutaween*, Saudi's religious police. Had they instigated this move towards the Islamic State, and would they dare to rise up against the Royal House?

The King called a second conference with Ministers Ibn Faisal and Al Ajman who had met with Hezbollah. Also present were the Prime Minister, the First Deputy and Crown Prince Salman, and the second Deputy of the Council of Ministers. The Deputies were younger brothers of the present king, sons of the country's founder, King Abdulaziz ibn Saud.

Seated on chairs covered in rich tapestries shown to best advantage against the dark wood panelling of the walls, were the aging princes in their white robes. Displayed on a circular gold table were dozens of red roses imported that morning from Europe,

---

[30] The Committee for the Promotion of Virtue and Prevention of Vice

specially chosen to echo the touches of red within the swirled blue and gold pattern of the thick carpet. The overall impression was ostentatious rather than sumptuous, but the princes of the Royal House had more on their mind than interior decoration.

"Obviously, we need to take this threat seriously," King Abdullah was saying, "despite the source." The eighty-eight-year-old king was still in moderately good health, but succession had become a growing concern to his followers. The Crown Prince was in his late seventies, and his physical condition showed in the pain reflected in the lines of his face. Many thought that it was time power moved on from the brothers of Abdullah to the next generation.

"Was Hezbollah able to furnish proof?" the Crown Prince asked.

The king glanced in the direction of his Ministers and drummed his fingers on the arm of the chair. He wore a white shirt with a high collar under a grey suit tailored for him in Paris. A golden outer robe deliberately linked him with the room's décor. The fine fabric of his white *ghutrah*[31] held in place by a black headband framed a pudgy face formed a canopy to his spectacles and draped over the discreet shoulder-padding of his suit. His moustache and beard, which was trimmed to an exaggerated keyhole shape below his bottom lip, were tinted jet black to cover any hint of aging.

"We were shown the evidence they claimed was taken from the man at the border concealed in a cell phone and a Qur'an," Minister Al Ajman said. "They also played us recordings of the man's confession under torture. This evidence could have been manufactured by Hezbollah for some ulterior motive."

"What do you think, Minister?"

"As your Royal Highness suggested at the outset, it would be foolish to ignore a threat of this nature."

"Minister Ibn Faisal?"

He hesitated for a moment. "As your Royal Highness is aware, I have little confidence in the Shia," he said abruptly, "but there are times when we are forced to use them. Hezbollah is possibly one of the few militias that has the strength to withstand the Islamic State for a sustained period of time. They could form a useful ally."

---

[31] White headscarf held in place by a doubled black cord, the agal.

"I hear Iraq has begun incorporating the Shiite population into the armed forces in the war against the Islamic State," the Prime Minister said. "*Insh'Allah*, there will not be a need to use them for long."

It was not necessary to verbalise the violent role the Shia minority had played in various uprisings in Saudi Arabia; the Sunni held them in quiet contempt and had as little to do with them as possible.

The Crown Prince asked the question that was burning at the back of all their minds. "In the face of an attack by ISIS, can we rely on the complete loyalty of our troops?"

"Without question!" King Abdullah snapped. His brother glanced across at him and perceived the flash of misgiving that crossed his expression even as he spoke.

"Nevertheless, if some elements are at work among the *mutaween*, it could mean that they have undermined the loyalties of others." Crown Prince Ahmed suggested quietly.

All the men present were part of the extensive House of Al-Saud. The total number of Saudi princes was in excess of seven thousand men, all descendants of Saud ibn Muhammad. The greatest power and influence in the land, with key ministries in this absolute Monarchy, was wielded by the over two hundred male descendants of King Abdul Aziz Al Saud, while the sons of Hassa, his most favoured wife, held the strongest positions as heads of the combined forces. Abdul Aziz, who had defeated the Rasheed tribe in 1901 and reclaimed the land lost to his father when he was still a child, had taken more than three hundred wives from the local tribes to ensure their loyalty. He sired fifty sons and eighty daughters, and basic law required that the king must be chosen from among his offspring.

King Abdullah's eyes narrowed dangerously. "The job of the *mutaween* is to enforce Sharia. If I discovered any disloyalty in their ranks, I would not hesitate to deal with it harshly. But, you know of course that as commander of the National Guard, the men have always loved me and looked up to me as their leader. I cannot entertain the possibility of treachery."

The men nodded in agreement. It was pointless to remind the King that most of those serving today were not yet born when he had commanded the unit.

"Perhaps, your Royal Highness, it would be advisable to employ militia from Hezbollah as a mercenary unit," Minister Al Ajman ventured. "We could simply bring them in if there was an attack by ISIS to swell the numbers of our troops."

The Prime Minister shook his head. "If there is really an intention among the ranks of the religious police to encourage an uprising in the country, it would not help to have a militia sitting in Lebanon," he pointed out. "I think we should use them to create an investigative unit to probe these allegations and discover the men behind it."

"I believe that could work," Crown Prince Salman said thoughtfully. "Many of the royal princes in high positions could be trusted to co-operate with such a group. If we can use Hezbollah to help us uncover this plot and defuse it, it would be worth whatever we have to pay them."

The King considered his brother's proposition and after a moment or two, nodded in agreement.

"Salman, work with the Ministers to draw up a proposal on those lines," he said. "Let me see it as soon as possible."

The princes bowed to their older brother and, as was the etiquette, walked backwards to the door until they were away from the royal presence.

* * *

Since the olive-picking several weeks before, the weather had grown too cold for picnicking and most socialising was done indoors around the ample fireplace. Amal had chosen not to come with Moussa on this occasion and Eugenia read Juan's expression and followed him to his bedroom demanding to know the reason.

"How am I to know?" he asked defensively. "I simply tried to tell her that I couldn't commit to a long-term relationship and she got angry."

Eugenia looked at her brother in disbelief. "Had you given her a suggestion that there might be a relationship of some sort before that point?"

Juan hedged. "She knew I liked her."

"Was there a demonstrative action?" she pressed. "Did you hold her hand or kiss her?"

"No," he replied irritably.

"And did Amal lead you on?"

"Of course not!"

"So, Juan, what on earth were you trying to achieve by telling her such a thing out of the blue? No wonder she's staying away!"

Juan stared at his sister and then looked away in embarrassment. "It was something the old man said," he confessed. "I thought she thought…" He shook his head. "I guess I've been an idiot. Is there any way of undoing what I've done?"

"Not that I can think of at the moment," Eugenia replied unsympathetically. "I just hope you haven't affected my friendship with Amal by blundering in like that."

"The thing is, I really like her," Juan said miserably. "I wanted her to know that a future relationship is possible on a different level, but I need to establish a career first."

"Perhaps you'd better write to her if that's what you feel," she said. "Make sure you think about it carefully first. For heaven's sake, don't over-compensate and promise things you might not want to follow through on in a couple of years!" And she turned and left the room.

Over a beef curry lunch Lex fired some of the questions at Moussa that were building up around the book.

"How does Islam view the monarchies in the Middle East?" he asked.

Moussa frowned thoughtfully. "They're seen by most scholars as unIslamic," he said. "And, if you think about it, the Saudi royal house, Jordan, and some of the Emirates that practice succession, are all propped up by America in particular, which makes them even more unpopular."

"So their position is insecure," Lex said.

Moussa nodded. "They compensate by building extravagant mosques in the West and throwing huge sums of money at the various militia; rather like throwing pieces of meat to a lion that's about to attack. Under the present climate, it's just a matter of time before some group attempts to take them down. When they do, they know they will come up against the U.S. and its allies." He set his empty plate down on the coffee table. He smiled at Adriana and shook his head when she offered him a refill, "That was wonderful, thanks. I've done really well."

"But Saudi Arabia is under Sharia law," Eugenia said in surprise. "I thought the radical Islamists would have no problem with their form of Islam."

"They follow an extreme form of Sharia law known as *Wahhabism*. But you're right Eugenia, the only difference between them and ISIS is the royal family and the king's control of Mecca and Medina. By instituting a Caliphate, ISIS has set itself in direct opposition. King Abdullah must be very aware of the threat to the House of Saud."

"Saudi Arabia hasn't gone outside its borders to impose its rule on others in recent times," Lex offered.

"No, certainly not recently, but ibn Saud used the same tactics as the Islamic States in the early eighteen hundreds when he conquered Karbala. They massacred thousands of Shiites including women and children and promised the same treatment to unbelievers. Abd-al Wahhab, who instituted Wahhabism, said that those who wouldn't conform to his view should be killed, their possessions confiscated and their wives and daughters violated. We like to call this extremism, but this is just true adherence to the basic tenets of Islam."

"Jordan and the Emirates are far more moderate," Juan said. "Are they less committed to the teachings of the Qur'an?"

Moussa nodded. "That's about it," he agreed. "They follow the positive teachings, reject the jihadi element, and stop short of applying Sharia law. Unfortunately, that makes them a prime target for reformists. Fundamentalism is not known for tolerance!"

Lex set a few more logs on the fire and, within minutes, flames licked around them testing their options this way and that. Eugenia gathered up the plates and went to make coffee, and the conversation drifted onto other things.

Juan had remained subdued throughout the afternoon and appeared relieved when Moussa left at last. He assured Adriana that he did not need supper and would see them in the morning.

"What's eating him?" Adriana asked bemused.

"Remorse," Eugenia replied and returned to the book she was reading.

Chapter 29   Betrayal

President Assad's government forces had been barrel bombing Raqqa regularly but from September the United States also began bombing raids on the city hitting essential services and damaging infrastructure. An oil facility run by the Islamic State was struck. Food and fuel prices rocketed and there was a scarcity of gas for cooking. As the weeks dragged on, the number of civilian deaths increased and conditions worsened.

"Why don't they leave us alone?" Nour demanded during one of the raids. "We didn't ask them for help. No one wants them here!"

There was nowhere to hide from the scream of the aircraft and the whistling fall and muffled explosion of the bombs; the flashes of fire and smoke from the stricken areas and the rumble of anti-aircraft fire.

Raif lay behind her on their bed and held Nour tight trying to still her panic. He could feel the pounding of her heart under his arm.

"It will be over soon," he reassured her gently. "Don't worry."

"I'm not worried," she snapped. "I'm angry. Who do these idiots think they are, anyway?"

Raif grinned in the dark but said nothing. At least, he thought, the Israelis gave a warning to Gaza residents before they bombed an area. Short notice in some instances, but notice was given. It made him angry that the Americans did nothing. In their supposed zeal to strike against the Islamic State, they showed that they cared nothing for civilians caught in the attacks and some of the strikes seemed to be deliberately aimed at making the civilian population suffer as much as possible. In a country where food shortages were beginning to hurt, grain silos had been hit and with winter coming in fast, several provinces had been left without power after a gas plant was struck. So much for precision bombing, he thought, unless these were intentionally targeted.

It was difficult not to make the comparison with Israel. Where was the international condemnation for the spiralling civilian deaths? To the outside world, the United States was seen as the white knight coming to the rescue of the Syrian people, but it often had a different spin from where the Syrians stood.

The planes began to wheel away and the sound of explosions was replaced by the wail of sirens as the emergency services moved out into the areas that had been hit. Fires often raged for hours casting a pall of smoke and ash over the city. Raqqa was reeling under increasing deprivations; hospitals were unable to cope with the number of casualties, and many feared it would soon share Aleppo's fate. Raif constantly thought about leaving but there were obvious difficulties. Nour was deeply attached to her parents and had no intention of going anywhere without them, and he, Raif, could not just walk away from his job with the Islamic State. How easy would it be to gain employment if they did return to the West? These issues preoccupied his thoughts. The Islamic State was a noose around his neck.

To add to the city's woes, there was a drain of manpower as the fight for Kobane continued unabated. There was a no-choice decision to be made if a young man was called up. They said yes, or died—or they entered the militia and died anyway. Many were simply not coming back from Kobane and soon it would be the policemen, who earned a healthy salary and the added bonus of a car, who would receive the call to arms. His own call could not be far off.

"Well, the Caliph's not dead," Raif announced when he came home from work one evening. "It seems to be an ISIS tactic to throw uncertainty on the fate of their leaders and then come back, arms swinging, ready to fight another round."

Nour wiped her hands on her apron and reached up for a kiss.

"So tell me," she said. "What news of our exalted leader?"

"He's urging his followers on to 'volcanoes of jihad', whatever that means," Raif replied. "Muslims in the Middle East are being called to rise up against the agents of the Jews and crusaders, including their slaves and dogs."

Nour raised her eyebrows, "Our Caliph has a way with words! It would be nice if the U.S. Air Force would leave Raqqa alone for a bit and concentrate on cutting ISIS off at the head."

"Play on words intended?" Raif asked innocently.

She muttered under her breath and returned to the pot that was boiling on the stove.

"Oh, and he's breathing fire against the Saudi royal house," he added. "Al-Baghdadi would like to see them dismembered."

"So, what do you think, are they next on the Islamic State's bucket list?"

He grinned. "I think they've got their hands full fighting those Kurdish women in Kobane. It could be a long time before they're free to tackle Saudi." Raif slid his hands around Nour's waist and rested his chin on her shoulder. "I cursed the day I joined ISIS until I met you," he said. "Suddenly, after that, everything made sense."

She turned and snuggled up against him. "It was pre-ordained," she announced. "We were written in the stars." There was a hiss behind her and Nour spun around and whipped the overflowing pot off the stove. "The rice!" she exclaimed. "It's your fault, Raif, for distracting me!"

"May our lives continue to overflow with distractions," he said solemnly.

Nour giggled. "Go away while I finish the supper."

A month later, Raif was called to the headquarters of Raqqa's Islamic State. He answered the summons with a feeling of dread. Although the work at the Sharia court was depressing enough, it meant he was away from the horrors of the military. He received a salary that was more than adequate in the depressed economic state that Raqqa was in since the occupation of the province. If they wanted him back into the militia, he and Nour would have to find a way to leave Syria.

"We need men," the *raqib* said. "There are two kinds of jihad to be fought. You are an ideal candidate for cultural jihad and we would like you to return to Spain with your new wife."

Raif stared at him blankly. "Return to Spain?" he repeated.

The official nodded. "Your papers say that you were located in Malaga. To the Caliphate, this is an important area. We plan to take al-Andalus back from the infidel. You were recruited there; you know the people and you speak the language. We want you to go back and engage with Muslims as well as non-Muslims to move the process forward. When the signal is given we must have men on the ground ready to arise and conquer the *kafur*[32]. Muslims who attend mosque are being prepared by the imams but many have not recognised the call. They must begin to wake up and understand their destiny."

After the first stunned moment, Raif began to grasp the implication of what the *raqib* was saying.

"You need me to return as an agent for the Islamic State?" his expression was incredulous.

"Exactly."

He hedged, seeking a way out of a new dilemma. "We don't have money for the return ticket."

"The Caliphate will ensure that your expenses are paid and we can put you in touch with our men in Malaga who will help you to find employment."

Raif thought of Nour. "My wife has parents here. I am not sure if she…"

The official regarded him impatiently. "You are newly married so I will forgive that remark. Your woman is of no consequence to the Caliphate. As the man, Allah grants you full control over the female. This is a command and if you should fail to obey for any reason, we will anyway send you to the front." He glared across the desk. "Choose your option."

Raif was frigid with anger but he dared not show it. This was the opportunity he had been praying for and Allah had undoubtedly answered. He hoped and prayed Nour would understand.

"When do you want me to leave?" he asked stiffly.

"You have two weeks to prepare," the *raqib* replied. "I will fill you in on the details shortly. Finish your week at the court and I will inform them that you have been transferred."

Nour stared at him in dismay. "You can't mean it, Raif! How can we leave—just like that! What about the bakery, who will help *Baba*?"

---

[32] Unbeliever

Raif took her gently by the shoulders, "I know how you feel, *habibti*. This is a shock to both of us, but they haven't given me a choice."

Nour's eyes welled up with tears. "I'm not prepared for this," she said. "This is the only place I know. What about your family, how will they receive me?"

"They will love you."

"I can't do it!" she said emphatically. "They can't force us to do what they want."

He shook his head. "If I disobey orders, you know full well what will happen," he replied. "But, Nour, I won't make you do anything you don't want to do. If you would rather stay here, I will understand."

She looked into his face for a long moment before she replied.

"Thank you for giving me a choice, Raif. I would never let you leave without me; you know I love you too much for that. Two weeks!" She looked around her at the little apartment that had become their home and knew that turning her back on it would be a wrench. "We must go and tell my parents."

He drew her close. "Friday morning?"

Nour's face rested against his chest and he sensed the tears that were falling as she nodded her agreement.

"Spain will be safer for you and Raif," Walid said. "Of course, you must go. You must follow your husband."

"But I don't want to leave you," Nour protested, tears rolling down her cheeks for the dozenth time since she and Raif received the news.

Walid took his daughter in his arms and comforted her. "Think of it," he said. "There will be no more bombing raids, and you can throw off the *niqab* if you want to."

She smiled up at her father through her tears. Nour accepted that even the forced marriage to Sherif was Walid's attempt to do what was best for her and she had forgiven him. The parting would be difficult for both of them. Her love for her mother was on a different level. She was a simple woman with no education, who evaluated everything from her limited understanding of the Qur'an. From as far back as Nour could remember their relationship had been one of tensions and mutual misunderstandings. Walid was her mother's god and, in her eyes, he could do no wrong; but as much as she was proud of her daughter, she held up the Book as judge and jury over Nour's behaviour.

"*Baba*, why does life never seem to offer the right choices?" she demanded. "I would go happily if I could take you with me."

"Your husband is the man in your life now," Walid said, but not without a deep twinge of regret. "He's the one you must follow. But I will be here for you whenever you are able to come back."

Chapter 30   Betrayal

Eugenia pulled into the parking area of Granada's faculty of arts and collected together her handbag, laptop and camera. She locked the car and crossed the tarmac to the main entrance. The arts faculty was located on the outer limit of the city separate from the main campus, in an imposing two-storey brick building that had been built as a psychiatric ward. Part of it continued to serve as a psychiatric hospital and the standing joke among the art students was that by the time you graduated you were so screwed up that they simply transferred you to the other side of the fence.

Eugenia's mind was doing one of those splits between the assignment, which was due by the end of the week, and the newly-released report on the fifty-seven countries intent on putting a worldwide ban in place against the negative stereotyping of Islam. Already, Islamic terrorism was being almost universally covered up in what appeared to be blatant whitewashing. Any association made linking terrorists or acts of terror with Islam was labelled Islamophobia, or racism, effectively stifling endeavours to find solutions to the endemic.

What had disturbed Eugenia was the case of a young Pakistani, who had renounced Islam and married a Christian woman in 2006. He and his family sought refuge in Spain from the death threats against him in Muslim countries. Recently he had produced an amateur movie exposing the dangers of Islam and, as a result, Imran Firasat's lawyers were fighting a Spanish extradition order. Revoking Islam was sufficient for a death sentence under Sharia law if he was returned to an Islamic country, but no Muslim walked away from the ultimate apostasy of criticising the religion. With a wife and three young children, Imran had everything to fight for; Spain however, wanted rid of him. While the case was being heard, Firasat remained in jail. He was a threat to national security.

"I felt it was my duty to warn of the dangers of not understanding or stopping what is known as jihad," he said. "It was never my intention to provoke the Spanish government."

"Why can't they figure out the obvious?" Eugenia had demanded of Lex when she read the article that morning. "The man is not a threat to Spain's security, it's Islam! Free speech has become obsolete. Why? Because Muslim extremists say so!"

"We still have free speech against Christians and Jews," Lex pointed out with a ghost of a smile.

Eugenia ignored him. "Now these Muslim countries have the audacity to demand a ban on any criticism of their religion. Even when pre-pubescent children are being married off to old men, and some are raped to death; when women are being stoned, or drowned in swimming pools, for standing up against the injustices of a male-dominated system. Have we lost our minds as well as our tongues?"

Knowing her father agreed with her was not enough. All the warning signs of a major catastrophe were there; Eugenia wanted to take a somnambulant world by the shoulders and shake some sense into it before it was too late. Her only outlet was her website and she threw herself into the fight with renewed determination.

In the beginning, it had bothered Eugenia that the arts faculty lacked the normal university buzz; lately, she preferred the quieter ambiance and with the Christmas break just ahead, the atmosphere was relaxed. She settled herself at her desk and took her most recent assignment out of her portfolio. It was a sketch project, working with perspectives from different angles. It had been a challenge to set up the guidelines but she had enjoyed the work and was pleased with the completed drawings. A couple of other students gathered round to take a look and discuss the results.

"Great work, Eugenia," her friend, Lisa, commented. "You grasped it better than I did. I'm afraid the Prof is going to have something to say about my layouts."

"Are you sure?" Eugenia said. "Can I take a look?"

At that moment, her cell phone rang.

"Sorry, Lisa. Give me a moment, it's my father."

"Hi Genie, I hope I'm not bothering you."

"Is there a problem, papa?"

"Not at all, Moussa has invited us over to his place this evening. Are you free?"

"I am."

"He's very excited. My main character is arriving in Spain in a couple of weeks."

"Your main character! Papa!" but she laughed despite her feigned indignation. "So, we're going to meet the terrorist."

"I guess we are but don't call him that in front of Moussa or the girls."

"Of course not, silly. Do you know any of the details? When does he arrive?"

"I don't know a thing, but I guess we will hear all about it this evening."

"What was all that about?" Lisa asked curiously as Eugenia returned her mobile to her handbag. "You're meeting a terrorist?"

"Sure, it's a regular occurrence in our family," Eugenia said sweetly. "Just one of my father's fictional characters."

Lisa laughed, "Of course! Your father, the writer. What's he working on at the moment?"

"Some Middle Eastern thing," Eugenia said.

"Seriously? Creepy subject. Come and take a look at my work." And Lisa led the way across the studio to her desk.

* * *

Ground was broken for the construction of the Pentagon on September 11, 1941 and, sixty years later to the day, the building was struck by terrorists. Another of those remarkable 'coincidences', Lex thought, much like George Bush senior's first public declaration of "a coming New World Order", which also just happened to be on 11th September 1990 at the outset of the war against Iraq. Bush had repeated his statement on September, 11th a year later, just in case the world had missed the auspicious date the first time around. Of course, these things only became apparent retroactively, but the markers were all there.

The Pentagon attack was undoubtedly the most blatantly rigged bit of theatrics ever perpetrated against the citizens of the United States of America. It was particularly baffling that anyone had ever swallowed the official story. A 757 jetliner, Flight 77, ploughed into the side of a four-storey building and disappeared without trace into an impact hole too small to take it. There was an explosion, a fireball, a massive inferno within the building that had somehow, in a partially demolished upper-storey office, left a stool with an open book unscathed on top of it. There were no scars on the ground in front of the demolished area, no wings or tail-plane debris, and no plane debris visible in the clean-up thereafter.

A plane flown by amateurs had approached the Pentagon one hundred feet above vehicles on the highway at an impossible flight trajectory, before impacting the building. Eye-witness stories conflicted, confused at what they had seen; sleight of hand in a conjuring trick. It was obvious that some sort of missile had struck the building, but certainly not a 757. Then, of course, the question remained. If Flight 77 did not hit the Pentagon, what really happened to the aircraft and its passengers?

The attacks were history. Many openly declared that the investigations had been whitewashed. This Order behind the scenes made it their business to create a mystery, to belittle those who perceived they were being duped, and gloat when they brought the event to pass exactly as predicted.

They rub our noses in it, Lex ruminated, *knowing there is nothing we can do to bring them down.* His mind went back to the card game that predicted the fall of the twin towers and the attack on the Pentagon. He was convinced now that it signaled a coming event. Lex thought back to the final card in the game that had caught his attention. He did not doubt that the tall black building shown on the skyline was the One World tower. Once again he recalled the image of the human skull in the billowing clouds overshadowing New York, and its heading:

"Goal—Population Reduction".

Chapter 31   Betrayal

F-15E fighter-bombers screamed in across the horizon. Their undersides presented a surreal, metallic, and deadly beauty. As they roared overhead, earth and sky seemed to merge into one reverberating shriek of protest. The sense of being held captive under such massive power and all-consuming noise was terrifying beyond anything Nour had ever experienced.

Raif was at work and she had left on an impulse, determined to see her parents. Being alone on the streets was risky at the best of times, but even before the raid, the religious police had not been in evidence. It was the first time she had found herself outdoors during a bombing raid and never before had the jets flooded in in such great numbers. Nour's legs refused to move; she stood rooted to the spot gazing up as though hypnotized at the horror that darkened the afternoon sky. Someone grasped her arm and steered her to the doorway of a shop. Her legs felt like rubber under her.

"Are you all right?" She saw the stranger's mouth move but the words were swept away on the vast wave of sound. She nodded a reply. The man gave a tight smile at the black-clad figure before him.

"Take cover!" he shouted and turning, he ducked into an alleyway and was gone from sight.

Already she could hear the first dreaded whistle of the falling missiles and the unearthly pause before the earth quaked with the explosion. Nour tried to think. It was two blocks from where her parents lived; she desperately wanted to be with them but fear immobilised her. Still, the aircraft streamed through the sky in deadly unison and the sun turned a dull brown with the drift of smoke and the heavy haze of choking dust. Buildings offered no cover; only a miracle would save you anyway if the one you were in took a direct hit. Television coverage of the bomb sites always showed people scrambling frantically, and uselessly, at the piles of rubble, but seldom did anyone make it out alive. All these fragments tumbled through Nour's mind at the speed of the bombers before coalescing into one lucid thought. "Go!" And she went.

A small dark figure edged along the walls of the buildings scurrying as swiftly as a beetle until, at the end of the street, there was nothing more to cling to. She was laid open to the enemy above, which seemed intent on only one thing—her ultimate destruction. She flung back her veil and ran through the empty streets, her feet raising little puffs of dust; past the familiar row of palms, past the road island with its brightly massed cerise petunias. Nour reached the corner where, just visible, was the tree under which she and Raif had sat behind her parents' house. She was consumed by only one thought, to put one foot down in front of another before they got to her. She heard the whistle above the roar of the engines and knew she was too late. The concussion of the blast lifted her from the ground flinging her backwards making her one with an avalanche of debris. Her body slammed into the pavement and everything dissolved into a tunnel of darkness.

Someone bent over her, his shadow resting on her face. Nour's eyes flickered open. She squinted into the light and groaned as pain knifed through her. The aircraft had gone and left in their wake an eerie world of silence.

"Lie still. You're going to be okay." The paramedic rested a comforting hand on her shoulder and glanced back to where Nour's right leg was pinned grotesquely beneath her body.

His words came to her across a vast distance. "My parents…"

"Were they with you?"

With an effort, Nour lifted her arm and indicated vaguely, "Their house."

He glanced briefly in the direction of the shattered remains of the building. An emergency vehicle was parked in the road and men were swarming over the rubble searching for some sign of life.

"Don't worry," he said reassuringly. "They will be fine."

Later, she vaguely remembered the inside of the ambulance, the drip swaying from side to side as they drove. Now and then the paramedic spoke to her, but her head was full of cotton wool and his words died before they penetrated that place of comprehension.

They had retrieved her cell phone from her handbag and answered the dozen missed calls from Raif.

"You need to come," the paramedic told him. "She's been hurt." He gave Raif the name of the hospital.

When she next woke it was Raif's face that hovered anxiously over her. He kissed her forehead lightly.

"*Habibti*, can you hear me?"

Agony wracked her body and twisted her brave attempt at a smile. Someone brought a small glass; Raif lifted her head and helped her to drink. Within minutes, the pain receded and Nour slipped into a quiet place of euphoria. Raif's face faded into a comforting mirage and disappeared completely.

They operated on the leg the following morning.

"The knee is badly damaged," the surgeon told Raif. "We'll do what we can to repair it." He looked desperately weary. The hospital was understaffed, and many doctors and nurses had fled to Turkey or Jordan when the Islamic State moved in. Others, recognising how great the need was, stayed on. After airstrikes such as this last one, beds were in desperately short supply and operating theatres functioned around the clock. Nour was one of the lucky ones; she had been picked up early.

"They're dead?" Her voice was a whisper. "Both of them?" He traced the back of her hand, scarcely able to bear to look into eyes that held such pain. "Be brave, *habibti*."

"Both of them?" she repeated.

Raif nodded. "They are both gone, Nour."

She stared up at him in disbelief. Silent tears gathered and spilled over, soaking into the unruly tangle of hair framing her face. "No," she breathed, "not *Baba*."

He reached over, resting his face against her own, feeling her tears wet against his cheek. Nour slid her arms around him, burying her face in his neck, and sobbed.

The burial had already taken place within twenty-four hours of death in accordance with Islamic rites. Raif had overseen the arrangements and attended the prayers while Nour was in theatre. He had been back to the house to see whether anything could be recovered but had found nothing of value. The surgeon had told Raif emphatically that Nour would not be ready to travel for at least three weeks.

"Postpone your trip," he said. "She must be given time to recover from the battering her body has taken, apart from the knee itself."

"Will the knee recover?" Raif asked with some trepidation.

He shook his head. "We've done what we could with our limited resources," he replied, "but it's insufficient. When you get to Spain, see a specialist as soon as possible. At the moment, we will have to brace it in one position and she will need to use crutches."

Raif left the hospital knowing what he had to do. When he arrived back at the apartment, he sent an email to his father.

The Islamic State's headquarters had become a prime target for strikes both by the Syrian forces and the United States and had been vacated. Much of the militia had melted into the surrounding villages and towns while others were billeted among the civilian population of Raqqa. Raif met with the commanding officer in a house near the Euphrates River and asked for more time.

"My wife's parents are dead and my wife has been seriously injured. We can't leave Raqqa on schedule."

The officer sighed irritably and tapped his fingers on his desk. "How soon can you leave?"

Raif recounted what the doctor had told him.

"Three weeks," the officer agreed. "No more. We will make the arrangements for your flight from Lebanon, but your wife will have to make the journey to Beirut by bus or taxi." He read the desperation in Raif's expression. "If that is a problem, leave her here," he said coolly. "It's my business to make these arrangements and you are not the only person I have to move. Make your choice."

Raif nodded. "It will be fine," he said. "We will get to Beirut."

Chapter 32   Betrayal

Amal and Layla were in a state of nervous excitement and Moussa, though doing his utmost to appear non-committal was unable to disguise his mixed emotions.

"Raif's married," Layla burst out even before they were through the doorway. "He's bringing his wife home!"

"Layla," Amal said sternly, "you should wait for papa to tell everyone."

"But it's true; he is coming with his wife," Layla protested.

Adriana and Eugenia exchanged amused glances. "This is big news," Adriana said bending down to Layla. "You must be really happy."

Layla nodded and, having achieved her intention to be the first with the news, looked only marginally chastened by her big sister's irritation.

"Amal, how do you feel about all this?" Eugenia asked.

"You haven't quite heard the whole story yet," she replied with a smile. "Juan not with you?"

Eugenia glanced keenly at her friend and shook her head. "He is studying at the moment," she said by way of explanation.

"Of course. Well, let's go and sit down and we'll tell you what we know."

"This email came in this morning," Moussa explained as he poured their drinks. "Raif expects to leave in three weeks' and, as Layla said, he has his wife with him."

"What's her name?" Adriana asked.

"Nour," Moussa replied. "But there's a problem. A week ago, her parents were killed in one of the U.S. bombing raids on Raqqa, and Nour was injured."

"Is she badly hurt?" Lex asked.

"Some cuts, bruises, and abrasions, and her left knee is badly damaged," Moussa replied. "She was operated on there but it was unsuccessful. Raif's hoping they will be able to do something for her here."

"Will they come to stay with you?" Lex asked. "You don't really have room, do you?"

"We don't," Moussa said ruefully. "We'll have to find them a place."

"She won't be able to do much if she has a damaged knee," Eugenia cut in. "She will need nursing, and I imagine she is going to have emotional issues to deal with too." She turned impulsively to Adriana. "Mamma, we have that room below the house. They could stay with us until Raif manages to get a job." Eugenia intercepted Adriana's dubious look and overrode it. "I don't have classes for a while so I will be able to give Nour a hand."

Lex glanced at his wife. "I think Eugenia would be the right person for Nour," he said. "And the path ramps down from the house, so there would be no problem getting wheelchair access."

Adriana nodded reluctantly. "If Eugenia feels she can manage, that's fine. The room won't take much preparation."

"Thank you," Moussa said sincerely. "You tell me what you need and I will get it done."

"Can we come and visit them at your house?" Layla asked anxiously.

"Of course you can," Adriana said. "You can come whenever you like."

Amal served dinner around the glass-topped dining room table. She was a natural hostess and her food was delicious. The city lights, and lights from several of the larger yachts, reflected on the quiet water of the harbour a long way below. There was much speculation about the bombing that had snatched away Nour's parents and how she would be coping with the horror of what had happened. That evening, however, all of them chose to avoid the one thing that preoccupied their minds. Raif had voluntarily fought on the side of the Islamic State. Even Moussa and Amal wondered whether they would know the man who was about to return. Adriana agonised over whether Lex had acted foolishly in allowing Raif and his wife to stay in Frigiliana knowing they could all live to regret Eugenia's impetuosity. It was one thing to write about a terrorist, she thought, but quite another to invite him to stay in their home.

* * *

Raif and Nour left Raqqa three weeks later after the doctors were reasonably sure the wound was not infected. Raif booked a double seat on the bus so that Nour could stretch the leg out. He sat behind her and watched her face as the bus jolted and rattled over the rutted roads; it was obvious by her pallor and the blankness of her eyes that she was in a lot of pain and even the pills that the hospital had provided failed to deaden it completely.

For Raif, the period after the bombing had been the worst he had ever had to live through. Nour's agony of body and soul had been his own. While she did not intentionally block him out, her loss was so deep and so devastating that she could not include him in the circle of physical and emotional pain. He acted alone in the preparation for their departure. Nour was able to get about with the use of crutches but she remained physically unable to participate and mentally too weary to care whether she stayed or left—or even whether she lived or died.

She lived and re-lived what she remembered of the bombing. The all-consuming whistling that filled heaven and earth, the power that lifted her effortlessly off her feet, slamming her back an instant later onto the ground. The choking dust and the flying fragments, the comforting presence of the paramedic, and the hypnotic swinging of the plastic drip.

In Aleppo, Raif helped her off the bus and asked a woman to take Nour to the toilet. He bought rolled sandwiches with falafel and mint-flavoured yogurt but Nour returned in tears. She had been unable to squat and the stranger had had to support her over the pan. And no, she was not hungry.

The bus turned south and headed ponderously towards Hama and then Homs before taking the road to the Lebanese border. Nour grew weary and her head slumped onto her chest. Raif pulled a pillow from their hand luggage and slipped it behind her neck. She smiled at him gratefully and ate a little of the sandwich to please him. He tucked a blanket around her legs and she slept out of sheer exhaustion waking only when the bus hissed and drew to a halt at the border. Again Nour needed to ask for help at the restroom, but this time there was a spacious toilet and a handrail and she managed a moment of privacy.

"My family will meet us in Malaga," Raif told her, "and my father has arranged for a wheelchair to be brought to the plane."

There had been a flurry of texts between him and the family as the date of arrival approached and Raif discerned their excitement at seeing him again. His feelings were mixed, he longed to be home but knew that he came to his family on new terms. The rift his actions had created would be difficult to close.

Hostesses did everything they could to make Nour comfortable on the flight and she slipped into a drug-induced sleep as the cabin lights were dimmed. Raif watched a couple of movies and then gazed for hours at his reflection in the darkened window, his thoughts shifting erratically between the past and an unknown future. He had just begun to doze when the lights were switched on and it was announced that they were preparing to land in Madrid.

There was the usual rush to collect baggage and go through immigration. The hard-eyed officer examined Raif's passport, glanced at his face, and back at the document.

"What were you doing in Syria?"

"I went over to get married." The story was pre-arranged.

"Where?"

"My wife comes from Raqqa."

The official now regarded him with interest, fascination almost, his dark eyes sharp under beetling brows.

"Raqqa?" he echoed.

"Yes."

He looked Nour over from head to toe. She had abandoned the niqab when they left Syria and stuffed the offending garment into a bin at the airport in Beirut telling Raif she never intended to wear one again—ever! She had chosen to dress in a long skirt and a cowl-necked pullover that she hoped was fashionable enough to appear presentable before Raif's sisters and had left her long hair loose. It was a momentous taste of freedom that served to mitigate somewhat the physical discomfort she was experiencing.

"Wait here please." The officer's tone was ominous.

"Is there something wrong?" Nour whispered.

"He will probably run some sort of security check on me," Raif said quietly. "Don't worry, Nour. I don't think they have anything to connect me to ISIS." He squeezed her hand reassuringly but she noticed that his palm was sweaty.

Was it possible that that suggestion of freedom was to be snatched away from them again? She hunched over in the courtesy wheelchair and fixed her eyes on her hands, willing her heartbeat to adopt the same inertia. In the queue behind them, people were becoming restless as they waited their turn. Raif tried not to notice the whispering and the glances in their direction. He closed his eyes and concentrated on steadying his breathing. When he opened them again, the officer was approaching, his face tight with irritation as he took his place behind the counter. He stamped the passport and tossed it down with a brief nod of the head. He looked over Raif's shoulder, his expression was dispassionate.

"Next!"

Raif retrieved their documents, picked up the bags, and manoeuvred Nour's chair with the other hand.

"Breath easy. We're through!" he whispered.

Before they caught their connection for Malaga, they buried Syria in a valedictory cup of coffee at a busy café in the terminal and this time a hostess trundled Nour to the waiting plane in the wheelchair while Raif coped with the hand luggage.

Malaga appeared for the briefest of moments before touchdown in a triumphant vista of cloud, mountain, and sea, and Raif's thoughts turned to the Islamic State's claim upon this city. *Insha Allah,* it would be a long time before they could turn their focus to Spain; they had still, after all, not managed to conquer Kobane! As for his intended role, Raif hoped there would be a way to extricate himself from it. His thoughts were lost in the roar of the jet engines. Nour grasped his hand tightly as the aircraft touched, lifted, bumped, and slewed slightly to the left before gripping the tarmac and lumbering to a halt.

Layla greeted her brother like a puppy, her body wriggling with pent-up excitement as he appeared at the door of the arrivals lounge. She flung her arms around him and buried her face against his chest. Raif laughed and hugged her in return.

"Layla, this is Nour."

With one finger pressed tentatively against her bottom lip, Layla shyly presented Raif's wife with a card she had made. Nour rose to the occasion immediately.

"Layla that is beautiful! Thank you."

Layla blushed with pleasure and immediately volunteered to push the wheelchair.

Amal took Nour's hand. "You must be so tired," she said. "We've decided to save celebrations until you've both had a chance to rest."

Moussa put his arm around Raif's shoulder as they left the terminal. He had seen the weariness in his son's eyes and the pale, pinched look of his young bride. They would need time, Moussa discerned, to begin the process of healing.

"It is so good to have you home."

"It's good to be back, *Baba.*"

They travelled in two cars. Amal settled Nour in the back of the car with her leg stretched out across the seat and her back propped up with cushions against the door. Layla chattered happily, twisting herself against the confines of the seatbelt so that she could see her new sister-in-law.

"Eugenia's going to be there," she said. "She's great, you'll love her too. And we all love Juan!"

Amal was thankful that no one could see the warmth that rose in her cheeks at the mention of Juan's name. She had seen nothing of him in the past several weeks and she deeply regretted her role in their parting.

"Are we going to be staying in their home?" Nour asked uneasily.

"They have a separate room with a bathroom below the main house," Amal explained. "Eugenia felt she could be of help when Raif is not there; until your leg heals, that is."

Nour closed her eyes and leaned her head against the window behind her. She felt the familiar weariness sap her body indistinguishable from the depression she had experienced for the past several weeks. Even the thought of having to meet another stranger was too much for her to cope with. She wished herself back in the familiar confines of the flat in Raqqa where she could lie and look at the ceiling-fan turning slowly round and round and think of nothing beyond the inane futility of its rotation. She met Layla's indefatigable questions and comments as sweetly as she was able until Amal intervened and suggested that Nour might need some peace after such a long journey. The drone of the car was soothing and she was jolted out of a light doze by a sudden unevenness of the road as they turned into the driveway of Lex and Adriana's home.

"You've been fast asleep!" Layla said in a slightly accusing tone.

Nour smiled. "I have, sorry."

"Papa and Raif are already here. They're taking the luggage down to your room."

Amal came round and opened the door for her. "Can you manage?"

"I think so, thank you."

"You do speak English I hope?" Amal asked suddenly aware that they had all slipped naturally into Arabic from the first moment of their arrival.

Nour nodded, "Of course, we all studied it at school. I doubt any of them will be teaching it now though."

"You mean in Raqqa?"

"And wherever the Islamic State has seized control."

Amal glanced at Nour sharply. "You don't sound as though you like them."

For the first time, Nour laughed. "This is the first taste of freedom I have experienced in months," she declared. "Raqqa is dominated by fear. I will miss my home city, but I could not live under such oppression forever."

"And Raif?"

"You will have to ask him," Nour said. "But I think you will find he has changed a lot since you last saw him."

Amal smiled. "Good to hear. Do I have you to thank for that?"

Nour shook her head. "Not really. I think the change came from earlier experiences."

Amal extricated the wheelchair from the boot of the car just as Eugenia came down the path towards them.

"I'm so happy to meet you," she said leaning down impulsively to hug Nour. "Raif and Moussa have taken the luggage. Shall we go and meet them?"

Layla skipped down the path ahead of them and Eugenia took charge of the wheelchair. "Raif said you were fine on crutches in the house."

"I manage quite well," Nour said. "I am still able to cook and clean and Raif gives me a hand with the heavier things." She glanced at her surroundings, "Your garden is very beautiful."

"My mother loves gardening. This is almost all her doing. You will meet her tomorrow. She and papa felt it would be better to let you settle in without too much fuss this evening."

The door was open and Raif and Moussa had stacked the suitcases just off the entrance. The room was small but compact. There was a comfortable-looking bed, a built-in wardrobe, and two armchairs. Cold chicken, fresh bread, and salad were laid out for them on a small table in an alcove to the right of the entrance.

"It's very small, but I hope you will be comfortable here," Eugenia said. "There's a two-plate stove and a bar fridge. You're welcome to use our washing machine."

"You have gone to so much trouble. Thank you." Nour was overwhelmed.

"We're going to leave you to unwind," Moussa said. "I will call you tomorrow, Raif. We have made an appointment for Nour to see an orthopaedic specialist on Thursday. It will be best to get things moving as quickly as possible."

Moussa reached into his pocket and handed Raif a bunch of keys. "The car the girls came up in is a wedding present to you and Nour," he said. "It's not new, but it's in good condition. You will need a car up here."

Raif glanced down at the keys in his hand and when he looked back at his father there were tears in his eyes.

"After all I have put you through?"

"You are back," Moussa replied. "That is all that matters now."

Chapter 33   Betrayal

Saudi King Abdullah was hospitalized with pneumonia and, at ninety years of age and with a history of health problems, the subject of succession, coupled with the plummeting oil price was foremost in the minds of most of his people. Despite the massive drop, Saudi oil production continued at its normal high level. Crown Prince Salman bin Abdulaziz Al Saud, who was expected to succeed the ailing king, gave his assurances that the economic interests of Saudis would be protected, but international markets remained jittery. Already, since June of the previous year, the United States was producing more barrels of oil per day than Saudi Arabia, and OPEC could not allow this radical climb to continue. In the past, falling crude prices had generally presaged slumps in the global economy with the smaller oil-producing countries succumbing first. By shaking the economic tree, the innumerable small shale-oil producers would be forced to drop out of the market placing OPEC back on centre stage.

Meanwhile, as a hedge against the future, Hezbollah stock-piled oil and weapons against the time they might launch against Israel or be forced to defend themselves against the Islamic State. They had proved useful in their investigative role in Saudi Arabia and already several princes had been charged with sedition and quietly executed. Investigations continued against the Sharia police, but the king had urged the Shia militia working behind the scenes, to proceed with caution and subtlety. It would not do to appear to be on a witch-hunt.

Saudi Arabia had many more concerns than succession and the oil price. Since the warning from Hezbollah, it was decided at the highest level to build a wall to keep ISIS at bay. Although the Saudi population consisted predominantly of conservative Sunni Muslims, and ISIS was admired by many, the higher echelons of the state regarded the militia with a great deal of suspicion. The monarchy was an offence to fundamentalist Islam and therefore the Caliphate was a threat. Although the Islamic State had grown out of Al Qaeda, and Saudi Arabia had supported the militia's part in the war against the Soviet Union in Afghanistan in the 1980s, the Salafist movement that evolved from it was dangerous. Saudi Arabia's oil wealth constituted only part of the nation's attraction. As the protector of Medina and Mecca, the nation was the spiritual heartbeat of Islam and its value to the enemy was beyond price.

"The kingdom of the two Holy Places must be protected," Hezbollah chief, Kamil Ghassan, stated categorically. "I am certain your Royal Highnesses would prefer not to plunge the Saudi nation into a war against the Islamic State. It would be far better to keep the baying dogs out."

The decision was not reached lightly. Hezbollah's warning of an impending invasion provoked them to action. A formidable border fence, patrolled by the Saudi Arabian military already existed but they knew it was not enough to hold ISIS back. The concept of a great divide was first considered in 2006 during the Iraqi civil war, and plans were brought back onto the drawing board. Engineers were called in, the planning phase was accelerated and, in September, King Abdullah fast-tracked the first phase of the wall's construction. Such a wall called for intricate planning and would cost a fortune, but weighed against the safety of the royal family, it was decided the step must be taken. The plans showed multi-layered barriers extending along the six-hundred-mile northern border with Iraq with seventy-eight monitoring towers and eight command centres.

"The centres will be linked using a fibre-optic communications network," the head of the security team reported in their initial presentation meeting with Prince Salman and the Second Deputy. "Top men from the armed forces must be trained to man it."

"How many men will be needed?"

"We anticipate it will require around three-and-a-half-thousand," the security head replied. "But naturally troops must be brought in on regular patrols as well. We will also need thirty-two rapid-response centres and three rapid-response intervention squads."

Even to the oil-producing giant, the cost was intimidating; especially at a time when the dramatic slump in oil revenue was not yet seen to have reached its lowest level. There was little choice but to proceed. Mecca and Medina, the jewels of the Kingdom, must also be protected at all costs. It was inconceivable that the nation should fall.

But while the royal family was fully aware that they might hold the external enemy at arms-length with their fortifications, the enemy within remained the unknown factor.

* * *

The Mediterranean had put on her royal garments. Dressed in sparkling blue turned translucent green over the shallows, she showed a delicate edging of lacy white where she beached the shoreline. The sun had chosen this day to discard its weakness and challenge winter head-on. Leafless trees lifted their arms in supplication to the heavens, and bushes, cleansed after the previous night's rain, enhanced their richness through diamante droplets that reflected every facet of light.

Raif drove down the freeway to Malaga and pondered the events of the first few days in their new home. Like the rest of his family, he had taken to the Wesley-Smiths instantly. Their warm hospitality and acceptance of Nour and himself despite, presumably, knowing his association in Syria with the Islamic State, stunned him. There was no sense of condemnation or rejection of him as a person. The night before, Lex and Adriana had gone to the opening of an artist friend's exhibition in the city, and Juan and Eugenia had invited Raif and Nour up to the main house for supper. After their meal, Juan had brought out his guitar and entertained them with songs by Sting and Radiohead and they had chatted until late. Eugenia had questioned them at length about Syria showing that she was well-informed. Both he and Nour were impressed with her sensitivity, allowing them, when they felt ready, to volunteer information about the death of Nour's parents. Nothing was said of Raif's mission to Syria but, given time, he would tell them how it had come about. He knew it needed to be aired to remove any uncertainty they might be feeling beneath the surface. It was something he would speak to his father about today.

Moussa was waiting for him at the entrance to the building.

"I thought we might go and have a cup of coffee at the restaurant down the road before joining the girls," he said, "that way we can talk without Layla interrupting every few minutes."

Raif laughed. They wandered down the avenue of trees, now almost bare, with just a leaf or two waving helplessly in the soft breeze. The smell of good coffee wafted from the café as they approached and Raif sniffed the air appreciatively.

"Are you okay to sit out here?"

"Sure, it would be a shame to waste such good weather."

Moussa ordered coffees and they tilted back on their chairs delighting in the sunshine which fought a silent war with the persistent winter chill.

"So," Moussa said, "tell me all that happened over there."

Raif nodded and stirred his coffee thoughtfully.

"It was tough," he admitted at length. "I don't know where to start."

"Try the beginning."

He shrugged a shoulder and grinned, "Good enough starting point I suppose." He began to describe the Iraqi training camp and briefly related the death of Rami Mansour at the hands of one of the officers. "That is where my questions began," he confessed. "Right at the outset."

Moussa nodded. "What did you do?"

"There was never anything I could do," Raif said. "You don't argue with ISIS unless you want to follow the same fate as Rami. I just went along with it all." He described the shock he had felt when he first entered Syria. We were made to believe Bashir Assad was to blame for everything and, at first, I swallowed that story. I mean, Assad is responsible for a lot of Syria's problems, but the various militia and the overall lawlessness, for a whole lot more."

Moussa nodded. "And the international community as well, for that matter," he pointed out. "There has been a huge amount of interference. They are determined to bring Assad down and they're supporting the militias for their own purposes."

Raif nodded, "A lot of our weapons came from the US," he said. "I don't know where they got hold of them though. They may have been seized during raids."

"Did you see any action?"

"I did, but it wasn't what I had expected."

Moussa watched him silently knowing that some sort of explanation was forthcoming.

"I don't think I'm ready to speak about it yet," Raif said at last. "I just wanted out and fortunately my prayers were heard."

"The media reports are full of the atrocities."

"It's ugly. I hope I never have to be part of anything like that again."

Moussa reached a hand across the table and gripped his arm. "You're free now," he said. "Presumably they don't have any further hold over you?"

"No," Raif lied. "You're right. I'm out of it for good!"

"And what about Islam?"

Raif looked up and met his father's eyes. "I could never deny my faith, of course!"

"Look at where your faith has taken you!"

"I don't believe denying the need for jihad means I must abandon Islam."

Moussa scratched his chin, "Jihad is an intrinsic element of Islam. You deny the necessity to kill the infidel and the Jew; you are already denying your faith in the Qur'an."

Raif was silent, not wanting to hear what he knew to be the truth. Moussa pressed his point.

"Christian communities that have played a vital part in our Middle Eastern culture for centuries are being wiped out in Iraq and Syria and this goes directly against the teachings of the Qur'an."

Raif nodded, "I know it does, *Baba*."

"And so are the Jews."

Raif bristled visibly. "Israel can't expect any special treatment after what it has done to the Palestinians!" he retorted.

"And what the Islamic Caliphate and the other militia have done to Christians, to Jews, and even to moderate Muslims—have they not exempted themselves also?" Moussa's voice remained steady but he gazed unflinchingly at his son and Raif was forced to drop his eyes.

"I have seen what they do," he replied. "Those things will remain with me forever."

"I'm not saying Israel is right in all its dealings," Moussa said gently, "but neither is Islam. You can't make one set of rules for Jews and another for Muslims."

"You still can't expect me to deny Islam," Raif said and there was a stubborn set to his jaw. "I love my faith and I love the Prophet."

"I am not asking you to do that, Raif. I have no right to ask anyone to enter my world of unbelief. I must say though, that I fear what religion is capable of doing to a reasonable man." Moussa drained the last of his coffee and called for the bill. "I read recently that the name of the Prophet Muhammad is mentioned only a few times in the Qur'an while the name of *Isa*, Jesus, is mentioned twenty-five times. Is that true?"

"No," Raif said shortly, "I am sure it's not." He changed the subject abruptly. "Lex and Adriana have been very good in having Nour and me with them out there. Do you think I should tell them what I have told you? I mean, that I am not tied to any militia any longer."

"I think that would be a good idea. Eugenia had some sort of brush with ISIS militants and it would be good to set their minds at rest."

"She had trouble with ISIS here?"

Moussa nodded. "Ask her to tell you about it sometime. But clear the air with them first."

He raised a hand as their waiter came through the swing door of the restaurant, and signalled for the bill. "We'd better get moving," he said. "The girls will never forgive me if I keep you all to myself."

In the hope that no one would be able to trace him, Raif had changed his cell phone number and stayed away from the mosques where he might have been recognised. With any luck, he thought, the contact would be broken and they would forget him.

On Thursday, Raif helped Nour into the back of the VW and they drove down to the hospital. Moussa met them in the foyer and wheeled Nour to the lift. He had already formed a bond with his daughter-in-law. He had yet to discover the feisty side that Raif insisted was an integral part of her character, but he understood the pain she was suffering in the violent loss of her parents. Moussa knew he would never overcome the agony of facing the mutilated bodies of his own parents who had perished in the bombing. In his empathy with this dislocated, lost young woman, he understood her at a deeper level even than Raif. He was gentle with her knowing she needed time to heal, whereas Raif often became impatient with her withdrawal from him and the world in general.

Nour was sent for X-rays before seeing the orthopaedic surgeon. After a careful examination of her leg, he straightened up and helped her into a chair on the other side of his desk. Raif looked at him questioningly.

"There's been a great deal of damage to the knee," the surgeon said, "but it is repairable. Nour will need a full knee replacement to get her back on her feet. I think we should schedule her for an operation as soon as possible." He looked at his diary, "I have February third free, it's a Tuesday. Does that suit you?" Raif nodded and the surgeon scribbled a note under the date. "See the desk as you go out. My assistant will make all the arrangements and give you a list of procedures that Nour must follow. I will see you in the ward on the second of next month." He stood up, shook Raif's hand, and rested an arm over Nour's shoulder as they prepared to leave the office.

"Don't worry, young lady, we will look after you!"

His comforting words caused tears to well up in Nour's eyes and she blinked them away. The operation was going to cost a great deal of money and the burden would fall squarely on Raif's father.

"When I am better, Raif and I will both work to repay you," she told Moussa fiercely as they took the lift to his apartment after her appointment.

He cupped her face in his large hands, "My dear, I have money put away for such things as this," he assured her. "You are Raif's precious bride and nothing is too good for you. There is no debt within the circle of family."

Nour put her head in her hands and the tears flowed freely.

Chapter 34   Betrayal

Layla answered the ringing of the telephone.

"Yes, this is the Ahmadi residence." She stood on one leg and tucked the receiver into her neck. "No, Raif doesn't live here; he lives in the hills near Frigiliana. Who is calling please?" she listened carefully. "I'll tell him you called... His number? Hold on." She flipped the pages of the message book beside the phone and read it out to the caller. "It's a pleasure. 'Bye."

"Who was that?" Amal asked as she came into the lounge. She loosened the towel from around her head, bent forward and began to methodically rub her long hair dry.

"A school friend of Raif's. He wanted his number," Layla replied.

"A school friend?" Amal straightened up slowly and pushed the strands of damp hair away from her face.

"Yes," Layla frowned. "Did I do something wrong?"

"No, I don't think so. Did he give you his name?"

"Ali, I think."

"Did you say anything else?"

"No," she said doubtfully. "I just gave him the number."

"Okay, but don't give Raif's number to anyone else," Amal warned, and before Layla could ask why she added, "I'm going to dry my hair, I'll be in my room."

Amal absently allowed the hot air from the hairdryer to waft over her head for a few moments before making a decision. She switched it off and called Raif on her cell.

"Did you know anyone called Ali at school?" she asked.

"I don't think so, why?"

"Layla just gave your number to someone claiming to know you from school days."

There was silence from the other end then Raif swore softly in Arabic.

"Could it be a problem?"

"I hope not, but there are people I would rather avoid at the moment," he paused. "Tell Layla…"

"I already have."

"I'll change my sim card again in the meantime."

"Do that."

Nour was watching him closely.

"What was that about, is there a problem?"

"Probably nothing. Layla gave some caller my number." Raif closed his cell phone and removed the sim. "I'll get a new card when we're next in town."

She glanced nervously in his direction, "I don't think they will give up easily," she said.

"I've left the Islamic State behind and that's where I would like it to stay."

He was fighting confusion on several fronts. It was difficult to find work when so much time was given to helping Nour. It was an awkward time for them both and she was often irritable or depressed. Raif knew she was in pain and that intimacy was difficult for her, but this knowledge did not help his feeling of rejection. And then there was that remark by his father about Jesus in the Qur'an. Raif had gone back to a nightly routine of study of the book to disprove Moussa's assertions. As he re-read passages he had glossed over before, he discovered that the Qur'an had nothing bad to say about *Isa*. In fact, there were supernatural miracles linked with him such as healings, whereas nothing of the kind was attributed to Muhammad. And although he had not discovered all twenty-five references at this point, there certainly were many allusions to him in the scriptures. Why then was there so much antagonism towards Jesus by Muslims?

* * *

Lex Wesley-Smith was keeping a fairly close eye on his main character. Raif Ahmadi was a troubled young man, of that he had no doubt. He appeared straight enough, but you could never really tell with these types and, if he were honest with himself, he would be happy to hear he had chosen to move on. Eugenia and Juan were convinced Raif was fine and Lex had always trusted their intuition in the past but he could not shake off the notion that he had placed his family in jeopardy by having Raif and Nour on the property. On the other hand, having one's main character right there to observe was a distinct advantage, therefore Lex watched and, whenever he could, involved Raif in friendly conversation. He waited knowing that the moment must arise when the real meat could be gnawed from the bone, so to speak. He wanted to know what Raif had experienced back there in Syria under the Islamic State and how it had influenced him. He liked what he had seen of Nour. She was very quiet, but that was understandable considering what she had been through.

Eugenia was walking up the path towards the house and a moment later she popped her head around the door of Lex's study.

"Hi papa, can I get you a cup of coffee?"

"I'd love one, thanks."

"Were you visiting our new neighbours?" he asked as Eugenia returned and placed a tray on the table under the window.

"Raif's out but I was having a chat with Nour"

"You two seem to be getting on well together," Lex observed.

"She's easy to talk to once you get past the shyness," Eugenia replied. "I really like her. In fact, I like them as a couple. Raif has made it clear that he wants nothing further to do with ISIS."

Lex stirred his coffee thoughtfully, but said nothing. He was still less inclined to accept everything Raif said at face value.

Chapter 35   Betrayal

*God is our Goal. The Prophet is our leader. The Quran is our
constitution. Jihad is our way. Death in the service of God is the
loftiest of our wishes. God is great; God is great." Muslim
Brotherhood*

As it turned out, it was Nour that opened the conversation with Lex.
Eugenia had invited her for coffee one afternoon when Raif was out.
She wheeled her through to the living room where a fire was burning
and Juan was stacking logs in the two-tiered wooden box against the
wall. He called a greeting and left to fetch another load. The white
Labrador was curled up on the hearth rug with the puppy, while one
of the cats had commandeered an armchair and was washing itself
contentedly. Flames leaped up the chimney showering the hearth
with occasional bursts of sparks.

"It's lovely and warm in here," Nour exclaimed as Eugenia helped
her into a chair and propped her foot up.

"It's been really cold over the last few days," Eugenia said. "You
must have cold winters in Syria?"

Nour nodded. "We have snow sometimes. I pity the refugees that
are living in camps over there at the moment."

Juan walked in rubbing his hands together against the chill. "How
are you, Nour?" and without waiting for a reply announced, "Did I
hear something about coffee?"

"Just on my way," Eugenia laughed.

Juan removed the cat and sat down opposite Nour.

"I hope you guys are comfortable down in the basement," he said.

"It's hardly a basement," Nour replied with a smile. "We have
beautiful views onto the garden and yes, we're really comfortable
there."

Juan glanced up as a young man ambled into the room and saluted
a greeting. "Oh yeah, Nour, this is Sam. He's a friend of mine."

"Pleased to meet you," she said politely.

"English?" Sam directed the question to Juan.

"No, Nour is from the Middle East. Sam is die-hard Spanish," he explained. "Claims to speak no other language."

"I speak American pop," he contradicted with a grin.

His trousers were several sizes too large and rested on his hips, but his exposed underwear did not seem to embarrass him. Sam flopped down onto the sofa and stretched out his legs. Despite the blond hair which protruded in erratic strands from beneath a navy baseball cap, which he wore back-to-front, Nour thought he looked likeable. He had an open, friendly face and a warm smile. He was clean-shaven except for a suggestion of stubble around the chin and his brown eyes held a hint of mischief. He leaped up as Eugenia came through and took the tray from her.

"Papa's joining us," Eugenia said as she cut generous slices of the cheesecake she had baked earlier.

"Never been known to miss out on cake, no matter how pressing the urge to write," Juan observed cynically.

"Watch it, young man!" Lex said, arriving just at that moment. He greeted Nour and Sam and helped himself to coffee.

"So, you've met Sam," he remarked to Nour. "As a rule, he's inseparable from his skateboard."

Sam smiled affably and Nour suspected his English was better than he let on.

"Are you good with the skateboard?" she asked him.

"I am the best," he replied in Spanish and hooked his thumbs under his armpits to drive the point home. Lex realised it was the first time he had seen Nour laugh and he warmed to the transformation he saw in her face. Perhaps, he thought, this was the right place for her and Raif after all; she was starting to come out of her shell.

A dull, grey rain was beginning to fall and Juan and Eugenia volunteered to drive Sam back to the village leaving Lex with Nour.

"I understand you are writing about Syria," she said shyly.

Lex stood up and set some more logs on the fire. "I am," he said. "I'd love to hear more about the country if you're up to talking about it."

Nour glanced down at her hands for a moment and then appeared to come to a decision. "Of course, I will help in any way I can."

"Tell me about Raqqa. What was it like before?"

"Before the militias came? It seems so long ago now," she said, "but I'm sure you know the history."

He nodded.

Nour thought back and described the city that was so firmly coupled with the Euphrates River. She spoke about some of her childhood memories, the crowded streets in the city centre, and some of the many sights and smells that made Raqqa what it was. She spoke of picnics on the banks of the river and bathing in its clear waters.

"I had never seen a dead body," she said, "and I only remember a few violent acts, once a neighbour beating his wife, another time a shoplifter being kicked by the owner of a shop. Nothing more than that, and they were shocking to me. Then the militias arrived." She shook her head. "My childhood ended there. I have seen so much since then—death, bodies... their heads impaled on the park railings, women and children beaten; crucifixions. It was impossible to avoid. And the bombs..." Her voice trailed away.

Lex moved closer to her and placed a reassuring hand over hers. "You don't have to talk if it is difficult," he said gently.

She shook her head and tears flowed silently down her cheeks. She had held her emotions in check for so long that those soundless tears were all that betrayed the anguish within.

Lex waited until, surprisingly, she allowed the words to flow.

"You learn to know the difference in the planes. There were so many bombs. They have different sounds—the barrel bombs used by Assad's forces, and those used by the American allies." She looked Lex straight in the eye as though her next words were intended as some sort of challenge. "I feel that I directed the bomb that killed my parents," she said bitterly. "I went out alone, which I should not have done. Women are not supposed to leave home without a husband or a father. But I wanted to see my parents! I know it is irrational, but perhaps if I had stayed where I was, it wouldn't have happened." She twisted her hands in her lap. "The aircraft followed me," she said. "They dogged my path before the bombs fell."

"And you were caught in the explosion."

She looked away from him then and an anguished cry broke from her lips, "Just before the house. I should have died with them."

"But you didn't die, Nour. And your parents wouldn't have wanted you to when you were just beginning a new life with Raif. You still have a purpose for living."

Her head was in her hands and her shoulders shook as she allowed the pent-up emotions to break forth into sobs that wracked her body.

Eugenia stopped in the doorway and looked at her father questioningly.

"Papa?"

"Don't worry, Nour's fine," he said gently.

"Did you say something that upset her?"

Nour shook her head and dried her tears on the sleeve of her jumper. "Your father's been helping me put my life back in some sort of perspective," she said. "It's going to take time, but I know I must begin to speak about the things that have happened."

"I'm going to make you some tea," Eugenia said firmly. "You must stay here until Raif gets back."

Lex sat back, his expression was grave but he spoke lightly. "Genie believes tea is a remedy for most ills," he said. "In that at least, she takes after her mother." He looked at her bowed head thoughtfully, "Nour, you could be a great help to me with this book. Together we could get the word out to a world that has hardly noticed what is taking place in the Middle East. If you are prepared to work with me, we could open people's eyes."

For a while, Nour appeared not to have heard, but then she lifted her head and looked at him. "You are right," she said. "I must move on. I can't wallow in self-pity forever, but I can make something of a bad situation. Perhaps we are here for a reason."

By the time Eugenia brought the tea through to the lounge, Nour had begun to compose herself and, when Raif returned an hour later, he found his wife looking almost relaxed for the first time since her parents' death.

* * *

Raif found a job with a small business in Frigiliana. Running the bakery in Raqqa had given him management experience and his facility with languages was becoming increasingly evident, which proved useful in his dealings with the public. He spoke English and

Spanish with a fair degree of fluency and was beginning to study French in his spare time.

"I'm not earning a fortune," he said to Nour, "but at least we can pay rent to the Wesley-Smiths now."

"And we're not so dependent on your father," Nour said contentedly. "When my leg is sorted out, I will look for work as well. Two salaries will be better than one."

Raif slipped an arm around her shoulder. "I will keep a lookout for a better position in time. We will get our own place and start a family. Perhaps you could work from home?"

"I would like to live up here in the hills. It would be wonderful to raise children here."

They sat contentedly watching the dusk deepen into night knowing deep down that dreams were dreams and reality was bigger and harsher, but that the process of dreaming created a fibre of hope to cling to.

The terror attacks in Paris in January that left seventeen people dead were followed by an outpouring of grief and solidarity. World leaders, with the notable exception of the U.S. president, joined with the people of Paris in taking to the streets. The Israeli Prime Minister made an appearance despite being asked by the French President to stay away and was lampooned by the press.

"He was gauche!" Juan declared. "He tried to force his way onto a bus ahead of others; he elbowed his way through the crowd to get to the front line. The man's an idiot!"

"You and the rest of the world would have had him stay away from the proceedings," Eugenia retorted. "Four Jews were killed by Muslim terrorists in an attack on a Jewish food outlet, "obviously he needed to show concern for his people."

"Eugenia, are you deliberately forgetting Israel's war against Gaza and their treatment of Palestinians? Of course, no one wants him to show his face in Europe."

"And you are refusing to see the Palestinian role in provoking reprisals by continually firing rockets into Israel?" she retorted.

"The Israeli response far outweighed the provocation!"

"It's a war that's being fought here, not a friendly tennis match. Besides which, the entire world is becoming as anti-Jewish as you are and still manages to persuade the masses that Muslims, no matter what acts of terror they perpetrate, are a peace-loving people. Perhaps you haven't taken Boko Haram's latest massacre into account either. Two thousand people in Northern Nigeria! *Two thousand people*, Juan—while world attention is riveted on the happenings in Paris. By Muslims who want to enforce their laws on others!"

"What on earth is going on here?" Adriana demanded as she came down the stairs from the bedroom. She glanced from one glaring face to another.

"Absolutely nothing," Juan said unconvincingly.

"We're firing shots across the border," Eugenia replied and stalked out of the room.

"When did she become such a staunch supporter of Israel?" Juan demanded.

Adriana raised her eyebrows. "Silly question, Juan."

"So, she had a brush with some Salafists; does that necessitate a completely anti-Muslim attitude."

"She was the one who asked us to bring Raif and Nour here," Adriana reminded him. "That doesn't sound like a blanket prejudice. I think she's seeing Islamic jihadism through different eyes now, that's all."

"Palestinians can't be tarred with the same brush as ISIS," he protested.

Adriana regarded him for a few moments before answering. "I don't know enough to answer you on that," she replied at length. "But I do remember them gunning down about twenty of their own people after the Gaza war."

"They were collaborators."

"So they said. But no proof was offered and there was no trial. I'm not saying that Israel is all good and they're all bad—there's wrong on both sides, I'm sure."

Juan shrugged irritably. "Genie is over-reacting at any rate. She needs to get over it."

Adriana smiled at her son. "I don't think that's going to happen, Juan. So maybe it's you who need to be more accommodating."

"What did Raif and Nour make of the Charlie Hebdo attack?" The weekend's events in Paris were fresh in everyone's minds.

"He and Nour were just as shocked as we were, I think. Papa, did you hear that the other Paris shooting took place in a kosher market? I feel as though history is beginning to repeat itself."

"It's certainly becoming unsafe to be connected in any way with Israel," Lex conceded. "And that goes for America as well as Europe."

Eugenia grimaced. "It's going to be a rough year," she replied. "Increasing terror and a shaky global economy."

"It could be worse," Lex said philosophically as he sat down at his desk.

Eugenia raised her eyebrows. "How do you figure that, papa?"

"Your grandmother might choose to visit."

"Don't let Mama hear you say that!" she laughed. "How's your book going, papa?"

"I'm hoping I might be able to finish the first draft by the end of this month," he said. "The only trouble is I have no idea how it's going to end."

"So, what makes you think you will finish it?"

Lex laughed. "I'll do the work and trust the book to do the rest. Perhaps it will take longer than I anticipate."

Eugenia shook her head. "Sometimes Juan and I wonder how we were ever born into such a crazy family. But never mind, I love you anyway." She kissed the balding spot on the crown of his head and picked up the tray. "See you later," she called as she left the room.

In a bold move that refused to be intimidated, Charlie Hebdo put out a new edition of their magazine. The cover picture conveyed the message All is Forgiven, with a cartoon of the weeping Prophet bearing in his hands the slogan made popular worldwide after the attack, *"Je suis Charlie"*. In the United Kingdom the magazine was sent in white wrapping to those who ordered copies and officials asked news agents to provide a list of subscribers' names. It seemed that even the small acts that might be construed as anti-Islamic were now bringing individuals under the spotlight.

Chapter 36   Betrayal

One thing that struck Raif forcibly as he re-read the Qur'an was that Mariam, the mother of Isa, Jesus, was the only woman referred to by name. There was not even a mention of the name of Prophet Muhammad's mother in the text. Yet chapter three of the Qur'an was given over to the Family of Mariam, and chapter 19 was simply headed 'Mariam'. Not only did the Qur'an assert that Mariam never committed any sin and went to heaven in bodily form, it also had much to say about Jesus in chapter 33. It called him the Word of God, the Spirit of God, and the Christ. Miracles were attributed to him, including healing and the raising of the dead. Moreover, the Qur'an itself said that Jesus went to heaven, that he was still alive and that he would return. Never were any such claims made of the Prophet.

Raif was shaken. It made no sense that Islam denied the teaching of its scriptures. If Jesus was Christ as the Qur'an said, why were Christians being persecuted? And if the Qur'an stated clearly that Jesus was the Word of God and the Spirit of God, why were Muslims whipping themselves into a fury over depictions of Muhammad but killing those who proclaimed Jesus?

Raif was sitting on the grass by the pond with the Qur'an in his hand when Lex came across him.

"Hi Raif, I see you're enjoying a bit of sunshine."

Raif's response was entirely spontaneous. "Lex, I'm trying to work something out. Perhaps you can help me."

"I can try," Lex said, sitting down on the grass beside him. "What's the problem?"

"I need to know what Christians believe."

"You might be asking the wrong person. I know some of the basics but I wouldn't count myself a believer. What is it you want to know?"

"My father told me you're not a Christian. May I ask why?"

Lex shrugged. "I suppose I'm a nominal believer. I'm pretty sure there's a God out there, but I've chosen to live my life my way."

"My father made the same choice," Raif said. "He didn't like what he saw of the contradictions within Islam so he chose to reject it all."

Lex glanced at him, "What made you choose differently?"

Raif shrugged. "We got a lot of teaching from the imams when I was at school. I was fired up by what they said."

"And when you went back to Syria?"

"I hated what I saw of ISIS but I was afraid it was my own failure to completely commit myself to Allah."

"Through jihad?"

He nodded. "I don't have the stomach for it. And I suppose that leads me to what is concerning me here."

"Go on."

Raif shook his head. "I'm increasingly confused. I decided to make another real attempt to discover a Qur'anic path that I could follow in good conscience, but there doesn't seem to be one." He paused and ran his fingers through his hair. "Did you know Jesus is written about in the Qur'an?"

"I know there's a mention of him," Lex said.

"More than a mention, really," Raif contradicted. And he went on to describe some of the things he had read. Lex glanced at him in surprise.

"That's interesting. Some of that is Catholic teaching—the part about Mary being without sin, and Jesus creating a bird from mud."

Raif looked puzzled. "It's all the same, isn't it?"

"Not really. I spent enough time in chapel during my school days to know that there are books that the Catholics accept that are not in the Bible. Muhammad was married to a Catholic wasn't he, which would explain why those things might have been included in the Qur'an."

Muhammad had married several women, even a pre-pubescent girl, but these were thoughts Raif had carefully suppressed for fear of dishonouring the Prophet. He changed the subject. "What about Jesus being the Word of God—is that Catholic teaching as well?"

"No, that's from the Bible. If I remember correctly, it says the world was created through the Word of God."

Raif drew a sharp breath. "That's incredible!"

It was Lex's turn to look puzzled. "Why? What did I say?"

"If the Bible says that the Word of God created the world, and the Qur'an calls Jesus the Word of God, the conclusion is mind-blowing," Raif said. "That means Jesus is the Creator."

"And therefore God," Lex concluded but he sounded less convinced. This was, as he had said, stuff he had heard time and again in his youth; old, rejected baggage, which he had no intention of taking up again.

Raif however, was eyeing him with quiet amazement. "One more thing," he said. "Why was Jesus treated as a criminal? From a Muslim point of view, crucifixion is an ugly thing. If he was God how could he die that sort of death?"

It was obvious that Raif was searching for answers, but Lex was out of his depth. "I only know that it was for sin," he said helplessly.

"The Qur'an says he was not a sinner"

"Not for his sin, for the sin of humankind. Look Raif, let me contact a friend of mine who will be able to give you the answers."

Raif nodded quietly. He rose onto his haunches and examined the grass between his feet as though he would find the answers there. Lex got up and dusted off the back of his trousers.

"Sorry I couldn't have been of more help, Raif."

"Actually, you have given me far more than I bargained for, Lex," he replied. "It's going to take me some time to digest."

Paradoxically, it was Lex who returned to his study troubled by the conversation that had taken place. It was annoying to realise that his words had resonated with Raif, without being able to understand why. More years ago than he cared to remember, he had outgrown the need for Christianity. There had been a brief flirtation around that vulnerable early-teen, prepubescent period when he had gone to chapel on his own and 'found Christ'. He vividly remembered the awareness of sin and the need for a Saviour, the joyful feeling of 'being saved'. It had quickly dissipated under mockery from his peers, and parents who had spoken scathingly of Alexander 'finding religion'. All in all, he had grown up and grown wise and recalled that embarrassing lapse for what it was—a childish grasp at a fairy tale.

So what made Lex write this chapter? Was it intended to portray more of Raif's character through his struggle, or was it some echo from the past that had resurfaced and left him feeling a little lost, like a child again back at boarding school, far from home, and deeply in need of comfort?

* * *

Sam arrived unannounced, shook the droplets from his hair, replaced his cap, and flopped into an armchair close to the fire.

"Hello, Sam!" He seemed not to notice the heavy irony in Eugenia's tone.

"Oh, hi Genie. It's pretty cold out there."

"Well you seem to have landed in the right place to warm up," Juan said with a laugh. "Is it coffee you're here for?"

"Sure, if you're offering!"

Juan looked pointedly at his sister who turned her back and ignored him.

"Okay Sam, it's over to us. Come and give me a hand."

Juan organized mugs while Sam examined the biscuit tins to see what they offered. "There was some dude in the village today asking questions," he said as he munched one of Eugenia's homemade ginger nuts.

"What sort of questions?"

"Well, you know, about the guy that's staying here."

Juan stiffened, "Raif?"

"Yeah, he was looking for him."

"Did you say anything?"

Sam rubbed his chin with the back of his hand. "It wasn't me he was asking. You know the guy in the coffee bar—what's his name?"

"Julio?"

"Yeah, him."

"Sam, listen to me! Get to the point will you? Did Julio tell this guy that Raif was here?"

"No, he didn't."

Juan gave a sigh of relief. "What did he tell him?"

"Nothing much. I don't think he liked the look of him. I didn't either. He was one of these hectic Middle Eastern dudes. You know, big beard, that sort of thing."

Juan swore softly. "Somebody else might have told him Raif was working in the village or that he was living here, which could mean trouble."

Sam's eyes widened. "You mean, like, there's someone after him?"

Juan looked at his friend in exasperation. "Yes, there could be someone after him! This guy doesn't sound much like a long-lost relative."

"So, we'd better tell the dude."

Juan nodded thoughtfully. "You're right for once, Sam. This isn't information we should keep to ourselves."

Juan went out to meet Raif when he returned from work and briefly conveyed Sam's message. Raif listened politely, but a muscle in his jaw reflected his disquiet.

"Could I ask you not to pass this on to the others," he asked. "I wouldn't want them to be alarmed unnecessarily. I know what this is about and I'll deal with it."

"Sure," Juan said. "But if there's a problem…"

"No, no. There's no problem. This is just someone I've been meaning to see. Thanks for letting me know."

Juan watched him walk down the path towards the room he shared with Nour and wondered if Raif was being completely honest with him. Until Sam spoke to him today, Juan realised he had almost forgotten the connection Raif had had with ISIS and now, despite Raif's dismissal of the news, he was concerned. Knowing his background, any big-bearded Middle Eastern dude, to use Sam's terminology, who was looking to connect with Raif, held potential for trouble.

Chapter 37   Betrayal

*"I say to the entire world as a warning: We are living under the
Islamic Caliphate. We will die for it until we liberate those occupied
lands, from Jakarta to Andalusia. And I declare: Spain is the land of
our forefathers and we are going to take it back with the power of
Allah."*
Islamic State video.

As he headed towards Malaga on that Saturday morning, Raif knew
that there was only one option open to him, and that was to fulfill his
obligation to the Islamic Caliphate. Any attempt to avoid the
inevitable would endanger himself and Nour and, worse, could spell
disaster for the Wesley-Smiths. The very thought that his actions
might affect the people who had shown them such care and
hospitality made Raif feel sick to his stomach and, although he was
loathe to move before Nour's operation, it was becoming clear that
they must leave their home in the hills as soon as possible.

He found a parking place at the mosque and crossed the grey and
white paving that led to the entrance. Architecturally, the Islamic
institute was Moorish in character and, within the mosque itself,
elaborately detailed, but Raif was in no mood for sightseeing. He
found his way to the offices and asked to see Dr. Ibrahim.

"Well, well, you have finally arrived!"

Raif did not miss the sarcasm. "My wife has been ill and requires
an operation," he explained briefly.

"I am sorry to hear it," Ibrahim remarked without managing to
convey a modicum of sorrow in his tone. "Kindly sit down."

Raif sat separated from the doctor by a wide expanse of desk. It
was strange, he thought, how human power can be conveyed in the
breadth of a desktop and the depth of reflection in its polished

surface. The doctor ignored the social niceties and drove straight to the point.

"You have wasted a great deal of our time and money," he said. We have sent men out to look for you. If you intended to lose yourself, you did not do an adequate job." He looked over the top of his spectacles and his eyes were cold and unyielding. "You were fully aware that your release from Syria was granted for a purpose. May I remind you that you contracted to serve for another year?"

Raif nodded. "I apologise for not seeing you earlier," he murmured.

The rebuke concluded, doctor Ibrahim moved on. "Allow me to first convey to you what we mean by the term 'cultural jihad'," he glanced down at the nails of his interlinked hands which rested on the desk. "Whether you live in Syria, Spain, or the United States, it makes no difference. You are a Muslim first and a citizen second. Muslims do not integrate into the society in which they live unless it is under Sharia law. Of course, you understand this."

"Yes."

"There are two parts to your job. The first is to change the dishonouring behaviour of those Muslims who have not recognised this basic tenet and draw them back to the true faith." His hands drew apart at this juncture and grasped at the air to dramatise his point. "If they do not choose to return, the Qur'an offers them no mercy. A time will come when they will die at our hand. You will make lists of those men and women who say they are Muslim but remain outside of the faith." He paused to see the impact of his words. Raif's expression did not change. "Of course, the second aspect of cultural jihad takes on another and more challenging form as we work together to change the trend of the society in which we live," the doctor continued. "These Western countries are the enemy of Islam. The reason we are here in the West is that the *kafur* raped and pillaged our resources and killed our people. Our war is fought from within and is now starting to bear fruit. The false liberty of the western nations is anti-Islam; it is an idol that must be destroyed." His eyes burned into him across the great divide of the desk. "Do you hear what I am saying?"

Raif nodded briefly.

"You have seen the filth of the West; the drugs, the alcohol, the films, the sports—all these are done in the name of entertainment.

In the eyes of Allah these things are dung. Also, all forms of government of the infidel, whether capitalism, communism, or a monarchy, are displeasing to Allah and must be destroyed.

He fingered his beard thoughtfully, "These attacks in Paris—of course Israel is behind them."

Raif glanced at him startled, "What makes you say that, Doctor? We saw the news from Paris. The attackers had Muslim names."

Doctor Ibrahim frowned darkly. "These sources are twisted, of course. Israel has everything to gain. These Jews still believe the myth that the land is theirs. They want the Jews to go back to Israel so they kill and accuse Muslims. These are their tactics." Raif was stunned as he wondered how the doctor could have reached such an outlandish conclusion. "Your work is to subtly change the western mindset to accept Islam so that a transformation to Sharia can be accomplished. This is the sword of Islam that you are asked to bear; to lay down your life as a martyr in the service of Allah that your name may light up before his throne."

As Raif left the building later, he felt as though he was suffocating. He had taken one step in their direction and he was like a fly trapped in the web of a spider. He had been given orders. There was nothing he could do to extricate himself, no one he could appeal to, none that could relieve him from this morass. The only way to get out of their clutches was through death. He toyed with the idea of suicide but as he considered what it would mean to Nour and his family that, he knew, was no option at all. If not death, then what? Obedience was out of the question.

As he drove slowly back home he began to entertain a new thought. What if he appeared to carry out his orders by creating a convincing storyline of his conquests? The possibility was both tempting and terrifying. It was not considered a sin under Sharia for a Muslim to deceive or to lie to a non-Muslim; truth was only deemed a necessity to one who shared the Islamic faith. Allah would certainly not forgive his deception to such a great man of God as Dr. Ibrahim. Yet, ironically, Raif found the idea of deceiving Eugenia or Lex far more disturbing because he liked and respected them. His father had emphasized honesty towards everyone, no matter what their belief or station, and that was a philosophy Raif had always attempted to live up to. This looked set to become another failure of that path.

The answer came to him in the early hours of the morning after a sleepless night. If there was a hell he, Raif, would rather go there than deceive the people he loved most. He would certainly rather go there than risk their lives. If it meant that to survive, he would have to play mind games with Doctor Ibrahim and the Islamic State, so be it; but, from now on, Raif was no longer a Muslim. He slid out of bed without disturbing Nour, donned a dressing gown, and walked into the garden. He spoke the words aloud to Whomsoever might be listening.

"I, Raif Ahmadi, renounce Islam," he said. "I will no longer be in bondage to its laws. From now on, I choose to be set free." He had not quite gained the courage to speak against Allah and his Prophet, but the decision had been made and it was binding. Despite the chill night air and the deep darkness of the night, Raif felt a touch of warmth such as he had never experienced before. It went deep into his soul and rested there. It felt like a well-spring of joy.

* * *

It came as no surprise to Lex that Freemasons had erected the Georgia Guidestones; it was just the sort of mystery drama the Craft relished. The protocols or "guidelines" inscribed on the monument in eight modern and four ancient languages, formed a basis for some future order in which the population of the world would be radically reduced. The Guidestones consisted of four granite slabs arranged around a fifth central column while a capstone completed the astronomically aligned arrangement. The small granite cube set into the prepared niche above and to the right of the English language protocol seemed to add deliberate emphasis to the call for the world population to be maintained at under five hundred million.

In Ancient Craft Masonry, the cube was associated with the legendary stone block in Solomon's Temple which King David was said to have unearthed during the digging of the foundations. It was said to be black, perfect in dimension, and inscribed on its upper face within a triangle or delta with the sacred tetragrammaton, the ineffable name of God. The Hebrew Talmudists had called it *eben shatijah*, the Stone of Foundation, because, they declared, it had been laid by Jehovah at the foundation of the world and was the stone that supported the four corners of the earth. Masons chose to believe that Solomon had placed it within the Holy of Holies where the ark was overshadowed by the Shekinah glory of God.

Lex was well aware that Freemasonry was firmly linked to Temple lore and heavily overlaid with Egyptology, so he was familiar with the pseudo-Biblical approach. Enoch was purported to have first consecrated *eben shatijah* and commissioned the building of an underground temple on Mt. Moriah to house it. Masons believed that Enoch's son, Methuselah carried out the building, which consisted of nine vaults, one beneath the other, accessed through apertures. Enoch, they said, instructed that the stone be placed beneath the lowest arch and he set upon it the triangular plate of gold, each side a cubit in length. The delta was then decorated with precious stones and engraved with the secret name of God. This legend formed the basis of the Royal Arch and Select Master's degrees of the Americanised York Rite. In both of these, *eben shatijah* the Stone of Foundation was considered to be the receptacle of the ark on which the sacred name is inscribed.

The thought came randomly to Lex when he was feeding the cat. The coffee was already percolating filling the kitchen with the enticing aroma of freshly ground, and the cups were on the tray. He set the dish of cat biscuits on the floor absently and gazed out of the window at the garden still touched by deep shadow in places where the sun's rays had not yet penetrated. The Catholics also had a stone—Peter. Lex took his phone out of his dressing-gown pocket and checked Wikipedia.

Jesus had said to Peter, you are Petros and upon this small rock, petra, I will build my church, and the gates of hell shall not prevail against it[33]. The name Jesus had given to Peter was, in Greek, Petros, meaning rock. The Catholic Church had taken this verse and built a doctrine upon it, giving primacy over the entire church to the Roman Pontiff. As succession from the line of Peter could be easily disputed and, in his letters, Peter himself said that *Jesus* was the rock

---

[33] Matthew 16:18

which the builders disallowed, serious doubt was thrown right there, on the doctrine of papal pre-eminence.

Taken in context, Lex read, the previous verse confirmed what Jesus meant. Peter had just expressed his belief that Jesus Christ was the Son of the living God and it was on this foundation, that the church was destined to be built.

Lex picked up the tray and headed upstairs to wake Adriana. Faith in Christ and not in a pope; he kept his thoughts to himself as they drank their coffee on the balcony. It was not worth annoying her on the subject of Catholicism—especially not first thing in the morning.

Later, he phoned Sandy Williams. He was a bit of a Bible scholar but a good friend nevertheless.

"Sandy, old man, how are you doing?"

"Fine, Lex. Nice to hear from you. It's been a while."

"We've been busy," Lex said, "but we must get together sometime. Look, I wondered if you could help me. Is there anything in the Bible to do with a cube?"

Sandy laughed. "The only thing I can think of, off the top of my head, is that the Holy of Holies was a cube."

"Holy of Holies?" Lex sounded puzzled.

"The heart of worship in the Jewish Temple," he said. "Why do you ask?"

"It's to do with a book I'm working on," Lex said, "I've been pursuing a line of thought that involves cubes which have been worshipped as gods."

His friend was silent for a moment. "That's an odd one for you," he commented at length. "It doesn't sound like the sort of thing you usually get yourself involved with."

"No, I suppose you're right," Lex replied. "But this Holy of Holies, could it have been a focus of worship?"

"No way!" Sandy said emphatically. "The Jews were very careful not to give concrete form to their worship. The Bible made it clear there was to be no representation of God, no idols of any sort. However," he added on reflection, "it was considered to be the place where the glory of God dwelt. Only the High Priest was permitted to enter, and then only once a year on the day when he made atonement for the nation of Israel. Even then, he had to be in a place of absolute right-standing before God."

Lex scrubbed at his chin with the palm of his hand. He was onto something here but could not be sure where it was leading him.

"So this cube was filled in some way with God's presence?"

"That's right," Sandy said. "Did you know there are plans to rebuild the temple?"

"No?"

"The Jews are fully prepared for the event, which is what adds to the antagonism between them and Islam."

"Because the Dome of the Rock stands in the way of its construction?"

"Exactly. An iconic Islamic structure is the only impediment, that is if you don't count the whole Islamic world!"

Lex switched his cell phone to his other hand and stirred his second cup of coffee of the morning. "I see what you mean," he murmured.

"You've heard of the Antichrist?"

"Sure."

"Well, New Testament prophecy has it that he will enter the Holy of Holies and declare himself God."

Lex felt the hair on the back of his neck prickle. "The God of the cube!" he breathed.

"What on earth do you mean?"

"As I mentioned, the cube is associated with a god," Lex said. "Usually Saturn, the hidden god. Presumably, if a man enters the Holy of Holies and says he's God, he is revealing himself as Saturn."

Sandy whistled. "That's a new spin, but I see where you're going with this. I would say Satan rather than Saturn though. In reality, Saturn is just a planet—Satan is the being that hides behind the so-called gods and goddesses of this world."

For some reason, Lex found it easier to believe in Santa than Satan so he side-stepped that one.

"One more question, Sandy. Could this Antichrist guy be a pope, by any chance?"

"There are prophecies that tie him in some way to the papacy, yes. Interesting, Lex! You must let me read the book when you've completed it."

"Sure, I'll email you a copy it once I'm satisfied that it's finished. Send me the references to those prophecies, will you?"

Lex picked up his coffee. In one sense the conversation was illuminating. Obviously, the Stone of Foundation was an allegory denoting a person. Equally clear now was that this person was a leader; god on earth in the likeness of Saturn or Osiris/Isis, who had been anticipated for generations—perhaps even thousands of years. Religions had pointed to his coming; mysteries had been woven around his person. What was more amazing, if Lex had it right, the building and bombing of the Twin Towers signalled his imminent revelation.

On the other hand, the whole thing was even more convoluted and confusing than ever. What was he pursuing? Was this an Islamic leader, a Catholic pope, Head of the Illuminati, or a political leader? All could be said to have triumphalist aspirations but they surely could not all be batting on the same team. It appeared the intention was to present him as the Foundation Stone of some form of world government. And if he was, as Sandy suggested, the expected Antichrist of the Christians, his obvious desire was to usurp the position of the Son of God.

Chapter 38   Betrayal

For a long time, despite the United States-led airstrikes, it appeared that Kobane would fall. Then heavily-armed Kurdish Peshmerga from Iraq moved in to aid the beleaguered town and with the backup support of the allied air strikes drove the Islamic State back. By January 2015, they had recaptured several strategic areas and brought a large part of the town back under Kurdish control.

Over a thousand ISIS fighters had lost their lives in the fray but far more important to the Caliphate was the loss of face which accompanied their defeat. The ISIS image of invincibility was damaged but not shattered. In a last-ditch attempt to regain the advantage, the Caliphate sent a large number of suicide bombers into Kobane detonating trucks of explosives and declaring they would fight to the last drop of blood for final control. With the last drop still largely intact, they retreated to lick their wounds.

If they were losing ground in Syria, the Islamic Caliphate in tandem with other Salafist organizations was successfully launching jihad on a different level in Europe. In the days ahead, this was destined to grow exponentially, releasing a reign of terror on an unsuspecting world. Paradoxically even as five of the seventeen victims of the attacks on Paris were laid to rest, the French President vowed to protect the Muslim community.

"It is Muslims who are the main victims of fanaticism, fundamentalism, and intolerance," he declared, adding that the whole country was united in the face of terrorism. Strangely the anomaly seemed to pass most people by—how could Muslims be the main *victims* of terror, when they were quite obviously the main perpetrators? The pigs were leading the rest of the farm animals into deeper and deeper confusion—it was Animal Farm all over again!

Lex wrote furiously over this period. He was appalled by reports of the Islamic jihadist militia, Boko Haram, running rampant in

Nigeria. Days later the rampage spilled over into Cameroon as the militia captured slaves, including many children, before melting back into their own shadowy world. Europe was focused in on itself and even African countries reported the Paris attack on Charlie Hebdo in greater detail than the atrocities perpetrated on the African Continent in the name of the Prophet. There seemed to be an increasing helplessness or unwillingness on the part of the authorities to act against these groups.

"The world has begun to believe the Islamic lie," Lex wrote, "They are starting to accept the Muslims' credo—we have a right to kill those who criticize us, to behead or crucify Christians because they are of a different faith; we have a right to kill every Jew because the Qur'an sanctions it! The West is being held to ransom. Islamic jihadists are not invincible, we do not have to bend over backwards to refrain from offence. Offence is not given as much as it is received."

As he re-read the words he knew he was angry. Angry about the Salafist sleeper cells that were springing up throughout Europe and the United States, undermining the lifestyle and safety of those, like his own family, who had nothing against Muslims as people, but everything against the imposition of the laws of another faith upon their lives.

He was angry about the book-burning that was taking place touted as a "purification of the earth" plunging the Middle East back into the Middle Ages and threatening to do the same to Europe and America. He was angry most of all at the politicians, the religious elect, and the educators, who proclaimed, in the face of violence and intimidation, the innocence of Islam, the religion of peace.

Around this time, an attack by ISIS against Saudi Arabia killed three border guards including General Oudah al-Belawi, commander of the border operations in Saudi's northern zone.

First Deputy, Prince Salman's breath hissed between his teeth when he received the news.

"A breach of that nature means only one thing!"

The Second Deputy nodded, "An inside job."

"Exactly! How else could they know he would be there?" Not for the first time, Salman voiced the concern they had had from the beginning. The fence could possibly contain an insurgency, but what use was it if the enemy was within the borders?

On 23 January 2015, King Abdullah died. Pictures online showed robed men gathered around a grave, austere against the bare desert sand, piled high with white stone and marked at either end by simple cement headstones.

"I'm told he did a lot to improve the rights of women in Saudi," Lex commented.

Moussa scowled. "Four of his daughters have been held under house arrest for the last thirteen years," he said. "In my opinion, that gives a clearer indication of his entrenched views on the subject of women's rights."

Raif glanced at him in surprise. "Why? What did they do?"

"Abdullah divorced one of his wives, Alanoud AlFayez, the mother of the girls," he answered. "Incarceration may have been to prevent them from following her to the West. I'm not sure."

"So, do you think the new king let them go, *Baba*?" Raif asked.

"I heard that Alanoud pleaded with Barack Obama to bring his influence to bear on Crown Prince Salman to release them," Moussa replied. "Obama seems to avoid any form of what he sees as interference in Saudi affairs. My bet is that they will stay exactly where they are."

Lex set his beer down on the table and gazed out over the harbour below. The three men were seated on the terrace of Moussa's apartment. It was a quiet Sunday afternoon and the women had gone off to the shops on some pursuit of their own leaving the men to 'babysit'. In the lounge behind them, Layla was happily stretched out on the couch watching the Lion King. She had seen it so often that she could quote screeds of dialogue verbatim, but familiarity did not seem to diminish her enjoyment of the movie.

"Is the West in Syria because of Assad, or because of Saudi Arabia?"

Father and son glanced at one another before Moussa answered. "Good question," he replied. "It could be a bit of each. As allies of Saudi, America doesn't support the Shiites. They've wanted the Syrian regime out for a long time. But with the threat against Saudi Arabia, there has been more activity from the U.S. in Syria. It could be intended to draw the militia's attention away from Saudi."

"There's something I heard while I was in Raqqa," Raif said thoughtfully. "We know that Obama has a Muslim background," they nodded. "It was said that he is *'Sayed'*."

Moussa whistled between his teeth and muttered something in Arabic.

Lex looked at Raif blankly, "What does it mean?"

"It's a title they use before the name of the Prophet Muhammad," Moussa replied. "It denotes the honour they bestow on his name. By calling the American President *Sayed,* they are saying he is a direct descendent of the Prophet!"

Lex laughed. "That throws a new complexion on things. Perhaps he's out to establish a Caliphate of his own!"

Moussa returned his glance more soberly. "If he is accepted by Islam as a descendent of Muhammad, you can be sure he's been planted into America for some reason," he replied. "There are a lot of questions about Obama that no one has been able to answer satisfactorily. Already his meddling in the Middle East has intensified the crisis."

"Against Israel's better judgment, America's in peace talks with Iran as well," Lex said. "So they're playing both sides. The Iranians want sanctions lifted and the U.S. wants control over their nuclear program."

"I'm inclined to think Israel is right to be worried about the Iran deal," Raif replied. "No Muslim is required to be truthful to an unbeliever. They will say what is necessary for their own purposes and have no problem doing the opposite once they have what they want."

* * *

They ran into one another at the art gallery in Malaga. Rain had fallen overnight adding a gloss to the flared pattern of the brown cobble-stoned street. It reflected the red of the traffic lights and painted a suggestion of the black overcoat of the man crossing to the gallery side. Trees were shedding droplets onto the pavements under the hint of a breeze but the skies were still grey and sullen with cloud.

Amal stopped in her tracks but it was too late to pretend she had not seen him. Blood rose to her face and her heart began to pound.

It was weeks since their meeting in the restaurant and they had both gone out of their way to avoid any further contact. Juan had made several attempts at writing to her but all had ended in the waste-paper basket. No words had seemed adequate, in his opinion, to correct the misunderstandings that had arisen between them.

"Amal!"

"Hello, Juan."

"Were you going to the gallery?"

She nodded. "My father has a new exhibition."

"I know. I was coming to take a look myself. Let's go in, it's cold out here."

He stood back for her to enter the narrow door off the street. The gallery was not very large; it consisted of two rooms and Moussa's black-framed photographs were displayed in stark relief against the white walls. A second artist, a local sculptor, had metal pieces set on white plinths and the whole effect was hard-edged but pleasing to the eye. The gallery was heated and they slipped off their coats and hung them on pegs at the entrance. Amal was profoundly aware of Juan's presence as they walked around the room gazing at the exhibits. He was so tall; she felt diminutive next to him. She passed comment on what she knew of some of the prints, the techniques her father used to soften landscapes, and the way he overlaid multiple shots of a scene to blur and feather a row of trees.

Juan stopped before a portrait of Amal, head bent to one side, hair loose over her shoulder and those eyes like dark pools. The image was at once mysterious and captivating. Yet again, he was struck by the sense of innocence inherent in the expression; there was no guile, no sexual allure to her beauty. Later Juan would say, faced with this portrait, he knew without a doubt that he loved Amal, but he still struggled with the sting of her last words to him at the restaurant: *Western men don't appeal to me at all, your values are different to ours.*

Juan stood there without speaking; Amal glanced in confusion at his closed expression and then turned away to stare sightlessly at a piece of sculpture. Juan joined her after a moment and spoke lightly.

"Your father is very talented, Amal."

They moved on, saying little, aware of the unspoken tension between them that neither of them knew how to bridge. As they completed their tour of both rooms, they nodded to the gallery owner, collected their coats and Juan took Amal's elbow. It was a small, protective gesture as they stepped out into the icy chill of the street.

"Do you have time for a coffee?"

"I don't, sorry. I have an appointment at ten-thirty."

His face conveyed nothing. He simply nodded and they parted ways. Amal was not surprised to feel a deep pang of disappointment as she walked towards her car. She could have made a simple call and postponed her hair appointment, but it was too late now. Glancing back, there was no sign of him.

Chapter 39   Betrayal

"You will pay the price as you walk on your streets, turning right and left, fearing the Muslims. We will conquer your Rome, break your crosses, and enslave your women, by permission of Allah."
Jihadist video—threat against Italy.

"France is the mother of terrorism. America is the mother of terrorism." Fists were raised and pumped the air; the chanting grew more heated. "France is the mother of terrorism. America is the mother of terrorism."
Black flags fluttered passively over the frenzied heads of the West Bank demonstrators. The Charlie Hebdo cartoons of the Prophet were still causing a backlash. In Islamic terms, the deaths of the cartoonists, and even the French Jews, who were killed for no particular reason, were justified. Hatred against the West was mounting as the victims were made responsible for their slaughter. Israel was to blame, the West was to blame, and it was their idols, *their* freedoms that had forced the righteous hand of Islam. In the malls of Europe and America, in the cinemas and the businesses, in the sports stadia, and the nightclubs, people continued blissfully unaware that a fuse was lit. It was a matter of time before the explosion, just a matter of time.

Raif made his first report to Dr. Ibrahim. He launched into well-rehearsed detail about how he was influencing the villagers.
"My employer is very interested in hearing about Islam," he said. "He and his family have always supported immigration to Spain."
"Unusual for the middle class," Ibrahim commented.
"Because there have been so many accidents in the crossings from North Africa, he's sympathetic to the boat people. As he said, many people never make it, and when they do they are not well-received. Not everyone is comfortable with the situation."
The doctor tugged at an ear. "What did you tell him?"

"I agreed with him and pointed out that these people come to Spain because it was once their home. Many people come in from Libya, for example, because they see Malaga as a safe-haven after all they have suffered."

Ibrahim listened attentively, occasionally nodding. His eyes remained slightly hooded as though he was reserving judgment; his mouth a thin line, partially hidden within his dark beard.

"You reminded him of our history."

"I did."

Doctor Ibrahim smiled thinly, "Have you had the opportunity to speak to others?"

Raif nodded without hesitation. "I make it a habit of going for a morning coffee to Julio's bar before work. That way I get to know more of the local villagers. There have been conversations since the Charlie Hebdo attack. Of course, they know I am from the Middle East and, at first, they were hostile. I have spoken about the sanctity of Islam. They are Catholics; they understand that religion cannot be treated with contempt."

"The men that attacked those cartoonists were martyrs!" The doctor said sharply. "The blasphemers deserved to die. The West will discover that blasphemy means death in our language." Raif wondered at the change in slant, on his last visit the doctor had been certain that Israel was behind the attack.

Ibrahim's face was bloodless, his eyes narrowed and he tugged at his beard. "Freedom of speech!" he spat contemptuously. "They call it freedom to draw cartoons of our beloved Prophet, bless his name. Their kind must die like dogs! We will slaughter them without mercy and let their blood run in the gutters."

He knew he should express his agreement, but the level of Ibrahim's venom caused Raif to retreat into silence. The doctor composed himself and inhaled deeply before grinding out his next question.

"And where are you and your wife living at present?"

"In the hills above the town. We have found a room there with some people." He kept it deliberately vague.

"Have you had an opportunity to speak to them also?"

"Unfortunately not. I don't see much of my landlord." Raif lied.

"I will need names and addresses," the doctor was not to be fobbed off.

Raif's heart sank but he remained outwardly composed. "I will get them for you. I'm afraid I never asked."

"Make sure you bring them next time," Ibrahim rejoined curtly.

"Of course."

Raif sensed the interview was at an end and he stood up to take his leave. It was dark in the office and as he stepped out into the sunlight, he reached into his top pocket for his sunglasses. He would make certain he and Nour found another place to stay before his next appointment. He could not allow anything regarding the Wesley-Smiths to fall into the hands of the good doctor.

Doctor Ibrahim pressed the buzzer on his desk and a young man, dressed in a pale blue Islamic robe and white skull cap answered the call. His face bore a youthful innocence that he had attempted to disguise under a thin growth of immature whiskers. Large liquid eyes were fringed with long dark lashes and black hair fell in natural waves over his forehead in stark contrast with a flawless milk-coffee complexion.

"Ahmed, do we have any of our people in Frigiliana?"

He thought for a moment. "I think there are two families," he replied. "I would need to check."

"Do that. I don't trust Raif Ahmadi. I have a feeling he is playing games with us. I need someone to watch him."

Ahmed nodded. "I understand. It should be a simple matter. The village is quite small. Do you want one of our men to befriend him?"

Doctor Ibrahim thought for a moment and then nodded. "If he's hiding things from me, he is not likely to confide in anyone else in a hurry, but let's try to reach him on a human level first. Tell whoever does it to be discreet. I don't want him to suspect anything."

"What are we looking for?"

"I'm not entirely certain. He can start by finding out where he is living, and who he speaks to in the village. We'll work from there."

"Raif, what do you mean, we must leave? You said we would stay until after my operation!"

"I know, *habibti,* but we're overstaying our welcome here. It's time to move on."

"There's never been any indication…" her voice trailed off. "Raif, you're lying to me! What has happened?"

He sighed. "They're trying to find me. You know these people. They don't give up easily."

Nour's face blanched. "You've seen someone from Islamic State and you haven't told me!"

He could not bear to look at the accusation in her face. "They sent a man into the village to look for me. If they find out where we are staying it may endanger you and the Wesley-Smiths'."

"You had no right to keep it from me! I'm your wife, Raif. If you start hiding things now it will escalate and eventually, there won't be a marriage anymore." She gripped his arm. "Raif, listen to me. You're not protecting me by keeping things to yourself; you're destroying our ability to work together. Do we have a partnership or not?"

He looked away from her. "Of course we do, Nour. I just want to keep us all out of trouble."

"Where do you want to go?"

"I thought we could move closer to the coast. I'm sure Amal would be happy to help you after the op. Eugenia is back at university anyway, and we couldn't expect her to take time off."

"I'm sure I'll manage. It's not likely to be any more difficult than it has been. But what about your job, Raif? It won't make sense to commute to Frigiliana every day and jobs are hard to come by in Spain at the moment."

"I'll start looking. There's sure to be something. In the meantime, I'll hold on to what I've got."

Many more questions nagged at Nour's mind. The sense of freedom she had felt on leaving Syria had been snatched from her and that nauseating sensation in the pit of her stomach had returned. She felt like a trapped animal. Would they ever manage to break free from the clutches of the Islamic State?

* * *

Lex ran into his friend Sandy Williams at the Malaga vegetable market.

"Sandy, I've been intending to call you to make a definite time for a get-together. Do you have time for a beer?"

"Always! I just have to pick up a couple of things for Leslie. We have people coming round this evening."

"I've been running errands for the wife myself," Lex said. "How about we meet at that bar across the road—you know the one?"

"Sure, see you there in half an hour."

Lex took his loaded basket to the car and walked back to the tapas bar. It was a popular venue for market-goers, somewhat dingy after the bright sunlight on the street, but warm and welcoming. The man behind the counter wore a black tee shirt with the sleeves deliberately rolled-up to display upper arms the size of the smoked hams which hung from the beams over his head. Lex ordered a platter of chopped meat and a couple of beers and found a corner table.

Sandy arrived moments later and stood silhouetted in the doorway, his eyes raking the tables in search of his friend. Lex waved a greeting and he wound his way between the tables, set the heavy bags of vegetables against the wall, and drew up a chair.

"So," he said. "This is a pleasant surprise! How are you and Adriana?"

"No complaints," Lex returned.

"And research on your book?"

"Going well."

The two men sipped their beers and compared notes on their children before Lex got to the point.

"I have a chap staying at my place who is expressing an interest in Christian stuff. I can't answer him but I wondered if you and Les could come and chat to him sometime."

"Sure, no problem. Who is this guy?"

"Raif Ahmadi. He and his wife are from Syria."

"Syria. Are they Muslims?"

Lex nodded. "He's been reading the Qur'an and found that it says a lot about Jesus. He's interested and wants to know more."

"Whoa, I don't know about that!" Sandy said holding up both hands in protest. "I don't think I'd be prepared to speak to a Muslim."

"Look, Raif's a nice guy," Lex said, surprised. "He's just interested. Anyway, I thought you guys liked talking about your religion!"

"Sure, we do," Sandy said uncomfortably. He took a long sip of his beer and picked up a cube of ham between finger and thumb. "But these days you have to be careful. Muslims get upset if they think you're trying to change them. I reckon it's not safe to get involved."

Lex raked his fingers through his hair. "I didn't take you for an Islamophobe," he said.

Sandy's laugh was uneasy. "No, don't get me wrong, I'm not. Just let's say I'm cautious. There's this case right now in Bremen, Germany, where a Protestant pastor preached that Christ is the only way to heaven. I mean this is Christianity—it's what we believe. But now, he's been accused of disparaging other faiths—intellectual arson, they called it. He's likely to face prosecution for preaching the Gospel."

"That's rough," Lex said, surprised. "I know there's a bit of a backlash against fundamentalist Christianity, but surely if he's preaching in church…"

Sandy shook his head. "There's this nervousness surrounding Islam. You can't put a step wrong. If you tell a congregation that Jesus is the only way to eternal life, you're told it is inciting others to violence. Speaking about Christianity is becoming dangerous. This Raif guy might be harmless or he might not. I'm just not ready to lose my head yet; I've got a growing family to worry about."

Lex placed his glass down on the coaster covering a typical postcard shot of the fort as he did so.

"What about this United Nations incentive to bring religions together?" he asked. "The pope seems to be endorsing it. That makes sense to me—religion has never brought peace to the world."

"United Religions Initiative? Yeah. It is the sort of thing the pope would go for," Sandy said. He traced a finger through the fine beads of liquid on the outside of his glass before setting it down on the table.

"You don't like the idea?"

Sandy shrugged. "Look, these things appear great from the outside," he replied. "There's a lot of enthusiastic, well-meaning people involved, but somehow I don't think God is."

Lex laughed. "What do you mean? They're believers. Do you think they left God out of the equation?"

Sandy pursed his lips and nodded. "I can see why people are attracted to anything that might propagate peace," he replied. "But notice something here, the stronger these movements get, the more

Christians and Jews are facing flack. What I see is a wave of persecution coming, not peace."

"But if all you Christians joined this UR initiative, surely it would begin to change things?"

Sandy was silent for several moments while he considered how to answer his friend. Lex was not a believer and Sandy had never been entirely comfortable in laying down the cold facts to someone that might find them offensive.

"I have to start and finish with what the Bible says," he said at length. "Firstly, Christianity by its very nature is exclusive, not inclusive. That doesn't mean it's like some sort of exclusive club with limited membership. Jesus Christ died for all sinners—that means none of us are excluded from the sacrifice he made. But many choose to exclude themselves."

Lex nodded. "Sure, I understand that," he said. "I'm quite content to be an outsider, I always have been."

"What it adds up to then, is the exclusive claim Jesus makes about himself. He says he is the way, the truth and the life and that no one comes to the Father except by him."

Lex shrugged irritably. "I can see why it gets people's back up!"

"There are many claiming to be Christians, Lex, but few who will choose to do things God's way. Plenty will follow a humanistic path."

"And in your opinion, this new initiative is anti-Christian!"

Sandy grinned. "This will raise your hackles even further," he declared. "It's prophesied that there will be a world church just like this United Religions movement. There is no way that I would get involved. I know you're familiar with that parallel initiative from the UN, the concept of a New World Order."

"Sure."

"Whether we connect the dots or not, what they are proposing is socialism, pure and simple! The Commies were behind the UN from the get-go. Just look at what's happening worldwide and tell me it's not Communist tactics we are staring in the face."

Lex surveyed his friend thoughtfully as he took another sip of his beer. What Sandy was saying came as no surprise, it merely confirmed what Lex had been noting for years; nothing had changed. The unions, the workers, and the universities were simply confirming by their words and action that Communism was advancing its ideologies all the more swiftly and successfully since they had persuaded that the world that it was dead.

He nodded. "Are you telling me that Islam is working hand in hand with Communism?" he asked sceptically. "The two are at total odds with one another."

"I doubt that they are knowingly doing anything of the sort," he agreed. "But I think there has been manipulation of world events and of the masses; it's possible they are being used. The culmination of these societal changes can only come about through some sort of catastrophe. Under normal circumstances, the world would never accept world government under a single leader."

"In other words, a man-made catastrophe?"

"Exactly!"

Lex appeared sceptical, "Enter the Antichrist?"

"Megalomaniacs have attempted it in the past. This time I reckon the nations have been well prepared."

"And you believe trouble is coming?"

"It's already here," Sandy said quietly. "Look, tell your friend, Raif, is it? Tell him to read the Bible. Perhaps you could get him a New Testament at the bookshop down the road? Then if he's still keen, I'll take a chance and meet with him. I can't avoid trouble forever. The time's coming when we will all have to decide what team we're batting on." He stood up and retrieved his packages. "Thanks for the chat, Lex. Keep an eye on things that are happening. Oh, and what you said about the pope was interesting. Don't be fooled by this present guy's lamb-like appearance. I'm certain he has a major role to play in the coming events. A major role!"

Chapter 40   Betrayal

"They chopped children in half. They chopped heads off. How do you respond to that? That is what we have been going through. That is what we are going through." The Reverend Cannon, Andrew White, Vicar of Baghdad.

"They were staying with the Wesley-Smiths up on the hill." Francisco, the proprietor, took a pile of printed leaflets off the counter and slipped them into a plastic bag. "They've moved."

"So Raif has left?"

"No, no. Just taken a few days off to get settled. He'll be back on Monday."

"So where are they living now?"

Francisco waved vaguely. "I'm not sure, closer to Malaga, I think."

Saleh Hassan smiled as he took the packet. "I am sure you are pleased to have the help. It can't be easy running the business on your own."

"You would know, Saleh. You've had that battle since the death of your wife."

"My daughter is growing. She is a great help already."

"She's a nice young girl. How old is she now?"

"Fourteen, almost fifteen years. It has not been easy for her without a mother, but she is coping." He set thirty euros down on the counter; Francisco rang up the correct amount on the till and handed him the change.

"Thank you for your business, Saleh."

Saleh Hassan wished him a good day and the doorbell jangled as he left. Francisco scratched his head as he went into the print room at the back of the shop. So far as he could remember Saleh Hassan had not been in for prints since Raif started work. He was not the only Middle Eastern man who had questioned him about Raif either.

There was that bearded chap, a stranger to the village, who had been in and asked questions some time back. But Saleh could have met Raif anywhere locally, he supposed. They were, after all, both foreign.

"Someone in the village was asking after you on Thursday," Francisco said when he and Raif had an early morning cup of coffee together. "It reminded me that I should have mentioned another visitor some time back, it just slipped my mind at the time."

"A man?"

"Yes, a bearded guy. Foreign like you."

Raif nodded. "Someone else mentioned it. A friend from Malaga, I went down to see him."

"Ah yes. No problem then?"

"None at all. Who was this other guy?"

"A local, Saleh Hassan. He asked if you had left. You've obviously met."

"Saleh Hassan," Raif repeated slowly. "No, I don't think so. Does he live here?"

"He owns the vegetable shop on the other side of the hill, there." He pointed up the road. "You may have seen it."

Raif hesitated and shook his head. "I'm sure word gets around. There aren't too many people from our part of the world in Frigiliana. Did he say anything else?"

"Not really," Francisco said slowly. "He just asked where you were living now."

"Oh?"

"I have no idea, of course. But you'll get to see him anyway," Francisco said cheerfully. "He has another lot of advertising pamphlets that he wants us to print. They're in the back."

"I'll get on with them then," Raif said. "When will he be in?"

"Sometime on Wednesday. He's possibly going to bring in quite a bit of business in the next few weeks. There's a mosque he belongs to that is just starting out. It's all in Arabic, of course, so I've no idea what it's about."

Raif rinsed his mug and set it down on the draining board.

"How many copies does he need?"

"A hundred."

Raif made a mental note to tell no one in the village where he and Nour were living. He picked up the notice written in bold Arabic script. It was an announcement of the opening of a mosque in a neighbouring village on the last Friday in February. An imam from Barcelona would be present to bring the first sermon and all were encouraged to attend. Raif recognised his name as one who was highly esteemed in Islamic circles. It would not be a moderate message, of that he was certain, and if this Saleh Hassan had asked for him by name, it meant he would receive an invitation to attend. He grimaced. The whole thing remained ridiculously complicated. All he wanted now was to be left alone so that he and Nour could get on with their lives; it seemed it was not to be.

Lex came into the shop in the afternoon to find out how the move had gone. They chatted for a few minutes about the two-roomed cottage Raif had found closer to Nerja.

"We're sorry to have left you," Raif said. "Nour won't forgive me in a hurry, she loved your place."

They walked outside and stood in a patch of weak wintery sunlight on the pavement.

"Why did you leave," Lex pressed. "Was it just to find something bigger?"

"Not entirely." Raif looked at him directly and lowered his voice. "I owe it to you to be honest," he said. "People have been looking for me and I didn't want anyone to connect me to your family. You understand?"

"Are you in trouble?"

"No, not at the moment," Raif replied quietly. "But it's not easy to step away from this organisation. They want their pound of flesh."

"Be careful, Raif. We don't want anything to happen to you and Nour."

Raif smiled gratefully, "Thanks, Lex. You will need to take care as well. That book of yours could lead to reprisals."

Lex nodded. "I know. I've given it a lot of thought, of course, and I don't want to endanger the family but I feel that the word needs to get out. People, governments especially, seem to be on a suicidal path. It's almost a deliberate blindness that causes them to deny what's right under their noses. Oh, by the way, I've got something for you." He put a hand into the top pocket of his jacket and pulled out a brown paper packet. "I spoke to that friend of mine, Sandy."

"The Christian?"

"Yes. He said this was a good place to start, and if you were still keen he would get together with you."

"What is it?"

"A New Testament. He suggested you start at the beginning and work your way through."

Raif raised his eyebrows. A New Testament—a Bible! Under the Islamic State just reading it would bring the death penalty, no questions asked. He took it gingerly and thanked Lex. Back in the shop he took the little book with its dark blue cover from the packet and turned it over in his hands. It was frightening to be in possession of such contraband but he was curious to see what made it blasphemous in the eyes of the imams. He wondered what Nour's reaction would be, or if she would even allow it in their home. At present, it would be safer to hide it at work and read it during his lunch break. He slipped the packet into the back of the filing cabinet. It would be safe enough there.

Francisco was out of the shop when Saleh Hassan returned on Wednesday morning and Raif greeted him as he arrived. Although he was dressed in slacks, a tee shirt, and sandals, his features were instantly recognisable as Middle Eastern. He was swarthier in skin colour than the average Spaniard, with thick dark hair that had begun to grey over the temples. His brows formed a dramatic sweep over eyes set back into sockets darkly smudged as though bruised. The mouth was sensual, heavy lips thinly disguised by an untrimmed moustache, and several days' growth of beard gave his face an unwashed appearance. He brought a pungent scent with him of some liberally-applied cologne.

"Marhabba."

Raif's smile was cautious as he returned the greeting.

"I'm here to collect my pamphlets."

"Mr. Hassan. Yes, they are ready." Raif passed the plastic carrier bag across the counter. Hassan removed one of the leaflets and scrutinised it.

"Fine, fine. Let me give you one of these so that you will not forget to take this opportunity to visit us," he said and passed the copy back across the counter.

"Thank you," Raif said. "My wife is about to have an operation to her leg. But, *insh'Allah*, I will be there." He reverted automatically to the almost superstitious use of 'if God wills' and instantly despised himself. He had no intention of invoking anyone's will and knew he would not be attending the meeting.

"Where are you from?" Hassan asked, "Syria?"

Raif nodded. "Damascus."

"I am from Iraq, Baghdad. Perhaps you will come and drink Arabic coffee with me at my shop. You know where it is?"

Raif thanked him for the offer and took the money for the leaflets. "I wish you well for the opening," he said politely.

"There will be a further need for printing," Saleh Hassan replied. "We have still to set up our computers and buy printing machines. It will take time."

"We are glad of your business."

"So come to the shop on Friday after mosque. We will talk of home."

Raif shook his head. "Thank you, but I will be working. Francisco is not a Muslim; I must keep to office hours."

Hassan's expression clouded. "So, what is this I am hearing? You don't go to mosque?"

"I have attended in Malaga," Raif rejoined truthfully, although without mentioning that the last time was before his trip to Syria.

Mollified, Saleh Hassan took his leave. The scent that accompanied his visit lingered on for some time after that, as did Raif's sense of unease.

Chapter 41   Betrayal

Nour spent the night before her operation in the hospital, an ordeal she faced with a mixture of trepidation and relief. Raif, Moussa, and Amal came for the visiting hour and presented her with a huge vase of flowers. The orthopaedic surgeon dropped by in the evening and introduced her to the anaesthetist, questions were asked and x-rays were examined.

After everyone had left, Nour lay in the hospital bed listening to the foreign sounds, the rattle of trolleys, the sharp click of the nurses' shoes on the tiled floor, and the rattle of bedpans. The deep regular breathing and soft snores of those who shared the ward with her, were broken now and then by a sudden cry or moan; unfamiliar sounds that snatched away from Nour any possibility of sleep. Late in the night, from the nurses' station across the passage, she detected the clink of cups and an occasional muted burst of laughter. In these surroundings, she felt more alienated and alone than at any time since her father and mother had been snatched from her.

It was a Catholic hospital and light from the street that spilled over onto the wall opposite illuminated a crucifix that hung above the bed. Nour tried desperately to avoid looking at the lifeless body hanging from that cross; it brought back vivid images of the suffering of those Syrians who had died that way. She had seen some of the bodies slumped on makeshift crosses in the centre square of Raqqa, their bodies coated in dried blood, flies gorging themselves at their eyes and slack mouths. It seemed grotesque to worship such a hideous symbol of death.

Why crucifixion, she wondered? Did the militias use it as a mockery of Christianity, or was there something else behind the bizarre use of a cross on which to cause a human being to suffer and die?

They wheeled her into the operating theatre at 8.30 the following morning. Nour lay on the operating table as they set up the screen between her upper and lower body and administered the spinal block. It was icy cold in the theatre and Nour shivered uncontrollably in her thin hospital gown. In a surreal moment she saw her leg supported by the surgeon's hand, rise above the screen; it was devoid of all sensation, as though it belonged to someone else's body. A second surgeon had joined the first and they conversed quietly between themselves. At the last moment, when all preparation was completed, they tucked a heated blanket around Nour's upper torso. A Catholic sister sat beside her and held her hand until the shivering stopped and she began to relax. Despite the lack of sleep, Nour had refused the offer of morphine and her mind felt exceptionally clear.

"So where are you from, darling?" the sister asked.

"Raqqa in Syria."

"And were you hurt in the fighting there?"

Nour answered the questions obediently, avoiding any mention of the death of her parents in the bombing. The memory was still too raw to share with strangers. She had a question of her own that must be asked.

"People in Syria are being crucified," she blurted out when there was a lull in the conversation. "Why a cross? Why did they crucify him?"

The nun looked surprised and she hesitated for a moment before answering. "It's like this," she said at length. "Jesus hung there as a link between heaven and earth, but his arms reached out to all mankind."

Nour was silent for a moment. The nun's words had a compelling effect on her.

"What kind of God allows himself to die in such a horrifying way," she asked more quietly.

This time there was no hesitation in the nun's reply. "A compassionate God," she said. "One who is prepared to share in our suffering."

Nour closed her eyes and retreated into silence. A God who reached out his arms to mankind: a God who shared in people's sufferings. This God, Jesus, sounded so intensely personal. But the Qur'an made it clear that God has no son. She had heard that those words were written three times around the Dome of the Rock in Jerusalem—Do not say that God has a son.

The sister remained beside her, respecting Nour's need for silence.

Some time later Nour opened her eyes again. "Why," she asked. "What was the point? Couldn't he have removed the world's sufferings if he was God?"

The older woman thought deeply before she replied. "Do you remember that mine disaster somewhere in South America?" she said at length. "Many miners were trapped for more than two months, two thousand feet underground. They managed to drill down to the men eventually and messages were sent back and forth. Then one brave soul was lowered down into the shaft at great risk and he brought the miners out one at a time." She tucked a strand of grey hair back under her starched white head covering as she spoke. "Jesus chose the same method. He couldn't just give a blanket pardon to people who didn't care anyway. Instead, he chose to rescue those who understood there was a cost to our wickedness—a price paid in blood to draw us back to our Father."

For a long time, Nour lay, oblivious to the work being done on her leg, and contemplated the nun's words in silence. Her father was gone forever; all she had left of him were memories. Could it be true that Jesus had paid a price in blood to draw her back to a heavenly Father, so much so, that he sent his Son to the rescue?

At length, the orthopaedic surgeon stood to his feet stretching his arms above his head to ease the cramped muscles.

"We are all done," he said. "Your knee is looking good, Nour, we've done a full replacement and removed some broken pieces of bone that must have been giving you trouble. In time you should be able to bend the knee again."

"Not straight away?"

"You will need some physio. It will take a bit of work to get it moving but it shouldn't take too long."

The screen was taken down and Nour was wheeled into a recovery area before returning to the ward. As the anaesthetic wore off, the old familiar pain returned. The agony of the early injury had faded into a blur until now. This time, there was adequate medication and when the pain was at its most excruciating, relief was at hand. Now, when Nour's gaze strayed to the inert figure on the crucifix, she felt

His presence with her. He was a God of compassion and He knew her sufferings. Her pain was nothing in comparison with His.

In the weeks after returning home, Nour began to see progress in her recovery. The knee was still excruciatingly painful at times but, with the physiotherapy twice a week, the joint was moving and Nour was learning to put weight on the leg again. Whenever she was home from university, Eugenia dropped in to see how she was progressing, and she and Amal took her out one morning to a restaurant overlooking the sea.

It was still too cold to sit on the terrace, but there were magnificent views through the glass sliding doors to where the weak midday sun turned the shallows translucent and the deeps, cyan. White-tipped swells, stark against the aquamarine, lifted and rolled under a sharp breeze.

It was her first real outing, and Nour felt her spirits lift. They ordered a garlicky bean soup, followed, for Nour's sake, "She has to taste it!" with paella Valenciana.

"Sam arrived yesterday just in time for lunch," Eugenia said with a smile that covered some heavy sarcasm.

"I feel sorry for him," Nour replied.

"Why?" Both girls looked amazed.

"Well, he's obviously from a poor family."

Eugenia burst out laughing. "What makes you think so?"

"Well," Nour looked embarrassed, not certain why her observation had caused such merriment, "his clothes. They must be handed down to him by someone much larger. And he's always so hungry," she went on weakly knowing by their expressions that she had somehow blundered, "which must be why he always arrives at meal times."

Eugenia doubled over with laughter and Amal fought unsuccessfully to control her mirth.

"What have I said?" Nour asked. "What is so funny?"

Amal explained in Arabic that the clothes were Sam's own and probably very expensive. "It's a skateboarding thing—American fashion."

Nour looked from one to another, her mouth twitched and she laughed with them. "And I suppose he's not half-starved either?"

Eugenia pursed her lips, "No," she returned. "His mother is a great cook. He practically grew up with Juan and thinks of himself as part of our family."

"Well, I've wasted a lot of sympathy on him," Nour retorted. "I hope he appreciates it!"

Her indignant response drew a fresh burst of laughter from the others.

"How is Juan?" Amal tried to sound nonchalant but neither Eugenia nor Nour were fooled.

Eugenia sighed and set her fork down on her plate. "I do wish you two would get together and resolve things," she said. "It's obvious how you feel about one another. He's fine. The job seems to be suiting him, and I do believe he's missing you."

"It's not that simple, Eugenia. There are big differences in our outlook and our background. I don't know if they could be overcome."

"It depends on your level of determination," Eugenia said. "If your feelings are deep enough you will find ways of dealing with the barriers."

Amal fell silent and toyed with the remains of her paella. Nour reached across the table and took her hand.

"You know my story," she said. "I didn't fight for Raif when my father wanted me to give him up. As a result, I entered into a disastrous marriage and almost lost your brother forever. Eugenia's right, Amal, barriers can be overcome." Amal squeezed her sister-in-law's hand and nodded.

"You're both right, of course. I miss him terribly. I just have no idea how to go from here."

Eugenia set her plate aside and called for the dessert menu.

"I'm going to celebrate Nour's first outing with an ice cream sundae. Who's going to join me?" Clearly, her brother and Amal were never going to deal with their issues unless they received a push. The time had come, Eugenia decided, to make things happen.

Chapter 42   Betrayal

"Islam is coming to take over Germany whether you want it or not! Your daughters will wear hijab" German Muslim.

'Fight them and Allah will punish them by your hands, cover them with shame, help you over them, heal the breasts of believers.' (Qur'an 9:14)

Western refusal to link Islamic terrorism to Islam was becoming increasingly bizarre and progressively more difficult to maintain with any dignity or logic. If the Qur'an said it and the deeds followed those scriptures faithfully, how were the acts of jihad perpetrated by 'terrorists' but not Islamists?

The murder of the Jordanian pilot, following so soon after the beheading of the Caliphate's two Japanese prisoners, plunged the Islamic State deeper into barbarity. A human being was broken and publically humiliated, caged like a beast, doused with petrol, and set alight. This depraved and hideous act, professionally filmed, was put out so that the world could view his death through social media, with the designation 'Healing the Believers' Chests.' (Qur'an 9:14)

In Saudi Arabia, the new king denounced the killing of the Jordanian pilot, saying it went against humanity and contradicted Islam. It was difficult to perceive how.

"Amal has taken Layla out for the afternoon," Moussa told Raif and Nour as they arrived. "There's a new children's movie showing. I can't sit through those things!"

They sat in the living room with sunshine pouring in from the terrace through the glass sliding doors. Nour's leg was propped up on a cushion; the most comfortable position for it since the operation. Moussa had brewed a pot of coffee and brought out a plate of Amal's biscuits.

"King Salman bin Abdulaziz condemned Islamic State's latest horror," he declared, "but I think the statement is hypocritical. The Saudis themselves still employ torture, public beheadings, floggings, and severing of limbs under Sharia law."

"They don't like ISIS," Raif commented. "They have every reason to feel threatened."

"Moaz al-Kassasbeh[34] was a Muslim," Nour said miserably. "We are Muslims. The Islamic State is not content with that, it wants to force us to be more Muslim than we are."

Her father-in-law smiled. "Exactly that, Nour. Jihadi Islam has embraced the essence of the Qur'an and is determined to inflict its radical message on the rest of the world. When they burnt this man they were saying to Jordan, if you don't take the Qu'ran in its entirety, we will impose it on you. Choose one way or another."

"Jordan gave its answer by taking to the air against ISIS," Nour said. "I was so proud when I saw the Jordanian Air Force make that fly-over of the dead pilot's house."

Moussa looked at his son. "Raif, what is *your* stand now?" he asked.

"You know, papa. I hate this brutality and I cannot be part of it."

"Have you cut all ties with these radicals?"

Raif avoided his glance. "You know I have, papa."

"Have they cut all ties with you?"

Nour glanced anxiously at her husband. "Have they, Raif? Please don't keep anything from us."

Raif stood up angrily and crossed the room to where the broad sweep of the Mediterranean Sea reflected the warm glow of sunlight in sequin-like sparkles off its deep blue robes.

"How long have we been back?" he demanded as he swung round to face them. "Have you seen me do anything out of line? What am I supposed to do to earn your trust—beg for it?"

Moussa looked quietly at his son and Raif bristled under his gaze. Nour felt an icy chill descend upon her heart. She looked down at the hands lying palm-up in her lap.

"You were lying to us, Raif," she said later as they walked to the car. "What are you trying to hide?"

---

[34] Slain Jordanian pilot

He glared at her. "What reason have I given you for distrust?" he snapped. "You and my father are making assumptions. Where do you come with the idea that I am hiding something? I explained why we needed to move. It was to avoid contact with the Islamic State. What more do you want me to say?"

Raif refused to be drawn into any further discussion on the subject and they drove home in silence. That night, in bed, he turned away from her for the first time in their marriage.

Nour trod carefully in the next few days wondering if she had misread Raif's response. Perhaps she had been wrong in judging him so readily. She made up for it in small ways knowing that his annoyance would blow over eventually, but she made up her mind not to say anything until she was certain an apology on her part was justified.

Raif sat in his car during his lunch breaks and began reading the forbidden New Testament that Lex had given him. Despite himself, he was fascinated by it. On Friday afternoon he unwrapped the packet of sandwiches Nour had prepared for him, opened the little book, and began to read the Gospel of John. What he saw shook him to the foundations.

"In the beginning was the Word, and the Word was with God and the Word was God.

The same was in the beginning with God. All things were made by him; and without him was not anything made that was made."

Raif sat gazing sightlessly out of the car window; Lex had been right and the Qur'an confirmed what the Bible said. Jesus was the Word, the Word was Creator, the Word became flesh—a human being. The Qur'an acknowledged this in part but what it did not say was that the Word was God!

Any further doubt was swept away when Raif remembered what the Qur'an itself said in Surah 10, Yunus, verse 94. It encouraged Muslims to look to the Jews and the Christians who read the *Torah* and the *Injil* (the Gospel) to confirm the Qur'an. Muhammad had believed in the veracity of the scriptures and even encouraged his followers to read them!

He was in the world, and the world was made by him, and the world knew him not.

He came unto his own and his own received him not. But to as many as received him, to them gave he power to become the sons of God, even to them that believe on his name.

Later, he used a quaint turn of phrase when he described the moment to Lex. "Suddenly, right there in the front seat of my car, I believed and felt the Son rise in my heart," he said.

Lex hid his embarrassment well at the time, but the young Syrian's sincerity shone through his face as though an inner light had been turned on. Lex put an arm around the young man's shoulders and gave him a brief hug.

"Our terrorist has been reborn," he said to Adriana and Eugenia later. "Strange thing; you can see it. He's a new man. It's just as if he has shed his past like an old garment."

Adriana smiled at his words and accused him of waxing lyrical but Eugenia was touched.

"I'm happy for him," she said. "If anyone needed to shed a burden, it was Raif. He always looked as though part of him was old –did you notice, papa? His eyes were dead. I think Raif has suffered so much shame and anguish because of what he has been through."

"He's totally messed up my story," was all Lex would say. But he uttered the words with a twinkle in his eye.

That same evening, when Raif returned home from work, he went through to the kitchen where Nour was preparing the evening meal. He slipped his arms around her waist and drew her to him.

"Can you switch off the stove for a minute," he asked. "There's something I need to tell you."

Nour looked up at her husband and read something in his eyes.

"Of course. Just give me a moment."

They went through to the little living room and he pulled her down next to him on the sofa.

"Firstly, I want to say sorry," he said. "Please forgive me, Nour. I have lied to you. I am in a difficult situation and I will need your advice to help me out of it."

She drew a sharp breath, "Raif! What has happened?"

He described the events of the past few weeks. The realisation that the Islamic State was on his trail and the options he had felt were open to him.

"As I said before, I had to protect you and the Wesley-Smiths," he said. "I couldn't see any other way to do it."

"But you are back in their drag-net!" Nour protested with tears in her eyes. "They won't allow you to simply walk away from them a second time."

He met her eyes and sighed. "You're right, Nour. We need to work together. We've shut one another off in the past few weeks."

She glanced up at him indignantly. "What do you mean? How have I shut you out?" When he did not immediately reply she averted her gaze and managed a little "Oh," before retreating into silence.

Raif reached out for his wife and drew her into his arms. "It's okay," he reassured her. "We've both messed up. I should have spoken to you as soon as I knew there was something wrong. You're a strong woman; you've proved that to me over and over again. I know we will be able to work this out together somehow. "

"But you've felt shut out too."

He nodded slowly. "You've gone through agony since your parents were killed; I've seen your struggle. But Nour, I need to share your load."

"And I haven't allowed you. I'm sorry, Raif." Tears flowed freely down her cheeks and she buried her head in the familiar hollow beneath his shoulder.

"We came back to Spain because this is where God wanted us to be," he said. "Now I must find out from Him how to get out of the mess I have got us into."

"God?" Nour looked at Raif in surprise. "What do you mean?"

"This may be even more difficult to explain than the lies and deception," he confessed. He dropped his hands, threw back his head, and looked at the ceiling. It was a make-or-break moment, literally. It was possible the revelation he was about to make would shatter their marriage and he had prayed hard that Nour would understand what he was about to say.

"Nour, I have been reading the *Injil*." She looked at him, stunned into silence. "I believe it," he said. "I believe it is true."

The blood drained from Nour's face. "I don't understand, Raif. What do you mean? You are a Muslim, how can you read that book?"

"I have asked God to reveal Himself to me," he said. "He has begun to do that, Nour."

She shook her head angrily. "No, Raif! What is this you are saying? I can't hear any more!" she pushed him away from her and ran to the bedroom slamming the door behind her.

Raif sat for many minutes in silence and then he dropped his head into his hands.

Chapter 43   Betrayal

'And I stood upon the sands of the sea, and saw a fourth beast rise up out of the sea, having seven heads and ten horns, and upon his horns ten crowns, and upon his heads the name of blasphemy. So he carried me away in the spirit into the wilderness: and I saw a woman sit upon a scarlet coloured beast, full of names of blasphemy, having seven heads and ten horns. And the woman was arrayed in purple and scarlet colour, and decked with gold and precious stones and pearls, having a golden cup in her hand full of abominations and filthiness of her fornication: and upon her forehead was a name written, MYSTERY, BABYLON THE GREAT, THE MOTHER OF HARLOTS AND ABOMINATIONS OF THE EARTH. And I saw the woman drunken with the blood of the saints and with the blood of the martyrs of Jesus: and when I saw her, I wondered with great admiration. And here is the mind that hath wisdom, The seven heads are seven mountains, on which the woman sitteth ...'
Revelation 13:1, Revelation 17:3-6,9

The graffiti on the Georgia Guidestones had set Lex off in an unplanned direction. He had a sense that there was a deliberate link between ISIS, the militia, and Isis, the goddess. Unveiling both, Lex decided, was something he wanted to achieve with this book. The goddess Isis was quoted in an inscription on the temple in Sais as saying, "I, Isis, am all that has been, that is or shall be; no mortal man hath ever me unveiled." That was not to say that no mortal man *would* never unveil her, and he, Lex, was up for the challenge.

It involved research and he began at the beginning. Isis was a member of the Ennead and part of the nine original Egyptian gods and goddesses from Heliopolis, the birthplace of the gods. She was best known as the wife and sister of Osiris and, after her husband's death, was usually depicted with a stepped crown representing the empty throne of Egypt. Occasionally, the goddess was shown wearing a headdress of cow horns enclosing a lunar orb and in this, she assimilated the bovine role of the deity Hathor.

Isis also appeared as a principle of the fruitfulness of nature among many ancient religions; she was goddess of the moon, magic, fertility, and healing, and was regarded as mother and protector of the Pharaohs. After the death of Osiris, she also took the role of goddess of the dead and funeral rites.

Adriana peered over Lex's shoulder as he sat at his computer.

"That's Stella Maris," she remarked in surprise. "Why the sudden interest in Catholic images?"

Lex swung round on his office chair and surveyed his wife in surprise. "It's not Catholic," he replied. "Stella Maris is Isis as she was adopted into the Roman pantheon. She was known as the Star of the Sea."

Adriana frowned. "It's Mary. Our Lady of the Sea."

"A lot of their roles seem to have mysteriously overlapped," he remarked cynically, "Isis was called Virgin of the world but she was said to have given birth to all things, including 'all those illuminated by the rays of the divine sun'."

"No one ever suggested that the Madonna gave birth to everything," Adriana answered imperiously.

"She gave birth to the divine Son," he returned. "Presumably that includes all those followers illuminated by Jesus."

Adriana stared at him. "What are you suggesting?"

Lex was not about to back down when he was on a winning streak. "Simply that the Catholic version of Mary is Isis in another of her many roles."

"*Usted está hablando absurdo!*[35]" she said, reverting to Spanish as she often did when annoyed.

"Well, we have the pope's Mother of Europe, adopted as the emblem on the flag of the European Union with the twelve stars around her head," Lex retorted. "Whether we are talking about Venus, Ceres, or Isis, the goddesses don't differ much from Catholicism's version of the Virgin Mary, Queen of Heaven and earth!"

---

[35] You are talking nonsense.

Adriana flounced out of the room at that moment, muttering something about having married a heathen.

In her maternal role, Isis was represented nursing the child, Horus. Parallels to the Madonna with the Christ child were obvious, especially as Roman Catholic images of Mary and Jesus had, in many instances, unashamedly adopted and renamed the pagan images of Isis and Horus.

What Lex had come to realise was that the goddess of a thousand epithets was one. Although she was represented in many aspects, ultimately she was worshipped universally as the Divine Reality, Queen of Heaven cloaked in the sun's rays and with twelve stars around her head. A serpent encircled the naked globe of the moon beneath her feet like the orbits of a spaceship caught in the gravitational pull of a dwarf planet.

* * *

King Salman Abdulaziz Al Saud, the new King of Saudi Arabia, paced the thick carpet in the ornate conference room of his palace. His face had developed an unhealthy pallor and he had developed an annoying tic below his left eye. Now and again he removed his spectacles and rubbed the eye in an attempt to dispel the irritation but its stubborn and relentless twitch, like an over-wound clock, continued to taunt.

"Hezbollah must go! We cannot trust them. They should never have been allowed a foothold in our country!"

Salman's deputies chose to remain silent. It was pointless to remind the king that he had played a major role in allowing in the advisors in the first place. "The Shia have never been trustworthy!" he expostulated. "Look what is happening. The more the Islamic State entrenches itself in the north, the more the Shia militants are consolidating their position in southern Iraq. They have seized Yemen. They are more dangerous, many times more, than ISIS." He mopped his brow, which was dripping with perspiration despite the air-conditioning.

"They are active, certainly," his Second Deputy noted cautiously, "but we must not allow the Shia too much credit, brother. Numerically, we all know the Sunni population is dominant throughout the Middle East."

The Shia militias, dubbed *al-hashad al-sha'abi*[36] by the Iraqi press, were backed and co-ordinated by the Iranians. They had moved to fill the vacuum created by the incompetence of the regular armed forces in Iraq under the increasing threat in the north from the Islamic Caliphate. There was a sense in the Middle East that a power that had lain almost dormant, like a snake in hibernation, was coming to life.

"It is their prophecies that worry me," Salman groaned. "They are empowered by their prophecies and what they see as the imminent return of the Mahdi."

The Second Deputy shot a furtive but meaningful glance in the direction of his older brother who was now positioned as the First Deputy to the new king. It was said that discussions around the Shia prophecies dominated the tea parties that took place in the women's quarters of the Saudi royal palaces, and that even the servants dared to whisper about such things in the corridors. In the Hijaz, King Fahd, the one with the name of an animal, was dead. King Abdullah who had taken the throne in his place had followed him to the grave; the prophecies had proved unsettlingly accurate. Next, it was said, there would be a period of turmoil in which no king would remain for long on the throne—and then the Al Mahdi, the Twelfth Imam of the Shiites, would return.

"We would be unwise to allow the superstitions of the Shiites to unsettle us, brother. We are building barriers against these militias and securing our borders. Other countries, including the United States, are looking at our installations with envy. They have nothing like our border control."

"They are not under the same threat as we are."

"Perhaps not, brother," the First Deputy said soothingly, "but we are well prepared for any eventuality and Hezbollah has encouraged the advanced training of our troops as well as our intelligence capabilities."

The king shook his head irritably, adamant that the militia must leave the country. "We can't allow the possibility of an uprising of the Shia militia within our borders," he said firmly. "For all we

---

[36] The popular mobilisation

know Hezbollah may already be working with them even now to overthrow our kingdom."

Chapter 44   Betrayal

Black cubes, symbolising the god, Saturn, were proliferating as sculptures throughout the globe, or so it appeared to Lex as he carried out an internet search. The goddess Isis who controlled the dark energies, and whose magical powers were said to exceed even those of Osiris, was represented by a black square. Six identical squares that made up a cube, implied perfect knowledge in the hands of man. Saturn, the supreme god and ruler of kings, was just another name for Cush, father of Nimrod. All the gods, it seemed, sprang from the legends of Cush, Nimrod, and his wife, Semiramis, and their worship continued under a multitude of names to the present day.

Lex was following a path that appeared to be endless. It was a trail of mysteries within mysteries, much like the Russian Matryoshka dolls within dolls. At times, he wondered why he pressed on with the investigation, except that he was becoming more certain there was something dark and tangible, and deeply involved with the present, behind it all.

Religions seemed to have been built on some hidden memory of this black cube—it was there in Islam's Ka'aba, in the rituals of Freemasonry, and in the black cube in the Meditation Room of the United Nations. Saturn, Lord of the Rings, "The Greater Malefic", was often represented as the Grim Reaper, and as the slayer of his father with his sickle. He was associated with death, limitations, restrictions, and decay—a god that had a lot in common, Lex thought, with the Islamic State.

* * *

"I'm taking you out to lunch tomorrow," Eugenia announced. Juan had just arrived home for an extended weekend visit and was sitting in front of the fire. Eugenia was drawing the curtains against the evening chill that seemed to descend the instant the sun went down.

"Why? What's the occasion?" he asked suspiciously.

"Can't I treat my brother now and again?" she asked.

"You've never done it before."

"Oh come on! I'm constantly doing stuff for you and your weird friends."

He raised his eyebrows. "If you say so!"

"So, are you going to let me take you to lunch, or not?"

Juan grinned. "Who's paying?"

"I will—just this once. You can drive me down."

Eugenia had chosen an intimate little seafood restaurant in Nerja, on a promenade overlooking the beach. For once the weather had co-operated and the day was pleasantly warm. Below them, people had spread brightly coloured towels among the boulders and some intrepid souls had stripped down to their swim shorts or bikinis and were soaking up the sun.

Juan and Eugenia were led to a corner table and handed the menus.

"They do a great seafood platter for two if you'd like to share one with me," Eugenia said.

"That sounds good."

Juan checked the wine menu and ordered a bottle of chardonnay. At that moment, Eugenia's cell phone rang.

"Oh hi," she said. Her expression changed. "No, actually I can't right now. I'm with Juan. We're about to have lunch." She listened for a moment. "Really? Can't it wait?" She paused. "Oh, all right. Give me a moment will you?"

"Hey! You're not going to walk out on me are you?" Juan asked. "What's going on?"

"It's Nour. She's got a problem." Eugenia took her jacket from the back of the chair and shrugged into it. "She's just round the corner. I won't be long." She kissed her brother on the cheek and left the restaurant.

Juan half stood up to follow her and sat down again. The wine waiter had approached the table unnoticed and was uncorking the bottle. The lunch order had gone through and, like it or not, he was stuck. If he knew his sister at all, he would probably have to pay the bill as well. He dutifully tasted the wine and gave the waiter the nod. Before he could stop him, he had filled both glasses and moved on. Juan sipped his chardonnay glumly and checked his watch. At that moment, a young woman entered the restaurant and stood at the doorway surveying the tables as though searching for someone.

Juan felt a small pulsation of shock at the sight of the all-too-familiar face. He leapt up and crossed the room towards her.

"Amal! What are you doing here?"

The colour rose in her cheeks.

"Juan. I was here to meet Eugenia."

"I don't believe it!" He grinned and shook his head. "We've been set up, Amal. Come and join me."

She followed him and sat down obediently. "Isn't Genie here?" she asked puzzled.

"She received a mysterious phone call from Nour and promised to return," Juan said, "but I suspect she has no intention of doing so."

"How embarrassing, I'm sorry."

"Don't be. I'm delighted to see you. I hope you are okay with having me as a lunch partner?"

Amal smiled. "It's not what I expected," she said, blushing. "But, yes. It's a lovely surprise."

"I'm afraid the lunch has been ordered," he apologised. "I hope you like seafood."

"When Eugenia told me about this place, she mentioned that they do a great seafood platter. I told her I love seafood. Your sister seems to have had it all carefully worked out."

Juan shook his head in amazement. "She didn't miss a trick."

Amal laughed. "So it would seem."

"I've missed you," Juan said. "I only realised how much I missed you when we met at the gallery. I should never have let you walk away."

"I have missed you too," Amal admitted softly, "but I thought my words had done too much damage."

He took her hand across the table. "I blame myself. I was totally arrogant. I never thought I'd say this, but I am so grateful to Eugenia for meddling. Can we start again from square one?"

"I would love to."

Their seafood platter arrived at the table accompanied by a wonderful aroma of lemon and garlic. Distracted, they failed to notice the young woman who stood observing them for a moment from the opposite side of the promenade. Eugenia smiled and set off across the road to where Adriana's car was parked.

"Did it work?" her mother asked.

"Perfectly!" she said with satisfaction and leaned back in the passenger seat.

"Are you sure Juan had his wallet with him to pay for the lunch?"

Eugenia laughed. "Don't worry, Mama, I paid before I left. Shall we go somewhere for lunch? I can't believe I sacrificed that seafood platter. I'm starving!"

Chapter 45   Betrayal

Alexander Wesley-Smith's novel was nearing completion. The trouble was, Lex had no idea of the ending or, as yet, what to call the book. During the writing, he had played around with various working titles but nothing had stuck. A book's title was important, but the way the story found closure, even more so. While the characters themselves were settling into a believable almost happily-ever-after pattern, the backdrop of Islam was a rising ocean.

Before he began work on the book, he had had a dream. He was on a small white boat on a dark green, angry sea. The boat was riding sideways over the rolling swells while Lex had his eyes fixed on even angrier waves gathering ominously some distance away. He clearly remembered seeing the letters xxx form in the white spume, but even while his eyes were fixed on that wave another lifted and approached the little craft at great speed. As Lex ducked into the comparative safety of the flimsy cabin, he felt the lash of the spray as it broke over the boat. For some reason, the dream taunted him as though it was an impenetrable warning of the future. He was missing a vital key and the book could not reach an end without it.

Lex, Moussa, and Amal sat on the terrace overlooking the garden. Spring was approaching with a smattering of warm days and Eugenia had taken Layla to see the peacock chicks that had hatched the previous week. Adriana brought out a tray of drinks tinkling with ice and pulled up a chair to join the group around the table.

"Did you ever check out the Georgia Guidestones," Moussa asked Lex.

"Actually, yes, I did," Lex replied. "Somebody had had a go at it with graffiti. Supposedly a cube with number 20 and 14 on the two exposed faces was mysteriously placed in a niche in a top corner. I think the whole purpose was to draw public attention to the monument itself."

Moussa smiled wryly. "Someone out there is intent on restoring interest," he agreed. "If the graffiti was intended to draw attention to the cube, they succeeded. The focal point seems to be this obsession with the reduction of the world population to five hundred million! I don't think it is co-incidence that the cube was positioned directly above the number."

"From a population of seven billion—frightening, if it's true!" Adriana said. "Who erected the stones in the first place?"

"There are definite links to Freemasonry," Moussa replied. And the man who commissioned them gave the name of R.C Christian, but no one seems to know much more than that,"

"After repeated vandalism of the site, a surveillance camera was put up," Lex added. "Despite that, supposedly no one was seen inserting the cube."

"Could RC Christian be a pseudonym for Roman Catholic Christian?" Adriana asked.

"I wondered about that," Lex replied. "But it could also point to Christian Rosencreuz, the professed founder of the Rosicrucian Order."

Adriana refreshed their drinks from the jug of sangria. "2014's come and gone," she commented as she sat down. "Whatever this stone was saying doesn't seem to have happened."

"I don't know," said Lex. "Perhaps something did happen."

"Like what?" Moussa asked.

"If the graffiti was intended to draw attention to the cube there may be a link. The one crude bit of painting said 'F the New World Order' the other said 'I am Isis'. It may be co-incidence that caused the Islamic State to call itself ISIS, but perhaps not."

"They certainly hit the headlines in 2014," Moussa agreed. "In which case perhaps the mention of the New World Order in the graffiti was also relevant?"

Lex pursed his lips thoughtfully, "Perhaps we shouldn't disregard the possibility of a link between ISIS, global government, and Freemasonry, in that case. Did you know in Freemasonry a cube is highly symbolic; allegorically it's a person known as the Stone of Foundation."

"xxx," Moussa said with a laugh.

Lex glanced at him sharply, "What do you mean?"

"I've read up quite a bit about Masonry and xxx is the Masonic designation for the Foundation Stone."

Lex whistled. "I don't believe it!"

"Why, what did I say?"

He shook his head. "Nothing, just a dream I had some time back. I was only thinking about it a couple of days ago."

"You said the cube could suggest a person?"

"Someone in the likeness of the hidden god—Saturn. I have an idea he's going to come as head of world government and masquerade as the Christ."

"Well, Christ is called the cornerstone in the Bible," Adriana said. "Perhaps that's why the stone is placed in that position."

Both Moussa and Lex glanced at Adriana with interest, but at that moment Eugenia and Layla came panting up the hill with the puppy frolicking around their heels, and the conversation was shelved.

"He bites!" Layla said laughing. "His little teeth are sharp!"

Eugenia picked up the wriggly Labrador pup. "Oh excellent— sangria! A drink is just what I need right now. It's hot out there today." She filled a tumbler and flopped into the nearest chair with the puppy still firmly grasped under her arm. Adriana passed Layla a glass of fruit juice and a couple of biscuits. The conversation changed to a discussion of the somewhat unseasonal weather.

Lex retreated into silence, happy for the interruption. He had no desire to launch into any deeper explanation but he was suddenly keen to delve a bit further into Masonic symbolism.

* * *

It was days before Nour could bring herself to speak to Raif again on anything but a superficial level. She felt deeply betrayed. If he had declared his intention to leave her, it would almost have been preferable to the notion that he would turn his back on Islam.

She was civil but distant. Raif tried everything to reach her but to no avail. She cooked and cleaned, limping about the house with only one crutch now that the knee was beginning to heal, but her attitude said it all—he was being punished. Eventually, the subject had to be aired and Nour recognised her duty to expose the deception Raif was under and persuade him to return to the faith.

"There has to be a way through this," she said. It was a Saturday morning and Raif had settled on the sofa after a breakfast of coffee and croissants; his newspaper folded in his lap as though he had forgotten his intention to read. He looked up at her.

"Are you ready to talk about it?" he asked.

She raised her eyebrows. "I suppose so, but I can't see any answers. You know what you are doing is wrong, Raif. So why are you choosing to go against everything you believe?"

Raif held out a hand to her, "Come and sit down, Nour."

She came reluctantly and sat on the edge of the seat determined in her indignation not to be seen to be too submissive.

"What do you want to know?" he asked.

"Why you have done this to me?"

He smiled. "It was not done against you, Nour. You know that."

"Well, it has hurt me!" she retorted.

"I know and I'm sorry."

Nour turned to him and looked him in the eye for the first time. "I don't understand, Raif. Why?"

"When we came back to Spain, there was one thing I wanted more than anything else," he replied. "I wanted to leave jihad behind and take Islam in its simplest form, but I couldn't. The *Surah* and the *Hadiths* condemned me. My duty in Islam is to carry out all Allah's commands and I was not capable of doing that." Raif stood up and paced the room. "As a Muslim, I was expected to see Muhammad as the perfect man and live my life as he lived his. But Muhammad's life was one of violence, warfare, and torture; he even condoned the rape of women who were considered enemies of Islam—I didn't want to be like him. I need you to understand my conflict, Nour. I was condemned by what I saw from the Qur'an as my weaknesses." He turned to face her. "Do you understand?"

"I am trying."

"I decided the simplest answer would be to denounce my faith."

"You did that?" Nour's face expressed her shock.

"I did. But it made no difference. I was still trapped by the knowledge that in denying Allah I was destined for hell."

"Oh, Raif." She dropped her head and massaged her forehead with her fingertips.

"There was no answer for me until Lex gave me that little book."

Nour was silent. Despite herself, she was beginning to see her husband's dilemma.

"As I read the New Testament, I found a man I could relate to. He was not weak, Nour, not a coward, but someone I could follow. He cared about people. When a woman was caught in adultery he didn't join the men that wanted to stone her to death; he asked the man who was without sin to cast the first stone and then waited while her accusers slunk away one by one."

"What happened to the woman?"

"He told her that he did not condemn her but that she should go and not sin again. I realised as I read about Jesus that he was demonstrating a path that is difficult to follow. Evil is in our nature; good is against it."

Nour looked at her husband silently. She knew he was right. Even those she loved best, like her father and Raif, were never perfect and why should they be when her own life was far from faultless?

"I never really wanted to be like Muhammad," Raif said, "but I want to be like this man." He paused and rubbed a hand thoughtfully over his chin. "Only the cross was difficult to understand. I don't know why Jesus gave himself up to his enemies like that."

"He was compassionate," Nour said quietly. "He wanted to share in our sufferings."

Raif dropped onto the seat beside her, "Where did you hear that?"

"There was a nun at the hospital. She told me other things as well."

Raif took Nour by the shoulders and gazed into her face in amazement.

"Did she say anything about sin?" he asked.

Nour nodded slowly. "She said he died for our sin but he couldn't pardon everyone because most people don't really care. Instead, he chose to rescue those who realised there was a cost to the wicked things we do."

"He paid the price. Death for our sin," Raif said with sudden comprehension.

Raif took his wife in his arms and held her. She buried her face in his shoulder comforting herself in the nearness and familiarity of his body. The fear involved in Islam was an accepted part of the religion—something Nour had never questioned. It was firmly bound up in the rules of Sharia, and Sharia was the same whether you were a radical Muslim or a moderate. There were rules and there were punishments for disobedience. Every Muslim was brought up knowing that stepping out of line brought about consequences—most of them terrifying. As Raif spoke, Nour understood for the first time that her deep-seated rebellion was against the imposition of all those impossible laws that had been thrust upon her from childhood. Raif tried to explain the differences, as he understood them, in Christianity.

"It seems so simple," he said. "You believe in Jesus and then you do what He wants you to do because you love Him."

"That's it? Nothing more?"

"I think it's just a starting point of something beautiful—a relationship with your Creator," he said. "I'm hoping beyond hope that you and I can share the discoveries."

"Please bring the book home, Raif," Nour said at length. "Let's read it together."

* * *

Although he had no real idea what he was looking for, Lex had returned to his study of the Georgia Guidestones. There was a compulsion to the investigation now, as though the completion of the book had gained an unexpected urgency. The first thing that caught his eye was the date that the notch for the cube was purported to have been cut.

"September 11, 2009!" he exclaimed aloud. "Someone out there loves this date."

There were conflicting dates for the placement of the new cube, but September 2014 seemed to be the most likely. A wedding had taken place at the Guidestones in August and the cube was said to have been positioned in the indentation in commemoration of the event. The fact that the bridegroom, who claimed to have commissioned the cutting of the cube, was one of three who had chiselled the original stone out of the niche five years before the event, only added, in Lex's opinion, to the stage management of an intended mystery. But why the September 11th anniversary, Lex thought, unless it was deliberate.

Reading back over his manuscript, Lex was almost surprised to rediscover his digression into the events of 9-11. He recalled the card game that had started him on that train of thought. The raid and the subsequent court case were undoubtedly carried out as a means to draw attention to a game that would have otherwise gone unnoticed. Lex contemplated another possibility. It was not only ISIS that had defined 2014. The opening of the One World Tower thirteen years after the 2001 attack was a singular event, but one that would have been disregarded by most outside of New York City. Thinking back to the prophetic card game and the prognostications by George Bush Snr. well-prior to the 9-11 attacks, the opening of the new tower should have been a really big deal. Was it possible that the numbers on the Guidestone cube were a reminder of that event or a signal to certain watchers? The name of the edifice alone said it all.

The One World Trade Center building had broken through its bands of iron in the earth and risen, at first discretely, until it reached the upper limits of the skyline. Gradually, storey by storey, black and overbearing, it grew in visual power until eleven years later it dwarfed and dominated everything around it. The four-hundred-and-eight-foot spire, which topped the building, bringing the structure to its record-breaking 1776 feet hearkening back to the signing of the Declaration of Independence, or the inception of the Illuminati, gave a very good impression of being a minaret from which the *muezzin* proclaims the *adhan*, or call to prayer. Once clad in glass, the main building's dark inner heart, so reminiscent of the picture in the card game, was concealed. Its façade was what the world desired to see. One remaining section of the building was still closed. Lex made a quick check of the internet for the opening date of the Observation Deck but none was given. The advertisements declared it would take place in early spring.

Chapter 46   Betrayal

Raif knew that he had to completely divorce himself from the Islamic State but the question was how to do it. Whichever way he looked at it there was danger involved, both for himself and Nour. He could not just walk away and expect ISIS to bless his departure, but neither could he ask Nour to uproot again and go into hiding just when she was beginning to settle. A strong bond was forming between Nour and his family. From the first moment, Moussa accepted her as a daughter. While no one would ever replace her own father, it was obvious that Nour loved Moussa and looked up to him, and Raif was loathe to take that away from her. The only other option was to approach the Spanish authorities and ask for protection. That was equally fraught with complications. Telling them of his association with the Islamic State might rebound on him in any number of ways, including deportation into the hands of the militia he was desperately trying to avoid.

Raif discussed it with Nour and they decided that pretence was deceit and therefore no longer an option; the only approach was the direct one. It was just possible that the Caliphate would release him without question.

When the time came for his next report back, Raif arrived at the mosque early and followed the now familiar route through the building to the offices of Dr. Ibrahim. Despite the chill in the morning air, he was sweating. The prospect of this interview filled him with dread and notwithstanding his assurances when he left in the morning, Nour was tense and pale. Dark rings under her eyes demonstrated what he already knew; for several nights she had slept badly, afraid that something was about to happen that would snatch Raif from her.

Dr. Ibrahim was behind his desk as usual. His expression hardly changed when Raif was shown into his room and his dark eyes reflected a coldness that did not fill Raif with confidence.

"Sit down."

Raif sat and waited while the imam completed writing notes on a pad in front of him. He set his pen aside and looked up.

"You have a report for me on your activities?"

Raif met his eyes. "Not this time, doctor."

"May I ask why not?"

"I haven't done any further work since I last saw you."

"I have made some enquiries in Frigiliana and discovered that what you claimed to have done before was, in fact, a pack of lies." Dr. Ibrahim tapped his well-polished desk with manicured fingertips. "Explain that!"

For a moment, Raif was incapable of answering. He knew instantly that Frigiliana's green grocer must have been employed to probe his activities. He was a garrulous man and one that people opened up to despite themselves. He cursed himself for imagining he could get away with anything where the Islamic State was concerned. There was nothing for it but to admit what he had done.

"I am sorry," Raif replied. "I am not the man for this job."

"What do you mean?"

"I mean that there are men better suited to speaking to others about the Islamic state. I can't do it."

Dr. Ibrahim's face conveyed nothing. The desk tapping had ceased but Raif did not know whether to take that as a good sign or a bad one.

"Perhaps," he said, "you would do better at another worthier vocation. A martyr's belt might be more suited to your nature?" The words were deeply ironic but almost sweetly uttered and Raif experienced the sensation of his bowels loosening under the intensity of his fear. When he spoke he was surprised to discover that his voice did not waver.

"No, Dr. Ibrahim. I think you know that that is not my path. I came to the Islamic State intending to surrender myself fully to the organisation. I have since realised that I cannot do that. I ask that you will release me from all further duties."

The doctor sat upright in his chair and stared long and hard at Raif without speaking. Then abruptly, he seemed to reach a decision.

"We have no further need of your sort!" His voice was carefully controlled but the tone was menacing. "If you show your face here again, we will kill you. Get out of my office!"

Raif stood up, wished him good morning, and left, shutting the door quietly behind him. He knew he should have been relieved; instead, he felt sick to the stomach. Nevertheless, he sat for a moment in his car and sent a text message to Nour telling her that the interview was over and the outcome was positive.

On the opposite side of the car park, a young man with a cherubic face unlocked his vehicle and slipped behind the wheel. He waited while Raif reversed, drove down the driveway, and turned right into the tree-lined avenue, before starting his engine.

Following him proved simple, a welcome diversion from what had promised to be a boring day. Raif stopped on a side road off Avenue de las Americas and Ahmed parked in the street opposite. No doubt the interview with Dr. Ibrahim had been a little tense, he thought. The doctor was an intimidating man; Raif Ahmadi would need a cup of coffee to settle his nerves. He smiled contentedly when twenty minutes later his quarry emerged from the doorway and walked towards his car. It was easy to see that the possibility of being followed had not entered his head. Raif Ahmadi simply crossed the parking lot without so much as a glance to left or right. As he drove, he routinely checked his rear-view mirror but, Ahmed guessed, his thoughts were elsewhere. Nevertheless, he hung back, putting two or three vehicles between them as a precaution.

Raif left the coastal road and turned into the Las Cuevas district. Behind him Ahmed slowed down and, as Raif stopped in front of his gate, he made a mental note of the house number and drove on.

* * *

The Observatory of the One World Tower opened to the public on May 30th, 2015 on the sixty-first anniversary of the formation of the Bilderbergers. Nothing out of the ordinary happened to otherwise mark the day. But this was the benchmark from which one could now 'see forever'.

ISIS had seized the Palestinian refugee camp of Yarmouk near Damascus in April after a prolonged siege in which more than a thousand refugees lost their lives. The crisis was deepening daily. Jordan and Lebanon had absorbed many Syrians but resentment was simmering as overcrowding increased. Assimilation on such an enormous scale was not possible; refugees were prepared to take on work at lower wages causing further discontent within the host countries. In June, the United Nations refugee agency reported from

Jordan that funding was running out. The urgency of the situation seemed lost on the international community while in the camps, hunger proved the provocation needed to make a move towards the West. What began with a stream soon became a flood.

Raif looked across the table at Nour's expression.

"Who was the letter from?" he asked. "It's obviously not good news."

She shook her head. "It's from my aunt," she replied. "Many died from the cold in the camp last year and this winter is expected to be worse. With their food assistance cut back refugees are leaving, hoping to reach Europe before the cold weather sets in."

"Your aunt and your cousin could come here," Raif suggested.

Nour shook her head. "I don't think they want to leave," she replied. "Sameer has been schooling some of the local children and thinks they should hold on. He likes to feel useful."

"And your aunt?"

Nour smiled ruefully, "There's no question. She will stay with her son."

"Perhaps the international community will wake up and help," Raif said. "Several countries that promised funding haven't made the donations. If the UN puts some pressure on them, it could ease things."

Nour nodded. "I'm sure no one wants the problem to get worse. We haven't seen many new immigrants here, but I know the numbers are on the rise in other places, especially Germany."

Raif reached for a second piece of the Arabic bread Nour had baked during the morning. He filled it with falafel and salad and rolled it expertly.

"They need to be quick," he said. "Europe could get more than they bargained for."

Nour pushed her plate aside, her food untouched. "I love it here," she said, "don't misunderstand me, but there are times that I long for the Syria that I knew as a child." Her eyes filled with tears and she wiped them away with the back of her hand. "I don't suppose the country will ever be the same again."

Raif reached out and took his wife's hand. "That sadness will probably always be with us," he replied. "But we can keep a little of the past alive with our memories and pass them along to our children. Who knows, perhaps Syria will recover—Lebanon did."

"There are still car and suicide bombings over there, and there's militia like Hezbollah. I'm not sure that the Lebanese have got their country back completely." She squeezed his hand briefly and let it go but her expression was bleak as she left the table. "Syria will never be the same again for me," she said. "It's stained with blood that can't be erased."

Chapter 47   Betrayal

The plight of refugees from the Middle East worsened dramatically as winter set in. For so many, the situation in Syria had become unbearable as starvation was added to their list of heavy burdens. The answer lay in Europe. They traversed the countryside in the snow, dressed as warmly as possible, carrying the very minimum in a backpack or a bag. Children were among them; babies in strollers, older children on foot, often howling in anguish as the cold bit into their feet and their parents pushed them at an unrelenting pace. Borders were beginning to close against them and if they wanted to make it to Germany they needed to be swift. More than seventy percent of the migrants swarming the now well-traversed routes across the Continent were men; most genuinely preparing to forge a new life in a foreign land before calling for their women and children to join them, others seeking jihad, an overturning of the established order for the advance of Islam: in short—terror. Proper screening was impossible with resources stretched to the limit. Men housed in camps demanded better food, improved sanitation, and improved living conditions: some groups melted away into the night and were lost to the tenuous systems of control. Perhaps some of the Paris attackers were among this group. At least one of those who imposed terror in the Bataclan that night was carrying a Syrian passport and had arrived with the refugees.

The Eagles of Death Metal were playing to an ecstatic crowd; faces upturned, arms raised they swayed like tendrils of some gigantic sea plant caught in the gentle currents of an underwater world. The words wove a Satanic invocation in their trance-like pattern; *I love the Devil, I'll kiss his tongue, I'll kiss the Devil on his tongue.*

The Devil came in the form of men bearing AK47s. Many assumed the first burst of gunfire was part of the performance until the screams of those mowed down under the deadly spray of bullets spread pandemonium. Terror came to the Bataclan, to a football stadium, and to the cafes and streets of Paris. Satan was invited. It was just the beginning.

* * *

Lex's attention to the paragraph he was typing was interrupted by a buzz on his cell phone.

"Sandy. Good of you to call. How are you?"

"Fine, thanks," he answered shortly. "Lex, you remember when we spoke about the Guidestones recently, you also mentioned the Protocols of Zion?"

"Of course. You have something for me?"

"I think I do. As I remember, it's an odd document, obviously intended to be seen to be Jewish in nature."

Lex nodded, "It speaks of Gentiles as though written by Jews," he acknowledged, "and as I remember it's signed in such a way as to imply a union between Jews and Freemasons."

"I glanced over it years ago," Sandy said, "but never really read it properly. It's the Jewishness of the document that struck me."

"So what's on your mind," Lex asked.

"The Jewish feast days were laid out in the Old Testament. Jews have followed them religiously over the centuries even when they weren't fully following the God of their fathers. This may be a co-incidence, Lex, but I don't think so." Sandy paused to gather his thoughts. "After our chat, I checked out the Georgia Guidestones myself. Some of the dates mentioned in connection with the Guidestones tie in with the Jewish feast days. I'm not sure whether it's significant in terms of your book."

"Try me."

"You saw the recent video of the groundskeeper removing the cube?"

"That amateur video on YouTube?"

"That's the one. Only the numbers 20 and 14 were visible from the ground but there were other numbers and some letters cut into the other faces of the cube."

Lex straightened up and rolled his office chair away from the desk. "I don't remember the exact numbers," he said "but I recall there were initials—MM on one side and JAM on the other."

"It's been suggested that the numbers on the cube could have been read in reverse. Two of the languages on the Guidestones are Hebrew and Arabic, both are read from right to left. There was also a mention on one of the sites that the Guidestones are set up to track Polaris. There was something about the counter-clockwise rotation of the earth if viewed from the Pole Star."

Lex gazed sightlessly out of the window. "So, in reversing the direction of the date on the cube, what do you get?"

"8/14/2016. I'll get to that. First, let me fill you in on some of the dates. The niche seems to have been cut when the stones were first made, and the piece cemented back in place. It was removed and left vacant for some time before the new cube was set in place on September 25th 2014. That date coincided with *Rosh Hashannah*, the Jewish New Year – a day which also marked the beginning of the *Shemitah* year."

"Shemitah?"

"A seventh year of rest for the land; a Sabbatical, if you like."

Lex was silent as he absorbed this information. Then, "You said there were others?"

"Well, a couple of others. The groundskeeper removed the cube and destroyed it on the 15th of September last year, a couple of days after the *Shemitah* year reached its conclusion and on the last day of the *Rosh Hashannah* celebration."

"So a year later, almost to the day?"

"That's it. It's my feeling that the Jewish feasts are being used deliberately."

"Not co-incidence?" Lex scratched the back of his head with his free hand.

"The reverse date on the cube," Sandy replied, "is the 14th of August, 2016. It falls on Tisha B'Av. It's a day of mourning commemorating the destruction of both the first and the second temple in Jerusalem. A supposed insider source on the Guidestones said that JAM stood for Judicie Anno Mundi, Judgment of the World,"

Lex whistled softly between his teeth. "Hell!"

"You could say so!" Sandy replied soberly. "Jesus said the temple would be destroyed, but in three days he would raise it up. He was speaking of his death and resurrection. Paul later reminded Christians that *they* are temples of the Holy Spirit. If there is anything to all of this, I would say it stands as a warning to Christians and Jews that they may be destined to reach their nemesis in the future."

Chapter 48   Betrayal

It was a Sunday morning. Nour stepped out into the sunshine. She had just washed her hair and small tendrils around her face were beginning to coil into life as it dried. It was easy to believe that spring was on its way; knobbles were appearing on leafless twigs bringing an imminent promise of blossom. Here and there tender new leaves had made a daring debut against the possibility of another cold snap.

Nour's heart was light; another promise was made by the swelling of her breasts and the gentle rounding of her belly. She and Raif were on the edge of one of life's greatest adventures—the advent of new life; a child of their own.

Raif had found work with a computer company in Las Cuevas so that their travelling was reduced and a higher salary meant they could begin to put money away for the baby's arrival. And although she still had to treat it with care, her knee had healed well in the year since the operation. All told, life was wonderful.

She sat down on the grass in their little patch of garden and ran her fingers through her damp hair lifting the strands to allow the sun to do its work. At first she did not notice the car that drew up on the verge opposite their house. A man approached the gate. He was very young, swarthy-skinned with the hint of an immature beard; he was dressed in jeans and a navy-blue tee shirt. Nour stood up.

"Can I help you?"

"I'm looking for Raif, is he in?" His smile was warm and reassuringly friendly.

She nodded. "What is your name? I'll let him know you are here."

"Dabria. I'll wait."

As she walked towards the house, Nour attempted to shrug off the niggle of uncertainty that sounded a warning in her mind.

"Raif?"

He came through from the bathroom. "What is it, *habibti?*"

"There's someone outside…" She broke off mid-sentence as she saw the flash of alarm cross his face. He caught her by the arm and urged her roughly in the direction of the bedroom. Nour stumbled as a flash of pain shot through her leg. She caught her balance and clung to the door jamb.

"Raif, what is it?"

"Get in there and lock the door!" he ordered.

Nour swung round in time to see two men running towards the open door of the house; a third was vaulting the gate. He dropped lightly onto the lawn just as the first two burst through the door.

"Nour! Do as I say!" Raif yelled.

She shook her head. "I am staying with you," she said quietly.

"She is right, this is the time to stay together," the man pulled a gun from inside his jacket and waved it at them almost casually. He leered at Nour and she returned his look contemptuously.

Raif looked at the youngster in the blue tee shirt certain he had seen him before.

"What do you want?" Raif demanded.

"We have known for some time that you are a traitor," the man said pleasantly. "We have been watching you. Your lies never fooled Dr. Ibrahim, he is too smart for the likes of you! We would like to know what sort of a Muslim you really are."

Raif was silent.

"We have come to hear you and your wife recite the *shahada* in the presence of witnesses," the one flourishing the gun wore an orange shirt, which reminded Raif incongruously of the overalls worn by Gitmo and prisoners held by Islamic State.

"Why?" Even as he asked the question his blood ran cold and he glanced at Nour. She lifted her chin defiantly as she faced the intruders. Only by the pallor of her skin did Raif know she was afraid.

"Speak what you know to be the truth," she said simply. "It's all right, *habibi,* I am with you."

For a long moment, Raif was silent. The two older men moved forward menacingly.

"Speak!"

Raif drew a deep breath. "I will not say the *shahada*."

A growl emanated from the throat of the young man and he went for the knife in his belt.

"Wait, Ahmed! We will search the place first."

Ahmed! That was where he had seen him! He was Dr. Ibrahim's sidekick. Raif had failed to recognise him in western dress.

The third man took the command as his personal mission. He was taller than the other two, broad-shouldered, with thick dark hair and a couple of days' growth of beard. Given a task, he set to it with alacrity. There was the sound of drawers and cupboards being opened and slammed shut followed by the occasional crash as some object hit the floor. The men waited. It was clear the delay was making them edgy.

"*Yella!*" Ahmed called. There was a grunt from the bedroom and the big man returned triumphantly bearing the little book between finger and thumb.

Nour moved closer to her husband and took his hand; the other was cupped protectively around her stomach as though to comfort the little soul in her womb. Her palms were clammy. Raif glanced at her and saw with pride her unbowed head.

The searcher held up his prize for the others to see.

"*Injil!*" he exclaimed triumphantly. "The Gospel."

Ahmed leaped forward and struck Raif with the back of his hand. "You believe this? You would go against *tawhīd*, the oneness of God?"

"*Al-'Ahad, Al-Wāhid*—Allah is one, he is single," the one with the gun intoned obediently.

Nour stood up to her full height, "The true God has a Son," she said. "He is loving and compassionate. He even calls us to love our enemies."

"*Shirk! Shirk!*[37]" Ahmed screamed. He lunged towards her and lashed out with his fists at her face. Raif pushed between them trying desperately to shield his wife with his body. There was a shot and he stumbled backward; Nour tried to hold him but he fell

---

[37] To attribute divinity to a created entity is, according to the Qu'ran, an unpardonable sin. Islamic teaching rests upon the principle of Tawhid – an uncompromising monotheism.

awkwardly against the wall. A strangled cry emanated from Nour's throat and she dropped to the floor beside Raif ignoring the searing pain in her leg as she lifted and supported his head. As she looked up at their assailants, she saw the long knife in Ahmed's hand.

The officer who brought the news of their death to Moussa later that night was not new to the task, but it was never one he relished. This had been a particularly ugly scene in which the male victim was shot and both corpses stabbed several times before being beheaded. It was enough for the moment to share the news. The gruesome nature of their death would be revealed in time, but it was his policy to allow the family to absorb and begin to deal with the initial shock. First things first.

He had slipped the little New Testament into a plastic bag at the scene. It would need to be cleared by forensics but he would ask them to pass it on to the family afterwards. Little things of that nature often proved a comfort at times like this.

Neighbours had heard the shot; the exultant cries of "*Allahu Akbar,*" and saw the car leave the scene moments later. They identified it as a Japanese model, silver-blue, and gave the detective three digits of the number plate. The police had launched an intensive search. It would only be a matter of time before the terrorists were picked up. This much information he passed on to Moussa and Amal before he left them.

Moussa called Lex in the morning. He spoke stoically and deliberately. They had both been murdered, he told him. Yes, he was coping but the girls were very upset. There would be an inquest and no, he could not shed any light on what had happened.

Lex, Adriana, and Eugenia drove straight down to Malaga to see them and Juan, who received the news at work, immediately dropped everything to be at Amal's side. They found the family numb with shock.

"I lost my son three times," Moussa said. "Once when I heard the imams had turned him and then again when he joined ISIS in Syria. There was always a possibility that the path he chose might lead to his death—I knew that. But Nour, she was innocent of all this…"

"She was expecting a baby," Amal whispered. "We were going to tell you this week. I can't believe this has happened!" Juan slipped an arm around her shoulders and she buried her face against his chest and wept. Layla had crept into a corner beside the sofa. Her knees were drawn up hard against her body and her usually expressive face was vacant with a level of grief she was ill-equipped to bear. Eugenia lifted the child into her lap and held her.

On the following morning, the newspapers were full of the lurid details. Moussa did his utmost to shield the girls against the press and answered their questions cautiously. He had the living to consider, and Raif's connection to the Islamic State would be better left unspoken.

On the evening of the following day, police cordoned off an area in downtown Malaga. A street battle ensued. The papers proclaimed in banner headlines the following morning that an officer was injured and two terrorists of Middle Eastern origin were shot dead. According to the neighbours of the young couple, a third suspect had been witnessed leaving the scene of the murder, a younger man, but his identity remained unknown.

Chapter 49   Betrayal

For several weeks, Lex's book remained untouched. He had no appetite for writing especially for a public blinded to what was taking place under their watch. The work was destined to be labelled hate speech anyway. In his thinking, Lex saw it buried with his other attempts at novel writing, with all those with multiple rejection slips from publishing houses against their name. It was the little book that breathed new life into him at just the right time.

Moussa asked Lex to meet him in town one spring day in early March. The almond trees were blossoming in virginal white against the silver of the olive trees and the hillsides were showing signs of new life. Below and to his left, the Mediterranean Sea was calm and splendid in a fresh shade of blue. The world had put on its beautiful garments.

They met at a pavement café and ordered rolls and café con leche. Lex noted the ravages that sorrow had left on his friend's features. His cheeks were hollowed and the lines around his eyes and mouth had deepened into grooves. But Moussa's eyes held a different message.

Lex cupped his hands around the tall glass of coffee.

"How are you and the girls doing?" he asked.

"A little better. Juan has helped Amal through this patch. He's been a continual visitor."

"Not a nuisance, I hope?"

Moussa shook his head. "Not at all! Even Layla has been better for his presence."

"I have a feeling you will be approached for Amal's hand in the not-too-distant future," Lex said. "I hope you are all right with that."

"Some time ago, I might have discouraged the match," Moussa said reflectively, "but I have seen a great deal of maturity in your son. I think they will manage to overcome whatever disparities there are in their cultural backgrounds."

"Adriana reminded me the other day that we managed it," Lex replied with a grin. "With her Spanish passion and artist's temperament, she was a fiery young thing. A practicing Catholic as well."

Moussa smiled. "And you, an atheist? Quite a combination!" He sipped his coffee and looked out over the placid water of the harbour. "That officer came back last week," he said.

"The one that brought the news?"

He nodded briefly. "He brought me this. Said it was found at the scene." He took the navy-blue covered New Testament from his jacket pocket and put it down on the table.

Lex felt a jolt of shock as he gazed down at the familiar book. He met Moussa's eyes.

"Did they die because of this?" His voice sounded hollow to his own ears.

Moussa shook his head. "They died because of Raif's ties to ISIS. The discovery of a Bible would have simply justified what they intended to do anyway."

Lex shut his eyes. "I gave that to Raif," he confessed.

Moussa smiled slightly, "I thought one of you might have done so," he said. "I didn't think it would be you."

"Raif was searching for answers," Lex replied. "He told me that Jesus appeared many times in the Qur'an and he wanted to know more."

"Was it new when you gave it to him?"

Lex nodded. "It hadn't been opened."

"It has been well-thumbed since," Moussa said and he picked it up. "I've been reading it myself. I wanted to see what it was that Raif found. There's this passage I read last night. Either Raif or Nour had underlined it.

'Though I speak with the tongues of men and of angels, but have not love, I have become as sounding brass or a clanging cymbal. And though I have the gift of prophecy and understand all mysteries and all knowledge, and though I have all faith, so that I could move mountains, but have not love, I am nothing. And though I bestow all my goods to feed the poor, and though I give my body to be burned, but have not love, it profits me nothing.'" He looked up. "What it

says is true, Lex. There are so many Muslims who are working and working; doing things for the poor, and giving *zakat*. It counts for nothing if the heart is not right."

"Not only Muslims," Lex said. "We're all guilty of trying to do things to assuage our consciences."

Moussa picked up the book again. "It goes on: '*Love suffers long and is kind; love does not envy; love does not parade itself, is not puffed up; does not behave rudely, does not seek its own, is not provoked, thinks no evil; does not rejoice in iniquity, but rejoices in the truth; bears all things, believes all things, hopes all things, endures all things. Love never fails.*'"

"Does it say something about being a child and speaking as a child?"

"You've heard it before?"

"Somewhere back in the shadows of my youth," Lex said. "It's a beautiful passage."

"'*When I was a child, I spoke as a child, I understood as a child, I thought as a child;*'" Moussa read. "'*But when I became a man, I put away childish things. For now we see in a mirror dimly, but then face to face. Now I know in part, but then I shall know just as I am known.*'" He looked up at Lex again. "I would like to believe this is true for Raif and Nour, and even for that unborn child. That they are in that place of love," he said. "That they are not lost at all. They are known."

Lex said nothing. He gazed down into his glass of coffee that had turned tepid as they spoke, fighting the well of emotion that was struggling in him. Moussa leaned over the table and gripped his elbow.

"Thank you for passing on this little book. It has given me hope. The last verse says it for me: '*And now abide faith, hope, love, these three; but the greatest of these is love.*'" He stood up. "I wanted to let you know," he said. "This, for me, has been something beautiful. Perhaps you will understand, I needed to be able to continue with life but I couldn't have done it without hope that they are not lost. Thank you."

Moussa walked into the restaurant, paid the bill and left. Lex sat alone gazing out beyond the yachts and ships docked at the quay. Gazing at a world where it seemed, there was still reason for hope.

Chapter 50   Betrayal

"Death is the sentence. We know there's nothing to be embarrassed about this, death is the sentence... We have to have that compassion for people, with homosexuals, it's the same, out of compassion, let's get rid of them now."
Dr. Sekaleshfar, expert on Shariah Islamiyya or Islamic Law, in a 2013 speech at Orlando Mosque.

If Lex had expected a single event to take place after the opening of the Observation Deck in the One World Centre, he was disappointed when the event passed without a blip on the RADAR. It was only as he looked back over the months since the May 29th opening that he became aware that the world had taken a dramatic shift in direction. It was in May that food began to run out in refugee camps across the Middle East and Syria in particular. Pleas from groups for the international community to comply with their promises of aid fell on deaf ears and the mass exodus began. Refugees had been arriving in Europe for months before this event but now there was a deluge. They swept into Europe in ever-increasing numbers swamping communities that had at first received them with open arms. By the end of the year, they were no longer termed refugees as it became obvious this was a migration from every part of the Middle East and North Africa. Structures had broken down within the donor nations, borders were breached, passports were found dumped, and the level of aggression rose as the demands made by many migrants increased.

On the other hand, the American President's legalisation of same-sex marriage in June threatened politicians, government structures, and churches that failed to comply. LGBTQ extremism was now aimed at undermining and removing gender barriers on every level, even absurdly demanding that biological differences between male and female should no longer be recognised. And because the liberal lie of a new, enlightened world was believed, society conformed to the deepening confusion with scarcely a murmur. The threat of offending Gays and Muslims became a subtle gag. Free speech now came with a cost.

At the same time, economic woes had deepened globally, food security was threatened, and acts of terror grew in frequency and intensity. The nations of the world had moved to the edge and were staring disaster in the face.

* * *

Juan took Amal by the hand and led her across the crowded street. The noise and clamour of the parade was becoming more distinct the closer they came to the Alameda; still the jarring sound of bells and the helicopters circling overhead predominated. Caught in glimpses through the throng were the distinctive regal colours of purple, crimson and gold that adorned the many thrones of Christ and the Virgin Mary which had been made and decorated over many months by different *cofradia*. Even from here, the sense of excitement was tangible. One *cofradia* had encountered another at an intersection of the streets and their huge 'thrones' were raised in salute; the two teams performing a ritualised back and forward step, six times, amid cheers from the gathering.

Juan and Amal were close enough now to see some of the men packed tightly against one another, sweating no doubt under the distinctive uniform of the different areas as they slowly bore their heavy burden on their shoulders through the narrow streets. From her window above, a woman tossed flower petals onto the carved figures depicting the passion of Christ and the weeping Virgin. Youths stood precariously on the narrow ledges of the buildings and pressed back as the swaying floats threatened to pin them against the wall.

"I never thought they would be so big!" Amal exclaimed, "So many men are needed to carry them."

"They are heavy!" Juan said with emphasis. "Some need two-hundred-and-eighty men in several rows to lift them and they are carried for hours. They pick only the young, really strong men from amongst the contenders for the job." He grinned, "I'm told they put the best-looking at the front."

"And they use the bells to co-ordinate their movements?"

Juan nodded. "Each of the thrones has one man who rings the bell with a hammer. That's the signal for laying it down and for taking it up again. There have to be moments of rest. Each of the men is carrying the equivalent of about forty kilos."

Amal stopped suddenly as a new group came into sight along an adjoining street. "Why are they wearing those tall hoods?" she asked.

Juan shrugged. "I've no idea. Many groups wear them. There are different colours representing different *cofradia.*" He laughed at her stricken expression. "Why? What's wrong?"

She took his arm. "They're creepy, just their eyes showing like that. Like those pictures you see in America where they burn crosses."

"You mean the Ku Klux Klan?"

Amal nodded. "The whole thing is a little strange. It has a sort of fascination, but it makes me feel uneasy."

"We can leave if you like," Juan said. "The crowd is very heavy anyway and I'm not sure how close we're likely to get to the Alameda."

"Let's see what we can see from here," she suggested.

They pushed their way through the crowd to gain a better vantage point and, for a while, watched in silence as the pageant moved slowly by; a rich diet of flamboyance and Baroque religiosity combined, somewhat incongruously, with military marches. They were followed by women and girls dressed in black and wearing the high comb *peineta* in their hair.

"It's like something out of a fantasy. Perhaps they should call it Spain's Game of Thrones," Amal commented with a smile.

"Without the violence," Juan returned. He looked thoughtful for a moment. "My Dad has this friend, Sandy, a Christian guy. He told me once that the Catholic Church has its root in the mystery religions."

Amal looked confused. "But it is Christian, isn't it? If this man is a Christian, why does he say such a thing?"

"He's not a Catholic," Juan returned as he watched the slow approach of a float bearing the Virgin. "Protestantism is different.

He said that the Pagan religions also had annual processions. They would bring out their gods and parade them before the people to raise their fervour. Those religions were really just sensual. Their goddesses, such as Cybele and Juno, like Mary, were known as the Queen of Heaven."

"Do you think this parade is just that? Is it intended to raise the senses of the people?"

He nodded. "I'm beginning to see Sandy's point; there is something creepy about it." He took her hand. "Come on," he said, "let's go and get something to eat. I'm sure we've seen enough for today."

They had turned away and begun walking back towards the parking area when the blast occurred. Suddenly the world of pageantry switched to real-life drama. Their decision to stay away from the Alameda, they realised later, may even have saved their lives.

They were rocked by the first explosion, but even before they had managed to grasp what they had heard, it was followed by a second, then yet another.

For an instant, Malaga seemed to fall eerily silent. Around Juan and Amal people were rooted to the spot; then came the mass awakening, mass terror. Panic, raw panic, pandemonium, women screaming, people running blind and directionless; in their terror of the unknown running even from themselves.

Within moments fear translated into action. Many men ran towards the Alameda to see if they could help; women collected themselves and gathered together in silent groups. Some, men and women alike, wept. Others took out their phones to call and reassure family members. The rise and fall of a multitude of sirens became a calming refrain in itself.

The evening papers were filled with reports of the carnage; the massive loss of life. Three suicide bombers had detonated their deadly load at the heart of the crowded avenue. Newspapers and websites across the world used one particular photograph of the many bodies strewn like garbage across the road. Raised at an angle among the fallen was a cross from one of the floats still bearing the image of the suffering Christ.

Chapter 51   Betrayal

2022

Dr. Ibrahim looked up from his laptop. "Sit down, Ahmed," he said. "I have an assignment for you." The younger man took his seat obediently.

"Yes, Imam Ibrahim?"

"*Insha Allah* the time has come for the greater advance into Europe. There will be a signal, a catastrophic sign to the followers of the Prophet, bless his name, that the uprising has come."

Ahmed breathed out audibly and his eyes shone as the words touched his soul. "Allah be praised!"

The Imam bowed his head in brief acknowledgment of the invocation. "I want you to sound the warning to our network here in Spain," he said. "Tell the leaders to check their arms caches, increase the levels of alertness among their followers and at all times, exercise caution until the moment is ripe. They will recognise the call to arms beyond any doubt. The imams must raise the level of excitement in the mosques without speaking too directly. Secrecy is paramount; the Spanish authorities must suspect nothing!"

"Of course, Doctor. I understand," he hesitated before asking the question that was foremost in his mind. "Do you know, Imam Ibrahim, what that signal will be?"

The doctor's face darkened perceptibly at the impertinence of the young man, but he checked the impulse to utter a sharp response. The question was one to which every Muslim, including Ibrahim himself, desired to know the answer. What is the sign that the end is coming? Will we see in our lifetime the promised great reward, the fruit of our zeal?

"Be content to exercise patience, my son," he said at length, "What is to be will soon be known. The waiting is almost over. In a very little while, we will see Islam transcendent; the decadence of the West will be crushed; all women will know their rightful place, and the Mahdi will make his appearance. Many Imams have believed that we must see another generation or two before Islam dominates the Western world by sheer numbers, and it is true of course that we would outbreed Europe in that time." His smile displayed his contempt. "With four wives to every man, we can breed twenty children to their one."

"But you are saying we will not have to wait so long, Imam Ibrahim?"

The doctor locked his hands together, stretched his arms out across the desk, cracking his knuckles as he did so. "Perhaps not, my child, the time may be far shorter than any of us have realised. I don't think it will be long before it all comes together."

Word had come to him from much higher up but with little more clarity than Dr. Ibrahim had passed on to Ahmed. An event was planned by Israel, one that would incite great anger but also bring unity to the Islamic world. He knew with certainty that the promised revelation of the Mahdi would take place during the ensuing conflagration. It was he who would lead the armies to victory in the name of Allah.

Dr. Ibrahim dismissed Ahmed after briefing him on the direction that the new orders must take and then he sat back in his chair, hands locked behind his head as he contemplated the future. The West, he thought with satisfaction, would be taken completely by surprise.

In fact, Ibrahim was wrong. Radical Islam was the pawn of another power, which also believed it held the reigns. Communist forces had taken control of almost every facet of the West by stealth. The formation of the United Nations through their agent Alger Hiss was their first great triumph. Through U.N. interference in weak nations, strong leaders were disposed and replaced by corrupted, compliant leaders who would serve the hand that doled out the money. It was the U.N. that contrived to bring a subtle form of Socialism to every facet of society. Liberalism was the seed that corrupted the youth through mind-bending drugs and music, to the adoption of a pseudo-Hinduistic religion. It was a small step from there to promiscuity and the demolition of the family unit.

It was Carl Marx who initiated the environmental movement from which Global Warming and Climate Change evolved. Indeed, 'ecology' was a word coined by the Marxists. Mikhail Gorbachev, while promoting bigger government and less freedom for the people, settled comfortably in the U.S. and penned the Earth Charter. Marxists hijacked the Democratic Party so that ultimately Democratic goals were almost indistinguishable from those of the American Communist Party.

For over forty years, Robert Muller, "the father of global education" used his mix of socialism and the arcane to promote "group consciousness" in the minds of children through his redirection of the education system from the United Nations. Under the orchestration of the Insiders, unrecognised by even those who moved close to the inner circle, Jesuits also worked within society to create a liberal/religious strata closely linked to the political. The plan was intricate, far-reaching, and had advanced to such a point that it had become self-perpetuating.

Then, from the heart of Hitler's Germany, one man began the training of future world leaders patterned after his own ideology. In a decade or more these men and women had begun to infiltrate the nations as thought leaders and heads of state. Out of this body would emerge an independent organisation that would have the power to dictate far-reaching radical policy and direction to kings, popes, and governments across the globe. It was both subtle and insidious—a serpent that held the nations immobile in its coils as it began to slowly tighten the grip.

Liberals threw their weight behind Islam despite the obvious fact that Islam was diametrically opposed to everything espoused by liberalism. Sharia law denied woman's rights, gay rights, and human rights in general. It allowed for the harshest punishment of any form of criminality. Liberal backing for Islam was irrational yet few appeared to recognise the contradiction because Islam was the ideal tool to complete the groundwork of a Communist takeover of the West—destruction of family, destruction of Christianity, and destruction of the State.

* * *

It never occurred to Alexander Wesley-Smith to look more closely at the architecture of the One World Trade Centre until Eugenia mentioned that the architect of the Oculus was Spanish.

"Oculus?" Lex asked, puzzled.

"You know, Papa, the terminal station for PATH which links to the Trade Centre."

"What does that have to do with an eye?"

Eugenia smiled patiently. "It was a feature used in Byzantine and Neoclassical times, a circular portal usually in a wall or a domed roof. There's one in the dome of the Pantheon which is open to the elements; it allows light into the building as well as an exchange of air."

"And this oculus in the World Trade Centre, what's that about?"

"It's amazing, papa! We were given a virtual walk through the building last week during one of our lectures. You should check it out online."

Lex swung round in his office chair and faced Eugenia thoughtfully. "Oculus, portals, and paths; they're all arcane terms."

"Could be," she replied quizzically. "What is it, papa? What's ticking over in that mind of yours?"

"I'm not sure yet, Genie, but thanks for the tip. I'll take a look."

The architect of the One World Trade Centre building had allowed for a wedge of light to penetrate the terminus building from the Memorial Garden, maximising the effect of the rays during the autumnal equinox. When Santiago Calatrava extended the terminal under the memorial garden, the oculus became the focal point with a soaring superstructure representing the white wings of D'Iune, the goddess, Juno. In the main hall beneath the ground, the curved steel-ribbed walls swept a gracious 160 feet to the glass ribbon of the closed eye, initially designed to open for a few hours a year in commemoration of the demise of the Twin Towers, but later modified because of the enormous cost implications.

While the response of New Yorkers was somewhat jaded by the expenditure, which had soared in tandem with the design and the length of time it had taken to bring the work to completion, Lex's initial reaction to the project was one of unreserved admiration.

"It's stunning," he said to Eugenia over supper. "But they will have their work cut out to keep everything as pristine as it is at the moment. White will be a nightmare for the cleaners."

"It's a bit like walking through the bones of a massive skeleton, don't you think?" she laughed.

"Did you notice the eyes set into the wall tiles?" Lex asked with his fork poised halfway to his mouth. "Commuters making their way through the maze of corridors will never feel alone."

"It's weird!" Adriana commented as she whisked the serving dishes off the table. "Papa showed me the pictures but I really didn't like it. I think it's sterile to the point of being unnerving. It does have a sort of beauty, but to me, it is the work of a massive ego with little sympathy for the human element."

"It appears to be all about the eye," Lex said. "The observation deck, the oculus, and the incorporation of the eyes into the design. Any idea what Calatrava intended us to draw from his work?"

Eugenia shrugged, "Our lecturer pointed us to the Egyptian hieroglyphs, he felt they are intended to represent the eye of Horus," she said. "I agree with you, Papa, I think it's a reminder that we are being watched."

Chapter 52   Betrayal

Eugenia took her seat in the university lecture hall. Their art history professor was a tall, lean man with rigid features, a tight smile that rarely touched his eyes, and greying hair that grew sparsely around the ears and neck which he valiantly persisted in drawing into a non-descript pony-tail.

His lectures for the previous term had covered the works of Michelangelo and da Vinci in some depth and now he proposed to move on.

"Donato di Niccolo di Betto Bardi, better known as Donatello, was from Florence. We're talking early Renaissance circa 1386-1466. He was apprenticed to Lorenzo Ghiberti. Donatello was best known for his bas-relief works."

The lecturer went on to describe and illustrate some of Donatello's better-known sculptures including David and the monumental seated Saint John the Evangelist. Among his superb works there was one piece that captured Eugenia's attention. After his return from Rome in 1453, Donatello began sculpting Judith and Holofernes for Cosimo de Medici. Like David, Judith was a tyrant-slayer but her preferred method was not five small stones and a sling. She had used the sword on her inebriated foe. Originally the statue was gilded but now the only remaining glint was on the tip of the sword as though the weapon had been dipped in gold. Judith's face appeared impassive as she prepared to decapitate the slumbering Assyrian general—she could have been slicing the head off a chicken for all the emotion registered there.

For Eugenia, this statue brought back the still-raw emotions attached to Nour and Raif's death. Decapitation was a sign of deepest contempt for one's enemy. It was strange how swords and beheadings had become newsworthy items once more in this twenty-first century when automatic weapons, tanks, and atom bombs seemed more relevant to the age; but it was generally the men who raised their swords to kill, not the women. Eugenia left the hall with her friend and walked out into the weak winter sunshine.

"What did you think of the lecture, Lisa."

Her friend raised her eyebrows. "Dull!"

"Really?"

"Prof Alvaro is so boring," she drawled.

"But Donatello wasn't," Eugenia said. "He did some amazing work."

"Oh sure. Yes, amazing!" Lisa was hardly listening and at that moment her eyes fixed on her real centre of interest.

"There's Sergio. See you!" She raised her hand, flung her jacket over her shoulder, and flicked the ends of her long hair with lacquered fingertips. Sergio greeted her with a return wave and as she met him, he took her arm. Eugenia gave a wry smile and dug in her rucksack for the car keys. Lisa was going to have to work if she was to make it through the year, but Eugenia was not entirely sure her friend was attending university for the degree.

On the way back to her digs, a single room in a boarding house that was hers for the 'varsity term, she considered Judith's beheading of Holofernes. What was the meaning of Donatello's sculpture? Eugenia's boots clumped on the wooden stairs as she made her way to the second floor. She unlocked the door, dragged off her boots, and slid her feet into her slippers. Helping herself to a handful of biscuits, she waited for the kettle to boil and, with a steaming cup of tea on the table beside her, flopped onto the bed. Eugenia settled down against the pillows, opened her laptop, and keyed in Judith and Holofernes.

The story held all the right elements. Judith was a beautiful widow woman who lived in Bethulia situated on a mountain overlooking the valley of Jezreel in Israel. The Assyrians under Nebuchadnezzar's general, Holofernes, had invaded the land and Judith's city was about to be destroyed. Holofernes had seen Judith and desired her, so this young woman grasped the opportunity given her to defeat the enemy. She brought him into her tent and plied him with drink. With the help of her aged servant, when Holofernes was in a drunken stupor, Judith took his sword, lifted up his head, and decapitated him. In that sense, she followed David who had finished off Goliath with the giant's own weapon.

No one seemed to be certain whether the Book of Judith was legend or truth. Perhaps it was purely allegory. That thought encouraged her to take a deeper look at the names of the characters involved. Judith was the feminine form of Judah and simply meant Jewess while the city's name, Bethulia, held the meaning virgin.

The name Holofernes offered no further clue except in Eugenia's mind it seemed to suggest holocaust, heat, and furnace. Jezreel though, sprang from two root words meaning to sow and Almighty. God will sow.

"Could it be prophecy?" She wondered. "What if this Jewish widow represented Israel?" Eugenia again voiced her thoughts aloud. Judith's enemy came in to plunder and destroy but Holofernes was betrayed by his passions. The Assyrians represented the area around Babylon—modern-day Iraq. *Same old foes, still bearing their swords and still decapitating their enemies.* She set her empty cup down on the bedside table. *Perhaps that's what it means,* she thought, *God will allow Israel to be avenged of her foes. The widow woman, the one deprived of a husband and left alone, could only be Israel!*

"Daughter of Zion your time's drawing near." Eugenia had heard those words somewhere before, perhaps in a song. It was a phrase pregnant with promise. Like Donatello's sword which still bore a tip of gold, raised over the impassive face of Judith, the book had survived as an added promise to a land increasingly isolated and beleaguered. The Almighty God will sow in the Valley of Jezreel.

Chapter 53   Betrayal

It has been several years since I attempted to write a conclusion, I toyed with the ending on and off but nothing satisfied me. After Raif and Nour's death, it seemed, at first, the reason for this book had perished with them, but I must finish what I began. Will it see the light of day? In some ways, I doubt it.

Juan and Amal were married less than a year after their experience in Malaga. It had left them deeply shaken, especially as it followed so closely on Raif and Nour's horrific murder, but they viewed the uncertainty of our existence as a reason not to delay. They are obviously deeply in love. It was, inevitably, a bitter-sweet affair without Raif and Nour but they were right in not using that as a reason for a further postponement. They are now the proud parents of two young boys.

Moussa found refuge in that "little book", as he insists on calling the New Testament. I couldn't fault some of the reasoning behind his choice. When those Coptic Christians were murdered for their faith on the beach in Libya, he pointed to one of the photos of the men in their orange jump-suits and the black-clad assassins preparing for the moment of their beheading. He asked me one question. "Who would you rather spend eternity in paradise with?"
"The answer's self-evident," I replied.
"Put those guys in paradise," he predicted, "and in no time, they would have raped their virgins and turned on one another. To me, that sounds more like hell!"
I was amused, but Moussa was serious. He has apparently chosen instead, like Raif and Nour, to become a Christ-follower. It has changed him and he seems to be at peace with himself. Oddly, it has made me aware of my emptiness; the peace I see in Moussa now has raised a strange longing in me. Eugenia has softened as well since Raif and Nour's death and the fear that once haunted her has gone. The little book seems to have touched us all…

It was the destruction of the Georgia Guidestones, in the early hours of the morning, on the anniversary of the Declaration of Independence, that precipitated this move of mine to write again! It has been dubbed a bombing, and a car was seen leaving the site moments later. With what could be termed undue haste the following day, the remaining arms of the monument were completely demolished, citing safety issues.

This is already seen as a right-wing plot but to what possible purpose? It could be seen as a deliberate deepening of the mystery we are being fed and a possible sign that the long-awaited take-over is imminent. If the destruction of the Twin Towers was a declaration of intent—could the bombing of the Guidestones constitute the moment of action, or am I reading too much into it?

Things are happening at breath-taking speed. The Russian/ Ukrainian conflict is increasingly likely to envelop surrounding nations especially as NATO increases the intimidation and aggression from their side. Yet everything combined—the massive fuel and food price-hikes, which threaten to increase world famine; the attempt to force farmers off their land; the controls under the pretext of world health; political instability; even the start-up of the Hadron Collider at CERN after three-years silence, all this and more, seems to point to something new and oppressive in the atmosphere. Increasingly, it is the World Economic Forum at the hub of all that is taking place. The man at its head claims to have set many of the present world leaders in place—all from his own stable!

From what I know now, none of these things are accidental. The preoccupation with dates boldly proclaims that these events have been carefully orchestrated with meticulous attention to detail. The move towards some sort of cataclysmic event is growing in momentum and we seem powerless to stop the machine.

Is this book my last? It could be. Our very lifestyle is being radically threatened. The breath we take today may not be granted tomorrow. Just a year or two back, I was a supreme optimist, certain that the world owed me something, even if it was just the publication of one of my books. So, when did the change come about? Perhaps that foundation, which I now realise was never on bedrock to begin with, was first undermined when Eugenia was attacked.

A shadow has descended upon the planet. People still congregate in the malls, flock to sporting events, worship at music concerts. Perhaps they will continue to marry, give birth, love and hate, but the darkness is deepening swiftly.

I see the wings of the goddess Isis overshadowing the earth. Isis, daughter of darkness, offspring of the hidden god, Saturn, is about to allow the veil that concealed her from our sight to be torn asunder.

Mankind has been betrayed. My book has its title—Betrayal of Fools.

Postscript   Betrayal

And when he had opened the second seal, I heard the second beast say, Come and see.
And there went out another horse that was red: and power was given unto him that sat thereon to take peace from the earth, and that they should kill one another; and there was given unto him a great sword.
Revelation 6:3,4

And I looked, and behold a pale horse: and his name that sat on him was Death, and Hell followed with him. And power was given unto them over the fourth part of the earth, to kill with sword, and with hunger, and with death, and with the beasts of the earth.
Revelation 8

On the American dollar note is the pyramid with the eye of Horus indicating a separated capstone; beneath it are the words Neuvos Ordo Secularis—New Secular Order.

The Giza Pyramid is 481.3 feet or 5776 inches from base to capstone. The One World Trade Centre, with its spire, measures 1776 feet, supposedly as a reminder of the American Declaration of Independence. Co-incidentally perhaps, the Illuminati made an appearance in Europe during the same year. As the Freemasonic calendar, Anno Lucis, adds 4000 years to our year, the establishment of the U.S. could be said to have taken place in the year 5776. 5776 was the Jewish year, 2015/16. It was also said to be a Jubilee year, the 70th since the time of Christ.

June 1, 2016 (01.06.2016) saw the opening ceremony of the Gotthard Tunnel in Switzerland. This was no ceremonial cutting of a ribbon by a group of dignitaries; it was a full-blown act of Satanic worship performed openly before "honoured" guests. Humans grovelled at the feet of demonic angelic beings; the audience was treated to scenes of terrified screams, wailing, and devilish laughter. A goat man enacted a death and resurrection. Images of flames licked against the walls of the tunnel, a backdrop to a marching zombie army clothed in the familiar orange jumpsuits of ISIS or Guantanimo prisoners: On a raised platform, semi-clothed men and women gyrated in a blatantly sexual dance. It was a calling up of the demonic from the pit of the underworld.

If hell was what the world desired, Saturn/Satan, the hidden god, was prepared to bring it to earth.

NASA played its own part in marking the year. After a successful manoeuvre on Independence Day, 4th July 2016 (5776), the spacecraft Juno went into orbit around Jupiter. Juno also adds her stamp to the 5th of July which, in mythology, is named the 'Flight of the People'.

The 7th July celebrates the Nonae Caprotinae, or personal festival, of the goddess (Juno of the Goat) and female slaves[38] appear to have been the focus of the celebration.

Juno's name is derived from D'Iune, the Dove; it is in this form that she was worshipped by the Romans and the Babylonians. Like the Antichrist, she carries the olive branch in her hand and comes in apparent peace. An even more notable epithet for Juno is Lucina; like Lucifer, she is known as the bringer of light. As the third person of the Assyrian trinity was represented by the wings and the tail of the dove, the terminal of the One World Trade Centre, was built to represent the person of the goddess.

Juno undoubtedly had a significant role in her coupling with her unpredictable husband Jupiter in the heavens. What was the real function of this craft? Is the projected two-year information-gathering of the Juno spacecraft simply adding impetus to the opening of an earthly portal? Juno is, after all, not only the "Queen of Heaven" but also the goddess of birth.

---

[38] The timing of this NASA event is particularly chilling as Juno is identified with Vesta, fire in the centre of the world. Philolaus speaks of her as "The Vesta of the universe. The House of Jupiter. The mother of the gods."

If Juno is simply intended to represent the present-day pinnacle of the Tower of Babel in the heavenlies, CERN, no doubt, will step in to complete the earthly end of the job.

Watchers have been waiting for the chosen year that the Capstone will be set in place upon the pyramid of the Neuvis Order Secularis. The completed One World Tower signalled the imminent revelation of this leader, represented by the black cube, and his arrival on the world scene will be the final attempt to wrest power over the earth from God.

An impersonator of Christ is about to take centre stage. He is the golden phallus of the reconstructed body of the ancient king Nimrod/Osiris. He will promise to bring peace to the shattered, fragmented, blood-let and exhausted nations of the Middle East, and the world. This global figure will be permitted 1,260 days in which to rule, before the promised judgment of Almighty God is poured out. His coming represents the last stage in the Betrayal of Fools.

In 1871, Freemason Albert Pike wrote a blueprint for three world wars to be deliberately fomented after his death. The Jews only returned to their land in 1948, yet he spoke of the third war in this way:

"The war must be conducted in such a way that Islam (the Moslem Arabic World) and political Zionism (the State of Israel) mutually destroy each other. Meanwhile the other nations, once more divided on this issue will be constrained to fight to the point of complete physical, moral, spiritual and economical exhaustion..." [See appendix 1]

Jesus Christ is the true corner-stone that the people of the earth have rejected. They would not build their lives on Him but instead chose idols of their own making.

*You watched while **a stone was cut out without hands**, which struck the image on its feet of iron and clay, and broke them in pieces. 35 Then the iron, the clay, the bronze, the silver, and the gold were crushed together, and became like chaff from the* *summer threshing floors; the wind carried them away so that no trace of them was found.* ***And the stone that struck the image became a great mountain and filled the whole earth.*** Daniel 2:34,35 (NKJ) Emphasis added.

The human race has chosen to reject God's plan and adopt the counterfeit—the outcome is of our own making. The warning from scripture is clear; the stone that was rejected will break down all that man has built up through his own wayward imagination and his desire for personal power. Jesus will ultimately fill the earth with His glory.
Maranatha.

There is a God in heaven that revealeth secrets... But as for me, this secret is not revealed to me for any wisdom that I have more than any living, but for their sakes that shall make known the interpretation... Daniel 2:28,30

# # #

Rest in the LORD, and wait patiently for Him;
    Do not fret because of him who prospers in his way,
    Because of the man who brings wicked schemes to pass.
Cease from anger, and forsake wrath;
    Do not fret—it only causes harm.
For evildoers shall be cut off;
    But those who wait on the LORD,
    They shall inherit the earth.
For yet a little while and the wicked shall be no more;
    Indeed, you will look carefully for his place,
    But it shall be no more.
But the meek shall inherit the earth,
    And shall delight themselves in the abundance of peace.
The wicked plots against the just,
    And gnashes at him with his teeth.
The Lord laughs at him,
    For He sees that his day is coming.
The wicked have drawn the sword
    And have bent their bow,

To cast down the poor and needy,
   To slay those who are of upright conduct.
Their sword shall enter their own heart,
   And their bows shall be broken.
   Psalm 37:7-15 (New King James)

About The Author
Betrayal of Fools

Like most human beings, I have always held a fascination for the hidden things—the gift is always best wrapped! This tendency to delve beneath the surface has led me to examine and expose the machinations of men of power—supposedly implemented for the good of the planet!
I am a follower of the Lord Jesus Christ. In Him, I live and move and have my being.

Other books by Lyn J Pickering

Another leader is about to arise. A man who will seize Europe and overpower her as a man takes a woman. He will dominate her and she will serve him. The man's name is War.

Pierre Zein, a Lebanese journalist, interviews Hussein ibn Muhammad, an Ayatollah claiming to be the Twelfth Imam of the Shiites and begins a quest to expose the European leader behind the prophecy. His search leads him into danger and to the ultimate realisation that the conspiracy has advanced far beyond the power of human intervention.

The year is 1981 and Lebanon is involved in a bloody civil war. Life in is a daily struggle and Pierre's work takes him out into the conflict areas on the streets of Beirut. When Danielle, a girlfriend from Pierre's past, contacts him, romance seems an impossibility. Love, drama and mystery lend this action-packed thriller an intensely human angle. **Well-written, deeply researched, Lyn J Pickering captures the both the richness and the menace of the Middle East.**

* * *

The **Nimrod Twice Born** series interweaves the dramatic events of Israel at the time of Jesus Christ with a World War II conspiracy thriller.

The skills of a Magician, Simon Magus, win him the favour of the wife of Herod Antipas. The magician initiates a conspiracy so intricate and so far-seeing that it will only reach its climax in our time.

Matthias von Ingolstadt leaves the horror of the trenches behind at the close of the World War I and returns to a Germany humiliated by the events that have left the country bankrupt and vulnerable. He meets and falls in love with Anna Lejkin, a Jew. What follows appears to solve their racial differences but ultimately leads to discovery, manipulation and disaster.

A Jew in Frankfurt, Germany, Michael Segal is caught up in the events preceding the war. His friendship with Gabriele have far-reaching consequences for them both.

Heinrich Himmler, the future SS leader of the Third Reich, forms a relationship with Ernst Röhm a battle-hardened veteran of WWI who has a penchant for young men. He promises Himmler the one thing he most desires – power.

Nimrod Twice Born is an intricate story of love, romance, witchcraft, power and intrigue. Lyn J Pickering employs history's trail of circumstantial evidence to combine both Christian conspiracy and historical fiction in one bizarre and riveting package.

Appendix 1

Extract from Albert Pike's Letter to Guiseppe Mazzini

Albert Pike--American attorney, Confederate officer, writer, and high-ranking Freemason. December 29, 1809 – April 2, 1891. Purported letter to Guiseppe Mazzini.

"The Third World War must be fomented by taking advantage of the differences caused by the "agentur" of the "Illuminati" between the political Zionists and the leaders of Islamic World. The war must be conducted in such a way that Islam (the Moslem Arabic World) and political Zionism (the State of Israel) mutually destroy each other. Meanwhile the other nations, once more divided on this issue will be constrained to fight to the point of complete physical, moral, spiritual and economical exhaustion…We shall unleash the Nihilists and the atheists, and we shall provoke a formidable social cataclysm which in all its horror will show clearly to the nations the effect of absolute atheism, origin of savagery and of the most bloody turmoil. Then everywhere, the citizens, obliged to defend themselves against the world minority of revolutionaries, will exterminate those destroyers of civilization, and the multitude, disillusioned with Christianity, whose deistic spirits will from that moment be without compass or direction, anxious for an ideal, but without knowing where to render its adoration, will receive the true light through the universal manifestation of the pure doctrine of Lucifer, brought finally out in the public view. This manifestation will result from the general reactionary movement which will follow the destruction of Christianity and atheism, both conquered and exterminated at the same time."

Appendix 2

Freemasonry is the heart of the conspiracy to war and One World Government.

This display ad was run in *The Jerusalem Post* newspaper in November, 1994.

"Masons of Peace"

In *The Jerusalem Post* (November 1994) was an advertisement placed by "The Grand Lodge of the State of Israel." The display ad was addressed *"To the Masons of Peace,"* and listed: *"The Honorable **Yitzak Rabin**, Prime Minister of Israel," "His Majesty, **King Hussein of Jordan**,"* and *"The Honorable **Bill Clinton**, President of the United States."*

The ad closed with these fascinating words: *"With warm fraternal congratulations on the signing of the peace agreement between Israel and Jordan."* Signed—***Ephraim Fuchs**, President of the Israel Order of Masons."*

In his remarks graveside at the funeral service in Israel for the assassinated Israeli Prime Minister Rabin, President Bill Clinton, wearing a Jewish yarmulke, a skull cap, referred to the slain Rabin as "Our elder brother." Of course, he was referring to the Brotherhood of the Lodge.

Encouragement

Many years ago, when I felt the call to write Opus Dei, I was aware it was not going to be universally received and that feeling was strengthened further when I began work on Nimrod Twice born. Betrayal of Fools probably completes the cycle begun more than thirty-five years ago. I don't write books that will hit the pop charts. However, I do hope Betrayal of Fools will serve its purpose and act as a warning of impending judgment.

God is both a God of Love and a just God. He has given us more than two millennia to repent of our rebellion against Him, but for the most part, the human race has chosen to thumb our nose at our Creator. Some are simply apathetic; others have chosen to be deceived, or to live a life of evil. Either way, the end is the same. Only by God's chosen path through His Son, Jesus Christ, can a man or woman be saved.

For some, my book may prove to be a beacon of hope, but I am under no illusions. As human-beings, we remain deliberately and determinedly ignorant. Even when judgment does come, most will refuse to bow the knee and acknowledge that God is who He says He is.

We have entered the last of the last days and He is still reaching out a hand to you. Allow Him to touch your heart and take you through the upheavals to come. It's not yet too late.